ROMANTIC TIMES PRAISES NORAH HESS, WINNER OF THE REVIEWERS' CHOICE AWARD FOR FRONTIER ROMANCE!

MOUNTAIN ROSE

"Another delightful, tender and heartwarming read from a special storyteller!"

KENTUCKY BRIDE

"Marvelous...a treasure for those who savor frontier love stories!"

HAWKE'S PRIDE

"Earthy and realistic....Bravo to Norah Hess!

DEVIL IN SPURS

"Norah Hess is a superb Western romance writer....*Devil in Spurs* is an entertaining read!"

SWEET DELIGHT

Spencer sat down at the table and said with his heart-stopping smile, ''I bet you baked us a pie.''

''No.'' Gretchen shook her head as she stirred a bowl of cornmeal batter. ''It's something better than that.''

A teasing glint came into Spencer's eyes. ''I can only think of one thing that would be better than a slice of pie.''

''Really?'' Gretchen looked at him, then blushed and looked away. There was a meaning in his gray eyes that made her catch her breath, and a tingling started in her lower body. ''And what is that?'' she asked recklessly.

''You know what,'' Spencer answered, his voice as smooth as honey.

''I'm afraid I don't,'' Gretchen said as she shoved the cornmeal mixture into the brick oven, then straightened up to smile at him in mock innocence. ''You'll have to tell me.''

Spencer looked significantly at her mouth, making Gretchen's pulse race.

Other *Leisure Books* by Norah Hess:
MOUNTAIN ROSE
KENTUCKY BRIDE
HAWKE'S PRIDE
DEVIL IN SPURS

LEISURE BOOKS  NEW YORK CITY

A LEISURE BOOK®

October 1993

Published by

Dorchester Publishing Co., Inc.
276 Fifth Avenue
New York, NY 10001

If you purchased this book without a cover you should be aware that this book is stolen property. It was reported as "unsold and destroyed" to the publisher and neither the author nor the publisher has received any payment for this "stripped book."

Copyright © 1993 by Norah Hess

All rights reserved. No part of this book may be reproduced or transmitted in any form or by any electronic or mechanical means, including photocopying, recording or by any information storage and retrieval system, without the written permission of the Publisher, except where permitted by law.

The name "Leisure Books" and the stylized "L" with design are trademarks of Dorchester Publishing Co., Inc.

Printed in the United States of America.

To Natalie,
with love

Kentucky Woman

Chapter One

Pennsylvania 1775

The early spring morning was barely gray in color when Gretchen Ames awakened, stretched sore muscles, and sat up. In the chill and gloom of the room she reached for the threadbare dress folded neatly at the foot of her straw pallet. Pulling it over her head, she rose to her feet, bent over to smooth the covers over her bed, then left the room, her bare feet making no sound.

She moved just as quietly as she climbed the worn stairs to the big, drafty attic room of the old, rambling three-storied farmhouse. The younger children of the Public Institution for Paupers slept there. It had been her task for the past five years to get the little ones up, dressed, taken to the outdoor privy, washed up at the pump a few yards from the house, then herded into the kitchen. All this before five o'clock.

A welling of pity rose up in Gretchen as in her mind's eye she saw them lined up like cattle at a feed trough, waiting for a nod from Cook to take their places on benches worn smooth from the countless bottoms that had slid off and on them. There they would sit and wait again, their hands folded in their laps, for the heavyset, stern-faced woman to nod her head, giving them permission to dig into the wooden trenchers of thin gruel with a few scraps of salt pork floating in it. Some mornings there would be a slice of coarse bread added to the meager meal.

It was a diet that kept them alive, but put no fat on little bones, and very little strength. And the evening meal of fatty mutton and a boiled potato barely took the edge off their hunger.

Gretchen knew well the pangs of hunger experienced during her eight years at the institution. After the drowning of her parents, and having no relatives she knew of, she had been sent to the—more commonly known—poorhouse.

From the day of her arrival it seemed that hunger always gnawed at her as she worked from dawn to dusk, six days a week, stopping only for half an hour at noon to wolf down a slab of cornbread and a glass of buttermilk.

Sundays were days of rest for some, wherein no field work was done. Everyday chores, however, went on as usual. There were cows to be milked, chickens to be fed, and eggs to be gathered.

This seventh day of the week was looked forward to with anticipation *and* dread. Dread, because the church itself was the most uncomfortable place imaginable. The building was unheated, and during the daylong services everyone, including the youngest tot, was expected to sit up straight on the hard benches and make no noises. If by chance a child should fall asleep, or wiggle in his seat, or drop a prayer book, he or she went to bed without supper. And losing that meal was a hard punishment. It was the one meal of the week when hungry bellies received a hearty serving of beef stew and all the cornbread they could eat. And to miss the milk and sugar cookies served that day was unthinkable. These sweets were the anticipations of the Sabbath.

Gretchen climbed the last step and pushed open the door of the drafty room. She peered into the semigloom at the double row of twenty-three children sleeping on straw pallets like her own. The little boys were on one side, the little girls on the other. The small bodies were hunched beneath thin, worn blankets, for the April nights and early mornings were still quite cold.

She hated to awaken them, to take them out into the chill air to stand shivering while waiting their turn at the pump to wash their faces and hands. She sighed. It had to be done; rules had to be followed here, no matter what.

Picking up a small bell just inside the door, Gretchen moved down the narrow aisle of sleeping forms, gently jangling it. Brown eyes, blue eyes, and those in between, popped open, then cold, pinched lips smiled at her. She smiled back, knowing that she was a favorite with them. Although it was against the rules, she always managed to give each love-starved child a quick hug and kiss as she helped them into their thin homespuns.

There was never any time for affection in this place, and Gretchen had missed that more than anything else since coming to the poorhouse when she was ten years old. Thankfully, she had enjoyed an abundance of love, hugs, and kisses from her parents before their death, for here, she had never again heard a kind word nor felt an affectionate touch. The Institution was operated by a Puritan church group who held a very religious outlook on the world. Hard work and a complete lack of enjoyment was the cornerstone of every man, woman, and child unfortunate enough to end up in the establishment.

Everyone worked on the poor farm; even the four- and five-year-olds had their duties. They were put to work in the garden patches, pulling weeds from around plants too tender for the sharp blade of a hoe that might damage them. The little ones fed the chickens, gathered the eggs, ran and fetched for Cook, and kept an eye on the toddlers.

Each fall the older boys and girls were issued two changes of clothing. These were all used articles, donated by the good ladies of the church. Shoes were to be worn only in the winter.

Gretchen smiled grimly. Her shoes were usually too big for her slender feet, and she was forced to put layers of paper on the soles. But that worked out very well, she discovered. The paper gave added warmth to her feet. And if the shoes looked cumbersome on her, who was to notice or even care? They all looked alike, more or less, in their hand-me-downs. Not one teenage girl there had the slightest notion of fashion. Most had been born at the poorhouse or had arrived there at a very young age. And having never been allowed to leave the farm's premises, except to occasionally go to work for a day at one of the grand homes in the area, they had no idea of what went on outside their small world.

Gretchen remembered a little of what it was like beyond the large acreage, the dreary, weather-beaten house. She could recall parties given at her parents' home, her mother's bright, ruffly dresses, the skirts rustling over full petticoats as she walked, the way she always smelled of roses.

And her hands were always so pretty, white and soft. Gretchen looked down at her own hands, at the broken nails, the knuckles stained a dark brown from grubbing in the soil. Her hands, more than any other part of her body, suffered the most in the winter. It seemed that whenever gloves or mittens were being handed out they were all gone by the time she stepped up to receive a pair. Consequently, four months out of every year her hands were chapped from the cold, the skin cracked and bleeding. As for that, warm weather never brought much comfort. After one day of gripping a hoe handle for hours on end her palms became blistered; and the blisters broke open, then formed great calluses.

A grimace of distaste flickered across Gretchen's face. Her workload could be cut in half if she followed the footsteps most of the teenage girls took. She could go to the overseer's cottage and entertain the fat man whenever he sent for her. But she had overheard those girls talking about their experiences in the man's bed and had made up her mind that she would hoe weeds until she dropped before she would ever take the beaten path to that cottage.

She had became more determined over the years when some of those foolish girls turned up with the fat man's baby in their bellies. He, of course, always denied the pointing finger, blaming the teenage boys for his dirty work. Reverend Fedders always believed him, and the girls were turned out, along with the innocent boys.

Gretchen wondered what had happened to those girls as she pulled a dress down over a small head. She had heard Cook say to one of the kitchen helpers that they were probably selling their bodies to whatever man came along.

She thought about those newborn babies that were sometimes left on the front porch of the poorhouse during the night; did they belong to the girls who had been sent away in disgrace? There were a couple in the nursery right now who resembled two of the girls who had been sent away recently.

Finally, the last child was dressed in his threadbare clothing. Taking a brush from the windowsill, Gretchen herded them down the creaking stairs, firmly dismissing from her mind that which she couldn't change. She had enough worries of her own.

The children went quietly along the narrow hall, holding their breath as they tiptoed past the room where the Fedders were still sleeping in their comfortable feather bed. Those two would not be rising until the sun was well up, Gretchen thought resentfully. Then Cook would serve them a hearty breakfast of meat and eggs and fried potatoes, plus big globs of butter to spread over hot biscuits.

As the last child filed through the back door to the privy, then to the pump to wash up, she hoped that one morning those two would choke on a piece of ham.

She had discovered a long time ago that there was no reason everyone at the poorhouse shouldn't eat as well as the Fedders. God knew there were plenty of vegetables and fruit raised on the farm, not to mention the many beeves and hogs that were butchered, as well as chickens, eggs, and milk. Her small charges should be plump, with dimples in their elbows, rather than so thin you could count their ribs. And the older children wouldn't look so gaunt if some of that food found its way to their table.

But that would never happen, she had also learned. Most of everything produced on the farm went to market. The money derived from the sale went to the church for the upkeep of the farm, or so it was claimed. It was Gretchen's private opinion that a good amount of it went into the Fedderses' own pockets.

As unfair as it was, cheating the inhabitants here had gone on ever since the establishment came into being, and it would continue to do so. "And you, you foolish girl," Gretchen whispered to herself, "stop worrying about it and start fretting about Gretchen Ames."

She stared down at the dew-wet grass, cold beneath her bare feet, an uneasiness pinching her delicate features. On her way to bed last night, Mrs. Fedders had stopped Gretchen in the hall and ordered, in her nasal voice, "Come to my office tomorrow morning at nine o'clock sharp. We must discuss your future."

Future? What future? she had wanted to demand of the haughty woman. *What kind of future does a pauper-raised female have?* Of course, she hadn't said any of it. She had meekly answered, "Yes, ma'am," and continued on to the long room under the eaves. There she stretched out on her pallet of straw that was exactly like the other sixteen placed in a row, two feet apart. Lying in the darkness, listening to her companions, some mumbling in their sleep, others snoring, she knew that her stay at the poorhouse was coming to an end.

When a teenage boy or girl reached the age of eighteen, which she had done last week, they were considered old enough to go out on their own. If one had a relative in the outside world willing to take him in, allowing him to stay until he found a place of employment, he was very fortunate. In her case, though, and in many like hers, there was no place to go, and she had no idea what to do once she walked through the wide gate of the farm.

Gretchen brought herself back to the present when the last little girl came running from the privy, pulling up her bloomers, her dress tail caught inside them. The boys had finished their call to nature in short order, most of them going behind the building to relieve themselves on the ground.

Gretchen motioned them to line up at the pump, and then as she worked the cold handle up and down, each child took his turn washing up in the frigid water.

The eastern sky was turning pink as she pulled a brush through the hair on each small head. As she hurried the youngsters toward the kitchen door, she wondered if this would be the last time she would escort them there.

Where might she be this time tomorrow?

Sometime later, as Gretchen ate her oatmeal with the other girls her age, she was conscious of the looks slid her way. Gossip was the only pastime or entertainment the inhabitants of the institution could indulge in. It always amazed her how quickly a few spoken words, a certain look, could travel from the kitchen to the barn to the fields. As far as she knew, there hadn't been a soul around when Mrs. Fedders had spoken to her the night before, but she'd swear that everyone in the place knew about her appointment with the woman this morning, and knew what it was about, as well.

She scraped her trencher clean, pondering on the cook. This morning, for the first and only time in eight years, the overworked woman had given her a half smile. Why now? she wondered. Was it out of pity? Did the woman know what was going to happen to Gretchen Ames? Was it so bad Cook felt sorry for her?

All these questions continued to nag at Gretchen's mind when later she stood in the backyard again, the little ones grouped around her, their teeth chattering like little magpies as they waited to receive their orders for the day. The older children had eaten and gone to the fields already, there to follow behind a plow, dropping seed into the ground. Anxiety began to grow inside her when one of the teenage girls arrived and took the children away to assign them to their chores and she was left standing alone in the yard, uncertain what to do. No orders had been given to her.

She started when Cook spoke behind her. "Gretchen," the woman said, not unkindly, "you're to help me in the kitchen until it's time to take your bath and wash your hair."

Gretchen nodded dumbly. It was true, then. She was being turned out today. She felt a trembling take hold of her body. Although there was nothing here that would make one hate leaving the place, still the poorhouse had provided security of a sort. She was used to the place; she accepted the hard work that paid for her straw pallet and meager meals.

With a slight drooping of her thin shoulders she turned and followed the cook into the kitchen.

The sun rose higher and Gretchen continued to scrub away at the wooden trenchers, placing them upside down on the long table to dry. Her fingers were shriveled like prunes when the kitchen clock struck eight times.

"It's time you go prepare yourself for your appointment with Mrs. Fedders," Cook said without looking up from the pan of potatoes she was peeling. She surprised Gretchen then by nodding her head toward the big fireplace and adding, "Take that kettle of warm water with you."

This was another first from the stern-faced woman, and it made Gretchen worry all the more. Never before, to her knowledge, had the woman ever given anyone warm water to wash up in. She had never shown any concern that many times in the winter a thin layer of ice had to be broken in the pail of water for washing.

Murmuring, "Thank you, ma'am," Gretchen dried her hands and picked up a hot pad. The big cast-iron kettle was heavy as Gretchen lifted it off the hearth, and dragged at her thin arms as she carried it to the room under the eaves.

Moving along the row of pallets, she came to the long bench where several scarred, wooden basins were lined up. She poured half the warm water into the one on the end, then picked up a sliver of lye soap and dropped it in the water. After stripping down to her petticoat she took up a rag hanging with several others on pegs in the wall and lathered it with the strong yellow soap.

She washed her face and throat first, then her arms and shoulders. Gretchen reached down the front of her wide-strapped petticoat and washed under her arms and then her firm, round breasts.

She washed there hurriedly, as she did when she came to the crotch area. The girls had been taught at an early age that it was sinful to linger in those two areas when bathing, and that they should never bare their bodies either. The body could be the Devil's workshop if one were careless of it was the only explanation ever given for the rule.

When Gretchen's entire body tingled from the scrubbing she had given it she lathered her hair, the color of ripe chestnuts, then rinsed with the remaining water in the kettle. After she had vigorously rubbed her wet head with a scrap of rough toweling she picked up the brush all the girls used and pulled it through her hair as hard as she could to keep the curls from popping out all over her head.

Her thick mop of hair had been the bane of her existence these past eight years. From the first day of her arrival at the poorhouse Mrs. Fedders had hounded her about it, always complaining that it wasn't kept neat and tidy. One day when that lady tried to control the curls herself and could not, she took the scissors to the beautiful long tresses.

Gretchen remembered the silent tears running down her cheeks as the long curls piled around her feet. Mama and Papa had been so proud of her hair. When the snip of the scissors finally ceased the hair left on her head was about two inches long. Mrs. Fedders had thrown up her hands in disgust when the short strands curled tightly around the girl's small head. She had stood trembling in terror, afraid that the angry woman might shave her head next.

At least that hadn't happened, Gretchen thought, whipping the damp petticoat over her head, then hurriedly taking up a clean one from the shelf under the bench. When she had pulled on fresh bloomers she took the dress from the wooden peg that bore her name above it and pulled the faded garment over her head. She stood a moment then, debating about her shoes. Should she put them on? Shoes were forbidden after the first of April, and it was now the middle of the month.

In the end she pulled on a pair of white, much-mended stockings, then slid her feet into a shabby-looking pair of shoes that laced up the front. After all, she wouldn't be beaten for putting them on. Although the boys were taken to the barn to receive the strap for some misdeed or other, the girls' punishment was added work applied to their already heavy load for any wrongdoing. They agreed among themselves that they would rather feel the strap to their backsides.

When the last lace was tied Gretchen rolled her soiled clothes into a bundle, then poured the wash water into a pail, which would be emptied by the girl in charge of making up the pallets later. She picked up the tea kettle and made her way back downstairs. In the kitchen she put the heavy vessel back on the hearth, forgetting to refill it, she had so much on her mind. After she had taken her sweat-stained clothing to the washhouse and placed them with the others waiting to be laundered she returned to stand beside the big woman still peeling potatoes.

"Do I look neat, Cook?" she asked timidly.

Pale brown eyes moved over her slender body in a dress two sizes too big for her, then looked doubtfully at her unruly curls for a second before answering quite gently, "Yes, Gretchen, you look neat." She nudged Gretchen toward the door leading into the back hall. "It's almost nine o'clock. When the clock begins to strike knock on Mrs. Fedders's office door. But don't open it," she cautioned, "until she tells you to enter."

It seemed to Gretchen, as she stood nervously chewing on a fingernail, that hours passed before she heard the whir of the clock announcing that it was going to strike. On the third musical bong she raised a small fist that trembled slightly and rapped twice on the heavy dark wood door. Several heartbeats passed before she was coolly bidden to enter.

She grasped the doorknob and, twisting it, stepped into a room that was toasty warm from a brightly burning fire in a brightly burning fireplace. She remembered her little charges' chattering teeth and knew that they still hadn't warmed up in their skimpy clothing, her resentment rising.

The harsh-faced woman sitting behind a pigeonhole desk didn't look up or let on in any way that she was aware of the nervous girl who had advanced within three feet of her. The quill she gripped in her smooth white fingers scratched uninterrupted across a sheet of paper.

While Gretchen waited to be noticed, her eyes were drawn to a pot of tea steaming on a tray, a plate of hot buns, and two small crocks of butter and jelly. When her mouth began to water she looked away, letting her eyes skim over the room.

The opulence here was glaringly different from the rest of the big, almost barren house. She had been in this room only once before: the day she had arrived here. But she had been so afraid of the stiff-featured woman who stared narrow-eyed at her that she hadn't lifted her gaze from the floor.

Gretchen was suddenly aware that Mrs. Fedders's wintry gaze was upon her, and she stiffened her spine to meet their cold regard. When the woman spoke it was in an equally cold voice.

"Gretchen," she began, "as you know you've had your eighteenth birthday and it is time you left us." Gretchen nodded, and the emotionless voice went on. "I've made exhaustive inquiries throughout the area for any household in need of a maid or kitchen help. I have been unsuccessful in finding you a place."

Gretchen waited to be told that she would now be turned out into a world of which she knew nothing at all. What she did hear from Mrs. Fedders, however, drained the color from her face.

"It has come to my attention that some of the wealthier householders have been indenturing healthy boys and girls when it comes time for them to go out on their own." The reverend's wife paused to run her eyes over Gretchen's body, its curves barely discernible beneath the oversized homespun. She frowned before saying, "You will be very fortunate if one of our good citizens indentures you. If you should be so lucky, make sure you are subservient to whomever buys your papers. If you are obedient and work hard, when your service time of five years is up you will receive a sum of money agreed upon, as well as some acreage of land."

Gretchen's brain had honed in on the word *indentured* and had gotten no farther. Every story she had ever heard about bonded people raced through her mind: hard work, small rations, and, sometimes, beatings. And almost always, if you were female, mating with the males of the household when ordered to. Hard work and meager meals she was used to, and most likely she could survive that, but she would not lend her body to have lust visited upon it.

A reckless defiance gripped her. "Thank you, Mrs. Fedders," she began, keeping her voice firmly calm, "for all the trouble you have gone to for me, but I do not wish to be a bond person. I will take my chances on finding employment."

Her eyes as frosty as dew in the early morning, the woman behind the desk glared at Gretchen. "I'm afraid, young lady, that you have little choice in the matter. There are already too many of you people wandering around out there, begging for money, sleeping in doorways. The good people of Brook County want an end to it. You should be grateful that the men of the community are willing to put up good money to provide homes for you paupers."

The irate woman paused to catch her breath, then continued, "Otherwise all you ingrates will be herded together and driven into the unopened wilderness to live the best you can. Believe me, you wouldn't last long out there with the heathen Indians and wild beasts."

Gretchen felt herself shrinking inside. Could such a cruel act be perpetrated on helpless young people? Wasn't there some kind of law in Pennsylvania that would protect them from almost certain death?

The stony face across from her said that there wasn't. An eighteen-year-old was considered an adult, and if one wasn't working, didn't have visible means of support, he or she was considered a vagrant and could be jailed or run out of town.

The town fathers would opt for the latter, of course. Anyone they jailed would have to be fed.

When Mrs. Fedders saw the helplessness that came into Gretchen's eyes, she gloated; she had won. She folded the piece of paper she had been writing on and, standing up, handed it to Gretchen. "Mr. Hayden, the man in charge of selling the bond papers, is waiting outside. Give him this document and he will take you to the town square, where you will join the others waiting to be bonded. Before the day is over you will have a new home."

She frowned impatiently when Gretchen only stared at her blankly, questions wailing in her mind. Was it her destiny to always be controlled by others? Was she never to try shaping it herself?

In a daze she felt her arm gripped firmly and she was led toward the door. She stumbled once as she was propelled down the dark hall and shoved through the door that opened onto the backyard. The door slammed behind her and she stood blinking in the bright sunshine.

An elderly man sitting in a wagon, the reins to a pair of horses held loosely in his hand, gazed at the lovely girl whose soft red lips trembled and hazel eyes shimmered with unshed tears. Tom Hayden sighed unhappily. She was a beauty, and some wealthy lecher would snap her up the moment she stepped upon the bidding block.

God, how he hated his job.

Chapter Two

The preacher closed his Bible, then Ben Atkins's sister was laid to rest.

The elderly man with snow-white hair and beard remained at the mounded grave long after everyone else had left, remembering. This was the third time he had returned to Pennsylvania in twenty years.

The first time was for the burial of his father. Five years later he had returned to see his mother laid to rest beside her husband, and now, ten years later, he was here to send his sister off to join their parents.

He stood staring sightlessly at the garden bouquets friends and neighbors had placed on the cold clay. He had lost so many loved ones over the years. Shortly after the death of his father his beloved wife, along with their eighteen-year-old daughter, had been killed by Indians.

The grizzled old man's thoughts lingered on the two women he had so adored. Mary, whom he had wed when she was sixteen and he twenty.

His young wife had been as adventurous as himself and had eagerly fallen in with his plan to strike out into the wilderness, to start their life together on a new frontier.

Against the disapproval of both sets of parents, they had packed their belongings on a sturdy mule and headed out, no particular destination in mind. They were in love and just being together was enough.

The third day on the trail they were struck with the beauty of the land they traveled, the gently rolling hills, the green valleys, the dense forests of cedar, maple, elm, and oak. That night, lying on their bed of cedar tips, close to a crackling fire, listening to the soft slap of water, Mary said sleepily, "Let's settle down right here, Ben, build our cabin close to the river."

"If that's what you want, Mary," Ben had agreed. "The thing is, I don't know where we are."

Two days later, as they were felling trees, a Shawnee brave came trotting through the forest and stopped awhile to watch them. Before he loped back into the woods he had informed them that they were in Can-tuc-kee, and that the nearby river was called the Ohio.

"So," Ben said, when the brave was out of sight, "we are in Kentucky. I've heard of that land, and also of the Ohio River." Mary smiled at him, and he began to wield the ax again.

In a little over three weeks he and Mary moved into their snug, three-room cabin that boasted wooden floors of maple that he had split into one-inch boards, then hewed smooth. Each room had a window with shutters that could be opened and closed. He planned that before winter set in he would cover the openings with oiled paper to let in the sunshine and keep out the cold air. He had also constructed an open loft over the main room.

The first two years Ben and Mary had worked from dawn to sunset, clearing land, plowing, and planting seeds. The only thing marring their contentment was that they were often forced to hide in caves when renegades were in the area. By some miracle their little cabin always escaped the red man's notice.

He and Mary began to feel safer as others came along and built their own cabins and tilled their soil. Today there were five homesteads scattered along the Ohio, plus a small fur post with an attached tavern on one end and a mercantile of sorts on the other. The soil was rich and produced fine crops. When their baby son came along they named him Spencer and knew complete happiness.

Their happiness grew when Spencer was two years old and baby Julie was born.

Ben lost all interest in life, though, the summer his daughter turned eighteen.

He and Spencer had gone squirrel-hunting one hot day. When they returned home in the late afternoon they had found the bodies of his wife and daughter sprawled on the ground in front of the cabin. They had been tomahawked to death, their scalps taken. As he and Spencer gathered them into their arms, he had thanked God that neither had been raped.

Ravaged with grief, Spencer had disappeared for two weeks. Where he had gone Ben never knew. But when his son returned he was no longer the young man who had struck out through the wilderness, his eyes wild with grief. It was a hard-eyed, aged-beyond-his-years man who had returned to him.

As for himself, he might as well have been buried with his wife and his daughter, for all that life mattered to him. He put away his plow, sold his livestock, and never farmed again. When the first frost arrived he turned to trapping with Spencer, a life-style that would keep him away from the cabin all day, a place of bittersweet memories, and would tire him enough so that when he went to bed he would fall instantly into a dreamless sleep.

It was then that he fully realized the change in Spencer. He felt a great guilt that he hadn't been able to help his son bear the terrible loss of his mother and his sister.

But it was too late now to change the path Spencer had taken. In the warm weather, before and after the trapping season, his evenings were spent at the post tavern, drinking and brawling with the other wild trappers, and lying with the tavern whores. Once his traps were set, he moved into a deserted cabin and ran his line from there. As was the habit of his friends, he moved in a whore with him so he could get his regular pleasuring without having to wade through snow and cold to the post.

It was to Spencer's credit, though, Ben thought, that he would never dream of dishonoring his mother and his sister's memories by bringing a low woman into their home.

A warm smile stirred in his beard and mustache. He was proud of his lean, six-foot-two-inch son. He had his father's straight nose and firm lips, and his mother's gray eyes and black hair curled loosely a couple of inches below his jacket collar.

However, Ben did not like the lines of dissipation he saw on the handsome face. They told a story of hard living, too much drink, and too many women.

As for himself, rheumatism had started bothering him about four years ago, striking him in the knees and fingers. There were mornings when he wasn't sure he could run his traps, he hurt so. If Spencer hadn't stepped in and helped him, he'd have had to bring in half his line.

Ben gave a startled jump, an uneasy shiver running down his spine when a hand descended on his shoulder. Were there haints here, spirits wandering around the cemetery where he stood alone?

He slowly turned his head, half afraid of what he might see. A wide smile of relief curved his lips. A boyhood friend stood smiling at him.

"Tom!" he exclaimed. "Tom Hayden. How are you, you old reprobate?"

"Fine, just fine, Ben. How are you?" The two old friends slapped each other on the back as they shook hands.

"Can't complain, Tom. My rheumatiz acts up sometimes. Got to expect that at my age, I reckon."

"I'm sorry about Bessie's passin'," Hayden said. "She was well liked in these parts."

"My sister was an easy person to like," Ben said as they turned from the grave and left the cemetery. "Who's the girl sittin' in your wagon?" he asked, recognizing the vehicle his friend had owned since he could remember. It still had a board missing on the right-hand side. "She one of your granddaughters?"

A scowl came over Tom's face. "I wish she was," he said. "Her name is Gretchen Ames. The poorhouse turned her over to me this mornin'. I'm to take her to the town square, where her bond papers will be bid on. You know, servant for some wealthy landowner for several years."

"And keep his bed warmed, too, I'll wager," Ben growled, the wrinkles on his brow deepening.

Hayden sighed. "Ain't no doubt about that. This one is a looker and scared half to death about her future. I sure feel sorry for her."

They were at the wagon then, gazing up at Gretchen. She smiled shyly at Ben when Tom introduced him, then looked away.

Ben's heart did a strange half beat. His daughter had been around this girl's age when the Indians killed her. Julie had been bigger, though. This one was so delicate-looking, a strong breeze might blow her away. He could see fear and dread of the unknown in her eyes, and there came over him the desire to protect this friendless girl who had no one to turn to.

His lips firmed with determination. Ben Atkins was going to take care of her, be her family. As long as he lived, no one would take advantage of her. Gretchen Ames would be the daughter he had lost so long ago. He would save this one from the lechers who preyed on helpless young women.

"Tom," he blurted out, "if the girl is willin', I'd like to take her back to Kentucky with me. I'll give her a good home and look after her like she was my own."

Tom's eyes widened. "You mean you want to buy her papers?"

"To hell with her papers. Tear them up. I don't want her to be a servant. I want her to be family. With sister Bessie gone I've only got Spencer now, and I get damned little comfort from that wild one."

Tom pushed his hat back and scratched his head thoughtfully. "What do you think, Gretchen?" He looked up at her, then exclaimed softly at the fear in her eyes. "It's not what you're thinkin', girl. Ben means every word he says. He only wants to give you a home. He'd never lay a hand on you in a lustful way. I've known him all my life and I don't know a finer man anywhere."

Gretchen studied the old man who had just offered her a home. She had contemplated jumping from the wagon and running away when Mr. Hayden had spotted his friend in the cemetery and stopped to talk to him. She was glad now that she hadn't, for as she looked into his eyes she saw a kindness that warmed her heart. He would be her friend, she knew.

She smiled shyly at Ben and said with warmth, "Thank you for your offer, Mr. Atkins. I gladly take you up on it."

Both men beamed at her, saying in unison that she would never regret it. "Are you a good walker?" Ben asked, raising his arms to help her down from the tall wagon seat.

Gretchen smiled thinly, remembering the miles she had walked behind a mule, dropping seeds into the rows of soil the plow had turned over. "Yes, Mr. Atkins, I'm a good walker," she answered. "Why do you ask?"

"'Cause I'm takin' you a fur piece and we'll be ridin' shank's pony."

Ben grinned at her. "Can you do it?"

"Don't worry, I'll keep up with you. I haven't got these long legs for nothing."

"You are taller than you look sittin' down."

"I'm five feet, six inches in my bare feet."

"Almost as tall as me." Ben chuckled. "I've shrunk a little, though, with the passin' years." His eyes swept over her body. "My buckskins won't be too big on you, I reckon. Lucky thing I got an extra pair with me."

"Buckskins?" Gretchen questioned. "Why should I wear buckskins?"

"Because your dress will be picked to pieces by brush. Buckskins are sturdy and smooth. Nothin' catches on them. 'Course once we get to my cabin you can go back to wearin' women's clothes." Ben looked at Tom. "Where's her duds?"

When Tom shrugged that he didn't know Gretchen looked down at the ground and mumbled, "I've got them on."

Ben pretended not to see her embarrassment and said smoothly, "That's good. Less to pack on my old mule. He gets ornery sometimes if I overload him." He turned to Tom and held out his hand.

"Do you think you'll ever get out Kentucky way? I'd sure like for you to come visit me and the girl."

"I just might do that one of these days," Tom answered, but both men knew that he wouldn't. It saddened Ben to think that most likely he and his friend would never see each other again as he watched Tom shake hands with Gretchen.

"Well, girl, let's get on the trail," he said gruffly, swallowing a lump in his throat. "My mule is tied up over there under that big oak."

As Ben led Gretchen away, Tom whipped up his team, wondering what he would tell the gimlet-eyed Mrs. Fedders. That one wouldn't like it one bit, losing the money from the sale of Gretchen's papers. By the time he returned to the poorhouse he had decided that he would say that an uncle of hers had showed up and taken her away.

Gretchen matched her stride to Ben's as they walked past large homes where wealthy families lived. She knew from listening to the girls who were sent from the poorhouse to clean these homes that inside there was beautiful furniture that had been shipped all the way from Europe.

She recalled how the girls always fought over who should work for the wealthy owners. Though the hours were long and the work hard, they didn't mind. They were given two good meals a day.

The prosperous part of town was left behind, then, and the little cottages of the common people began to appear. After another mile they reached the outskirts of the town which lay on the last level of sparsely timbered land. Here was a cluster of log cabins owned by small farmers. Each cabin was surrounded by fields of corn and wheat, just beginning to push through the soil.

And beyond lay the wilderness.

Ben heaved a long sigh of relief. "Boy," he said, "it's good to get away from all them houses and people. I swear they affect my breathin'." He drew in a deep breath, as though to emphasize his claim.

Gretchen, having been crowded in with people most of her life, wasn't sure what Ben was talking about. But as they pushed on through the forest, Ben following the trail he had broken two days earlier, she became aware of the serenity of her surroundings; the pungent odor of rotting leaves, the sharp tang of pine and cedar. As Ben had done, she took a deep breath and discovered that her companion was right. One did breathe better in the wilds.

Ben did not stop for a noon meal, but when the sun shone straight overhead he handed Gretchen several strips of pemmican and a handful of parched corn that he took from the bag slung over his shoulder. The Indian version of beef jerky was new to her, but she found it delicious and very filling.

They walked on, the old mule plodding along behind them. They skirted deep ravines, overgrown with brush and tall ferns, moved through open ridges and deep hollows. A heavy gray twilight was deepening when Ben said that they would be making camp a short distance ahead.

Gretchen heaved a sigh of relief. She was dead tired. She felt that they had walked at least twenty miles. But she hadn't minded one mile of it, she reminded herself. Each step she had taken had put more distance between her and what might have been a terrible future. She had a feeling of going home with this kind old man, something she hadn't known for a long, long time.

Within ten minutes Ben was leading the way to a wide bluff. "I camped here on the way in," he said, squatting down and raking together the remains of burned wood. After he had pushed some dry leaves and twigs beneath them he reached into his shoulder bag and pulled out a flint and a striker. He struck them against each other a few times and sparks flew, igniting the leaves. He hurriedly fed it some more dry twigs, and in a short time he had a fire burning brightly.

Standing up and brushing off his hands, Ben said, "I'll get the coffee started and then fix our beds before it gets too dark to see what I'm doin'."

"What can I do?" Gretchen asked, anxious to let her benefactor know that she wasn't lazy, that she would do her share of work.

"Well," Ben said thoughtfully, "do you think you could unpack the mule and take him to that stream a few yards off and let him have a drink? He's gentle and won't kick or try to bite you like some of them do."

"Don't worry about that. I've been handling livestock practically all my life," Gretchen assured him.

Ben grinned, pleased at her answer. "These Kentucky hills have a way of gettin' rid of them who don't belong," he said, "but you're gonna fit right in." He took a hatchet from one of the packs on the mule's back and walked off through the forest.

The wilderness seemed to close in on Gretchen with Ben's disappearance, and she was grateful for the mule's presence. To break the silence she talked soothingly to the animal as she unburdened his back. Then, taking up the lead rope, she led him to the water she could hear rippling over stones and rocks.

She laughed softly when, after the little animal had drunk its fill, he lay down in the grass along the stream and rolled his body back and forth. It was his way of limbering up stiff muscles. When he lunged to his feet she hobbled him a few feet from the leaping flames of the campfire that was now pushing back the descending night. She eased the bit from his mouth, and he was cropping grass and she was sniffing the brewing coffee when Ben returned with an armful of cedar branches.

The early spring nights were still chilly, and Gretchen sat close to the fire as she watched Ben arrange the boughs into two separate piles behind the fire and close to the stone walls of the bluff. When he had smoothed them out to his satisfaction he tucked a blanket over each cedar pallet, then added another one.

"There," he said, straightening up, "we'll sleep warm and comfortable tonight." He walked over to where Gretchen had piled the sacks and bundles and squatted down beside them. "Which would you rather have for supper," his eyes twinkled at Gretchen, "beans and fried salt pork or fried salt pork and beans?"

Gretchen pretended to give the choices serious thought. "I think I prefer salt pork and beans," she said after a moment.

"A good choice," Ben agreed, just as seriously. "I think I'll have that too." They broke out in laughter, one deep and cracked with age, the other light and lilting with youth.

Ben took a knife from the sheath at his waist and cut open two tins of beans a neighbor woman had given him. He spilled them into a blackened pot and sat them on the edge of the fire. While they slowly heated, he used the knife to slice up half a slab of salt-cured pork. The girl looked half starved, and the first thing he was going to do was put some meat on her slender frame.

Gretchen thought that she had never smelled anything so mouth-watering as the meat sizzling in a banged-up skillet, mingling with that of freshly made coffee. When a short time later she dug into a tin plate heaped with meat and beans, she knew she had never tasted anything so good. Ben hid his grin, pretending not to see how she wolfed everything down.

They were topping off the meal with coffee, the first Gretchen had ever tasted, when suddenly the silence was shattered by a most terrifying sound. Gretchen jumped, spilling her coffee, narrowly missing her leg.

"What was that?" She looked wild-eyed at Ben.

"Don't be scared." Ben replenished the coffee she had spilled. "That ole wolf ain't gonna come around our fire. He's only lost from the pack and howlin' so they'll answer him; direct him back to them."

Ben had barely stopped speaking when three long, drawn-out yowls echoed through the hills. He looked at Gretchen as if to say, "See, I told you so."

The wolves continued to call to each other for several minutes, then it grew quiet again. "Well," Ben said as he added more wood on the fire, "it sounds like he's back in the pack."

"Are you sure they won't come around the camp?" Gretchen looked nervously over her shoulder, peering into the blackness of the forest.

"Naw, they wouldn't attack us if they did. They only attack humans if they're cornered, or terribly hungry, like in the winter. The woods are full of game now and they eat real good."

Ben rose and began gathering up the utensils he had used in preparing supper. "I'll take these down to the stream and wash them," he said. "Do whatever you have to do while I'm gone."

Gretchen blushed at his meaning, even though her bladder was ready to burst. She was ready to dart behind a bush when Ben paused and turned around.

"One other thing. I left a pair of my buckskins on your pallet. You might as well change into them tonight. They'll keep you warmer than your dress will. Besides, from now on it's gonna be rough goin'."

How much rougher could it get? Gretchen wondered as she hurried to answer nature's call.

She shivered in the cool night air as she changed into the buckskins, but a few moments later she was toasty warm beneath the blanket, marveling at how much more comfortable this cedar bed was compared to the flattened-out straw tick in the poorhouse. As she watched Ben place the washed pieces around the fire to dry, her eyes grew heavy. In the serene calmness of the wilderness she drew up her knees and curled her hands under her cheek. If the wolves came around camp that night, she wasn't aware of it.

The next two nights and a day and a half passed in much the same way. Night camp was made in the same spots Ben had used on his way to Baker City. On the third day, in the early afternoon, a rain that had threatened for two days poured down. Ben and Gretchen were soaked to the skin when, half an hour later, they came to a cedar swale, shaded and lonely-looking under the gray, lowering skies.

"There it is, girl!" Ben exclaimed proudly, "your new home."

Gretchen peered through the falling rain at a rustic cabin that was much larger than most they had passed along the trail. It looked as sturdy as the trees it blended into, she thought. She was surprised to see smoke rising from the stonefield chimney. She had assumed that Ben lived alone.

Ben was equally surprised. He hadn't expected that Spencer would be home. He had said that he was going to rendezvous with a bunch of trappers over near Squaw Hollow.

The old man was suddenly nervous. How would his son take to having a young girl move in with them? His bearded chin tilted belligerently. He didn't care what he had to say; the girl was staying. He took Gretchen's arm and hurried her along, the old mule practically stepping on their heels, anxious to get to the dry warmth of the barn.

Chapter Three

The hour was gray, the air chill, when Spencer Atkins walked outside and closed the cabin door behind him. He paused on the porch and adjusted the pack on his back to a more comfortable position. It wasn't heavy. It held only a coffeepot and a pouch of coffee, a battered frying pan, a cup, and his bedroll.

He would eat off the land for the next two days of woods-running. Once he arrived in Squaw Hollow, he would find plenty to eat. The wives who accompanied their husbands to the yearly rendezvous would feed him. They would fuss over him like he was a beloved son.

Spencer's white teeth flashed in a crooked smile as he stepped off the porch and struck off in a westerly direction. Most of the good women would like to look on him as a beloved son-in-law. It had taken some doing over the years, ignoring the broad hints that he should take himself a wife. There had been times when a mother persisted in shoving her daughter at him that he'd had to come right out and say that he wasn't interested in marrying and settling down; that he liked it fine, living with Pa.

That's why I've always stuck with easy women, Spencer thought to himself. There were no parents pestering him to marry one of them. It also kept harmony among the mothers with marriageable daughters. There would be no jealousy or hurt feelings.

Still, he mused pensively as his long legs ate up the distance, he'd like to take a decent woman to bed once. He had noticed that his neighbor's young daughters always smelled so nice and clean, looked so fresh. Of course, they giggled a lot. That would soon become tiresome.

I wonder what it would be like, having a virgin, Spencer thought. New husbands were always bragging about their wedding night, boasting that no other man had been between the legs of their young wives before them.

Spencer's lips twisted wryly. He guessed he'd never experience making love to a virgin. The nearest he'd ever come to lying with a respectable woman was Trudie Harrod, and she wasn't all that respectable. There was hardly a single man in Piney Ridge who hadn't wrinkled her sheets.

But since her father had left her the largest farm in the vicinity when he died, Trudie was accepted by her neighbors, though privately she was discussed in unflattering terms. And whenever it was possible without being too obvious about it, she was left out of social gatherings.

He'd been visiting Trudie off and on for close to a year now. He found her as experienced as any whore, and her bed was much softer. He was becoming a little uneasy about her, though. She had begun to make marriage noises. If she kept it up, he would make no more trips to her cabin.

Spencer had just entered a cleared piece of land when a nesting partridge fluttered into the air several yards ahead of him. He stepped back among the trees, concealing himself behind a large birch. What had startled her? Not he. He was too far away from her nest.

After giving the area close scrutiny and seeing nothing out of the ordinary, he stepped back into the clearing, muttering, "Probably a wolf scared her."

But when he crossed the clearing and entered the opposite forest, a flash of buckskin darting among the trees caught his eyes. He quickly stepped behind another tree. There were still some Indians in the area whose hatred for the white man was as strong as the day he'd first set foot on their land.

Last year a dozen or so rebellious young braves had pulled away from their tribe, scorning the Shawnee chief's desire for peace with the white man. For close to a month they had gone on the rampage, terrorizing the community. They had set fires to three outlying cabins, raced their ponies through crops and gardens, and killed livestock. When they killed two men and a teenage boy and raped two women the area men had had enough. They banded together and went hunting them down. One by one they caught and hung ten of the Indian outlaws.

Things had calmed down then, with only occasional pilfering of anything they could get their hands on or setting fires to fields. The white man must still be on the alert when out in the woods. He ran the risk of being shot or catching an arrow in the back.

When several minutes passed and he saw no more movement in the forest he moved out, stepping as quietly as any Indian. He told himself that he had probably seen a young Indian maid out digging roots or picking berries.

It was around noon when clouds began to gather overhead and the sky turned a slate-gray color. "Hell," Spencer swore, "damned if I'm not gonna get rained on."

Minutes later, as he walked on, a stealthy crackling of brush brought Spencer looking for cover, asking himself if he had seen a renegade

Indian earlier, after all. He checked the position of his knife in case he had to do hand-to-hand fighting with a brave.

As Spencer stood as still as the tree he had concealed himself behind, the thought of danger gave him slight concern. Since an early age he had been able to take care of himself. Nevertheless, he was never careless. It was the careless man who got himself killed.

When some time went by he checked his silver-plated pocketwatch. According to it, twenty minutes had passed with nothing stirring around him. Still, he wondered, why had the birds resumed their singing and twittering? Of course, there could be several reasons for their silence, he thought. One being the overcast sky and the threat of rain, making them roost early.

Satisfied with his reasoning, Spencer stepped from behind the tree just as it began to rain. Huge drops pattered on the dry leaves covering the forest floor. "I'll be drenched," he muttered and broke into a trot. Moments later, with a wry twist of his lips, he slowed down to a walk. It didn't make any sense to run; he wouldn't stay any drier. He doubted there was any shelter within miles of the open land he now traveled.

Suddenly, while in midstride, three things happened simultaneously. He heard the report of a rifle, felt a searing pain across his forehead, and his knees buckled under him. He lay stunned, his cheek pressed into mud and wet grass, listening to the receding sound of running feet.

When there was no sound except that of the falling rain Spencer lifted trembling fingers to his forehead. They came away dripping blood. When he lifted his head he saw a pool of red where his cheek had lain. He staggered to his feet. He had to get the hell away from here. Whoever had shot at him might get it in his head to return, to make sure his shot had done the job it was meant to do.

Spencer stood a moment, fighting off dizziness as he swiped at the blood running down his right eye, almost blinding him. When his head cleared a bit he struck out toward home, peering through the blood and rain, his ears straining to hear any sound.

It was early afternoon when Spencer finally staggered into the cabin with a sense of profound gratitude. He immediately filled a basin with water from the pail sitting on a workbench under the kitchen window. Next, he pulled open a shallow drawer at the table's edge, took out a piece of white flannel, and dropped it into the water. Then he stood in front of a small mirror affixed to the wall beside the window and began to bathe his wound.

After a couple of swipes of the cloth he found that he only had a surface wound, despite all its bleeding. It probably wouldn't even leave a scar once it healed.

Spencer continued to press the wet cloth to his forehead until only a thin oozing of blood remained. He reached up to an open shelf and took down a small jar of salve, a concoction that his father had mixed up. After smoothing it liberally over the long, thin line the bullet had scored across his brow he built a fire in the fireplace.

He had just changed into dry clothing and was standing in front of the leaping flames, his wet buckskins steaming where he had spread them, when the kitchen door opened.

He spun around, his hand on his knife, then stared. His father and a tall, thin teenage boy stared back at him.

"How come you didn't go to the rendezvous like you planned?" Ben demanded right off, closing the door and shrugging out of his wet jacket.

Spencer looked at Ben and frowned, wondering at his pugnacious tone. And why was there a troubled, guilty look on his father's face? he wondered. After a minute he pushed the black hair off his forehead, revealing the red line and smeared salve.

"I started out to go this mornin', then around noon I got this from some sneakin' sniper." He gave a shrug of his shoulders. "I guess I could have gone on, but I was bleedin' like a stuck hog, and I figured I'd better get back home."

"Let me take a look at it," Ben said, only concern on his face now. While Spencer held his hair back, the old man scrutinized the wound closely. He stepped back then and remarked, "A half inch deeper, and it would have shattered your brains."

Spencer let his hair drop back down, a crooked grin twisting his lips. "Maybe," he said, "even if I do have a thick skull like you're always sayin'. Who's your friend?" he asked to change the subject. He looked more closely at the silent figure, who hadn't stirred since entering the kitchen.

He saw rain-flattened hair, cold, pinched features, and a thin body lost in wet buckskins much too large. He started in shock when he spotted softly rounded evidence that said this was no young boy standing behind his father.

His regard went back to Gretchen's face, and his lids narrowed when the green-hazel eyes stared back at him for a moment, then looked away with complete indifference.

His face flushed in annoyance. It was the first time in his life he had been snubbed by a woman. And to be snubbed by a skinny beanpole who looked like a drowned rat only added to the insult.

An overwhelming desire to wipe that aloof look off her face came over Spencer. He turned to Ben and asked with cool deliberation, "Where'd you pick up this weedy-lookin' thing?"

A flush scorched across Gretchen's face. She knew she was no beauty, with her short-cropped hair and bone-thin body, but what right did this arrogant man have to so cruelly point it out? She opened her mouth to demand an apology, but the words never left her mouth.

"Are you comparin' this girl to your whores and squaws?" Ben yelled. He jabbed a crooked finger at Spencer's broad chest, making him take a step backward. "Gretchen is the granddaughter of a friend of mine. Before he died, I promised him I'd take care of her." The lie slipped smoothly from Ben's lips.

"And you, you damn fool, if you can't see her beauty, it's because of the sort of women you're used to wallerin' around with."

As soon as the words had left his mouth, Spencer regretted that he had insulted the girl. It wasn't his nature to point out a woman's unattractiveness, but, by god, he didn't like Pa's description of him wallowing around with women. It made him sound like a . . . rutting bull.

So, even as he asked Ben's pardon, not bothering to look at Gretchen, there was resentment in his tone. "You could have told me who she was as soon as you walked in, instead of jumpin' all over me for not goin' to the rendezvous."

"Well, you surprised me," Ben said lamely. "I didn't expect to see you here."

Spencer looked at the thin figure shivering in the wet buckskins. He didn't like the idea of having a female underfoot all the time. Especially one who looked at a man as though he wasn't there.

"Where's she gonna sleep?" he growled.

"She's gonna sleep in the loft room where your sister used to sleep. I'll clean it out tomorrow.

"Gretchen," Ben continued, turning to the girl, "let's get you out of them there wet clothes before you catch pneumony." He handed her a fustian towel and motioned toward a door that stood ajar. "You can go into Spencer's bedroom and dry off. You'll see a doeskin shift hangin' on the wall that should fit you. Some squaw or other lost it in Spencer's bedroll the last time he went to a rendezvous."

Gretchen took the towel and walked toward the door Ben had indicated, feeling the trapper's eyes boring into her back. He had made it plain that he didn't want her here, but she didn't care. He didn't have to worry about what the future held for him. He was a man, strong and very sure of himself.

She was sure of one thing, she told herself. He wasn't going to drive her away, no matter how hard he might try. She finally had a home and she was going to keep it.

Gretchen paused at the door when Ben called after her, "In that trunk under the window you'll find some long johns. You can sleep in them tonight." She nodded and pushed open the door.

She found Spencer's room; like the kitchen and the large family room, it was spotlessly clean. It was sparsely furnished, however. It contained the trunk Ben had spoken of, a bed with a small table beside it, which held a candle holder and a candle. The cedar-plank floor was bare except for a dark blue woven rug placed beside the bed. His clothes were hung on pegs driven into the log walls.

Gretchen shivered in her wet clothing and as she stripped off her borrowed buckskins, goose bumps popped out on her flesh as she hastily dried off her body, then gave her head a brisk rubbing. She could feel her hair springing into its usual curls as she looked for, and found, the Indian dress Ben had mentioned. She pulled the soft doeskin garment over her head and smoothed it down over her hips, feeling half naked without her petticoat and narrow-legged bloomers.

The fringed and beaded dress clung to her, and looking down her body, Gretchen discovered delicate curves she hadn't been aware of in the shapeless dresses she'd been used to wearing. She became aware also that the dress showed a lot of skin. She tugged at the vee neckline, pulling it toward her chin. To her dismay, the supple leather fell back down in place, displaying a shocking amount of cleavage.

"Oh dear," she murmured on discovering that the hem only came a few inches below her knees. What would Mrs. Fedders say if she could see her standing here, the curves of her breasts showing, her legs and feet bare? And Ben's son would really curl his lip at her now.

"Well, let him," she muttered. "I can't stay in here all night." She found the long johns where Ben had said they would be and, folding them over her arm, she picked up the towel and wet clothing and walked to the door. Her hand on the latch, she paused. She could hear Ben and his son talking, and not in friendly tones.

As she listened, she caught the tail end of what Ben was saying. "And don't forget for one minute, Spencer, that she's family now. Don't try to work your spells on her."

"Dammit, Pa," Spencer came back heatedly, "don't you think I've got any honor about women? Besides, skinny females never did appeal to me, so you've got nothin' to worry about. I'll never lay a hand on your precious little rag-tail Gretchen."

Ben muttered some inaudible word and then it grew quiet. Gretchen waited a couple of minutes, then pushed open the door.

Both men looked up at the click of the latch. Ben smiled at her, but Spencer's eyes widened until they bugged when she stepped into the room. *She is exquisite,* he thought, gazing at the fair face with its delicate features, eyes the color of new leaves on an oak tree, with a slumberousness to them even when she was looking at him with scorn, which she was doing now. He moved his gaze from her chestnut-colored hair to move over her body. He lingered a moment on the firm breasts pushing against the doeskin before moving down to the gently rounded hips. Hunger leapt in his eyes and his breathing became heavy when he saw the slightly discernible mound at the apex of her thighs.

Her slender delicacy called to the raw male in him like no other woman had ever done before.

Spencer realized with a start that Ben's frowning gaze was on him, and he hurriedly switched his intent look to the dancing flames in the fireplace. He sat down, crossing his legs to hide the beginning of an arousal that pushed against his buckskins. It didn't help his condition when Gretchen bent over to spread her wet clothing on the hearth to dry. Never before had he seen such a fetching little rear end, he thought as she took the time to smooth the wrinkles out of the dress.

When Gretchen straightened up Ben grinned at her and said, "I expect you're hungry for a real meal by now. What would you like for supper?"

"It doesn't matter," Gretchen answered, "but whatever we have, let me cook it."

"Well, if you don't mind." A pleased smile stirred under Ben's beard. "Me and Spence do get tired of our own cookin'. I'll go fetch you a pair of my socks to put on so you don't get splinters in your feet, then we'll decide on supper."

When Ben went off to his bedroom Gretchen told herself that she wasn't about to stay in the room with this man whose eyes had just stripped the shift off her body, nor did she want to hear any more of his sneering remarks. With her chin in the air she marched into the kitchen.

She gave the room a more thorough scrutiny than she had when she'd first stepped in out of the rain. The presence of Ben's big son, the contempt he had shown when he realized she was a female, had blinded her to her surroundings.

A good-sized table, handmade but well-constructed, stood beneath a window, with four chairs placed around it. There was a hutch with open shelves above it where pewter plates and cups were neatly stored. There was a cooking fireplace in one corner, with a small stone oven built inside it. Standing next to it was a long, narrow workbench with pots and skillets hanging above it.

That she was pleased with the kitchen showed in the smile that curved Gretchen's lips. She would derive a lot of pleasure from preparing meals in here.

She looked up when Ben entered the kitchen, a pair of gray woolen socks in his hand. "They'll be big." He grinned as he handed them to her. "But they'll protect your feet and keep them warm until your shoes dry." He squatted down in front of the fireplace. "I'll get a fire started, then we'll go down in the cellar and see what we can find for you to cook."

When Ben's fire burned and crackled he took one of the candleholders from the table and lit the candle from a flaming twig, then lifted and laid back a trapdoor situated just in front of the worktable.

Gretchen followed him down a short flight of shadowy steps and gasped at the abundance of foodstuffs inside the stone-walled room. Her disbelieving gaze ranged over bins of apples, pears, turnips, and potatoes. In one corner stood a tall crock whose strong odor told her it was filled with sauerkraut. Beside it sat a wire basket of eggs and two covered brown crocks. She was to learn later that they held butter and milk. Gretchen lifted her eyes to the raftered ceiling and gazed in wonder at a half side of beef, a slab each of bacon and salt pork, plus a sugar-cured ham. Her mouth watered. Ben's cellar held more food for two people than the poorhouse provided for all its children.

"Well, girl, what will it be?" Ben broke in on her thoughts. "Should I slice us off some beef steaks? They'd taste right fine with some baked potatoes and a dish of stewed turnips."

Steaks, Gretchen said to herself. She could hardly remember what beef tasted like. Certainly she hadn't eaten any since arriving at the poorhouse. Cook often prepared steaks for the Fedderses, though, and the delicious aroma would float through the house, making everyone's mouth water.

She nodded her agreement, thinking that at least she knew how to cook them. She'd had kitchen duty many times over the years and she had learned much from Cook, simply by watching her. The Fedderses were fond of fancy meals.

Ben's knife flashed in the candlelight as it sliced through the side of beef. When he held three thick steaks in his hand, he looked at Gretchen and said, "Grab up the vegetables and I'll get the potatoes buried in the hot ashes."

As Gretchen peeled the turnips, quartered them and put them in a pot of water, she said, "Your son doesn't want me here, you know."

"It would seem that way," Ben agreed, "but he couldn't keep his eyes from strayin' in your direction all the time. He knows you'll be a big temptation to him, and he knows better than to try anything with you. Probably that's why he's mad."

"You're mistaken, Ben." Gretchen's hand went self-consciously to her cropped curls. "He couldn't possibly be attracted to me. You forget that he called me a skinny beanpole."

There was amusement in Ben's short laugh. "That was before he saw you dried off and wearin' that there squaw dress." He ruffled her red-brown curls. "You don't know much about men do you, girl?"

Gretchen blushed and shook her head. She didn't know anything about men.

Soon a mingling of delicious aromas was drifting through the cabin. Gretchen turned the steaks that were sizzling in the frying pan, then said to Ben, "Supper will be ready to eat in about ten minutes."

When Ben went to call Spencer to the table his son was gone. He had left by the front door.

Chapter Four

The rain slowed to a drizzle as Spencer's long legs climbed one hill and then another, his feet kicking out at tree roots and rocks in his irritation. He had left the cabin over an hour ago, not even sure why he was fleeing his own home. Now that his anger had cooled, he knew that his action had been much like that of a five-year-old throwing himself down and drumming his heels on the floor in a tantrum.

But damn Pa's hide, he had seen how drawn Spencer was to the uppity witch his father had brought home and it had tickled Pa no end. Pa's silent laughter was really what had sent him bolting from the cabin.

Spencer didn't like the way he had been attracted to the green-eyed beauty. Something warned him that he could easily get caught emotionally by the delicate, lovely Gretchen, and he disliked that thought even more. Of all the women he had known, none had ever touched his heart, and he intended to keep it that way. He liked his free and easy life, a life that did not include a wife and family.

He'd have a hell of a time keeping his hands off the new addition to their home, he knew, for when she had stepped out of his bedroom in that skimpy Indian shift his blood had burned like a forest fire running before the wind. Even when she gave him one of her see-through looks he had still wanted her.

Damn Pa for being a soft-hearted old fool.

Spencer's head was throbbing again, and his stomach rumbled from hunger. He hadn't eaten since early that morning. Could Gretchen Ames cook? he wondered.

Spencer was surprised to find that his aimless walking had brought him back to the hill opposite the cabin. Dim candlelight shone through the kitchen window; an early dusk had come on because of the rain and the gray skies. He paused and leaned against a tree, giving a sour grunt when he saw Gretchen's slender figure pass in front of the window. He had hoped that she and Pa would have eaten by now and that he could have the kitchen all to himself. He didn't care to spend any more time than necessary with a female whose every look found him wanting.

But hell, he thought as he pushed away from the tree, he was too wet and miserable to stay out any longer. He'd ignore the little witch, pretend she wasn't even there.

As he started down the hill, a little voice inside him whispered, *Oh yeah, I'd like to see you try it. There's not a man alive who could ignore that one.*

When Spencer pushed open the heavy door and stepped into the kitchen Ben and Gretchen sat at the table, in the middle of eating the evening meal. "We were just too hungry to wait for you, Spence," Ben apologized as he looked up at his son. "Fact is, I thought maybe you had gone to the post and wouldn't be back until tomorrow sometime."

Ignoring Gretchen and his father's thinly veiled innuendo, Spencer grunted, "I'm gonna get some dry clothes on." There was laughter in the look Ben and Gretchen exchanged as he stamped out of the kitchen.

Their faces were clear of all emotion, however, when after a few minutes Spencer returned and sat down at the table, where a plate had been placed for him just in case he returned. He jabbed his fork into a bowl of roasted potatoes and, spearing one, he was about to place it on his plate when Gretchen rose and snatched up the piece of pewter. He reared back in the chair, a glowering frown scoring his forehead. He forgot his intention of ignoring her, for the little witch didn't intend for him to eat.

Ready to flay her with his tongue, to do the same to his father if he interfered, he bit back his angry words when Gretchen knelt in front of the fireplace and, from a skillet there, forked a steak onto his plate. When she plunked the meat down in front of him he scowled at his father, who was trying to hide his amusement by bending his face over his own meat and potatoes. He knew he should say thank you, but damned if he would. He picked up his knife and fork and dug in.

Ben frowned at his son's rudeness but let it pass. Gretchen did the same, although she would have liked to call him all sorts of things as a silence settled over the table and wasn't broken until Ben asked, "How's your head, boy?" knowing that to be called *boy* would rile his son all the more.

"It's fine, just fine," Spencer snapped, although he had a pounding headache.

Ben was the first to sit back, rubbing a full stomach. "I can't remember when I've had a finer meal, honey." He smiled at Gretchen as he took his pipe and tobacco pouch from his shirt pocket. "Not since Mary used to cook for me, I expect."

He filled the clay bowl with cured long-green tobacco that he had grown, tamped it down, then walked over to the fireplace and lit it with a burning twig. When he returned to the table and sat back down he looked at Spencer, who was just finishing his meal, and asked, "What about it, Spence, wasn't that a fine supper?"

Spencer's eyes flashed briefly to Gretchen and then away as he shrugged indifferently. But the lift of his shoulders slighting the meal was a lie. It had been the tastiest piece of steak he'd ever eaten, but damned if he'd say so.

A minute later, however, he was almost paid back for his arrogance. When Gretchen served their coffee he had to hurriedly jerk his hand back to save it from being scalded as the hot liquid was carelessly splashed into his cup.

"Watch what you're doin'!" he exploded angrily.

Gretchen gave him an innocent, wide-eyed look, as if to say, "I don't know what you're talking about."

Again, Ben had to hide a grin. When Gretchen returned the pot to the fire, then resumed her seat, he said, "I've been thinkin' that I'll take you around to meet our neighbors tomorrow, maybe drop in at the post to meet the folk there. What do you think?"

Gretchen thought of her faded dress drying in the other room, the way it hung on her thin frame, the waistline coming almost to her hips, and cringed at the thought of meeting strangers in it.

It hadn't bothered her how she had looked at the poorhouse. All the girls looked the same, more or less, in their donated dresses. But Spencer Atkins's scornful look and words had made her aware of how poorly she must look, not to mention her cropped-off hair.

"Well, what do you think, Gretchen?" Ben reminded her that he was waiting for an answer. "Do you want to go visitin' tomorrow?"

"If you don't mind, Ben, I'd like to get settled in before I meet any of your friends." She smiled at him and started to add, "To enjoy the peacefulness here that doesn't exist where I come from," but caught herself in time. Ben, bless his heart, hadn't told his hateful son where he had found her only minutes before she was to be sold into bondage.

That knowledge would have curled his chiseled lips all the more.

"It's up to you, honey," Ben said. "We can go visitin' anytime. Ain't anybody in these parts plannin' on movin' I don' reckon. Besides, it'll probably take all day tomorrow cleanin' out the loft room for you. We've been usin' it as a kinda storage room and I expect it's in a pretty bad state."

He puffed out a cloud of aromatic smoke from his clay pipe before looking at Spencer and saying, "You want to give us a hand with the loft?"

Spencer raised his head and narrowed his eyes at his father. He'd heard the trace of amusement in the cracked voice. "I'm headin' for the rendezvous again in the mornin'," he said gruffly.

"I see." Ben nodded and stuck the pipe back between his lips. "I expect me and Gretchen can do it by ourselves."

Spencer's face was a dark study as he prepared his own pipe. He hadn't planned on going to the rendezvous. His head hurt like hell, but that was the first excuse that had come to him. It wasn't a bad idea, though, he decided on second thought. The little witch was begging for a set down, and if he was around her much longer he'd give it to her.

He sighed inwardly. He'd have Pa on his back then, and he didn't need to be on the bad side of them both.

"Well, say hello to the men for me," Ben said, standing up and knocking his pipe out on the kitchen hearth. "Explain to them that I ain't up to all that carousin' anymore."

Spencer nodded, and Ben looked at Gretchen. "Light another candle, honey, and we'll go up in the loft and see about fixin' you a bed."

Gretchen took a candle and holder off the mantel, aware that Spencer's eyes were on her as she lit the candle from the one on the table. Ignoring him, she carried it into the main room, then followed Ben up the ladder to the room that was to be hers.

A room all by herself, shared with no one.

The loft overlooked the family room and, except for an opening to allow entrance, only a foot-high railing enclosed it. Gretchen appreciated that. She wouldn't have to be afraid of rolling off the bed in her sleep and falling to the floor below.

"I hadn't realized it was such a mess up here," Ben said, standing amid old trunks and a pile of fustian sacks stuffed with what appeared to be rags. There was a jumble of rusty, broken traps, a dusty spinning wheel and a loom, and in the northwest corner of the room furniture had been shoved and covered up with sheets that were now yellow with age.

"I ain't been up here for a while," Ben said, looking around as though searching for something. "There's some furniture up here someplace. This was my daughter Julie's room, her little place of privacy. I remember she had it real cozylike up here. We'll clean the junk out tomorrow and you can fix it real purty for yourself."

"Is that the furniture over there?" Gretchen pointed to the corner.

"Yeah, that's it," Ben answered and moved across the floor to remove one of the covers to reveal a bedstead and a thick feather mattress. "Do you think you can help me put this together?" Ben looked over his shoulder at Gretchen. "I can call Spence up to help me."

Gretchen shook her head. She didn't want that one doing anything for her. "I can do it," she said, placing the candle on a debris-free spot on the floor, well out of the way of being accidentally knocked over and setting fire to the loft.

The pieces were heavy as she and Ben put the bed together, but Gretchen was strong despite her thinness. Hours of grueling work in the fields at the poorhouse had strengthened her arms and legs to a point where she could work ten hours a day without becoming overly tired.

When it was assembled the bed was a lovely four-poster. Its tall headboard had flowers carved in its center and it was stained a bright red. The foot rail, about eighteen inches high, had the same design. Woven back and forth across its framework were strips of rawhide for the mattress to rest on.

As Gretchen and Ben tugged the ticking of goosedown onto the frame, he remarked, "We'll have to change this for a straw mattress before long. Feathers can't be beat for sleepin' on in the winter, but they get mighty hot in the summer."

Having never, in her memory, slept on such, Gretchen made no response.

Ben walked across the floor and lifted the lid of one of the trunks. He reached inside and pulled out two pillows and placed them on the floor, then added a sheet and a blanket to them. "Do you want me to help you make up the bed?" he asked.

"No." Gretchen shook her head. "Go on back downstairs. I'll take care of it." She could hardly wait to be alone, to admire the bed, the first one she would be sleeping in after ten years of finding her rest on the floor.

When Ben's head disappeared down the ladder she shook out the sheet and smoothed it over the thick mattress and neatly tucked in the edges. Just as carefully, she spread the blanket over it. As she guided the pillows into the cases, her mind raced with plans of what she would do to this room; in Ben's words, how she would purty it up.

For one thing, she'd had plenty of experience with a spinning wheel and a loom. In her leisure time she would work at them, making cloth and rugs. The cabin was neat and clean, but it had been too long without a woman's touch. She was going to try and rectify that by prettying it some.

Giving the bed a final pat, Gretchen picked up the candleholder and started down the ladder. There were dishes to be washed and the kitchen to be neatened up.

Spencer, sitting before the fire, his stockinged feet propped on the hearth, looked up, his eyes honing in on the long legs flashing down the rungs. His pulse leapt at the thought of them wrapped around his waist. *Damn,* he thought, *I'll be glad when she starts wearing that patched dress of hers again.*

Gretchen smiled at Ben as she passed through to the kitchen, but she didn't look Spencer's way. She knew that it irritated him when she ignored his presence, but, strangely, it gave her supreme satisfaction to rile the big trapper. She muffled a giggle as she prepared a pan of soapy water. He riled so easily.

After the dishes were washed and dried Gretchen set the table for tomorrow morning's meal, then, stifling a yawn, she blew out the candle and walked into the family room. "I'm going to bed now," she said to Ben as she folded the long johns he had lent her over an arm. "What shall I make for breakfast in the morning?"

"Whatever it pleases you to make, honey." Ben smiled at her with affection. "You're the woman of the house so you make the decision, and me and Spence will eat it."

"Thank you, Ben." Gretchen spoke over a lump that rose in her throat, unable to say more. She would burst into tears if she tried. It had been a long time since anyone had treated or spoken to her so kindly. She hadn't glanced Spencer's way once, but she felt his scorching gaze follow her up the ladder.

Ben saw the hot look in his son's eyes as he watched Gretchen climb to her room and he frowned. "How come you didn't ride down to the post like you always do?" he asked suspiciously.

"Because my head aches," Spencer snapped out, avoiding his father's knowing eyes. He wasn't about to admit that he'd stayed home just to sneak looks at the most beautiful female he'd ever seen.

Ben studied his son for a moment, then allowed that probably his head *did* hurt. Nevertheless, he knew his son, and he didn't like the way he eyed Gretchen like a hungry wolf. He'd make sure he kept a close eye on him where the girl was concerned.

"Put some more salve on the wound," he said as he stood up. "That might help some. I'm goin' to turn in now," he added after a long yawn. "It's been a long day for me."

"Good night, Pa." Spencer's tone was much softer as he watched Ben limp toward his bedroom. His father's rheumatism was acting up.

Up in the loft room, Gretchen forgot about the rude man below as she pulled the Indian dress over her head, then dragged on Ben's long-legged underwear. She yanked the heavy socks off her feet and slid under the sheet and blanket. Curled on her side in the warmth of the feathers, a great peace flowed over her. The flames from the fireplace below sent flickering lights along the roof beams as she closed her eyes in sleep.

The rising sun had reddened the crest of the hills when Gretchen stirred, then turned over on her back. She fought wakefulness, trying to hold on to the dream she was having of her parents; she was a little girl again and each day was filled with love and laughter.

But like the morning mists, the dream drifted away and she was left with cold reality. Those days were gone forever, replaced with the harshness and drudgery of the poorhouse.

She turned back on her side, curling deeper into the featherbed. Her eyes snapped open. She wasn't lying on her old thin pallet of straw in the poorhouse. She was no longer a part of that wretched place. Ben Atkins had rescued her. He had saved her from something maybe far worse by giving her a home. A home deep in the wilderness of Kentucky, a cabin of which she would be mistress.

She wanted to shout her happiness as she threw back the covers, scooted off the high bed, and ran on light feet to the small window tucked under the eaves. Swinging open the shutter and kneeling down, she found that the rain had ceased. She drew in a deep breath of the scent of wet grass and earth and cedar and pine.

She hugged herself. Oh, but she was going to love living here. It was so beautiful, so peaceful. In the distance she could see the Ohio sliding serenely along in the valley below. Then, as she watched the reflection of the sun on the water, her eyes suddenly widened. A canoe had shot into sight, a nearly naked Indian lifting and dipping a paddle, swiftly pushing the vessel along. Her heart began to pound, her pulses racing fearfully. Was it the red man's intention to slip up on the cabin and set fire to it?

I must go wake Ben and Spencer, she thought in near panic. She had jumped to her feet when she remembered a conversation she and Ben had had on the trail, and she calmed down. She had asked him if there were any Indians where he was taking her and, if so, if they were dangerous.

He had answered, "We have plenty of them in our area, but outside of stealing anything they can get their hands on, if they are treated fair they're right hospitable. Actually, the Shawnee have more admirable traits than a lot of white men. As soon as an Indian child is old enough to understand, he is taught that deceitfulness is a crime, and that absolute honesty to those of his tribe is the basis of good character."

Ben had chuckled before adding, "They do believe, however, that they are only responsible for good conduct to their own people. When it comes to a white man or an enemy tribe, it's a different story. Especially if it's one he doesn't like, one who has done him dirt at one time or the other."

"What about you?" she had asked. "Do they like you?"

"Well enough, I think. I've never done them any harm. In all the years I've been here they've never bothered me. And they get along fine with Spencer. He can speak their language." This had been said proudly.

I'm not surprised, Gretchen thought now as she turned from the window and started unbuttoning the long johns. *He's a savage himself.*

When she had divested herself of her sleepwear and laid it on top of a trunk, she stood there naked, berating herself for not bringing her dress and petticoat up to the room with her. She grimaced. She'd have to don the skimpy doeskin again.

After she had yanked the garment over her head, feeling wicked that it was the only thing covering her nakedness, she pulled on the heavy socks and silently climbed down the ladder. As she walked through the family room, gray with the early dawn, she heard Ben's rumbling snores coming from his bedroom, and her lips curved in a smile. They had been comforting sounds on the trail at night when they had settled down in their cedar pallets. The sonorous sound had seemed to push back the darkness, the distant howling of wolves.

In the dimness of the kitchen, Gretchen made out the candleholder in the middle of the table, the tinderbox lying beside it. She lifted the tin lid, took out the flint and piece of steel and, holding them over the candle, struck them together. It took but a few sparks to ignite the wick. She picked up the holder and moved over to the fireplace, setting it on the mantel. She had been a little apprehensive about building a fire this morning. She had never made one before, but she had watched Ben make campfires and she didn't imagine it was much different than getting one lit in a fireplace.

She stared in surprise when she looked down at the hearth and found no ashes spilling out as there had been when she finished making supper the night before. Not only had they been cleared away but the framework for a fire had been laid. All she had to do was start a fire under it.

"Bless you, Ben," she whispered, removing the candle from the holder and laying its flame against a pile of dry wood shavings. The thin slivers caught immediately and ate into the carefully laid pieces of split wood placed on top of them. Nodding her satisfaction, she hurried to fill the big black tea kettle with water from a full pail on the worktable, blessing Ben again, for she had no idea where their water supply came from.

When she had hung the heavy vessel on a crane built into the fireplace and swung it out over the flames, she took off her socks and hurried outside to answer a call to nature. She spotted the necessary in back of the cabin and made her way to it. When she opened the narrow door all sorts of items fell out and scattered over the ground. She frowned her annoyance, then walked behind a clump of bushes just putting on new leaves. After breakfast she would ask Ben to clear out the little building.

A few minutes later, back in the kitchen again, she filled the coffeepot with water, ground some coffee beans to add to it, then placed the pot on a bed of red coals she raked to one side. That was the way Ben had made coffee when they made camp.

As she washed her face and hands in a basin of warm water, the aroma of seeping coffee wafted through the cabin. And a little later, humming softly to herself, she had bacon sizzling in a skillet.

As she turned the strips of meat, she wondered when Ben and Mr. Arrogant would leave their beds. Already the sun was glistening on the grass and beating at the window. If she still lived at the poorhouse she would have been out in the fields for a few hours already, or in the barn helping to milk the fourteen cows in residence.

She was stirring up a batch of flapjack batter when Ben entered the kitchen, Spencer a few steps behind him. "Mornin', honey." Ben ruffled her short curls. "It sure smells good in here. And look, Spence," he said to his stony-faced son, who had stepped past him and was filling the washbasin with water, "we're gonna have flapjacks with our bacon."

Spencer made no response, only proceeded to wash his face. *Beastly clod,* Gretchen thought to herself as he dried his face, then opened the window and flung the water outside. He picked up a comb lying on the windowsill, ran it a few times through the longish hair that lay on his collar, then sat down at the table.

When Ben would have washed up in cold water also, Gretchen stopped him. "I've heated some water for you to use," she said. "You should keep your hands as warm as possible. Getting them cold only aggravates your rheumatism."

"Well, thank you, Gretchen." Ben was touched at her thoughtfulness. It had been a long time since he had experienced tenderness from a woman. It was going to be real nice having her live with him and Spencer.

He glanced at his son and knew from the expression on his face that he wasn't of the same mind. He felt bad that Spencer had taken this cold attitude toward the girl he was beginning to look upon as a daughter.

I'm wondering, though, he thought to himself, *if maybe Spence is a little afraid of her and that's why he acts like he does. He's never been around decent women very much, single ones, that is. They're way different from squaws and whores, and he probably doesn't know how to act around Gretchen.*

When later the three of them sat eating the tender 'jacks smothered in maple syrup, along with slices of crisp bacon, Ben looked at Spencer and asked, "How long do you figure to be gone, son?"

"I don't know." Spencer helped himself to more flapjacks. "A week maybe. It'll take a couple of days to get to the Hollow, then the same to return."

"How's your head feelin' this mornin'? You did a lot of tossing around."

Spencer's lips twisted in a half smile. "How do you know that? You didn't stop snoring once your head hit the pillow."

"You're wrong." Ben's eyes crinkled in a grin. "Your mutterin' and groanin' woke me up a couple of times. I couldn't figure out whether you was carryin' on in pain or pleasure. Sometimes it sounded like both. What was you dreamin' about, anyway?"

Spencer gave Ben a murderous look, then slid Gretchen a fast glance. She sat calmly, eating her breakfast. Did Pa suspect that he had been dreaming of her? He took a swallow of coffee, then said, "I was probably dreamin' that I was throttlin' an onery old man."

He touched a finger to the thin red line at the edge of his hairline and brought the conversation back to Ben's first question. "My wound is tender, but my head doesn't ache anymore."

"Nevertheless, I'd stay out of fights for a while if I was you. A fist or a club upside your head wouldn't benefit you any."

Spencer grinned but didn't comment on the old man's remark. It was hard to stay out of fights at a rendezvous. The trappers would be drinking and spoiling for fights. He would, however, stay away from the quarrelsome ones as much as possible.

All this time Gretchen hadn't said a word. Her mind was busy, planning how she would fix up the loft room as the men's conversation passed over her head. She hadn't noticed, as Ben had, that his son's eyes often strayed her way.

She was nibbling thoughtfully on a piece of bacon when Spencer finished his coffee and rose from the table, remarking, "I'd better get goin'"

Ben stood up also. "I'll walk you outside." Spencer nodded, his eyes on Gretchen, who looked like she was miles away. He felt compelled to say something to her before he left, not just walk out the door. He had, after all, begun the coldness that existed between them.

But when Gretchen didn't look at him, didn't even seem to be aware of him, he spun angrily on his heel and stalked out of the kitchen.

Ben grinned and followed him. It was going to be mighty interesting, watching his son fight his attraction to Gretchen. A battle he was going to lose, from the looks of it. Before that proud rooster knew what was happening Gretchen was going to have him clucking like a hen . . . if she had a mind to, of course. Right now she didn't have much use for him, but that could change. Spencer could be quite persuasive if he set his mind to it.

Outside, Ben and Spencer stepped off the porch and walked behind the cabin to relieve themselves. "I've got to clean out the neccessary for Gretchen," Ben said. "Can't have the girl goin' behind a bush like a squaw."

"Yeah, it would never do for Miss Uppity to heist *her* skirts in the woods." Spencer's lips curled.

"That's right," Ben agreed, pretending he hadn't heard the cynicism in Spencer's words as they walked back to the porch.

Spencer picked up his rifle and the gear he had set against the door. Hitching the grub bag onto his shoulder, he grinned at Ben and said, "Well, I'm off. Take care of yourself while I'm gone."

"You do the same, son." Ben touched Spencer's shoulder, then remained on the porch until his son had moved out of sight before going back inside.

Chapter Five

As soon as Gretchen had washed and dried the breakfast dishes and made up the two beds, she and Ben climbed to the loft room armed with a broom, a pail of hot, sudsy water, and several rags Ben had found for her. They paused in the middle of the room, wondering where to start clearing out the accumulation of items that had found their way up the ladder over the years.

They decided, finally, that all loose trash would be tossed to the floor below to be burned in the fireplace later. Ben's rusty, discarded traps and other larger materials would be tossed out the window to be hauled away when they were finished cleaning the room.

Dust flew as articles that had been moldering for years went sailing over the short railing or flying out the window. In just a short time sweat began to gather on Gretchen's forehead and Ben was removing his shirt.

An hour later the big room contained only the bed, a rocker, a dresser, a small table, and two trunks, plus the spinning wheel and the loom. Gretchen looked at Ben, a smile of pleasure on her lips. "I'm going to sweep the floor now and you can burn the trash, if you want to."

"I'll get right to it," Ben agreed and climbed stiffly down the ladder.

Altogether, Gretchen spent close to two hours in her new bedroom, sweeping the floor, dragging furniture to where she wanted it, washing the window, then dusting everything. She had positioned the bed against the wall that allowed her to look out to the east, to see the sun rise in the mornings, and the stars come out at night. She had placed the table beneath the window, with the rocker next to it. And the dresser she pushed to the wall opposite the bed.

She now stood, looking the room over, visualizing the bright scatter rugs she would weave and place on the wide-plank floor. She would hang curtains at the window and make cushions for the rocker. The spinning wheel and loom were going to get a good workout.

She clasped her hands to her chest. "Oh, but it's going to be grand!" she whispered.

Dusty and sweaty but still full of energy, Gretchen descended the ladder and walked into the kitchen. A growling in her stomach told her it was time to eat lunch. Where had Ben got to? she wondered, stepping out onto the small porch.

Gretchen was stretching sore muscles when she saw Ben down at the barn, talking to a woman. She was about to step back into the kitchen when Ben saw her and called out, "Come on down, honey, and meet one of your neighbors."

Oh, dear, Gretchen thought, glancing down at the dirt-stained Indian garment she hadn't bothered to change out of, at her feet encased in Ben's gray woolen socks. Didn't Ben realize how awful she looked? Maybe men didn't notice appearances, she thought, but she was sure that women did.

Taking a deep breath, she stepped off the porch and walked toward the barn, conscious of the woman's eyes upon her.

Ben put an arm around her shoulders when she came up to them. "Gretchen, this is Trudie Harrod. She lives down the valley a piece."

There was an inflection in Ben's tone that made Gretchen give him a fleeting look. For some reason he didn't like this woman, who was running slightly contemptuous eyes over her attire. When he said, "Trudie, this is Gretchen, come to live with me and Spencer," pale brown eyes narrowed on her face.

"I thought at first you was a rag-tail Indian." The slightly plump woman's eyes moved over the doeskin shift again. "Are you a half-breed?"

"She damn well is not," Ben bristled. "If you had good eyesight, you'd know she's not."

Trudie gave a careless shrug of her shoulders. "What was I to think, what with the Indian dress. All the other neighbors are goin' to think the same thing if she goes around wearin' such heathen clothes."

"All the other neighbors will have sense enough to know that Indians don't have curly hair. And besides, this ain't her regular garb," Ben said coldly, his tone saying that only someone soft in the head would think otherwise. "She's been doin' some cleanin'." He paused, then added the words that he knew would irritate the rude woman. "That shift Gretchen is wearin' belongs to one of Spencer's squaws."

His words had the effect on Trudie that Ben wanted. Fury added color to her pale eyes and pasty cheeks. She had chased after Spencer Atkins ever since she and her father had moved to the hills from the Carolinas. And more times than she liked to remember, he had preferred a dirty squaw over her.

Her hand clenching the handle of the short riding crop she carried, Trudie snapped in a voice barely controlled, "You'd never catch me wearing a garment like that for any reason." Without another word, she turned and stamped toward her mare, her ample rear end bouncing with her angry stride. She awkwardly swung into the saddle and brought the crop down on the mare's flank. It lunged away, tearing down the valley.

"Bitch," Ben said. "You watch out for her, Gretchen. She's a mean one. She'll do you harm if she gets the chance."

"But why would she want to harm me?" Gretchen asked in surprise as she and Ben walked back to the cabin. "She doesn't even know me."

"She knows you're young and beautiful and that's a threat to her. She's got it in her mind that she is gonna marry Spence, and she'll hurt anyone who stands in her way. She brought her old black mammy with her when she and her pa moved here, and it's rumored that she don't hesitate to take a ridin' quirt to the old woman if she does somethin' that displeases her. That's how mean she is."

"That's awful." Gretchen stopped and stared at Ben. "Why do the neighbors let her get away with such cruelty?"

"Their hands are tied," Ben answered. "Every time someone asks the old soul if she's all right, she smiles and says that she's just fine. We know she's lyin', but what can we do?"

No more was said until Gretchen and Ben stepped into the kitchen. Then Gretchen said, "I won't be any competition to Trudie. I don't know where you got the idea that I am beautiful." She reached a hand up to her head. "For heaven's sake, my hair is shorter than your son's, and you know how he described me."

"I don't know what set Spencer off the first time he saw you. But when you got dried off he sure changed his mind about you lookin' weedy. I seen it in his eyes. He looked like a pole-axed bull."

"But he still doesn't like me. I can feel it all the way to my bones. It's going to be very difficult, the three of us living together."

"It's gonna be all right, honey," Ben assured Gretchen as she set out sliced ham and cold cornbread for their noon meal. "I don't think Spencer dislikes you at all. He proved that by cleanin' out the fireplace and layin' the makin's of a fire after you went to bed last night. And he brung in a pail of water from the spring back of the house so you wouldn't have to do it."

"Spencer did that?" Gretchen's eyes widened in surprise. "I thought you had."

"Naw, it was Spence. I was so tired last night, I forgot to do it. I think he was ashamed of how he had spoken to you and the way he had acted. He'd never come out and say it in words—he's too stubborn—but he'd try to show it by his actions."

"Maybe we can live in harmony," Gretchen said, motioning to Ben to sit down and eat. Privately; she thought it very unlikely. Ben's son set her teeth on edge.

The western sunlight fell in long bars of gold through the trees as Spencer came out of the forest and looked down on Squaw Hollow. A smile of anticipation curved his firm lips. There were at least a hundred white men down there, not counting the large group of Indians who were camped off by themselves, nor the handful of white women and a bunch of squaws. The white women were trappers' wives, a hardy bunch who could take the rough life of their trapper husbands. The squaws were there to take on any man who offered them a few coins. He hoped there were some he'd never lain with before.

He was more than ready for them. It had been a while since he'd had a good tumble.

Spencer was within shouting distance of the rendezvous when he was spotted. "Hey, men, here comes Spence finally," a deep baritone yelled, and a man came loping awkwardly toward him.

"You squaw-ridin' son of a gun, how are you?" The mountain of a man threw his arms around Spencer in a bear hug that made the air rush out of his lungs. "Have you wore out all the women yet back in your Kentucky hills?"

"Hell, yes, he has." A tall, thin man stuck out his hand when Spencer was released by the giant. "You don't think he came all this way to see you, do you, Kile? He's lookin' for new territory to explore."

"That's right, Ike." Spencer grabbed the long hand and shook it heartily. "Any new ones floatin' around, or have you two already worn them out?"

Kile let loose a bellow of laughter that fit his size. "We sure as hell have been tryin'. I've been makin' a regular hog of myself."

The longtime friends ambled toward the campground, questions and answers floating between them. How was trapping in their region this past winter? What prices were being paid for furs this year? The answers were that trapping was good, as usual, and the price of furs wasn't too bad.

They approached the huge campfire, and other friends and acquaintances noted Spencer's arrival and called out greetings. He was handed a glazed jug of moonshine. Lifting it to his mouth, he took a long swallow. He choked, and his eyes watered, as the fiery liquid ran down his throat.

"Good Lord, Pete." He handed the jug back to the man who lived in Squaw Hollow. "That's strong enough to burn out a man's gut."

Pete, a short, genial man who ran the post in the vicinity, guffawed loudly. "You just ain't used to good likker, Spence," he said, clapping Spencer on the shoulder. "Come say howdy to Little Bird. She'll be right pleased to see you."

"Are you still keepin' her happy?" Spencer grinned down at the man who didn't quite come to his shoulder. "How many younguns do you have now?"

Pete thought for a minute, then said, "I believe Little Bird will have her eighth sometime next month. I can't keep up with the birthin's. Seems like ever' time I turn around, she's havin' another."

"Well, hell, why don't you stay out of her bed sometimes? You do know that's how you make babies, don't you?"

Pete's laughter rolled out again. "I've been told that. You reckon it's true?" He gave Spencer a sham questioning look, then roared with glee again as he took Spencer's arm and led him away from the group, who were passing the jug around.

"Let's stay the hell away from that bunch," he muttered. "Some of them are gettin' as drunk as hoot owls, and there's gonna be a fight breakin' out between them before long."

Spencer remembered his father's advice about getting into fights and was happy to walk away.

They arrived at Pete's small campfire, and his Indian wife, a smile on her round, pleasant face, greeted Spencer quietly. He always wanted to smile every time he saw the pair together. The woman was raw-bone thin and stood a head taller than her short, squat husband. All their friends wondered what they saw in each other, but it was plain that a deep affection existed between them.

Pete patted Little Bird's bulging stomach. "You feelin' all right? You ain't gonna have the papoose here at the rendezvous, are you?"

The Indian woman gave him a playful push. "If I did, you probably wouldn't even be aware of it."

Pete slapped a hand on his thigh with a tickled action. "Damned if she ain't right." He laughed. "When she birthed our fourth I was out huntin', and I didn't notice the little scutter for almost a week."

Without warning, a picture of Gretchen floated before Spencer, her delicately boned body big with child, his child. The image lasted but a flickering second before he pushed it away. He could just imagine that cold beauty giving birth and her husband not knowing about it. She'd probably carry on like a spoiled child with a scratched knee. She'd make sure that everyone within hearing distance knew that she was suffering.

And God help the poor bastard who had planted his seed in her. He'd probably never be allowed to share her bed again.

"Will you eat supper with us, Spencer?" Little Bird broke in on his disparaging thoughts of Gretchen.

"Thank you, Little Bird." Spencer pulled his mind away from the picture of Gretchen lying on his bed, her arms open to receive him. "But I promised Matty Smith last year that I'd take my first meal with her and Will at this rendezvous. In fact, I guess I ought to be lookin' for their camp. From all the good smellin' odors driftin' 'round, it must be gettin' time to eat."

Little Bird nodded and invited him to eat with them tomorrow. Pete got off the rock he'd been sitting on, saying, "I'll show you to the Smith camp."

As the two men wound their way past other small fires, they were stopped often by trappers who greeted Spencer and wanted to talk awhile. In between pauses, Pete asked, "Did you bring a squaw along to warm your bedroll tonight?"

Spencer shook his head. "I didn't bother. I figured there would be plenty here already."

"You're right about that. A man can't step behind a bush to relieve himself without a squaw jumpin' out at him."

Pete looked at Spencer and grinned. "I've got one picked out for you. She's Little Bird's cousin. She lost her husband to a grizzly a few months back and ain't been with a man since. If you say the word, I'll keep her at our camp until you're ready for her."

"Sounds good, Pete. I'll probably come get her 'round midnight," Spencer said, then spotted Matty Smith kneeling before a cook fire. He and Pete parted and he approached his longtime friend.

Spencer's moccasin-shod feet made no sound on the trodden-down grass as he came up to the mother of four daughters who was turning strips of meat in a long-handled frying pan. "You got enough meat there to share with a hungry trapper?" he asked, a smile in his voice.

Matty Smith started and jerked her head around, then a smile of welcome gathered on her face. She stood up, exclaiming, "Spencer! It's good to see you, you hell-raiser." She opened her arms to enfold him in an affectionate hug. She released him and stepped back, studying his lean, handsome face. "You're lookin' good for yourself," she said, then frowned slightly. "I don't suppose you've taken a wife yet."

Spencer shook his head, the slashes in his cheeks deepening as he smiled at the plump little woman. "Hard likker hasn't weakened my mind that much."

Impatience and a little worry looked out of Matty's brown eyes. "You're a fool, Spencer Atkins," she said. "You're thirty-two years old. You should be married by now and have a couple younguns instead of whorin' round with squaws and tavern sluts. The trail you're walkin' is gonna lead you to an early grave. If you had yourself a good woman, she'd look after you, cook you good meals, warm your bed at night."

"Also give me a pain in the rump with all that coddlin'," Spencer broke in on Matty's tirade. "What you say is true for some men, but I'm not cut out for marriage. I like it just fine, livin' with Pa. I do as I please, when I please, changin' my bed partner when the notion suits me."

"Yeah, each one worse than the last," Matty snorted. "What's wrong with the decent single women?"

"I couldn't tell you." Spencer gave the irate woman a devilish grin. "I've never had one. What do you think is wrong with them?"

"Damn you, Spencer," Matty bristled. "I can never get a straight answer from you." She shook a finger at him. "You mark my words, someday you're gonna fall so hard for some young woman, you're gonna bay at the moon like some love-starved wolf, and I hope she won't have anything to do with you."

A pair of green eyes and chestnut-colored curly hair flashed in front of Spencer. "I'll never let it happen," he said flatly.

Matty wondered at the cold determination in his voice. Then, shrugging, she turned back to her cooking, and she changed the subject. "We'll be eatin' in bout half an hour. Why don't you go look for Will?"

Spencer heard the cool dismissal in his friend's tone and felt bad about it. But though he had a great fondness for the woman who worried about him, he wasn't going to get married just to please her.

As he walked away, he gave an angry jerk of his shoulders. He was getting damned tired of hearing, "Ain't you married yet?"

The impatient frown on his face faded when a male voice called out, "Hey, Spence, ole friend, I been waitin' for you to show your ugly face all week. What held you up?"

"How are you, Will?" Spencer smiled and shook the hand held out to him. Then he brushed the hair from his forehead, revealing the red line scored by the rifle bullet. "Some damn buzzard took a shot at me. Made me waste a couple of days."

"The Injuns on the warpath out your way?"

"I don't think so. It could have been a white man."

"Let's hope so." Will Smith pointed to the group of Indians camped off by themselves, their wild, shaggy ponies tied to the branches of a tree. "Them fellers seem peaceful enough. They brought in some fine pieces of fur. And I gotta give Pete credit, he gave them the same price he gave the rest of us. And he wouldn't sell them any firewater either."

"I hope no one else does either," Spencer said. "They go crazy after a couple of drinks of corn squeezin's. We don't need any fights breakin' out between them and the whites."

"How's your pa?" Will asked as they ambled toward the main campfire, where the majority of the trappers sat or stood around, discussing the price of furs, trap lines, and women. Some were still sober, but others were glassy-eyed from too much drink.

"Rheumatism is slowin' Pa down considerably," Spencer answered Will's question. "He can't wade the icy creeks anymore, so he's had to shorten his line. I'd help him if he'd let me.

Hell, I'd even run all his traps. But the old cuss is too damned proud."

Will nodded in understanding, then said, "Pride or not, the time is comin' when he'll have to depend on you. He's got no one else."

"I don't know about that." Spencer's face darkened. "When he came back from attendin' my aunt Bessie's funeral in Pennsylvania he brought back with him an old friend's granddaughter. He's treatin' her like family."

"Is that right?" Will looked his surprise. "Ben's pretty old to be takin' on the responsibility of raisin' a youngster. A little girl, at that."

"She's not a little girl," Spencer corrected shortly. "I think she's around eighteen."

Will gave him a quizzical look. "Your tone tells me you're not too happy about it. Is she ugly or somethin'?"

"She's pretty enough, I reckon," Spencer answered brusquely, "but she's a cold, uppity bitch. She's a man-hater, if you ask me."

Will kept his grin hidden. It would seem that his friend had finally come across a female who hadn't thrown herself at him and it was sticking in his craw. Something very interesting might come of this girl Ben had brought home, he speculated with an inward, pleased nod of his head. He couldn't wait for the next rendezvous to see what had happened between this girl and his old friend.

"It's too bad rheumatiz got hold of Ben," Will said with a sigh. "It's the bane of our trade.

Ain't many of us escape it. I'm forty-seven years old, and sometimes in the winter months my legs stiffen up on me. Matty's been puttin' money aside for years now to start a little store in the future, keep me out of the snow and cold."

He gave Spencer a sidewise look. "Did you ever notice that a married man outlives a bachelor two to one?"

"No, Will, I can't say that I have." Spencer's eyes narrowed suspiciously.

"Well, it's true. A wife looks after her man, makes him take care of himself, not drink too much."

"Aw, Will." Spencer turned on his friend. "You've never been on me before about gettin' married. You gonna start now?"

"Well, no, not exactly." Will looked sheepish. "It's just that . . ."

A squeal of pain had interrupted Will. He and Spencer spun around, their eyes finding and riveting on a woman trying to get away from a bearded, cadaverous-looking man who had her on the ground and was flaying her with his fists.

"That's Zeke West," Will said, anger in his voice. "He's new to these parts, and the woman he's manhandlin' is his wife. He's a dangerous and unpredictable bastard. He can kill a man without a bit of feelin'. Most of the time he takes his meanness out on Callie."

"I wonder what she's done to set him off?" Spencer wondered out loud.

"*She* ain't done nothin', you can bet on that. The poor woman hardly opens her mouth. He's probably lost all his fur money gamblin' and he's takin' it out on her."

The woman was skin and bones, Spencer noted as he continued to watch her struggle against her husband. One eye wore a greenish-yellow color beneath it, the result of it being blackened at an earlier time, and she had a purple bruise on one cheek and her other eye was swelling fast.

It had grown quiet around the campfire as the others watched the woman being battered. Although the faces of most of the men wore expressions of anger and disgust, none stepped forward to stop the abuse she was receiving. It was the law of the hills that no one interfered between a man and his wife, no matter what.

Spencer couldn't remember ever being as coldly furious as he was now. The one weakness in his hard armor was pity for the abused, the oppressed, whether it be human or animal. This poor woman wouldn't live long in the hands of her brute of a husband.

When Zeke West drew back his foot to kick the woman Spencer forgot the rules of the hills. He started toward the man with long, angry strides.

"That will be enough, mister," he ordered, stopping a few feet away.

It grew so quiet the silence hurt the ears as the bearded man spun around, his face surly and snarling. Everyone leaned forward when he growled, "You tryin' to tell me how to treat my woman, mister?"

"I am." Spencer waited on slightly spread legs, his fists planted firmly on his hips. "I wouldn't treat a dog the way you're treatin' that woman."

"Well, she's not your woman." West took a threatening step toward Spencer. "And I'll treat her any way it pleases me."

"Not in front of me," Spencer said quietly, his father's warning ringing in his ears.

Closely watching the man, his eyes widened a bit when West made a jabbing grab for the knife shoved in his belt. "I'll fix you, you bastard," he grated out. "You won't be able to stick your nose into anybody else's business."

Spencer's nerves tightened as the man sprang at him. This would be no rough-and-tumble fight. He could see in the man's eyes that he meant to kill him if he could.

"Watch him, Spence," Will called out behind him. "He's damn good with that pig-sticker."

Spencer sidestepped the first rush, then they were circling each other, West's hand clenching his knife, Spencer's hand on the handle of the gun shoved in his belt.

It happened so fast, everyone gasped. Spencer tripped over a tree root and tumbled to the ground. As he lay there, stunned and breathless, West swiftly straddled him and lifted his knife to plunge it into Spencer's heart.

"Shoot the bastard, Spence," male and female voices shouted. With a heave of his body, Spencer was free of West's weight and jumping to his feet. When West came at him again his hand, lightning fast, moved to his gun.

His shot hit the brutal man's heart before the knife left his hand.

There was silence for a moment as the acrid smell of gunpowder hung in the air. Then everyone was talking at once, slapping Spencer on the back, congratulating him on ridding the hills of a piece of vermin.

Spencer looked at the wife, still on the ground. How did she feel about losing her husband? It was possible she loved the man even though he treated her so badly. His answer was clear on the battered face. Callie West had joyous relief in her eyes as tears of thanksgiving ran down her gaunt cheeks.

Spencer shoved the pistol back in his belt as the trappers gathered around the dead man. "Let's get the hell out of here, Will," he muttered, hating the fact that he had taken a life even though it had been done in self-defense.

"What about Callie?" Will asked. "If we leave her here sittin' alone, some lowlife is gonna take advantage of her situation."

"Hell, I don't know what to do with her." Spencer looked over at the woman, who was now sitting up. Her previous look of relief had been replaced by one of uneasiness. She, too, had evidently realized that there might be other

Zeke West–types among them. He wondered how old she was. She looked fifty, but could very well be thirty. A woman would age fast living with such a man.

"Well," Will said, "Matty will have supper ready right about now. We'll take Callie along. She don't live far from us. Maybe she'll want to go back to the shack where she and West had been livin'."

Spencer suddenly wanted to get away, away from the crumpled figure of the man he had killed and the revelry that had started up again, the slain man forgotten.

"Will," he said, "I've lost my appetite. Do you think Matty will mind if I pass up supper?"

"Sure, she'll understand, Spence. But go easy on that rotgut, all right?"

Spencer nodded and started walking away, giving the campfire and West's body a wide berth. He didn't want to drink. In fact, the rendezvous he had so looked forward to had turned sour on him. He stopped, turned around, and called to Will, who was helping Callie West to her feet, "I've decided to go home, Will. I'll see you next year."

Will watched his friend walk away, thinking to himself that Spencer Atkins had changed somehow. Some of the wildness had gone out of him.

Chapter Six

Early-morning mists still hung over the valleys when Gretchen awakened, but the hilltops were bathed in light. Through the open window she could hear bird song as nests were being made, could feel the gentle breeze that wafted over her bed.

A happy sigh feathered through her lips as she let her gaze wander around the loft room. Shafts of sunlight struck through several lengths of missing caulk between the logs. The corners of her lips lifted softly. Poor old Ben probably wasn't even aware of the bare spots. He had said yesterday that he hadn't been up here in years. She knew, however, that, like the privy, all she had to do was mention the gaps and he'd be up here taking care of them.

Gretchen stared up at the rough rafters. If she never had any more good luck in her life, just meeting Ben was enough. He had supplied her with something she had dreamed of since she was ten years old. He had given her a home. That was worth more than anything else in the world.

It wasn't going to be easy, though, living with his hateful son. She had a feeling that he was going to make her life a misery. She played with the frayed edges of the blanket. She wished he wasn't so handsome. He had the nicest smile when he turned it on his father. His teeth were so even and so white against his dark skin. It would be much easier to dislike him if his face was pockmarked and his teeth rotten.

"Stop it!" she muttered, "and get yourself going. Handsome or not, he's an arrogant devil and you shouldn't have any trouble disliking him." She sat up and slid off the bed. She had overslept, and she had planned to wash clothes today. There was a small mountain of them out on the back porch.

As Gretchen stripped off the underwear and pulled the threadbare calico over her head, she wondered if the dress could stand up to another washing. She was desperately in need of clothing, but she hated to mention it to Ben. He had done so much for her already.

When Gretchen walked into the kitchen Ben had just finished starting a fire in the small cooking fireplace. He gave her a wide smile and said, "Mornin', honey. You're lookin' mighty sprightly. Did you have a good night's sleep?"

"I certainly did, I can't remember when I've had better." She smiled fondly at him. "What about you?"

"Not too good. That's why I'm up before you. The feathers in my mattress have shifted around and there are thin patches that kept me from gettin' comfortable. Then my left leg was gnawin' at me too. It's the one my rheumatiz bothers the most. It and my hands."

"I can't help your pain," Gretchen said regretfully, looking at Ben's bent and gnarled fingers, "but I can take care of your mattress. The first thing after breakfast, we'll fill a ticking with straw. You do have some, don't you?"

"Oh, yes. The barn's full of it. My young neighbor, Collin Grady, sharecrops my land. I get a third of what he grows. Can't even use half of it. I give most of the vegetables to the Indians who live down the river a piece."

"Don't you put any of it away for the winter months?"

Ben shook his head. "I don't know how to go about it. Mary always took care of that."

"Well, I know how to do it. You learn how to do everything in the poorhouse," Gretchen said with a sour laugh. "From now on, what we don't eat I'll put away for the winter."

Ben smiled his pleasure. Around about February every winter he'd give his right arm to chomp down on some green beans cooked with salt pork.

Gretchen picked up the big tea kettle from the hearth, and as she filled it with water from the wooden pail she said, "After we've had breakfast and changed your mattress I plan on washing clothes. Did your Mary have a big iron kettle that she used for boiling her whites in?"

"Yes, she did. It's out in the barn. And there's a long-handled wooden paddle to stir the clothes with. They ain't been used in years. Me and Spencer have a squaw take our duds down to the river and scrub them. She gets them clean, but of course she never irons nothin'. That don't bother Spencer none, though. He only wears buckskins."

"What about soap?" Gretchen asked, not interested in what his son wore. "Do you have plenty of that?"

Ben nodded. "There's several bars of yellow lye soap in one of the cabinets. My neighbor, Bessy Crawford, keeps me supplied." As Gretchen ground a handful of coffee beans in the small mill, he asked, "Do you want me to fill the wash kettle with water and light a fire under it?"

"Would you please? It will be nice and hot by the time I get around to using it."

The midday sun was hot and glaring as Gretchen wrung the rinse water out of one of Ben's shirts. She had gotten a late start on doing the laundry, for she had decided after breakfast that she and Ben might as well change all three mattresses and be done with it. It had taken them the better part of the morning making the switch. But it was done now, and the bed linens were boiling in the big black vat.

She spread the wet garment with the other clothes that were drying on bushes that circled the backyard. Ben had promised that the next time he went to the post he'd purchase some rope and string it between the trees so that she could hang the wash properly.

Gretchen stood a moment, stretching her tired back, looking up at the bright blue sky. Her eyes caught on a chicken hawk, high up, circling and circling. "I bet there's a farm below him," she thought out loud, "and he's just waiting to swoop down on a baby chick." Back at the poorhouse one of the chores for the five- and six-year-olds was to watch over the chicks and to chase away the feathered predators.

She had loved the baby chicks, holding them in her hands, feeling their softness against her callused palms. And she hadn't minded the early crowing of the roosters, even though it meant another day of drudgery. Their clarion call seemed to give her the forbearance to meet whatever the day held for her, giving her the promise that better times lay ahead.

When she went back to the tub of clothes still waiting to be washed she wondered if Ben would mind getting her a few hens and a rooster.

Gretchen sat on the top step of the porch, watching the sky fill up with night. She was tired, all the way to her bones. But it was a satisfying tiredness. In the kitchen, fresh-smelling clothes were folded in baskets, waiting to be ironed.

She leaned back against a supporting post, enjoying her solitude. Ben had gone to bed right after supper, also tired. He had worked all day, inside the cabin and outside. She hadn't needed to call his attention to the missing chinks in the loft room. He had seen them when they were changing the mattress, and all morning he had been up and down the ladder, carrying clay to fill in the cracks. He had also carried numerous pails of water from the spring for her use, and he had cleared out the little outhouse and cut down the weeds that blocked the path to it.

And though she knew he was tired, there had been a radiance about Ben that had been missing before. It was as though he had taken a new interest in life.

Off in the distance a wolf howled, and Gretchen was reminded of Spencer. She wondered if he had arrived at the rendezvous, and if so, what he was doing now. Her lips curled. He was probably getting drunk and wallowing around with some squaw.

She ignored the little twinge in her chest at that thought. She had probably eaten too much at supper.

About ready to rise and seek her own bed, Gretchen paused and turned her head to listen. The frogs down by the small stream that empied into the great Ohio were beginning to tune up. Anticipation gleamed in her eyes. Tomorrow she would go looking for poke greens. The tender shoots always appeared with the first croaking of the bullfrogs.

But as she climbed the ladder to her room she remembered that Ben planned on taking her to meet some of their neighbors tomorrow. She hoped that the women would like her, she thought as she carefully pulled the worn dress over her head, and not treat her like the Harrod woman had.

Gretchen hung the dress on a peg in the wall, wondering what the neighbor women would make of it, then fell into bed, wearing her petticoat.

Dusk was beginning to veil the lowlands when Spencer began to look for a camping spot. His stomach growled. He couldn't wait to get a fire started, to roast the squirrel that swung from his hand. Not a bite of food had entered his mouth today. Yesterday he had eaten the remaining pemmican he had packed in his grub bag. After a while he spotted the entrance to a cave and nodded his satisfaction. It was an ideal camping spot. He could build a fire in front of it and sleep in peace all night. Sleep that he needed badly. Last night's rest had been broken by nightmares of the man he had killed. Although the man needed killing, Spencer wished that he hadn't been the one to mete out justice.

Placing the squirrel and gear inside the cave and propping the rifle at its entrance, Spencer went in search of firewood; enough to cook his meal on and to keep a fire going throughout the night. Not only was there the threat of wolves sneaking up on him, but panthers also roamed the hills.

When he had gathered sufficient fuel for the night Spencer made a pile of dry twigs and leaves, then reached into a pocket and brought out the flint and striker he always carried. The sparks created by rubbing the two pieces together soon caught on the dry tinder and burst into flames.

Twenty minutes later, his back to the cave entrance and making sure he did not look into the flames—for they would blind him to anyone trying to sneak up on him—Spencer's white teeth stripped the tender meat off the squirrel carcass. When he had drunk a cup of coffee from the pot he had brewed he spread his bedroll on the cave floor, added more wood to the fire, then sought his blankets.

The man he had killed did not enter his dreams this night. Instead, flashing green eyes and chestnut curly hair swam in and out of them. He was up at first dawn, anxious to get started for home. He would not let it enter his mind that the young woman Pa had brought from Pennsylvania had anything to do with it. After all, what man in his right mind would be anxious to feel those contemptuous green eyes flaying the flesh off him?

He drank the rest of the coffee that had kept warm from the fire that had burned all night, then gathered up his gear. After scattering the fire and kicking dirt over the live coals to ensure no forest fire would be started, he struck out for home, his rifle in his hand.

It was past noon when Spencer came to the fork in the trail. He paused a moment, then instead of taking the one that would lead him to the cabin, he turned onto the one that would take him to the fur post. After all he'd been through, he needed a couple of glasses of raw whiskey.

The post was a long building, constructed of logs and sitting about fifty yards from where the Monongahela and the Alleghany joined to form the Ohio River. A few miles down the river was Fort Pitt. As Spencer stepped upon the narrow porch that fronted the building, he noted several boats and one dugout pulled up on the bank. A grin split his handsome, whiskered face. He would have the company of his trapper friends as he drank his whiskey.

The long building was divided into two rooms. The largest one, which Spencer stepped into, was where the fur trading went on, as well as being stocked with items the hill women might need: candles, lard, dry beans, slabs of salt pork that hung from the rafters, flour, cornmeal, baking powder, and salt and soda. On a table there were bolts of dress material, needles and thread, and bone buttons.

Placed upon a shelf there were some sunbonnets, and on a shelf below them were a few pairs of women's shoes and men's boots. When a barge came up the river once a month, bringing supplies and mail, it would also bring things that people had ordered to be brought to them from St. Louis, Missouri. These would be items the post didn't carry.

With a wave of his hand to the man who ran the post, a big, burly man by the name of Jacob Riely, Spencer passed on into the tavern separated from the storeroom so the women customers wouldn't have to mingle with the rough trappers, the men who imbibed too heavily of "corn likker," and the whores who entertained the men.

He was greeted with welcoming calls from both the men and the tavern whores. He was respected and well liked by the men, and was a favorite with the painted ladies.

"How was the rendezvous?" he was asked as the men made room for him at the rough plank bar. "How many fights did you get into, and how many squaws did you plow?" were the next questions.

Spencer debated telling his friends the whole story of what had gone on while he was away, but decided that he didn't want to talk about it. The news of his killing a man would drift up the river soon enough.

So he lied and told them what they wanted to hear. When he said he'd had so many squaws he'd lost count one of the tavern slatterns squeezed in beside him and ran her hand down the front of his buckskins.

"I hope they didn't wear you out," she murmured, stroking him through the material.

Spencer was surprised that his manhood didn't rise immediately. He'd been without a woman for several days now. But though his friends laughingly urged him to take the whore into the back room and give her what she was looking for, he felt no desire to bed the woman. He was about to remove the caressing hand when he heard a gasp behind him coming from the doorway.

He turned his head and swore under his breath as he looked into a pair of green contemptuous eyes.

Spencer had never felt shame or embarrassment before. He felt both emotions now. They were so strong his hand was rough as he knocked the whore's hand away with an angry curse.

No one else had noticed Gretchen standing in the door, statue still, her gaze frozen on Spencer and the whore, and someone laughingly said, "Come play with me for a while, Ruthie."

The man blinked in surprise when Spencer growled, "Shut your stupid mouth, Sam."

"What in the hell has gotten into you, Spence?" the trapper complained, then followed the direction of Spencer's startled gaze. "Who was that?" he gawked as Gretchen wheeled around and hurried back into the storeroom.

Chapter Seven

The Ohio flowed along, serene and unhurried, as the canoe slid into the main current with ease. Ben picked up the paddle next to where he knelt in the center of the vessel and dipped it into the water. For some time all that was heard was the *swish click, swish click* as he propelled the canoe down the river.

Gretchen sat quietly in the prow, her eyes skimming the thick vegetation that grew at the water's edge. Birds flitted among the trees, and once she saw a deer bounding off through the forest, its short tail waving like a little white flag.

Her feeling of guilt that she should be back in the cabin ironing clothes slipped away. She had worked hard all day yesterday and deserved a break from toil. After all, she no longer lived at the poorhouse, where every minute of every day must be spent at some labor or other. She had to keep reminding herself that she made her own decisions these days.

She broke the companionable silence. "I didn't know the Ohio was so wide."

Ben eased up on the paddle, moving it enough to keep the canoe in the center of the river. "Farther on, miles away, is the Mississippi," he said. It makes the Ohio look like a small stream in comparison." After a pause he added, "I like the Ohio better, though."

"Why is that?"

Ben shrugged his thin shoulders. "I can't rightly say. Maybe because me and Mary built our cabin within seein' distance of it, raised our Julie and Spence with it lookin' on. It just feels like family somehow." He gave an embarrassed laugh. "Sounds crazy, huh?"

"Not at all," Gretchen denied his charge. "If you live with something most of your life you're either going to hate it or love it. Fortunately, you love this muddy old river. I have a feeling that I'm going to learn to love it too . . . although it frightens me a little right now. It's so powerful."

Ben chuckled. "Wait until next spring when the ice in it starts breakin' up. You can hear its crackin' thunder for miles around. And you ain't seen nothin' fearful until you see it in full flood, sweepin' big trees along, cattle and hogs, even a log cabin sometimes. One year, about twenty years ago, it flooded so high it come within a couple feet of the cabin porch. You know how high up the cabin sits."

Ben grew silent and began working the paddle again. A few minutes later they rounded a bend in the river and he stepped up his rhythm as ahead, on their left, there was a narrow strip of burned land with charred tree trunks scattered about. A decrepit-looking cabin sat among them, and as the canoe shot past the windowless shack a tall, reed-thin man stepped through its door. Gretchen tried to count the brood of children that spilled out behind him, but Ben had thrown all his strength into paddling and the canoe pratically skimmed over the water. She thought she counted eight or nine, but thought she must be mistaken. That small cabin couldn't possibly house so many children.

"Ben," she said, turning her head and looking at the dark-browed man rapidly lifting and dipping the paddle, "why didn't you stop to visit that neighbor? I think he wanted to talk to you."

"I can't bear Ira Mott."

They were well past the depressing-looking farm when Ben let up on the paddle. "Ain't nobody in these hills who can abide the man," he said.

"Why is that?" Gretchen looked at him curiously.

"The man is downright mean to begin with. He keeps that passel of younguns in that two-room cabin that looks like it's gonna fall in on itself any minute. I hear tell the older children sleep in the barn."

"That's an awful lot of people to live in two rooms," Gretchen agreed. "I think I counted eight or nine children."

"Ten, last count, and Hattie and Elvira is both probably bigged with another. Every spring they come up with swollen bellies."

"Then there are two families living there," Gretchen said, wondering why that should be. How long would it take to build another cabin?

"I guess you could say that," Ben snorted. "There's two different mothers. Ira uses his sister-in-law too. He's after to raise a bunch of sons as soon as possible to help him work his farm."

"That's awful!" Gretchen gasped. "I can't imagine why his wife puts up with it."

"Ain't much Hattie can do about it. Ira don't hesitate to beat her if she goes against him. Same thing with his young sister-in-law. Elvira is scared to death of him. She was only thirteen when she had her first get. He's a mean one."

"Can't anything be done about that man? He should be arrested and put in jail."

Ben shook his head. "First off, we ain't got no law here in the hills. Just the law of might.

Most things are settled with a knife or gun, or fists."

"Well, then, why don't the men in the vicinity do something? Put the fear of God into him somehow?"

"We woods people tend not to interfere with a man and his family," Ben answered, then his beard spread in a wide grin. "One time when Ira had beat up Hattie real bad Spence liked to have killed him with his fists. Of course, he didn't let on that he pummeled Ira because he had blackened his wife's eyes and broken two of her ribs. Instead, he claimed that Ira had stolen from his traps. But everybody knows the real reason he tore into the wife-beater."

Gretchen didn't want to admit it to herself, but her regard for the arrogant trapper went up a notch. When none of the other men would go to the woman's defense, he had. He had let that horrible man know what it felt like to have one's face battered.

Silence grew between them again and lasted until Ben nosed the canoe toward the riverbank. "This is where Deke and Bessy Crawford live." He pointed to a cleared patch of land. "Both fine people, although Deke runs off at the mouth. He can talk all day and not say a word worth listenin' to. I sure hope he ain't home."

As the canoe scraped gravel, Gretchen gazed up at a sturdy little cabin nestled at the edge of a pine grove. There was no comparing it to the rickety shack and weed-filled yard they had passed a short time ago. There was a profusion of jonquils blooming around the Crawford porch and the grass had been recently scythed. As she stepped out onto land, she sniffed the pleasant odor of freshly cut hay.

They were hailed from the cabin door as Ben pulled the canoe out of the water. "Darn," Ben muttered, "he's home. Get your ears set for a hammerin'."

Dressed in homespuns, a thin strip of rawhide holding up his trousers, Deke Crawford walked to meet them with a strut, as small men often did.

"Hey, Atkins," he called, "how you been? Ain't seen you for a while. I was tellin' Bessy this mornin', I was sayin' what you reckon has happened to Ben. You suppose his rheumatiz is actin' up? I sez maybe I'll go up the river and see how he is. Now ain't it somethin'? Here you are, come avisitin' us. And bringin' a purty girl with you. I bet that Spence finally went and got hitched. Is that what happened? Did this little gal hog-tie him?"

Gretchen looked at their neighbor in wonderment. How could anyone talk so fast and so long without coming up for air? She glanced at Ben and wanted to laugh at the pained look on his face.

When Deke did stop talking for a second and actually did draw in some air, Ben spoke before he could start again. "No, I ain't been laid up with rheumatiz. I've been to Pennsylvania to attend my sister's funeral. And no, Spencer ain't got himself married. This is Gretchen Ames, the granddaughter of an old friend of mine who just passed away. I've sort of adopted her."

"Well, I do declare. Knew you had a sister, and I'm right sorry she's passed away. Too bad, though, the purty young thing there ain't married to Spence. They'd make a handsome couple, wouldn't they though. Spence ought to have settled down a long time ago. A man his age oughtin' to be runnin' round like a wild Indian. Ain't no future in doin' that. Why I was tellin' Bessy just the other day that Spence . . ."

"Where is Bessy?" Ben interrupted impatiently the flow of words that didn't seem to have an end.

"Bessy? Let me think now where she is. Oh, yes, she's out lookin' for ginseng. Lots of money can be made diggin' 'sang. 'Specially if you can dig up some four-prongers. She ought to be back directly. Said she wouldn't be gone long. 'Course now, she might have run into them Mott younguns and stopped to talk awhile. They look for 'sang too . . . as well as mayapple, sassafras, anything that will bring in money for their onery paw. I hear tell he wants to hire out that oldest boy of his, and him bein' only ten years old. I ask you now, how much work could a body get out of a youngun that age?"

Again Deke stopped to get his breath, and Ben hurriedly jumped in. "It's been nice talkin' to you, Deke, but me and Gretchen have to get goin'."

"Do you now? That's a shame. Bessy will be sorry she missed you. But hold on a minute, I see her comin' yonder."

Gretchen looked to where Deke pointed and saw a little woman tripping along and wanted to laugh. She was reminded of a banty hen scurrying along, chasing a bug, her short legs taking such fast little steps. She wore a blue-sprigged calico dress that hung to her ankles and a white apron tied around her waist. On her head she wore a slotted bonnet and in her hand she grasped the gathered ends of a fustian bag, no doubt filled with 'sang.

A bright smile lit up Bessy Crawford's face as she came near and recognized Ben. "How are you, Ben?" she called; then, coming up to them, she looked closely at Gretchen.

"I'm fine, Bessy, and how are you?" Ben smiled at the vibrant little woman.

"Oh, I can't complain, Ben. Got my garden in, our cow just dropped a fine little girl calf this mornin'." She gave Gretchen her attention again. "Who is the young lady you've got with you?"

"She's the granddaughter of an old friend of Ben's," Deke answered before Ben could. "He's 'dopted her. Ain't she a purty little thing. Her hair is purty too, all curly. But it's too short. Ought to let it grow, girl. Long hair is a woman's crownin' glory."

"She's had typhoid fever," Ben testily told his lie. "All her hair fell out and it's just now growin' back. Besides, Gretchen would be good to look at even iffen she was bald."

"There, Deke," Bessy snapped at her husband. "That ought to hush you up for a while, always runnin' your mouth. Go sit on the porch and give your tongue a rest. From the looks of these two you've just about talked them to death."

Deke stamped off toward the barn, muttering to himself, and Bessy said, "Come on in and set a spell. I've got a dewberry pie coolin' on the table."

As Gretchen had expected, Mrs. Crawford's cabin was as neat and clean inside as the flower beds around her porch. Bessy motioned her and Ben to sit down at the kitchen table, then went to wash her hands, scrubbing them with a bar of lye soap. She took three pewter plates from a shelf and, cutting the pie, she placed a slice on each one. Dark blue juice oozed out of them as she put out forks.

As Gretchen ate the delicious pastry, she learned that Bessy had a lot to say also. But unlike her husband, she conversed. She was interested in what others had to say and she listened closely when they spoke.

Ben and Bessy talked of commonplace things: the weather, their neighbors, a church picnic that was coming up, and wasn't it awful that Hattie Mott and her sister was bigged again, and shouldn't Ira be hung by the you-know-what.

Then Bessy looked at Gretchen, who had sat quietly, listening to her and Ben, and asked, "Can you sew, Gretchen?"

"Yes, ma'am, I can," Gretchen answered promptly, a little proudly. She sewed an exceptionally fine seam. "I was taught how to at . . ." She stopped short. No one knew, not even Spencer, that she had been raised in a poorhouse. "My grandmother's knee," she quickly finished her sentence. "Why do you ask?"

Bessy blushed and nervously tucked in several gray strands of hair that had escaped the bun at her nape. "It's just that I noticed that your dress is way too big for you and I thought I could help you take it in if you didn't know how to sew."

Gretchen blushed, embarrassed. Bessy was being kind, saying that the dress didn't fit her. The garment was falling apart and the woman knew it. She slid a look at Ben and saw from the dark look that had come over his face that he was annoyed with his neighbor.

There was a hint of belligerence in his tone when he said, "We're well aware that Gretchen needs new duds. We've already made plans to stop at the post and buy her some dress goods," he said, telling his second lie. "We went off and forgot her clothes back in Baker City," he lied again.

Oh, my dear friend, what a liar you are, Gretchen thought, tears pricking the backs of her eyes. She couldn't remember anyone ever coming to her defense like this man did.

"I didn't mean to hurt your feelin's, Ben," Bessy apologized. "I just wanted to help if I could."

"Don't fuss, Bessy," Ben spoke more softly. "Me and Gretchen thank you for carin'."

"Thing is," Bessy said, a sadness in her eyes, "I always wished I had a daughter to do things for. 'Course Deke always wished for a son." She sighed. "God didn't see fit to send us either one."

"I always thought it a shame you and Deke never had any younguns. You'd have made fine parents," Ben said, popping the last piece of his pie into his mouth. He smiled at Gretchen then and stood up. "Time we get goin' to the post, honey. If you're like most women, I expect it will take you a while to pick out the things you need."

Bessy followed them outside, urging them to visit again. "When you get settled in, Gretchen, we'll have to see to it that you meet the young people in the neighborhood." Just as they were leaving, the little woman said, "When Spencer comes back from the rendezvous tell him to come over and let me know how my brother Bill and Matty are doin'. I ain't heard from them in a coon's age."

"I'll do that, Bessy," Ben answered, then seeing Deke coming from the barn, he took Gretchen's arm and hurried her along. "I don't want to get caught by that one again," he grunted, helping her into the canoe.

Again Ben sent the bark-craft skimming down the river, and it was but a short time before the rude frontier post came in sight. He pointed to the long building, explaining that it served the combined function of store and tavern. When he nosed the canoe onto the gravelly riverbank he added, "We need only go into the store part. From the looks of the vessels tied up, there'll be a bunch of trappers gettin' drunk in the tavern. I don't want them onery cusses seein' you. Them hellions would follow us home."

As he took Gretchen's arm and guided her up the beaten path she asked, "What's that building off by itself?" She had seen a man come out of it, lacing up his buckskins, and thought that the building was quite large to be an outhouse. "Does somebody live there?"

"Well, sort of." Ben looked uncomfortable. "The tavern women sleep there."

Gretchen wondered what a tavern woman was, and when she saw the man enter the back of the post by a side door she asked, "Are the women married?"

"Uh, no," Ben answered and hurried her along.

Gretchen gave him a puzzled look, wondering at his nervous tone. Before she could question him further it came to her what Ben meant by tavern women. A more common name would be whore.

She let the subject of the solitary cabin drop and followed Ben into the post.

Gretchen sniffed the odor of apples, coffee beans, and leather goods. "It smells awfully good in here," she said when she became accustomed to the dimness of the room.

"It does now," Ben agreed with a short laugh, "but you should have smelled it in here a month back when the trappers brought in the pelts they'd trapped all winter. The women wouldn't come near the place until Jacob packed them up and sent them down the river to St. Louis."

"Does this Jacob person own the post?" Gretchen asked, making straight for the shelf stacked with brightly colored material.

"Yeah. He's a rough one, but he's honest. Treats everybody fair. He's good to his squaw, too, and to the tavern women. He don't let them be abused. Some men want to . . ." Ben broke off in confusion, and Gretchen hid her amused grin when he said with relief, "Here comes Jacob now."

Gretchen looked at Jacob Riely and thought that she had never seen a bigger man in her life. He had to be at least four inches past six feet and weigh well over two hundred pounds, all solid muscle. His face was not what one would call good-looking. His nose had been broken at one time, and there was a knife scar running the length of his left cheek. Nevertheless, there was an attractiveness about his craggy features.

She guessed that his age was around forty.

The big man's blue eyes sparkled with appreciation as they traveled over Gretchen's face. "What's this little beauty doin' with an old codger like you, Ben?" Jacob teased, his voice soft for such a large man.

"You can just pull your eyes back in your head, Jacob." Ben grinned. "This here is Gretchen, my newly adopted daughter."

"Is that so?" Jacob offered his big hand to Gretchen. "What you wanna bet that ole Spence changes his mind about decent women?"

"I don't care if he does or not." Ben's eyes shot fire. "For I tell you this, ain't no man gonna play fast and loose with this girl."

"Hell, Ben, no man in his right mind would want to. A feller would want to get her to a preacher as fast as he could."

Gretchen felt her ire rising. If they were referring to Spencer Atkins, they were crazy. She would never marry a womanizer like him, not that he'd ever ask her. When she married it would be to a man who was settled, hard-working, and willing to stay home with his wife and family. He wouldn't be the sort whose main interest in life was carousing around and sleeping with loose women. Any woman foolish enough to marry Spencer Atkins would worry herself sick wondering who he was sleeping with when he failed to come home.

Ben put a hand on her shoulder. "There's no hurry about Gretchen gettin' married." He smiled down at her. "I want to keep her with me for a spell."

"You'd better keep your rifle handy then." Jacob smiled also. "Every trapper and single man in the area is gonna beat a path to your door."

To Gretchen's relief, Jacob's name was called from the tavern room. She was tired of being discussed as though she were blind and deaf.

"Pick out as much material as you want, Gretchen," Ben said when he saw her dithering between a calico and a gingham. "Money is no problem if you're worried about that. Pick out enough material to make yourself four or five dresses, and anything else you need. And don't forget shoes. There's some real pretty ones on the shelf up there."

With a nod and a smile, Gretchen's eyes flew over the colorful selection before her. No one wore such bright hues in the poorhouse. The garb there was mostly grays and blacks.

Half an hour later she had chosen five dress lengths and enough thin muslin for two night-gowns and a change of underclothing for each day of the week. She had also placed on the counter needle and thread and bone buttons for the dresses. Jacob was totaling up the bill when a burst of laughter sounded from the room beyond. Curious, and without Ben noticing, Gretchen moved to the door separating the two rooms, pushed it open, and peered into the long room. She gasped as she saw Spencer and a woman who stood close to him, her hand stroking the front of his buckskins. He gave her a startled look, and she turned and hurried back to stand beside Ben, her face beet red.

"You oughtn't to have looked in there, Gretchen," Ben scolded gently. "Things that go on in there ain't fittin' for a nice girl to see."

Gretchen nodded in full agreement. She'd give anything if she hadn't opened that door. Not only had she been shocked to see the woman stroking Spencer, but she had felt an emotion she refused to call jealousy.

"Can we go now?" she asked Ben anxiously, afraid that Spencer would enter the room and give her a mocking smile.

"Sure, honey." Ben noted her nervous agitation and wondered what she'd seen in the tavern. He started to pick up the parcels, then paused when Jacob spoke.

"Ben, ain't you gonna have a drink with Spencer and the men before you leave?"

"I didn't know Spence was in there." Ben looked his surprise. "I didn't expect him back for four or five days."

"Well, he's in there drinkin' with the men." Jacob laughed, then added, "And with one of the whores hangin' on him."

Ben looked at Gretchen again and imagined what she might have seen in the tavern. "I think I'll pass up the drink this time, Jacob," he said, picking up the three paper-wrapped packages, "and Spence will probably be comin' on home pretty soon."

Jacob stood in the doorway, watching the old man and the young girl walk toward the river, thinking to himself that his friend Spence would meet his match in this one. He wished that he could be a mouse in the Atkins cabin for a while, watching the mighty Spencer fall. There was no doubt in his mind that the slender girl climbing into the canoe would bring the big trapper to his knees.

Gretchen had noticed Ben massaging his hands several times that day and knew that they were hurting him. She moved to the middle of the canoe and picked up the paddle. "I'll do the work going home," she said, dipping it into the water.

It looked for a moment as if Ben would protest, then he stepped past her and took the seat she had occupied on their way down the river. As they swept past the Crawford cabin, Deke waved to them from his yard, but passing the Mott shack a short time later they saw no one, only hearing the fussing and crying of youngsters.

As Gretchen dipped and lifted the paddle, swinging it from side to side, Spencer wouldn't leave her mind no matter how hard she tried to push him out. What were he and that woman doing now? Were they in bed together? The questions niggled her brain. The woman was such a scraggly-looking thing with her greasy hair, her harsh features garish with the heavy paint she had applied to it. And she was old, at least thirty-five.

What do you care what the woman looks like, or what she and Spencer get up to? Gretchen's conscience asked, then added mockingly, *He doesn't mean anything to you . . . does he?*

No, he doesn't! Gretchen silently bristled back, and firmly put Spencer from her mind.

Mists were beginning to roll over the shadowed valleys, but the sunshine was still warm on the hills when Gretchen turned the canoe toward the place where Ben kept it. When she and Ben had climbed onto the riverbank she effortlessly dragged the vessel out of the water.

"Hold on there, Gretchen," Ben protested. "That's no job for a skinny little female."

"Why not? It's not heavy, and I'm strong."

"You are strong." Ben watched her turn the canoe over with ease. "Your delicate look is deceivin'."

Gretchen gave him a wry little grin. "I not only learned how to work on the poor farm, I gained a lot of strength doing it. A strength I needed to take care of myself. A lot of sneaky, mean kids live there, and I had to be as tough as them or they'd make life miserable for me."

"I'm right sorry to hear that, honey," Ben said, panting a little, finding it a bit difficult to keep up with Gretchen's graceful, lithe stride as they climbed the gentle slope to the cabin, "but you won't have to fight anyone anymore. You have me now, and I won't let anything happen to you."

"I'm mighty grateful, Ben." Gretchen slowed her pace when she heard Ben's shortness of breath. "But it will take me a while to get used to that fact."

They had entered the yard and Gretchen was about to step up on the porch when Ben said, "Here comes Spence."

"How is that possible?" She turned around and stared at Spencer, emerging from the trees a few yards away. "He was still at the post when we left."

"The distance is shorter iffen you walk," Ben explained. "The trail to the post is a straight run, whereas the river twists and turns, makin' it twice as long."

"Who is that with him?" Gretchen asked when a young man followed after Spencer.

"That's Collin. Collin Grady. I told you about him. He's the one who farms my land on shares. He's a fine young man, honest and hardworking. Lives with his widowed mother. Stay a minute and meet him."

The two men walked up to Gretchen and Ben, and Spencer, his face a stony mask, looked on as his father said to the very good-looking young man, "Collin, I want you to meet Gretchen. She's an orphan and she's makin' her home with me and Spence."

Gretchen looked up at the curly-haired neighbor, who had held his hand out to her shyly. His palms were callused from hard work, but his grip was gentle as he took her hand.

"I'm right pleased to meet you, Gretchen," he spoke softly, a blush coming to his face.

"I'm right pleased to meet you, too, Collin." Gretchen smiled into deep blue eyes, liking his shyness, so different from Spencer's arrogance.

Ben looked at the young couple, a pleased smile on his lips. Gretchen needed to meet some young people.

Spencer watched the pair also and thought with a frown that young Grady was holding Gretchen's hand an unnecessarily long time. His frown deepened when she continued to smile at their neighbor.

"Are you gonna give her hand back, or are you goin' to hold it the rest of the day, Collin?" he asked, pretending to be joking.

Collin's face turned the bright red of a ripe tomato and he dropped Gretchen's hand and took a step back. Gretchen gave Spencer a scalding look, then said to Collin, "Will you stay and have supper with us?"

Acceptance flashed in the young man's eyes, but then he caught sight of Spencer's scowling face and shook his head. "Thank you, Gretchen, but Ma will have supper ready right about now."

When Spencer walked away, a satisfied look in his gray eyes, Collin said, "I'd like to come by some evenin' to visit, though."

"You do that, Collin," Ben said before Gretchen could answer. "We'll discuss what you plan to plant on my acreage this spring." To his way of thinking things were moving a little too fast between Gretchen and their young neighbor. He wanted Gretchen to marry someday, but not for a long while.

"Er . . . ah . . . yes." Collin pulled his eyes away from Gretchen, who was disappearing into the cabin. "I do want to talk about that."

Gretchen turned the pork chops in the long-handled skillet, then set the table. Collin Grady was a nice young man, she was thinking, and handsome too. Not in the way that Spencer was handsome. Spencer had a hard, wolfish look, while Collin's face still held a wholesome, boyish quality. She'd bet he didn't drink and brawl, or go to bed with whores.

Still, it was the hard-featured face that kept pushing the softer countenance from her mind.

"It sure smells good in here," Ben said, entering the kitchen after she had called out that supper was ready. As usual, Spencer didn't second his father's remark as he took his place at the table.

And, as usual, Gretchen ignored him.

While Ben and Spencer discussed the rendezvous, Ben asking after Will and Pete and Kile, and Spencer still not telling of the fight in which he had killed a man, Gretchen's mind was on the new material lying on her bed in the loft room.

Maybe after she washed the dishes she would cut out a dress and sew it tomorrow in her spare time.

Chapter Eight

Heavy white dew covered the grass when Spencer rolled out of his blankets. In open places he saw the tracks of several wolves. He shivered involuntarily. Had he awakened just in time? As he rolled up his bedroll he told himself that he'd better keep his eyes peeled. The varmints might decide to track him.

He quickly raked together the burnt pieces of wood from last night's fire, cut some pine tips from the tree he'd slept under, and shoved them under the wood. He struck his flint beneath them and flames shot up. He picked up the coffeepot sitting nearby and placed it on the flames to heat the coffee that remained from last night's supper. While it warmed he answered a call to nature, then walked to a nearby creek and washed his face and hands, thinking that he must resemble a grizzly as he felt the bristle on his chin and cheeks.

Spencer had been gone from home for two days and two nights; his excuse to Ben was that he was going to scout out a new trapping area. Actually, he'd known that he'd better get away from Gretchen for a while. He was going out of his mind with wanting the little witch. He went around in a half-aroused state all the time. He had even gone to visit Trudie Howard, thinking his lusty neighbor could take care of his problem. And though in an hour spent with her she had brought him release two times, he had come away still unsatisfied, still wanting to take Gretchen Ames to bed.

And Pa would shoot him if he ever tried it.

The pot was steaming by the time Spencer returned to his small camp. Filling a pewter cup with the bitter brew, he sat down on a fallen tree trunk and stared into the flames, his mind on a problem he'd never had before.

Lately, just climbing between a pair of feminine legs and thrusting himself inside her wasn't enough. He thought of the countless women he'd had. He thought also of all the youthful companions who had whored with him. After a while they had fallen in love with decent women and each had married one.

What was wrong with him that no woman had ever touched his heart, given him the desire to become a husband and a father? he asked himself.

An inner voice answered his question contemptuously. "That will never happen to you as long as you continue to associate only with worn-out whores and Indian squaws. All your life you have run from decent women, afraid that one will trap you."

When a small face with short chestnut curls and green eyes flashed before him Spencer stood up, telling the nagging voice to go to hell. Somewhere along the trail he'd find a willing squaw who would give him relief and he'd have no more foolish notions that something was missing in his life.

He kicked out the fire, strapped his gear onto his back, picked up his rifle, and started down a trail that had been there long before any settlers had come along. For hundreds of years Indians had taken it to the blue grass hunting grounds. He walked swiftly. Suddenly he wanted to get home. He told himself that he was hungry for a decent meal, but he knew he lied. He was hungry for the sight of a green-eyed witch who had no use for him.

It was around noon and Spencer's stomach was making hungry sounds when he heard muted laughter and smelled tobacco smoke. White man or Indian? he wondered. Friendly or hostile?

Alert, his free hand on the knife at his waist, Spencer advanced silently and slowly. The voice of a white man became clearer and clearer. That didn't relieve his mind a great deal, though.

There were some whites in these hills who were worse than any brave on the warpath. There were some who, given the chance, would cut your throat for the pouch of tobacco you carried in your pocket. As a general rule an Indian only killed a white man if he had done him or his people dirt.

Spencer rounded a bend in the trail and stopped short. Off to his right in a small clearing sat a small one-room cabin. It had recently been erected; he could tell by the fresh bark and the notches that had been cut where the logs rested on each other. He would have known that anyhow because two weeks ago there had been no building there. It sat within yards of his trapline.

The sound of voices drew Spencer's attention to the back of the windowless building. A man—a stranger to him—and an Indian woman leaned on a split-rail pen, watching three horses chomping on a pile of cut grass that had been carried to them. He wondered why the man had chosen to build his cabin so far away from the settlement. Generally folk liked to live in the same vicinity of others for safety and human contact. He also had a feeling that the man wasn't a farmer; there was no evidence of land being cleared of trees. Nor did he appear to be a trapper. He looked too soft to walk miles every day, tending to traps.

Whatever the man did for a living was no business of his, Spencer told himself. He made sure he made enough noise as he approached the man and woman. One never slipped up on a man in the wilderness unless he meant him harm.

His scuffing footsteps were heard and the two faces swung around to stare at him. The man, bearded and of medium height and weight, said something to the woman, then pushed away from the fence, his hand dropping to the knife at his waist. He walked toward Spencer, stopping within feet of him.

"What do you want here, stranger?" he asked roughly.

"I think you're mistaken about who the stranger is here," Spencer answered coolly. "I've never seen you in these parts before and I was born and raised in these hills. As for your question, I don't want anything." When he received no response he added, "I could do with a drink of water, though." He wanted to keep the man talking, find out what he could about him. Strangers weren't always welcome in the closely knit community.

The man studied him a moment, then nodded his head. "Come on inside."

Spencer had to duck his head to walk through the crudely hung door, and he wasn't surprised to find that the floor of the cabin was dirt. The western sun shone through the door, showing plainly the sparsely furnished room. There were two bunk beds attached to the wall, gray horse blankets spread over the mattresses of cedar tips. There was a roughly constructed table and two split-log benches. A pail of water sat on the table, a gourd dipper lying beside it. Something simmered in a pot hanging over a small fire in a poorly drawing fireplace. The man was an amateur when it came to building a shelter and that which would make him comfortable.

The taciturn bearded man motioned to the pail, and after saying, "Help yourself," he walked back outside.

Spencer ignored the water pail, instead letting his gaze rake the room, looking for some evidence that would tell how this man made his living. He saw nothing that would even give him a hint of the man's occupation.

"My name is Jeeter Grundy," the man said when Spencer walked back outside. "Me and my brother Arnold is horse traders. Me and him share the squaw. If you got a dollar on you, you can take her in the shack and have a go at her."

Spencer looked at the woman, who gave him a gap-toothed smile and thought to himself, *God, I hope I never get so desperate I'd take a woman like her to bed.* Besides being the ugliest female he'd ever laid eyes on, he could see that she was simple. He wondered if she had been born that way, or if that almost vacant look came from being knocked around by the Grundy brothers.

"She knows all the ways there is to please a man," Jeeter prompted. "You just have to tell her what you want and she'll gladly do it for you. Me and Arnold trained her right."

Spencer shook his head. "Thanks, but I've just come from layin' with one of the tavern whores," he lied.

"Do you think you'd be interested in buyin' a horse?" Grundy asked. "I got a fine-lookin' horse I'll let you have cheap."

Spencer shook his head again. "People 'round here mostly walk."

"Well, I'm hopin' to change their minds about that," Grundy said. "Sellin' horses is the way me and brother Arnold make our livin'."

"Good luck to you then." Spencer turned to leave.

"You ain't told me your name, mister," Grundy reminded him.

"Spencer Atkins. Me and my Pa live a couple of hills away."

There was a quickening in Grundy's pale blue eyes before he quickly shuttered them with lowered lashes. He stood a moment, then with a nod acknowledging the introduction, he turned and walked into the cabin.

Spencer walked on, an uneasiness gripping him. The stranger had recognized his name and had tried to hide the fact. Why?

He was still pondering the question when he climbed the hill to the cabin and home.

Gretchen sat in her room, sewing the gathered skirt to the bodice of her new dress. She had to force herself not to hurry, not to do a shoddy job of the first new garment she'd had in ten years.

She had chosen a length of dark green calico with a tiny white flower in it, and she was quite excited as the dress took shape. She had worked on the bodice last night until the candle flickered and then died. Between chores today she had sewn the garment, anxious to get it finished, to wear something that didn't threaten to fall off her body any minute.

Subconsciously she wanted to be wearing it when Spencer returned home.

Gretchen glanced out the window, and with a sigh she rose and spread the half-finished dress on the bed. The sun would sink shortly and Ben would be in from hunting, hungry as a bear. The evening meal was practically made already, she reminded herself as she placed the needle and thread on the dresser. This morning she had taken the time to go to the little meadow down by the river to hunt greens. When she had returned to the cabin her basket held dandelions, lamb's quarter, and poke. For the past two hours they had been at a slow simmer, along with a big chunk of ham to give them added flavor. All she had to do was bake a pan of corn pone and supper would be ready.

Her mouth watered as she thought of the wild strawberries she had found also. Wait until Ben saw them. Some were no bigger than the end of her little finger, but they were as sweet as sugar. Served with a big dollop of thick cream they would be fit for a king.

Gretchen had also made another welcome discovery as she hunted for the greens: a sassafras bush. She had dug up some of its roots, and they were soaking in a pail of water on the back porch. After supper she would scrub them until they were pink, then tomorrow morning she would put them into a gallon of water and let them simmer for an hour or so.

There was no better spring tonic than sassafras tea.

Gretchen climbed down the ladder and walked into the kitchen. She was still smiling about the surprise she had for Ben's supper when Spencer stepped through the door. Before she could erase it he was smiling back. Her heart gave a jolt at the warmth of it, then settled down to a most pleasant feeling in her breast. How nice it would be if he smiled at her more often.

"Something sure smells good." Spencer sniffed the air as he hovered inside the door.

"It's ham and greens," Gretchen hurried to say, hoping he would not turn and leave as he had always done before. "And I have a dessert surprise for you and Ben." The smile was still on her lips.

A little sigh of relief rushed through her when Spencer sat down at the table and said with his heart-stopping smile, "I bet you baked us a pie."

"No." Gretchen shook her head as she stirred a bowl of cornmeal batter. "It's something better than that."

A teasing glint came into Spencer's eyes. "I can only think of one thing that would be better than a slice of pie."

"Really?" Gretchen looked at him, then blushed and looked away. There was a meaning in his gray eyes that made her catch her breath, and a tingling started in her lower body. "And what is that?" she asked recklessly.

"You know what," Spencer answered, his voice low and as smooth as honey.

"I'm afraid I don't," Gretchen said as she shoved the cornmeal mixture into the brick oven, then straightened up to smile at him in mock innocence. "You'll have to tell me."

Spencer looked significantly at her mouth, making Gretchen's pulse race.

"Oh, stop your teasing," she ordered, brushing at her immaculate white apron in confusion, making Spencer grin. But before he could pursue the subject Ben spoke from the doorway, a pleased smile on his face.

"It sure is good to not see you two snarling at each other for a change."

Gretchen was relieved to see the old man, for she didn't know how to flirt and she knew she was getting in over her head. Spencer, however, wore a faint look of annoyance. It was just his luck that Pa would come along just when he and Gretchen were getting to know each other a little. He would have liked to pursue this new acquaintance with her, learn more about her. He'd had no idea the cold little miss could be so friendly. He suspected that beneath that aloofness there was warmth and passion, a passion so hot it could scorch his very soul. Perhaps it was best that Pa had come along when he did.

While Ben and Spencer washed up at the dry sink, Gretchen set the table and dished up the ham and greens. The corn bread was done, and she sliced it into squares. Supper was ready.

This meal was eaten in a friendly atmosphere, an easy conversation flowing between the three of them. The strawberries and cream were greeted with enthusiasm, making Gretchen ask Spencer with sparkling eyes if they weren't better than what he'd had in mind.

He gave her a lazy look from beneath long lashes. "I admit that the berries are sweet and delicious, but what I had in mind would be ten times better."

Gretchen blushed and stood up to serve the coffee, which was sitting on the hearth keeping hot. Spencer watched her graceful figure in the worn dress and Ben grinned in his beard.

It was while they were drinking the strong brew that Ben looked at Spencer and asked, "While you were at the rendezvous, did you hear any talk about a big fur company moving into Kentucky, takin' over the trappin'?"

"No, there was no talk about that, that I heard. I'm sure that kind of rumor would have been on everybody's lips. Where did you hear it?"

"I ran into Deke while I was out huntin'. He said he's heard it, but he couldn't remember where."

"That one," Spencer said with a wave of his hand. "He probably dreamed it. I don't know how he could hear anything. He's always talkin'." Ben agreed, and no more was said about it.

When the coffee had been drunk Ben went out onto the porch to watch the sun set and to smoke his pipe. Spencer stayed on at the table. When Gretchen stood up and started to gather up the dishes he rose and began to stack the plates. She gave him a startled look and he shrugged.

"Before you came along I did this after every meal. I'm quite good in the kitchen."

And in the bedroom, too, I'll bet, Gretchen thought, then blushed a deep red. What was wrong with her? she asked herself. She had never had such thoughts before.

As Gretchen washed and Spencer dried, he entertained her with stories of their neighbors. Her laughter rang out often at some of the tales he told her. He didn't mention Trudie Howard, however, and she wondered why.

When the kitchen was in order once again Gretchen removed her apron, and she and

Spencer walked out onto the porch and joined Ben. They sat in comfortable silence listening to the sounds that twilight brought. When Ben knocked out his cold pipe and announced that he was going to bed Gretchen jumped to her feet, saying that she was going to turn in also. Spencer gave her a mocking smile that she pretended not to see. He knew that she was nervous of being alone with him in the dark.

"Good night, Gretchen," he said softly. "I hope you have sweet dreams. I know I will."

That he was hinting that she should dream of him, that he intended dreaming of her, Gretchen had no doubt. She said a hasty good night, thinking that likely she would dream of him.

Gretchen hung the last wet garment on the clothesline, a shirt of Spencer's. She stood looking out over the valley below. Ben should be coming home from hunting soon. Her breast rose with a sigh. When Spencer would return from the fur post she had no idea. Today was the first time he had left home for a week.

She had used the last of the salt last night and he had left this morning to go purchase some more. With a jab to her heart she remembered the day she had looked into the tavern room of the post and seen the whore fondling him. Would he spend some time with the woman before returning home?

He was a very virile man, after all. And though he soft-talked scrawny Gretchen Ames, gave her lips long, lingering looks, touched her at every opportunity, she knew that he was only teasing her. She was a fool if she thought he had any serious intentions toward her.

Still, the past week spent in his company had been the happiest time of her life, and when Spencer made an occasional trip to the post she would somehow learn to bear it.

Gretchen was peeling a pan of potatoes for their supper when a knock sounded on the open door. She looked up, startled, and grew still. A tall, rawboned man stood there, anxiety on his face.

"Miss," he said, "I think something has happened to the old man that lives here. He's layin' in the hay out in the barn."

Gretchen dropped the paring knife and, gathering up her skirt, her long legs flashed across the floor, her feet hitting the porch once as she hit the ground at a run.

It was eerie and quiet in the dimly lit barn when Gretchen rushed inside. "Ben!" she called anxiously, "where are you?"

There was no answer, no sound except that of the man who had followed her. She could hear his heavy breathing. She turned to ask where he had seen Ben, and without warning he was upon her, bringing her to the floor. She felt the seams falling apart on her worn dress, felt the bodice pull apart as buttons popped off and rolled away. A low, despairing moan escaped her as she realized that the man had lied to her, that he had lured her here to rape her.

The man was strong and he worked swiftly, silently. Within seconds he had straddled her body and was gripping her wrists with long-fingered hands. As she thrashed her body about, trying to dislodge him, her eyes widened in horror when he took away a hand to rip open the fly of his homespuns. When he roughly tugged at her legs, trying to pull them apart, she let out a piercing scream, hoping Ben was nearby and would hear her.

Her legs trembled at the strain of trying to keep them together as the man pried at them, trying to pull them apart. She knew they would give out soon, and she would be at the mercy of this brute who was determined to have his way with her.

She had opened her mouth to scream again when a maddened roar sounded from the barn door. The man on top of her grew still and released her hands. He started to rise and was helped to his feet by a hard fist coming up under his chin, landing him on his back.

Gretchen sat up and scooted out of the way as Spencer stalked toward her attacker, a murderous vengeance twisting his features. He was almost upon the stranger when the man jumped to his feet, his hand snaking at the knife stuck in his belt. As she watched with breath held, the wicked-looking blade glittered in his hand a moment, then went slicing through the air. Her heart seemed to stop, for surely the wicked-looking blade would enter Spencer's heart.

But even as the knife left the man's hand, Spencer was throwing himself sideways and the weapon whistled past his head, the blade twanging into the post where Gretchen cringed in terror. She watched Spencer rise to his knees and throw himself at the man, bringing them both to the floor. They rolled and wrestled, Spencer's hard fist lashing out time and again at the hate-filled visage.

Though Spencer was an expert with his fists, the stranger bested him at wrestling. When they rolled near the door the thin man gave a twist of his body. He was free of Spencer's grip and was sprinting from the barn.

Relief washed over Gretchen in waves, releasing the tears that had been struggling to fall. She dropped her face in her hands and sobs shook her slender shoulders. Spencer stood in the doorway shouting, "I'll get you later, you sneakin' bastard." He turned then, and dirt-grimed and sweaty, he knelt beside Gretchen and pulled her into his arms.

Cradling her head in his hands, he gently pushed it to lie on his shoulder, then awkwardly stroked her back in much the same way he would calm a dog or a horse. Never before had he ever tried to console a weeping woman.

Gradually, Spencer became aware of the soft breasts squashed up against his chest. His heart began to pound and his loins to throb in an urgency he had never experenced before. There wafted to him the clean, fresh smell of Gretchen's body, and not fully aware of it, he slid his hand down her side; stopping at her slender waist.

She is so soft, he thought, his palm edging up her rib cage, pausing within an inch of her breasts. His eyes were drawn downward and his breath became ragged as he saw through the thin material of her camisole a sweetly formed breast, the dark pink of its nipple. For the first time in his life he wanted to taste, to savor that part of a woman.

He cupped her chin and raised her face, wanting also to kiss her red lips. But should he kiss her? he asked himself. It was bound to lead to something else. And hell, he was fourteen years older than her. It would be blasphemous for a womanizer like himself to take her innocence. She deserved a better man for that, a younger man, not one who was already beginning to see gray in his hair. And besides, would he know how to make gentle love to such a delicate body, a virgin? He'd never had to worry about that before.

As Spencer continued to gaze down at Gretchen, he realized that he didn't want another man to be the first with her, even though he knew that he shouldn't be the one to initiate that very special time in her life.

Spencer caught his breath when suddenly Gretchen opened her eyes, an answering passion in them. He couldn't believe that the cool, aloof Gretchen Ames wanted him. All logic drained away from him. His arms holding her possessively, his mouth came down and covered hers with a hot intensity.

Although the lower part of her body had stirred, then throbbed in arousal at the warm closeness of Spencer's body, desire scorched through her when he drew her lower lip into his mouth and sucked it in a slow rhythm. Her arms came up around his shoulders as she pressed her body as close as she could to his.

"Ah, Gretchen," Spencer said on a long, tortured breath, his kiss deepening as he slipped her arms through the torn bodice and pushed it down to her waist, bringing the camisole with it.

He lifted his head, and in the dimness of the barn her perfectly shaped breasts looked like alabaster. He stood up, bringing Gretchen with him, and gazed at their beauty as his hands cupped them, their weight resting in his palms. Gretchen gasped a thin moan when he bent his head and drew a pink nipple into his hot mouth. She stretched up on her toes, bringing her breast closer to his lips, at the same time making a closer contact to his hard, throbbing maleness.

Spencer grasped her hips, and as he transferred his mouth to the other nipple, he bucked his hips against hers in time with his drawing lips.

When Gretchen was almost sobbing her need for release he swept her up in his arms and carried her to a pile of hay in a shadowed corner. Laying her down, he knelt beside her and, sliding his hands up her thighs, he undid the drawstring to her narrow-legged bloomers and pulled them down her legs and off her feet. He stood up then and hurried out of his buckskins. Her pulses racing, Gretchen watched him, fascinated, seeing his muscles rippling beneath his skin. Her eyes moved down his trim body and widened at the thick, long shaft protruding proudly from the thatch of tight curls at the apex of his thighs.

In just moments she would feel that muscle inside her, she thought. Surely her body couldn't receive it.

But, oh, how she wanted it inside her, needed it inside her, she told herself, and she opened her legs when Spencer came down to her.

Spencer positioned himself in the nest of her hips, and taking a nipple into his mouth, drew on it as he slid a hand down to her triangle of curls and began to stroke the little bud hidden there. Gretchen gave a low moan of pleasure, her face pressed into his shoulder. When she grew moist he raised up on his forearms and whispered, "Take me in your hand, honey, and guide me inside you."

He feels so hard and yet so soft, Gretchen marveled, taking his hard arousal in both hands and bringing it to the opening of her treasure.

Spencer hung over Gretchen, on fire to plunge his aching self deep inside her. But he knew that he had to go slowly; otherwise he might do her great damage.

"It's goin' to hurt, honey," he whispered, "but only for a moment, I think. Are you ready?"

Her eyes large, Gretchen nodded her head.

Spencer slid his hands under her hips and, lifting them, he eased himself into her.

Gretchen felt herself expand to take him and was thinking that it didn't hurt at all when his hardness came up against the protecting membrane. She let out a sharp cry of pain when, with one quick shove of his hips, Spencer broke it.

"I'm so sorry," he whispered in the curls above her ears, holding her close, his body stilled. "I'm sure the hurt will go away in a minute. I've been told that."

Doesn't he know from experience? Gretchen wondered, feeling a thin trickle of blood moving down her inner thigh. Was it possible she was his first virgin? If so, would that make her special to him? She prayed that it would, for he had become special to her.

As Spencer had promised, the hurt did begin to fade away in a short time, and Gretchen raised her arms and wound them around his shoulders, sending him the signal that he should continue.

Keeping his weight on his forearms, Spencer stretched out on her body, wrapping his arms around the small of her back and moving within her in slow, gentle strokes. Gretchen brought her legs up around his hips and mewed her pleasure with each drive that went farther and farther inside her.

Spencer felt his climax growing, eager to be released. But he wanted Gretchen's first time to send her spiraling heavenward, to feel her release so intensely that she would always be eager to make love with him.

He continued the slow rise and fall of his hips.

Time passed, and he was sure he couldn't hold back much longer when he felt the tightening of Gretchen's sheath around him. She was ready. He moved his hands down to her small rear and, lifting it off the pile of hay, bucked his aching shaft inside her with deep, quick strokes.

When their release came it was so strong, so satisfying, they could only shudder as they clung to each other.

Then, his body slick with sweat, Spencer slumped against the slender body beneath him, his head buried in her shoulder. A weak smile curved his lips. Gretchen felt so wonderful, he didn't know if he could withdraw himself from her.

It struck him then that he had spilled his seed inside her, a thing he had never done with a woman before. He had been so intent on the unbelievable release Gretchen was giving him, everything else had left his mind.

What if he had gotten her with child?

And what if he had? he asked himself. He was going to marry her anyway. She was the first woman to have ever given him complete satisfaction and he wasn't about to lose her to another man . . . Collin Grady, for instance. It had been plain that the young farmer was smitten with Gretchen.

As he lay on the now limp body, thinking that he would be able to make love to this beautiful woman any time he felt like it, he felt his manhood stiffen and grow hard inside her. He dropped his head to rest between her breasts and drew a nipple into his mouth, suckling it. Gretchen's lips curved in a slow, lazy smile and she bucked her hips, inviting him to start stroking.

He wasn't so gentle this time. Bending over her and lifting her lower body to fit into the well of his hips, he began thrusting, deep and hard. Gretchen caught his rhythm and, bracing her feet on the ground, she rose to meet each surge of his body.

"That's it, honey," Spencer whispered hoarsely. "Take it, take it all."

Gretchen and Spencer were nearing their climax when, outside, Ben's old mule twitched his ears at the shuddering groans coming from the barn. Ben frowned. Spencer knew better than to bring a squaw around the cabin now that Gretchen was living here. She could have walked in on them. He'd give the rutting pair time to finish, then that dad-ratted son of his was going to get a tongue-lashing.

This time Spencer rolled off Gretchen after they had reached heaven and then descended again. He was utterly spent. And Gretchen, although she, too, was exhausted, wondered if her legs would ever come together again, so relaxed that she couldn't move a finger or wiggle a toe.

Spencer dropped a kiss on her nose, then sat up and reached for the buckskins he had so hurriedly stripped off and tossed in the hay. As he pulled them on, he wondered how to ask Gretchen to marry him.

He never got the chance. A maddened roar from the barn door brought him swinging around, a guilty flush spreading over his face. His enraged father was striding toward him.

"Now, Pa." Spencer started backing away from him. "It's not what you think. I was just about to ask . . ."

The rest of his sentence was pushed back down his throat as Ben's fist landed on his mouth. He staggered back and landed hard on his rear end.

"How could you shame me like this?" Ben stood over him, his fists clenched. "I bring an innocent girl into our home and the first chance you get you're at her."

"But dammit, Pa, I didn't force her." Spencer picked himself up. "Ask her. She'll tell you that she was willin'. Besides, I want to . . ."

Ben shut him off with a disbelieving glare, then turned to Gretchen. Tears of shame were running down her cheeks as she struggled into the clothes Spencer had taken off her. She got to her feet, clutching the edges of the torn bodice together, her throat so choked with tears, she couldn't speak. She stood, looking imploringly at Ben, trying to make her eyes say what her voice couldn't: That what Spencer had said was true, that she had been a willing partner.

The wretchedness on her face told each man a different story. To Ben her tears were those of an innocent young girl who had been taken advantage of. To Spencer, she shed sham tears, deliberately putting all the blame on him.

Black rage rose inside him: rage at Gretchen, rage at himself. Hadn't he always known that so-called decent women were deceitful, treacherous, not to be trusted? What a damn fool he had been. He spun on his heel and started walking out of the barn. He had to get away from the little liar before he slapped her face.

He was ready to step outside when Ben called after him. "Pack your duds and get the hell out. I don't want to see your face around here again."

Spencer stopped, frozen in his tracks. He couldn't believe he was being ordered from his home, that the conniving little witch had caused a rift between him and his father. He left the barn, his back stiff with a blazing anger. If that was the way Pa wanted it, that was the way it would be.

Midway to the cabin he heard Gretchen utter a wailing cry, and his lips twitched bitterly. "Lay it on thick, little girl," he muttered. "Make sure Pa hates his only remaining relative, that when he's gone you'll inherit his cabin and land. That's why you were willing to give your virginity to me; so that you could point your finger."

Ben watched his son disappear into the cabin, a sadness in his eyes.

With a ragged sigh, he turned back to an almost hysterical Gretchen. He shucked out of his shirt and held it up for her to slide her arms into the sleeves. When her trembling fingers had finally buttoned it he handed her his handkerchief.

"Dry your eyes and blow your nose, honey," he said quietly. "We'll stay here in the barn until he leaves."

Like a little child, Gretchen did as she was told and then was able to swallow the lump in her throat and to speak. "What Spencer said was true, Ben," she spoke in a low voice, avoiding his eyes. "I was willing."

"I never thought for a minute that Spencer raped you, Gretchen," Ben said wearily. "He seduced you, which is almost as bad. My son is a womanizer. He knows all the ways there are to get what he wants from a woman."

Gretchen wanted to deny that Spencer had worked a spell on her, to tell Ben that their coming together had been right and natural. But, she asked herself, was that how he had looked at it? Maybe to him it was just a tumble in the hay, something soon forgotten and not apt to happen again. Maybe Ben was right. What she knew about men and sweet-talk was nil.

Still, she couldn't help holding on to her belief that Spencer hadn't used her as he did all his other women.

Ben hated to ask, but he had to know if Spencer had torn Gretchen's dress. "How did your dress get torn, Gretchen?" he asked gently.

Gretchen shuddered, remembering the man's attack on her. In as few words as possible, she told him how she had been tricked into going into the barn, the man's attempt at raping her, and Spencer's timely arrival that had stopped him. She spoke briefly about the fight, how the man had gotten away from Spencer and run off into the woods.

"You say the man was a stranger to Spencer?"

Gretchen nodded. "He'd never seen him before."

"That's strange. I ain't heard of no newcomers in the area," Ben said, then grew silent as he saw Spencer step out on the porch, a large canvas valise tucked under his arm. His heart grew heavy. He would miss his son dreadfully, but Spencer had done an unforgivable deed. As if seducing Gretchen wasn't enough, he might have gotten her with child. Only time would tell about that, he thought with a sigh.

When he watched Spencer saddle his stallion and lead him out of the pen, then disappear into the forest, he said to Gretchen, "He's gone now. Let's get on up to the cabin."

Twilight had arrived when they stepped up on the porch and entered the cabin.

Chapter Nine

Spencer's anger had cooled somewhat as the stallion plodded on, but resentment still rode him. Pa wouldn't even let him explain the events that had led up to his making love to his precious little Gretchen. He would have listened to him if the false-hearted little bitch had sided with him instead of sitting like a block of wood, crying and carrying on as though he had raped her.

Twilight was settling in when Spencer topped a hill and pulled in his mount to get his bearing. He hadn't been aware of where the stallion was taking him, he had been so furious. His gaze swept over the valley below. To his right, a mile or so away, were Trudie Harrod's cabin and outbuildings, and to his left, a couple of miles away, was the sturdy little one-room cabin he used when he trapped. It was there he brought a squaw to take care of his needs during the winter.

Well, he thought, it looked like he'd be spending all his time there from now on. He remembered that when he closed the place up he had taken away all foodstuff in case a bear came around. If a hungry bear smelled food, he'd go right through a window to get at it, and wreck the cabin in the process.

He nudged the stallion, Buckskin, and the big animal started down the hill. He would stash his clothes in the cabin, then ride to the post and purchase the staples he would need.

His small cabin looked lonely, sitting in the twilight shadows, as Spencer rode up to it. The lonesome call of a whippoorwill added to the feeling of isolation as he slipped out of the saddle and stepped up on the small porch. When he pushed open the heavy door he heard the skittering of mice as they looked for a hole to dive into.

He made his way in the darkness to the table beneath the shuttered window and fumbled for the flint and striker that always lay next to the candleholder. He struck the two pieces together a couple of times, and the sparks created ignited the candlewick. Holding the candle shoulder high, he skimmed a glance around the room. It was just as he had left it a few months ago. The Shawnee never bothered any of his things. He liked to think that it wasn't out of fear of him, but rather out of respect and liking for him.

Placing the candle on the table, Spencer walked over to the bedframe fastened to the wall and flipped open the feather mattress he had rolled up after he had put away his traps for the season. He'd have to get a straw mattress for the hot months, he thought, walking over to a metal trunk and throwing back the lid. Folded on top of the deep interior was a pillow, a sheet, and a blanket. He picked them up, knowing that at the very bottom were heavy quilts and blankets for the winter months.

Spencer deftly made up the bed, then unpacked his clothes, hanging shirts and trousers on pegs in the wall. He stacked his underwear and socks on a shelf built over the bed, then carried his shaving materials to the window and placed them on a shelf beside it. A shiny piece of tin hanging over it reflected his face.

That taken care of, he walked across the floor to where several sizes of gourds were lined up against a wall. Every housewife in the hills had some; when the insides had been scooped out and the shell properly dried there was no finer receptacle in which to keep one's staples.

He lifted the lids off each one. As he had expected, all of them were empty. He stood a minute, ticking off in his mind what he would need to buy at the post. Flour, coffee, salt and pepper, sugar, baking powder and soda, lard, dried beans, and salt pork. Glancing at the short candle stub in its pewter holder, he added candles to his list.

He gave the room a final glance, then walked out into the night and climbed onto Buckskin's back. As he turned the mount onto the river trail that led to the post, Spencer's stomach rumbled with hunger. He wondered what the little witch had made for supper. She was an excellent cook, he'd give her that. *And an excellent bed partner,* his inner voice added mockingly.

That, too, Spencer had to admit. As much as he despised her, he'd give a winter's catch to have her in his bed tonight, to make love to her until he couldn't move.

"I'll visit Trudie tonight," he muttered as the post came into view. "She'll make me forget that little green-eyed witch." But as he entered the post, he doubted if there was a woman alive who could make him forget the way Gretchen sent him soaring to the skies.

As soon as Jacob Riely saw Spencer, he started talking about the little beauty who had come to live with him and Ben. "Ain't never seen her like in these hills before," the big man declared. "You and Ben are gonna have a hell of a time keepin' the bachelors away from her." A wide grin split his face. "You're gonna have to keep your rifles loaded and propped next to the door."

"That'll be Pa's job," Spencer said shortly. "I've moved back to my cabin."

"You have? How come? If it was me, I wouldn't move a foot away from that little beauty. I'd just sit around, lookin' at her all day."

Pretending an indifference he was far from feeling, Spencer remarked, "If I can't take them to bed, I got no interest in them."

Spencer's nonchalance didn't fool Jacob. He had seen the scowl that had come over his face the minute the girl was mentioned. He grinned slyly and said, "Ol' Ben put you off-limits, didn't he?"

"The hell he did," Spencer denied hotly. "I just felt too crowded with another person in the cabin, havin' to be careful not to cuss in front of her, make sure I didn't run around in my drawers."

"Uh huh." Jacob continued to grin, then dropped the subject. "I expect you've come in for some provisions."

"Yeah. You know what I'll need. I'm out of everything." He started to go through the door into the tavern, then turned back to the counter. "Has your squaw got anything to eat in the back room? I'm starvin'."

"Got some venison stew. You want a bowl of it?"

Spencer nodded. "A big bowl of it."

Jacob disappeared through the door in back of the counter, and when he returned Spencer took the steaming bowl of meat and vegetables into the tavern and sat down at a table. He was greeted loudly by his trapper friends, who gathered round him. When, like Jacob, they started talking about Gretchen, calling him a lucky son-of-a-gun to have such a beauty living with him, he fastened them with chilling eyes. "Pa wouldn't care to have Gretchen discussed in a tavern." His voice was as cold as his eyes.

There was a moment of silence as each man remembered Spencer's quick temper, and his ability with his fists. And though no man there wanted to come up against them, their respect and liking for the trapper would have stilled their mouths anyway. Some of them wondered if he knew that the girl had been the main topic of discussion ever since she had been spotted in the doorway.

"When you was at the rendezvous, Spencer, did you hear anything about a fur company movin' into the hills?" one of the men asked, switching the talk from Gretchen.

Spencer shook his head. "I didn't hear any talk about that. Where'd you hear it?"

"Big Otter from the tribe down by the river told me it was spoken of around their campfire. Seems like this stranger has been goin' 'round to different villages, askin' if they had any furs for sale and would they be willin' to do business with a fur company next season. Said they'd give them a good deal."

Spencer pushed his empty bowl aside. "I doubt any big fur company is gonna come in here. It was probably some man from downriver schemin' to get his hands on some furs real cheap before they could be brought in to Jacob. If some big outfit was plannin' to move into Kentucky, everybody at the rendezvous would have been talkin' about it."

"I take it there were no strangers at the gathering," someone spoke up.

Spencer started to shake his head, then remembered the man he had killed. According to Will Smith, that one had been new to Squaw Hollow. Had he been scouting out the territory there, testing the waters for any dissatisfaction among the trappers? Were they content with the prices paid them for their winter's work?

"I did see one stranger at the rendezvous," he told the trapper, not mentioning that he had killed the man. "He was there with his wife. Come to think of it, there are a couple of new men livin' near here. They've built a rough shack a few miles from our place. I only met the one brother. He calls himself Jeeter Grundy. Claims to be in the horse-tradin' business."

"That don't sound likely." Jacob had joined the men. "People 'round here mostly walk. Besides yourself, there's only two other people who own horses: Trudie Harrod and Collin Grady. Everybody else prefers to walk. I think maybe we ought to keep an eye on Grundy and his brother."

"I think you're right." Spencer stood up. "I'll wander over there tomorrow and take a look at his mounts, pretend that I'm interested in buyin' one. If he tries to strike too hard a bargain we'll know he's not what he claims to be." He looked at Jacob. "You got my things together?"

The big man nodded. "They're in a poke on the counter."

"Thanks, Jacob, I'll settle with you the next time I ride in." He lifted a hand to his friends, and against their protests he left the room, picking up his provisions on his way out.

When Spencer climbed into the saddle he turned his mount's head in the direction of the Harrod place. He had decided that he would pretend that he was courting Trudie, to show Gretchen Ames that their lovemaking had meant no more to him than it had to her. And it would gripe Pa. He didn't like Trudie worth spit. He wouldn't like it at all that his son might marry a woman who had shared her bed with so many men.

Spencer had barely knocked on the door when it was flung open. "Well, my goodness, Spencer, come on in," Trudie greeted him jubilantly. "You ain't come visitin' in a coon's age." She hugged his arm against her plump breasts as she led him to a chair. "Sit down and I'll bring you a cup of whiskey." When Spencer had seated himself she asked, "What's in your poke out there on your horse? Has that fancy piece Ben moved into your cabin already ran him out of provisions?"

Spencer's brows drew into an irritated frown.

His voice was sharp when he answered, "Those are provisions I'm bringin' to my cabin. I've moved in there."

"Now ain't that nice," Trudie began with a pleased smile, then she narrowed her eyes. "Have you moved a squaw in with you?"

"Nope, I'm all by my lonesome." Spencer forced a rakish grin to his lips.

"Well then, I guess I'll come visitin' you once in a while." The smile was back on Trudie's lips as she leaned against his chair arm, her large breasts only inches from his face.

"No." Spencer ran a hand up Trudie's thick thigh and wasn't surprised to find that she wore no underwear. "I'll come visit you. I don't aim to have any women in my place. I figure visitin' you a couple of times a week will take care of my needs."

Trudie's eyes took on a glow. "It's about time you realized that." She stroked a hand through his hair. "Let me get your whiskey, then I'll show you the new quilt on my bed."

Spencer sipped at the clear liquid despite knowing that Trudie's impatient gaze was upon him. He was sorry he hadn't gone on to his cabin, for Trudie had no appeal for him tonight.

Finally, the glass was empty and he couldn't stretch the time any further. When he placed the glass on the floor Trudie grabbed his hand and tugged him into her bedroom. He cocked an eye at the bed, then at her.

"Trudie," he teased, "you lied to me. That's

the same quilt that's covered that bed for over two years."

Trudie gave a girlish giggle and whipped her dress over her head. "It's also the same mattress we've lain on for over two years." Her petticoat followed the dress in a pile at her feet as she stood naked before him.

Her heavy breasts were losing their firmness, and they bounced as she came up to Spencer and started to unlace his shirt. When it was pulled over his head and tossed onto a chair her fingers moved to the lacings of his buckskins as she said huskily, "It's been a long time since you made my bed bounce."

Spencer stepped out of his trousers and Trudie frowned. His long length was still limp. All the other times he had come visiting her he was hard and pushing against his fly as he walked through the door. "How much whiskey have you had tonight, Spencer?" she asked crossly, curling her fingers around his dead member. "I hope you're not goin' to disappoint me." She squeezed and stroked him.

Spencer was afraid that he would, since he felt no stirring in his loins, no stiffening in that part Trudie was trying her best to bring alive.

Maybe he wants some special coaxin'," Trudie said when her fingers got no results, and she knelt down on the floor.

His hands on his hips, Spencer watched her mouth work on him and felt nothing. When a couple of minutes had passed he said, his face red from embarrassment, "It's no use, Trudie, I guess I drank more than I realized."

Trudie released him and stood up, an angry light in her eyes. "I hope you remember that the next time you plan on comin' to see me. It's for sure I won't offer you whiskey again."

"I'll be ready for you the next time," Spencer assured her as he pulled on his clothes. He looked at her pouting face and said, "I'll be by in a couple of days and we'll take a long ride together. Like a courtin' couple," he added, which brought a pleased smile to her lips.

When Trudie heard Spencer's big stallion thunder away she rushed into the kitchen and pulled back a blanket that curtained off one corner of the room. She leaned over and shook awake the old black woman who lay curled on a straw pallet. "Get up," she ordered harshly. "Go bring Carter to me."

The old mammy looked at Trudie's naked body and knew what her mistress wanted. The bitch was in heat and she wanted the deaf-mute to cool her off.

When the elderly woman had stumbled her way to the shedlike structure attached to the barn and shook awake the man sleeping there he, too, knew what was wanted of him at the cabin. He grinned loosely as he pulled on his homespuns. He wouldn't be getting any more sleep the rest of the night. But he'd be well contented when morning came. And so would the bitch.

Carter had left his fly open and the evening air was cool on his protruding shaft as he followed the messenger to the cabin. Trudie was waiting for him, and as he stepped inside she pulled him down on the rug before the dead fireplace. They were coupling before the mammy could return to her bed of straw.

She shook her head. This had been going on for seven years, ever since the day Carter had shown up at the Harrod farm and written on a slate that he was looking for work. Mr. Harrod had asked him if he had been born without speech. Carter shook his head and wrote that the same Indians who had killed his parents when he was ten had cut out his tongue. Trudie had eyed him avidly. He was big, around twenty years old, and couldn't talk. He would be the perfect outlet for her driving lust when no other man was available. He could never tell that he lay with her, and she would see to it that his slate disappeared.

At first Trudie would sneak down to Carter's quarters when her father was asleep and stay with him until dawn broke. Shortly after the young man had arrived, Mr. Harrod had died, and the hired hand was summoned to the cabin whenever his services were needed.

The old woman turned over to her side to take her weight off the fresh whiplashes she had been dealt this morning for not fetching Trudie's breakfast quickly enough to please her. She fell asleep to the sound of popping floorboards as the hired hand pounded away at the woman who clutched his shoulders, urging him on.

Meanwhile, Spencer had arrived at his cabin and had turned Buckskin into the small shed built onto the cabin. He started a fire in the fireplace to ward off the cool spring dampness and put away his provisions. He poured himself half a glass of whiskey from the bottle Jacob had stuck in with his supplies, then sat down and stared moodily into the fire.

What was wrong with him, he asked himself, that his man part had refused to be aroused by Trudie? He was only thirty-two years old, for heaven's sake. He should desire a woman for many more years. Hell, that old trapper who lived in a cave in the backwoods was sixty-eight and always kept a young squaw, who claimed that he bedded her every night.

When a chestnut curly head with hazel-green eyes appeared in the flames he swore a hoarse oath and went to bed.

But the vision followed him there and remained with him all night. When he awakened at sunrise his manhood was hard and stiff with morning desire. A relieved smile curved his lips as, with Gretchen's face before him, he curled his fingers around his throbbing shaft. There was nothing wrong with him after all.

Chapter Ten

Gretchen sat on a rock overlooking the Ohio a few yards away. A basket of morel mushrooms rested beside her. Behind her the sun was setting through the fringe of the forest.

She turned her head to the right and listened as male voices sounded on the water, muted and indistinct. Then, simultaneously, she recognized the tongue as being Indian and saw a dugout sweep around a bend in the river. She sat quietly to avoid attracting attention as she studied it.

This was the closest she'd ever been to a native, and as the vessel swept by her, she thought that the young braves, dressed only in loincloths, were quite handsome. She wondered if the young maids in their village thought so too. Did their pulses leap and race when they looked upon the nearly naked bodies of the young men, as hers had done when Spencer stood above her, his clothes flung aside, his shoulders wide, his stomach flat and his hips narrow?

Gretchen's loins twisted as she recalled that hard body covering hers, and the rapture it had brought her. A bleakness came into her eyes. Who was he transporting to that height these days? she wondered. He had been gone a week now. Ben missed him, she knew, and she felt guilty that she had caused the rift between the two. It had entered her head many times to leave so that father and son could renew their former close relationship. The only problem was that she had nowhere to go.

Besides, she had become so fond of Ben, as well as the snug, cozy cabin that she was mistress of. She would miss them both dreadfully if she went away.

The sun dropped behind the trees. Twilight was approaching when Gretchen stood up, telling herself that she must talk to Ben again, make him understand that she had been a willing partner in her and Spencer's lovemaking.

As she approached the cabin, she could hear the creaking of the rocking chair that sat on the porch. She smiled when Ben called out, "Where you been, girl? We was just gettin' ready to go lookin' for you. Thought maybe an old grizzly had got a hold of you," he added humorously.

"We?" Gretchen's heartbeat picked up. Had

Spencer returned home?

Her pulse slowed in disappointment when Collin Grady stood up and said shyly, "Hello, Gretchen. I stopped by to bring you and Ben some butter and a pail of fresh milk."

Gretchen made herself smile and say "Thank you" to the handsome young farmer. "As soon as I put away my mushrooms, I'll pour the milk into a bowl and you can take your pail back home with you when you leave."

She felt Collin's blue eyes following her as she went through the door and, like most women, was glad she was wearing a dress that fit her, that made her pleasing to the eye. She had finished sewing the dress the day after Spencer stormed out of their lives, and had another one cut out, waiting for her to get to it.

She wished fleetingly that Spencer could see her in the new dress, then scowled at the idea. She could still see the contemptuous look he'd shot at her before striding out of the barn.

Stop letting that bother you, an inner voice ordered. *Maybe he didn't seduce you, but he used you. If he cared for you, he would have stood up to Ben and told him that he did, that lust had nothing to do with it.*

"You're probably right," she muttered as she poured the milk into a brown crock and set it aside to be carried to the cellar after Collin had gone. She washed out the wooden pail with soapy water, then rinsed it well and dried it. She carried it out onto the porch and put it down beside Collin, then sat down on the step beside him, keeping a wide space between them.

As Ben and the young farmer talked, Gretchen sat quietly, gazing up at the sickle moon now visible in the dark sky. Tree frogs were giving out their little chirps, almost drowned out by the croaking of the big bullfrogs down in the swamp. She leaned her head against the porch post, soothed by the night sounds, unaware of the sidewise glances Collin sent her moonlit face.

"Don't you think that's a good idea, Gretchen?" Ben spoke, reminding her that she wasn't alone on the porch.

"I'm sorry, Ben, I'm afraid I was woolgathering. What did you say?"

"I was sayin' to Collin that maybe I'd make us a small garden. Put in a few things like onions and radishes, some beans and sweet peas, a little okra. I love fried okra." He looked at Collin. "Do you think your ma could spare me a few seeds?"

"What about some potatoes and turnips and yams?" Gretchen broke in, warming to the idea of having vegetables practically right outside the door.

"No need to plant them seeds," Ben said. "Collin keeps me supplied with them."

"I'll bring the other seeds over to you tomorrow sometime," Collin said. "Ma has her garden in and she's got plenty of seeds left over."

"How is Agatha these days?" Ben asked their young neighbor.

"She's been feelin' poorly. Been down in her back. Worked too hard gettin' the garden planted, I guess. I told her to wait a few days until I got my plowin' done, but she said the moon was just right, and she went ahead and pushed herself to do it."

Ben said no more about Agatha Grady, but had anyone looked at his face they'd have seen that he had little liking for the woman.

"I saw Spencer the other day." Collin let the subject of his mother drop also. "He was sittin' with Trudie on her front porch. Is it true he's moved in with her?"

There was a taut silence for a moment, then Ben said, "I don't know if he's dumb enough to do that or not." His tone said he didn't want to discuss the matter any further. He gave a loud yawn then, signaling that it was time Collin went home.

Collin took the hint and stood up. "I guess I'll be gettin' on home, spend a little time with Ma before goin' to bed." He looked down at Gretchen. "It was nice visitin' with you, Gretchen," he said, surprising her. She hadn't said six words to the young man.

"Thank you for the milk, Collin." She smiled at him. "Don't forget your pail."

When Collin was well out of hearing Ben said, "I pity the woman who is foolish enough to marry him."

"Why is that?" Gretchen looked surprised. "He seems like a very nice person. I think he'd make a very good husband. He cares for his mother."

"That's the problem. He cares too much for that shrewish mother of his. She'll make life hell for the wife he brings home, for he never stands up to her. She's got him believin' that she's sickly from havin' to work so hard to raise him after her husband left her. He feels guilty."

"Did she work hard?"

"Heck no. No more than any of the other women in the area. She always had a farmhand to do the heavy work until Collin got big enough to do it."

"I expect all the young women like Collin," Gretchen said. "He's a very nice-looking young man."

Ben nodded. "After Spencer, Collin's their next choice." He gave a short laugh. "I gotta say, though, most of the mothers discourage their daughters from marryin' either one of them. They think that Spencer is too wild, that he'll never settle down, and as for Collin, whoever marries him will be marryin' Agatha too.

"There's this one little gal in Piney Ridge, though, that is willin' to take on his ma. She's a quiet little thing and positively dotes on Collin. I think he's pretty taken with her too. I see them walkin' along the river in the evenin's sometimes, their arms around each other's waists, talkin' and laughin'."

"Do you suppose Spencer did move in with that Trudie?" Gretchen wasn't interested in Collin Grady's love life.

"Damned if I know, Gretchen. If he thought it would aggravate me, he'd do it out of pure spite." Ben stood up and knocked the dead ashes out of his pipe. "I'm gonna turn in and get a good night's sleep so I can get an early start on the garden in the mornin'."

"I'll be in directly," Gretchen said. "I'm going to sit a little longer, enjoy the evening." What she really wanted was to be alone and mull over what Collin had said about Spencer and Trudie and try to figure out men. It appeared that they could make love to one woman on Monday, then another on Tuesday.

The sun had risen and the morning fog was lifting as Gretchen followed Ben to the shed erected between the cabin and the barn. He pushed open the door and began sorting through an assortment of tools and other articles that had been tossed inside over the years.

"Everything looks a little rusty," he said, examining a plow, then picking up a hoe to run a thumb over the cutting edge. "They'll need a little honin' done to them."

The sun was an hour higher by the time Ben

had sharpened the plow and hitched it to the old mule. "Giddap there, Jimbo." He snapped the reins over the broad rear, and the mule stepped out. The now sharp blade bit into the rich soil, making deep furrows through the weeds that had taken over the long-neglected garden.

When a couple of swipes had been made across the soil Gretchen rummaged through several small packets of seed that had been placed in a larger sack. Ben had found them on the porch earlier and she wondered at what hour Collin had left them there. She picked out a bag of beans and one of corn kernels, then began walking the length of the first furrow, dropping one of each into the ground. Later, the cornstalks would support the climbing beans.

When the sun was straight overhead and it was time for the noon meal, over half of the garden had been plowed and seeded. Another couple of hours and the job would be done. As Gretchen walked to the cabin to set out a cold lunch of ham and bread and a jug of cool buttermilk from the cellar, Ben unhitched the mule and led him down to the branch stream for a drink of water.

Neither Ben nor Gretchen had been aware of the slate gray eyes that had watched them all morning from back in the fringe of the forest.

The sun sparkled on the river as Spencer walked alongside it, stepping as lightly as any

Indian. When Gretchen and his father disappeared into the cabin he decided he would go and test the man who claimed to be a horse trader. He was going to offer to buy the little mare that had caught his eye the day he stumbled onto the newly raised cabin. If Jeeter Grundy refused to sell the little mount, he'd know for sure what he now only suspected. A big fur company was trying to horn in on the free trappers.

Spencer knew the chief, Big Otter, well, and knew that the man didn't lie. If he said that his people were being approached by a stranger to sell their furs to him, then it was true.

Four years ago, farther west, a large fur company had moved in, setting up headquarters in St. Louis, Missouri. So far they had stayed in that area, dealing with the Indians and trappers there. Rumor had it, however, that the white trappers and the Indians weren't happy they had signed on with the Missouri Fur Company. They weren't being paid what they had been promised, and they didn't like the fact that they were told in what area they could lay their traps. If they objected too strenuously, they found themselves having little accidents, or they discovered furs missing from their traps.

Spencer's jaw clamped down and his lips firmed in a tight line. If the big company tried to move into Kentucky, they'd have a fight on their hands.

Spencer spotted Jeeter's cabin a few yards

away and stepped off the trail to let his gaze travel over the area. The three horses were still in the split-rail pen and he thought with a wry twist of his lips that Grundy wasn't doing a brisk business.

Ready to step back onto the trail, Spencer waited while a man stepped through the cabin door, buttoning up his trousers. He knew he had never met this man before, but he looked vaguely familiar. When Jeeter stepped out from behind the man he saw the resemblance between them. It must be Jeeter's brother; no wonder he looked familiar.

Spencer stepped out of the forest and hailed the cabin. Both men looked up, then the brother gave a startled jerk and, mumbling some words to Jeeter, he walked away, disappearing among the trees. Spencer frowned. Why wouldn't the man want to meet him?

Jeeter called out a greeting and Spencer put the question aside until later.

"Well, Atkins, have you come to buy one of my stallions?" Jeeter moved away from the cabin.

Spencer shook his head. "As I said, I've got a stallion. I'd like a closer look at the little mare. I might be interested in her."

From the corner of his eye Spencer saw the stillness that came over Grundy's body, saw the uneasy flicker in his eyes before he said, "Sure thing. She's a little beauty." He leaned on the rail fence and added, "But I must tell you, she's got no speed to her. She can't run worth spit."

"I wouldn't be runnin' her much," Spencer said. "Too many hills around here. I'd mostly ride her to run my traps this winter. My trap line covers a lot of miles. A man's pretty beat when he finishes the day."

A slyness pricked Grundy's eyes at the mention of trapping. "You wouldn't have to work so hard if you wasn't a free trapper. You ought to get in with a big company. I hear tell they pay almost double what the small fur trader pays a man. That means he only has to work half as hard."

"There's not much chance of that around here." Spencer pretended no interest in Grundy's advice. "There's no big fur companies in these hills."

"But what if there was?" Grundy probed. "But what if the Missouri Fur Company out of St. Louis approached you, would you be interested?"

Spencer shrugged. "I doubt it. I wouldn't like workin' for someone else. What about the mare?" He switched back to the trim little animal.

A disgruntled look on his face, Grundy grudgingly turned his attention back to the three horses. "Well," he said, "I gotta be honest with you. She ain't got much stamina. I doubt she could stand bein' out in the cold all day."

Spencer slid Grundy a narrowed look. There was no doubt in his mind that the man didn't want to sell the mare, nor was he in these hills to do any horse trading. He was here on the orders of the Missouri Fur Company to convince the trappers in the area to work for them. If enough men signed up, they would move in.

Well, by God, Spencer thought, *he's gonna sell me that mare or he's gonna come right out and say what he's doing here.*

"She looks sturdy enough to spend a few hours in the cold." He looked at Grundy. "Throw a saddle on her and I'll try her out, see if she has a smooth gait."

For a split second it looked like Grundy would find more reasons why Spencer shouldn't buy the animal. But after one look into the gray eyes that had turned the color of old pewter he dragged a saddle off the fence and lifted it across the mare's back. After slipping the bridle over the proud head he led the mare out of the pen.

"Here," he said ungraciously, "don't run her too hard. Like I said, she ain't all that strong."

Bullshit, Spencer thought, feeling the muscles bunch and ripple as he climbed into the saddle. This little mount could run flat out all day if called upon to do so. As he put her through her paces, a canter, a trot, and finally a hard gallop, he could understand why Grundy didn't want to sell her. She was a fine piece of horseflesh.

"How much do you want for her?" Spencer

trotted the mare back to where Grundy stood waiting.

"She won't come cheap." Grundy practically growled the words as Spencer swung to the ground.

"You couldn't ask too much for her, considerin' all the faults you said she has." Spencer gave Grundy a dark look, daring him to deny it.

Every time Grundy pointed out a favorable quality the mare possessed to back up the high price he'd put on the animal, Spencer tossed back the man's own claim of the mare's limitations.

Grundy's face wore a sullen look when finally a deal was struck, one that included a saddle and was much lower than the price first asked. The scowl on Grundy's face deepened when Spencer demanded proof of purchase from him.

"Don't you trust me, Atkins?" Grundy growled.

"That's right, I don't," Spencer answered. "I trust no man when it comes to horse tradin'."

It was late afternoon, and Ben and Gretchen were finishing up the garden when Spencer secreted himself and the mare in a grove of cedar and sat watching them. Pa hadn't touched a plow since Ma died, he thought, and now at age seventy he was plodding along behind the old mule, preparing the soil for the little witch following along behind him, dropping seeds into the ground.

But he looked happy, Spencer had to admit. He didn't seem to be missing his son. Spencer's eyes shifted to Gretchen, and raw desire flared in them. She had put on weight since he'd last seen her, and the Indian shift she had donned to work in was pleasantly filled with her soft curves.

As he remembered making love to that velvet-smooth body, his loins convulsed into knots. It wasn't the first time this had happened to him. It happened every night in his dreams. Twice he had tried to seek relief through Trudie, and both times he had embarrassed himself when he had failed to perform. Not knowing that she had her hired hand to slake the desire he had aroused in her, he wondered how much longer she would put up with him.

He decided that she was hoping he would ask her to marry him.

Spencer leaned forward when he saw Gretchen and Ben leaving the garden patch, Gretchen going toward the cabin and his father leading the mule to water. Gretchen would start supper now, and after Pa had turned the mule into the pasture he would sit down to a hearty well-cooked meal.

The mare stamped her hooves and swished her tail at the flies nipping her rump. Spencer leaned over and patted her arched neck, calming her as he waited for Gretchen to call his father to supper.

It was near dusk when Ben washed up on the porch, then went inside to eat the stew whose spicy aroma Spencer could smell from his cover in the cedars.

He nudged the little mount and walked her toward the pen adjacent to the barn. Even as he had dickered price over her, in the back of his mind he'd known that he wanted the animal for Gretchen.

He called himself a fool as he turned the mare into the enclosure. He had laid out good, hard cash for a female who cared nothing for him.

Chapter Eleven

Spencer followed the beaten path to the post, his long strides making no noise on the thick mat of pine needles. Every once in a while he looked over his shoulder. He had a feeling that he was being followed. But nothing ever moved in the fast-darkening forest. He told himself that it was all in his imagination.

Nevertheless, he heaved a sigh of relief when the dim light from the post came into view. A wide smile of anticipation curved his firm lips as he stepped onto the narrow porch. From inside the tavern room he could hear the rowdy voices of his trapper friends, and the high, shrill laughter of the whores who were entertaining them.

He nodded at Jacob's squaw, standing behind the counter, and passed on into the barroom.

Slim Peters, his closest friend, removed his hand from under a tavern woman's skirt, dumping her to the floor as he stood up. When he met Spencer at the bar Spencer wrinkled his nose and said, "Phew, Slim, go wash that whore's perfume off you, then I want to talk to you and the fellows."

Slim kept his grin and said nonchalantly, "You'll get used to it. It's not like you haven't smelled the same way yourself a hundred times."

"I can't believe that." Spencer made another face. "I must have been drunker than a skunk if I did, or else had a very bad head cold."

When Jacob had poured them each a glass of whiskey the tall, slim man asked, "What do you want to talk to us about?"

"Yeah, what's in the wind, Spence?" one of the other trappers asked.

Spencer swallowed half his drink, then turned around to face the men standing behind him. "I've discovered that the man who calls himself Jeeter Grundy is not what he claims to be. He is not a horse trader. He's a scout sent here by the Missouri Fur Trading Company."

"Then the rumors are true. They do plan on moving in on us," Slim muttered darkly.

"Did he come right out and say so?" Jacob asked, a worried frown beginning to furrow his forehead. If it was true, he would lose a lot of business. The majority of the trappers brought their furs to him.

Jacob Riely had been a fur trader in his youth, tramping through the backwoods, trading for furs from the Indians out of a pack of trinkets strapped on the back of a mule. But he had soon decided there was more profit in letting the furs be brought to him. He hated to think that all his hard work and the long years put into the fur post would be for nothing. He listened intently to Spencer's answer.

"No, nothin' like that." Spencer shook his head. "But he asked me a lot of questions that left me in no doubt why he is here."

"What kind of questions?" Slim asked.

"He wanted to know how I'd feel about a big fur company comin' in, and would I deal with it if it did."

"I hope you told him to go piss up a tree," Jacob grumbled darkly.

"Not in those words, I didn't. But I did tell him that I wouldn't work for any man. That I'm a free trapper and I intend to stay that way."

"Good for you, Spence," one of the other trappers said. "I like it fine just the way things are now. I've heard tales of how them there big companies cheat the men who sign up with them."

When all the other trappers agreed Jacob sighed his relief and treated them all to a glass of whiskey. He leaned on the bar across from Spencer and said, "What about the Indians? Do you think they'll listen to his hogwash?"

"I don't know, but I'm gonna visit Big Otter when I leave here. He usually listens to me when I tell him about the white man who is out to do him dirt."

"I sure hope he listens to you this time," Jacob sighed. "I don't want to lose their business either. They bring in some fine furs."

Spencer finished his drink a short time later and left unobtrusively. But his departure was noted eagerly by the man who lurked outside in the shadows.

Arnold Grundy had heard every word that was spoken in the tavern. When Spencer struck off toward the river where Big Otter's village was situated he followed him.

Spencer had walked for about twenty minutes when there drifted along the river the sounds of chattering women, laughing children, and barking dogs. A few minutes later he came upon the Shawnee village sprawling along the Ohio. The sun had set and in the twilight a gray fog was rising from the river and drifting toward the village. It gave the tepees and the men sitting around the campfire an eerie look. The many rib-thin dogs running about caught his scent and came toward him, their hackles raised. The men were instantly alert and jumped to their feet.

"It's Spencer Atkins," Spencer called out. "I wish to speak to Big Otter."

"Come forward, Spencer Atkins," a deep voice called, and the braves settled down around the fire again. To the smallest child, the Indians knew that the white trapper was a friend, and that he came in peace.

Spencer entered the circle of the campfire and sat down next to Big Otter, crossing his feet Indian-fashion.

"What brings you out after sunset when the wolves prowl and the big cats are looking for food?" the chief asked.

Spencer took the long-stemmed pipe the chief handed to him and, after drawing on it, said, "I brave the animal's domain because it is urgent that I speak to you as soon as possible."

"And what is the reason for this urgency?" Big Otter asked when Spencer handed the pipe back to him.

"It's about the stranger who has come among us," Spencer began. "He will approach you about sellin' your furs to a big company located in St. Louis, Missouri. He will ask you to sign papers promising that you will sell only to the Missouri Fur Company."

When Spencer ceased speaking Big Otter said, "The stranger you speak of has already been here. He promises us much more money for our furs. More than we get from Jacob or at the rendezvous."

"Do not trust this man, Big Otter," Spencer spoke earnestly. "Once you sign their paper they will pay you with worthless beads and rotgut whiskey that will drive your braves crazy. And not only that; this company will tell you where you can trap. You will no longer have the freedom of the whole forest to catch your furs." After a short pause he added, "I think you should stick with Jacob the same way the trappers are gonna do. He always treats us fair."

A silence grew as Big Otter gazed into the fire, drawing thoughtfully on his pipe. Spencer tried not to show his impatience, knowing that an Indian took his time making up his mind. He leaned forward a bit when the chief took the pipe from between his teeth and began to speak.

"It will be as you ask, friend. You have never given us bad advice. We will continue to do business with Jacob Riely. He is, as you say, a fair man."

Relief was in Spencer's voice when he said, "You won't be sorry for makin' that decision, Chief. We don't need strangers comin' in here, rapin' forests and streams of all wildlife."

Spencer stood up. "I think I'll head home now. Will you ask your *Moneto* to keep the wolves and panthers off my trail?"

Big Otter nodded solemnly, then said, "It is told around the campfire that you have left your father's home."

"Yes, I have moved into my cabin."

Spencer knew that the chief expected him to add to that short sentence, but the Indian would think him weak if he said that he had left his home because of a woman. If a squaw caused trouble between two men in an Indian family, it would be she who would be ordered away.

Saying no more, he lifted his hand in farewell and walked off into the darkness, the half-starved dogs sniffing at his heels. Deep in thought of what might lie ahead if a large fur company did try to invade the hills, he was unaware of the man who followed him.

Spencer was within a half mile of his cabin when there sounded the report of a rifle, then a bullet struck a tree only inches from his head. He spun around, raising and cocking his own rifle. In the pale light of the sickle moon he made out the shadowy figure of a man disappearing through the dense forest. It would be useless to try to follow him. The man could be lying in wait for him.

Spencer's face was grim with anger as he walked on. He was getting damned tired of being shot at. In his heart he knew that it was one of the Grundy brothers who had tried to kill him, but proving it was another thing altogether.

When Spencer sought his bed, however, the Grundy brothers were no longer on his mind. He was lost in the thought of a slender, green-eyed child-woman. Had she gone to bed yet? Was she maybe thinking about him? Would she like the little mare he had left in the pen? When he finally drifted off to sleep his dreams were full of Gretchen.

Chapter Twelve

Gretchen and Ben had eaten breakfast and were lingering over their coffee when Gretchen broke the easy silence between them. "What kind of animals do you trap, Ben?"

Ben leaned back in his chair, scratching his white beard. "Well," he began, "there's more than you can count on the fingers of one hand," he said. "There's muskrat, beaver, raccoon, skunk, opossum, and weasel, to name a few."

"So many?" Gretchen looked surprised. "I've never heard of some of them. Do you take them straightaway to Jacob?"

"Good Lord, no." Ben laughed. "He don't get them until the season is over. The trapper has to flesh them out and stretch them over the proper-size board, then hang the pelts up to dry out. Then he takes them to the fur post and sells them to Jacob."

"My goodness," Gretchen exclaimed, "what in the world does Jacob do with so many coming in at one time?"

Ben laughed again at Gretchen's ignorance of the fur business. "He don't keep them very long. He sells them to another buyer, who ships them down the Ohio, onto the Mississippi, and then to the Missouri River. They finally end up in St. Louis. From there most of them are sent overseas to England. Especially the beaver pelts, which are made into hats and capes for the wealthy Englishmen."

Gretchen was silent for a moment. Mrs. Fedders at the poorhouse had worn a long fur cape in the winter. Could some of Ben's furs have gone into the making of that beautiful garment?"

"I wonder if those pampered men and women know how much hard work it takes so that they can keep warm."

"Hell, they never give it a thought," Ben said grumpily. "They couldn't care less that by the age of forty most trappers are crippled up with rheumatiz from spending hours in freezing weather and wadin' in icy streams."

"But I'm wondering if they are any happier than we are," Gretchen said after a short silence in which Ben stared moodily out the window.

"I don't know." Ben brought his attention

back to his coffee. "Chances are they ain't. I expect they have to work like the devil to hang on to their wealth, keep up with their rich friends."

Silence claimed them again and wasn't broken until the whinny of a horse broke into their thoughts. Hope flared in both their eyes. Spencer had come home.

Ben rose quickly to his feet and stepped out onto the back porch. Gretchen remained seated at the table, stirring her coffee so vigorously, it splashed out on the tablecloth she had placed on the table less than an hour before. She wasn't about to run outside to joyously welcome home the arrogant womanizer. She could still feel the shame of him using her, then going to Trudie Harrod's bed the very same night.

She was pouring herself another cup of coffee when Ben called out excitedly, "Gretchen, come quick!"

Hot coffee splashed on her hand as she plunked the pot back on the table. Spencer was hurt! She raced out the door, afraid of what she might see.

She saw Ben, alone, standing at the small pen, rubbing the ears of the prettiest little mare she'd ever seen. She jumped off the porch and ran to stand next to Ben. "Where did she come from?" she asked in awe as she gazed at the pure white animal.

"Damned if I know. Her saddle and bridle are here on the fence."

The mare nickered softly and moved over to Gretchen. She gently nudged Gretchen's shoulder with her head. Ben smiled as she raised a hand and scratched the pointed ears. "She's taken a likin' to you," he said.

Gretchen nodded, a pleased smile on her lips. She had never had a pet, nor been around horses before. She knew only the stubborn, plodding ways of mules. She instantly fell in love with the beautiful, gentle mare.

With wistfulness in her eyes, she said, "I wonder who she belongs to?"

"That is a mystery," Ben answered thoughtfully. "I've never seen her around here before. But she didn't just wander into the pen on her own. Someone had to unsaddle her and let down a rail for her to get in here."

"Can we keep her?"

"I reckon. Unless someone comes along and claims her. Could be she's been stolen and the thief left her here because he was bein' followed by the owner."

Disappointment clouded Gretchen's eyes. This beautiful little animal would never belong to her. The owner was bound to show up and take her away. She stopped stroking the sleek neck and dropped her hand. There wasn't any sense in becoming more attached to the little white beauty.

Gretchen turned away from the pen and almost walked into a bearded man who had noiselessly come upon them. At her startled gasp, his beard was stirred by a leering grin.

"I figured that trapper wanted that mare for some woman." His eyes slowly ranged over Gretchen's body. "Can't say that I can blame him."

"Who are you, mister?" Ben spoke sharply, stepping in front of Gretchen and blocking the ogling eyes of the stranger. "What do you know about the animal?"

"I know a lot about her. She belonged to me until I sold her to a trapper by the name of Spencer Atkins. I believe you're his pappy."

"I am," Ben answered, then said to Gretchen, "Why don't you go on up to the cabin, honey. I'll be along directly."

Gretchen lost no time hurrying away. But she couldn't walk fast enough to escape the gimlet eyes that were stripping the clothes off her. She felt somehow dirty.

She was clearing the table and sliding the dirty plates and utensils into a pan of hot, sudsy water when Ben walked into the cabin. "I don't like that one," he said, sitting down at the table. "He's got shifty eyes."

"Did he say why he's come here?"

"He claims that he's a horse trader, but I don't believe him. He struck me as bein' more of a horse stealer. It wouldn't surprise me if he don't try to steal the mare back."

"So we can keep her?" Gretchen asked, hope in her voice.

Ben nodded. "I expect so. If Spence wanted her for himself, he'd have put her in his own pasture."

"But why did he . . ."

"Give her to you," Ben finished her sentence. "Probably it's his way of sayin' he's sorry for what he done to you."

"Ben," Gretchen said crossly as she wiped the table, "I've told you before that Spencer didn't do anything that I didn't want him to do. You must stop putting all the blame on him."

"I reckon," Ben said after a while, "but he's got known ways about women. I should have knowed he'd get around you."

Gretchen dropped the subject. Ben was right in one respect: Spence had got *around* her.

The hot sun beating down on her head and shoulders did not deter Gretchen's delight in riding the little mare she had named Beauty. She had only ridden stiff-paced mules before, and without a saddle at that. Riding Beauty was like rocking along in a rocking chair, the mare had such a smooth gait.

She had tried hard not to think of the man who had left the mare for her, but that was almost impossible under the circumstances.

While she and Ben were sitting at the breakfast table this morning, he had taken a long swallow of coffee, then asked awkwardly, "Have you . . . er . . . had your . . . monthly visitor, honey?"

For a moment she hadn't known what he was talking about. It came to her then that he was asking if she'd had her menses. She had blushed and answered that she had. At the relief that came over the old man's face, she realized she should have told him as soon as she got it. She had known Ben worried that his son had gotten her with child.

Gretchen came to the spot where the trail forked. One path went straight on, the other leading off through the forest to the river. She turned Beauty onto the river road, thanking God that Spencer's seed hadn't taken root inside her. Ben would have made him marry her, and from then on her life would have been hell on earth. He would have continued to carouse around, flaunt his women under her nose.

The shame would be too hard to bear, she told herself as she reined in where a dense growth of willows shaded the trail. It was so cool here, the river so serene as it glided by. Perhaps here she would be able to shake Spencer from her mind. Beauty shook her head and snorted, and Gretchen rode her down to the water and let her drink her fill. When the mare suddenly lifted her head, her ears pointed, Gretchen looked fearfully over her shoulder. Who, or what, had startled the animal?

She relaxed a bit when she saw Trudie Harrod riding toward her. Gretchen reluctantly turned Beauty from the river and walked her to join the woman she disliked so intensely.

"Well, I heard that you've been ridin' around on a fancy piece of horseflesh," Trudie began, not bothering with a polite greeting. "Old Ben is quite generous with you, ain't he?"

Gretchen wanted to reply that actually Trudie's lover had given her the mare, but she decided not to stir up any more trouble than they already had. She suspected that Spencer wouldn't like his woman knowing how Gretchen Ames had come by the little mare.

"Ben is very kind to me," was all she answered.

"Unlike his son, huh?" Trudie taunted, her pale eyes watching Gretchen's face for a sign that her words had upset the young girl.

And though Gretchen trembled inside with anger, she managed to say calmly, "I'm afraid Spencer and I didn't hit it off too well."

"Spencer calls you an uppity bitch," Trudie commented, looking pleased at Gretchen's admission. She had suspected that the little beauty was the cause of Spencer's not being able to perform anymore; he was enamored of the stranger old Ben had brought into their home. "Spencer is livin' with me," she added. "Did you know?"

"Ben and I have heard that rumor," Gretchen admitted, wanting to knock Trudie out of the saddle and scratch her smug face. But she sat quietly, giving no indication of the turmoil going on inside her.

"Well," Trudie said, growing tired of trying

to get a rise out of Gretchen, "I'd better be gettin' home. Spencer will be wantin' his lunch right about now . . . and his dessert." She giggled. When Gretchen only looked at her, her face free of emotion, Trudie jerked her mount's head around and sent it at a hard gallop in the direction of her farm.

Gretchen watched them disappear down the river trail, wishing the horse would stumble and pitch its rider into a briarpatch. Her eyes desolate, she turned Beauty around and headed for home. The pleasure of her ride was gone. She saw none of the beauty that had entranced her before Trudie had interrupted her.

When Gretchen rode up to the cabin and dismounted she found Ben looking morosely at the garden, which was in desperate need of water. He had been surprised at how satisfying it had been, working the soil again after so many years. He hated the thought that all his vegetables might die.

A hot breeze pressed Gretchen's skirt against her body and lifted her curls as she walked up and stood beside Ben. He looked at her with worried eyes.

"If we don't get rain pretty soon we're gonna lose everything we worked so hard at gettin' started."

Gretchen looked up at the clear blue sky. There wasn't a hint of a cloud, no promise of the needed moisture. Next week July would arrive and it hadn't rained in a month. All the farmers were complaining. If they lost their crops, it would be a lean year for man and beast.

Gretchen knew there were no words of comfort she could give Ben, so she said instead, "I expect you're ready for lunch."

"Yeah," Ben answered dispiritedly, and she glanced at the pot of ham and beans cooking over a low fire. With the exception of breakfast, which she made before the cabin heated up, she now prepared their meals outside. The cabin became unbearable when the fireplace was in use. Ben had told her that all the hill wives cooked outside in the summer, and she found that she enjoyed cooking in the shade of the big oak in the corner of the yard.

One had to be careful of flies and bugs getting into the food, but it was worth fighting them off, for she liked the freedom of moving about and not having to be careful about dropping something on a well-scrubbed floor. They still ate their meals inside.

"After I eat I think I'll ride over to the post and jaw awhile with whoever is there," Ben said, turning away from his wilting garden. "It ain't gonna help the beans and corn, standin' here gawkin' at 'em."

Gretchen smiled to herself as she led Beauty through almost ankle-deep dust to turn her into the pasture. Ben liked his little snort of corn "squeezin's" once in a while, while he gabbed with his old cronies. She didn't fault him for that. She yearned for the company of her own sex once in a while too.

She had met most of the neighborhood women, and though they had been polite, they hadn't been as warm toward her as Bessy Crawford had been. They had invited her to visit them, but she got the feeling that they had done this out of respect and liking for Ben. None of them had come to call on her, although she had invited them. She had racked her brain for reasons why the women didn't like her.

Later, when Ben climbed on his old mule and rode away, his stomach full, Gretchen brought the dress she had been working on out onto the porch. She had only to hem the skirt and the sleeves and sew the buttons on the bodice. When finished it would be her prettiest one yet: a pink and blue gingham. She would save it for special occasions, although she didn't know what they would be. Piney Ridge didn't have a church, or a resident preacher. In nice weather a traveling preacher came through every few weeks, Ben had told her, holding services outside under the shade of the trees, with the small congregation sitting on the grass. Sometimes he married a couple or baptized a baby.

She remembered that Ben had said last week that Reverend Applegate was due to come through any Sunday now. Maybe she would attend the meeting, Gretchen thought. See faces other than Ben's . . . and Collin Grady's.

That young man was in the habit of coming

by a couple of times a week to sit on the porch and talk to Ben and to slide glances at her when he thought she wasn't looking.

Was he courting her? she wondered. Was that how courtships were handled? She had no knowledge of how such things took place. At any rate, she hoped he wasn't sweet on her. Collin was a very nice young man, handsome and hard-working, but she had no romantic notions about him.

Gretchen was so occupied with her thoughts, she was unaware of the dark clouds gathering in the west. When a streak of lightning crackled across the sky and thunder rolled through the hills she looked up, startled. Then a wide smile curved her lips. Rain was sweeping in sheets across the valley.

"I must bring Beauty in!" she exclaimed, putting the dress aside and jumping to her feet.

Had she taken the time to think, common sense would have told her that the mare would seek shelter beneath a tree. But the mare was more than a means of travel for her. Beauty had become the pet she had never had. Just as she would bring in a cat or a dog during a storm, she had the same compassion for the little horse.

Sprinting through the rain and the puddles that were already forming from nature's onslaught, Gretchen reached the pasture gate. She peered anxiously through the sheets of rain, looking for the mare. She thought she saw a long white tail swishing about beneath a large beechnut tree, and she cupped her hands around her mouth and called Beauty's name. The little horse came galloping toward her, its eyes rolling in fright as the lightning zigzagged across the sky and the thunder cracked and rolled. When the gate was opened for her she ran alongside her mistress to the shelter of the barn.

Gretchen was soaked through as she put her pet into its stall. Her dress clung to her like a second skin, and her curls were flattened and streaming water. She wiped the rain from her eyes and grabbed up two gunnysacks. She began wiping the mare down, talking soothingly to her as the storm continued to rage on outside.

She stopped, then, midway in a stroke at the white coat. All the windows in the cabin were open and her unfinished dress lay on the porch. She dropped the sacks. She would finish drying off Beauty later.

She was on her way to the door, to make the dash to the cabin, when a flash of lightning lit up the barn. She gasped and came to a faltering halt. The broad figure of a man had just stepped inside the barn. She opened her mouth to scream, then a well-remembered voice drawled, "Don't be frightened, Miss Ames. It's only me."

"Spencer?" she squeaked, peering in the gloom of the barn.

* * *

Spencer drew a sleeve across his sweating forehead. "Damn, it's hot," he muttered irritably, feeling smothered in the heavy air that hung around him like a blanket. He slapped at a mosquito, wishing it would rain and cool the land. He looked west at the sky. There were some gray clouds gathering, but they didn't look too threatening.

He turned his attention back to the crudely erected cabin. He had been watching it for over an hour and had seen no movement around the place. He swiped at his sweating face again, then leaned forward suddenly. Jeeter Grundy had stepped outside, buck naked. As he watched the man relieve himself on the ground, the squaw came and leaned in the doorway, also minus clothing. When the pair walked back inside the cabin he didn't have to guess how they had been entertaining themselves.

Spencer remained in the blistering heat another half hour, waiting to see if anyone approached the cabin. As with all the other times he had watched the Grundy shack, no one appeared.

He was reaching the conclusion that the Grundy brothers were the only ones who had been sent here by the fur company out of St. Louis. He stood up and shouldered his rifle and was about to step out on the trail when he heard the sound of heavy, plodding hooves.

A smile lit his face when his father, astride

his old mule, rode into sight. He eased back down on the rock he'd occupied for over an hour and feasted his eyes on the beloved, wrinkled face. He had missed his father dreadfully, and though the old man didn't know it, he had checked on the cabin every day to see if everything was all right with him . . . and Miss Uppity.

When Ben disappeared down the narrow trail Spencer found himself walking toward the cabin he had lived in all his life. He had a devilish desire to torment Gretchen, to bring her down off her high horse. He wanted to face her, too, to demand why she hadn't spoken up that day when Pa had found them together in the barn.

Spencer had walked close to a mile in the near-stifling heat when the sky began to darken. He was another quarter of a mile from the homeplace when the lightning flashed and the thunder rolled. When the rain came slicing in he lifted his hot face to catch its soothing coolness for a moment. He broke into a run then, the rain peppering down on him, soaking him to the skin within minutes.

He was only yards away when he spotted Gretchen and the mare running toward the barn. And he was only moments behind her when she opened the barn door and led the mare inside. As he stepped into the barn, a flash of lightning lit the darkness. In that split second of brightness he saw Gretchen clearly revealed in her wet, clinging dress, her nipples hard and tight from the coolness of the rain. The blood began to rush through his veins and pound against his ears. Desire tore at his loins. He had seen in that momentary light that her bodice was unbuttoned halfway down because of the heat, and her breasts were barely covered.

"Don't be frightened, Miss Ames. It's only me," he said, his voice thick as he advanced farther into the barn, dripping water on the hay that covered the floor. "It would seem that we've both been caught out in the rain."

Gretchen took a step back, and swallowed convulsively. "What are you doing here? What do you want?"

"To answer your first question," Spencer replied, stopping in front of her, "I'm here to get out of the rain. And as for your second one, you know what I want." He lifted a hand as though to stroke her cheek.

The action had been intended only to provoke Gretchen, to erase the haughtiness from her beautiful face, but the nearness of her, her own special scent, affected him profoundly. His palm gently cupped her chin. When he put his other hand on her waist and lowered his head toward her Gretchen knocked his hand aside and took another step backward, coming up against Beauty's stall. "Forget that, Spencer Atkins," she said, a catch in her voice as she remembered the fires this man could ignite

A Special Offer For Leisure Romance Readers Only!

Get FOUR FREE Romance Novels

A $19.96 Value!

Travel to exotic worlds filled with passion and adventure —without leaving your home!

Plus, you'll save $5.00 every time you buy!

Thrill to the most sensual, adventure-filled Historical Romances on the market today...

FROM LEISURE BOOKS

As a home subscriber to the Leisure Romance Book Club, you'll enjoy the best in today's BRAND-NEW Historical Romance fiction. For over twenty years, Leisure Books has brought you the award-winning, high-quality authors you know and love to read. Each Leisure Historical Romance will sweep you away to a world of high adventure...and intimate romance. Discover for yourself all the passion and excitement millions of readers thrill to each and every month.

Save $5.00 Each Time You Buy!

Six times a year, the Leisure Romance Book Club brings you four brand-new titles from Leisure Books, America's foremost publisher of Historical Romances. EACH PACKAGE WILL SAVE YOU $5.00 FROM THE BOOKSTORE PRICE! And you'll never miss a new title with our convenient home delivery service.

Here's how we do it. Each package will carry a FREE 10-DAY EXAMINATION privilege. At the end of that time, if you decide to keep your books, simply pay the low invoice price of $14.96, no shipping or handling charges added. HOME DELIVERY IS ALWAYS FREE. With today's top Historical Romance novels selling for $4.99 and higher, our price SAVES YOU $5.00 with each shipment.

AND YOUR FIRST FOUR-BOOK SHIPMENT IS TOTALLY FREE!

IT'S A BARGAIN YOU CAN'T BEAT! A Super $19.96 Value!

LEISURE BOOKS *A Division of Dorchester Publishing Co., Inc.*

GET YOUR 4 FREE BOOKS NOW—A $19.96 Value!

Mail the Free Book Certificate Today!

4 FREE BOOKS

A $19.96 VALUE

Free Books Certificate

YES! I want to subscribe to the Leisure Romance Book Club. Please send me my 4 FREE BOOKS. Then, six times each year I'll receive the four newest Leisure Historical Romance selections to Preview FREE for 10 days. If I decide to keep them, I will pay the Special Member's Only discounted price of just $3.74 each, a total of $14.96. This is a SAVINGS OF $5.00 off the bookstore price. There are no shipping, handling, or other charges. There is no minimum number of books I must buy and I may cancel the program at any time. In any case, the 4 FREE BOOKS are mine to keep — A BIG $19.96 Value!

Offer valid only in the U.S.A.

Name ______________________

Address ______________________

City ______________________

State ____________ *Zip* ____________

Telephone ______________________

Signature ______________________

If under 18, Parent or Guardian must sign. Terms, prices and conditions subject to change. Subscription subject to acceptance. Leisure Books reserves the right to reject any order or cancel any subscription.

1093FF

A $19.96 VALUE

4 FREE BOOKS

Get Four Books Totally FREE— A $19.96 Value!

▼ Tear Here and Mail Your FREE Book Card Today! ▼

PLEASE RUSH
MY FOUR FREE
BOOKS TO ME
RIGHT AWAY!

AFFIX
STAMP
HERE

Leisure Romance Book Club
PO Box 1234
65 Commerce Road
Stamford CT 06920- 4563

inside her. She must never let that happen again.

"You don't mean that," Spencer said softly, bringing both hands to rest on her shoulders, pinning her to the stable wall.

"I do mean it, and if you don't take your hands off me I'm going to call your father."

"He'd have a hard time hearin' you all the way from the post," Spencer said, staring at her mouth.

Her eyes glittering like a cornered bobcat's, Gretchen tried to push him away, but she might as well have tried to push over the big oak in the backyard. Spencer didn't budge an inch.

"Damn you, Gretchen Ames, you've made my life a misery," he rasped, and he pulled her into his arms. His head came down and she tried to escape his searching lips, but his head followed hers, and in seconds his mouth was fastened on hers in a wild hunger.

As his tongue slipped between her lips Gretchen made a desperate protest, knowing where the kiss would lead. But she was helpless to break it off. Spencer's large hand held the back of her head, making it impossible for her to move as his tongue slowly stroked in and out in rhythm with the movement of his hips.

Against her will a warmth began to grow in Gretchen's lower body, and with a little sob of surrender her arms came up to wrap themselves around his shoulders. Her fingers tangled themselves in his wet, black hair.

Spencer groaned low in his throat, and parting his legs he placed his hands on her small rear end and pulled her up against his aching, throbbing maleness. As he continued thrusting against her, he brought one hand up to undo the remaining buttons on her bodice. He parted the wet material, then lifted his head to gaze down at the round white mounds with their pink, pouting nipples. *I shouldn't do this,* Gretchen thought wretchedly as she cupped her breasts and lifted them, inviting him to do with them as he wished.

"Oh God," Spencer whispered, his head coming down, his open mouth covering one of the passion-swollen peaks. All conscious thought deserted Gretchen as he began to suckle her. She was lost in the pleasure of his drawing lips, his caressing fingers on her other breast. She made little murmuring sounds and held his head close to her.

When both breasts had been given close attention and Gretchen was so weak she was afraid she was going to crumple at his feet, Spencer raised his head and stepped away from her. She gave a small protesting sound, then relaxed when he began tugging off his wet buckskins. She hurried out of her dress. When it fell to her feet in a sodden mass she looked at Spencer.

He stood bare before her, his legs slightly parted so that she could see how much he desired her. She stared at his long, thick shaft, desperate to feel it inside her. It jerked when he saw her puckered nipples and he realized she wanted him as much as he did her. Wordlessly, he swept her up into his arms and carried her to the same pile of hay that had known their first lovemaking. Laying her down and gently spreading her legs, he positioned himself between them. He hung over her then, looking deeply into her desire-ridden eyes, willing her to admit she wanted him.

When her arms came up and her hands rested on his shoulders he gathered her hips in his hands and she moved her hands down between them and curled her fingers around his throbbing strength. She stroked him a moment, then guided him inside her.

With a sigh that came all the way from the soles of his feet, Spencer began stroking inside her moist heat.

He moved slowly, rhythmically, telling himself not to hurry, to make this coming together that he had dreamed of so often last as long as possible.

Nothing else existed but the two of them as Spencer's body rose and fell, Gretchen meeting his every thrust. As the minutes passed, their bodies became bathed in sweat and the air was filled with huskily whispered words of intense pleasure from both their throats.

The time came when Spencer was afraid he couldn't hold back much longer. When he felt Gretchen stiffen he knew that she had reached her limit too.

With a shuddering groan, he began to buck faster and faster inside her. In moments the barn rang with the cries of their release.

Spencer slumped on top of Gretchen, his heart racing, his body jerking involuntarily in the aftermath of spent passion. He was weak with a contentment he had never known before. As his breathing slowed he told himself that he had just glimpsed heaven in Gretchen's arms.

But when Gretchen's heartbeat settled down to a steady rhythm and her mind took over from the passion that had held her body captive, shame scorched through her. Her body's weakness where Spencer Atkins was concerned had caused her to let him use her again. A tear slipped down her cheek.

She brushed it away as anger and resentment began to boil inside her. She hadn't wanted him to kiss her, had tried her best not to let him. But damn him to hell, he knew that once he could get his mouth and hands on her she would be like putty beneath his touch.

When Spencer raised himself up on an elbow and smiled down at her, she glared back at him, her eyes stormy and spitting fire. When his surprised expression questioned her she raised a hand and slapped him hard across the face. He was so stunned, she was able to roll from beneath him, grab up her dress, and dash from the barn. Her hot tears mingled with the rain.

Spencer stood up and walked to the barn door to watch Gretchen's graceful body streak toward the cabin. A pleased smile lifted the corners of his lips as he stroked the welts her fingers had left on his cheek. Gretchen Ames could protest all she wanted to, but she knew, as well as he did, that he could make love to her anytime he wanted to. And he intended to do it often.

Chapter Thirteen

It was the middle of August and still scorching hot—the dog days. Gretchen and Ben worked in the almost bare garden. There were a few remaining tomato plants, but the cucumbers had been picked three weeks ago and had turned into pickles. The row of cabbage had been gathered, sliced thin, and packed in salt brine. The barrel was stinking up the cellar as it became sauerkraut. A row of onions had been dug up last week and dried. They now rested in the coolness of the cellar. And in a bin beside them were enough potatoes to last them through the winter.

Gretchen wore a pleased expression as she picked the last of the string beans and Ben followed along behind her, snapping off the ears of corn hanging on dry stalks that rustled in the hot air. This winter he would shuck the yellow kernels from the cobs and feed them to the old mule and the little mare.

The gunnysack of beans Gretchen dragged along behind her would be strung on long pieces of heavy string and hung up to dry. When the cold months arrived they would be soaked in water until they were plump again, then cooked slowly with a piece of salt pork or a chunk of ham. They would be very tasty, as well being nourishing.

Gretchen came to the end of the row and took off her bonnet. She fanned her hot face with it as she looked out over the garden. She and Ben had worked hard on their garden patch, but it had paid them well for their labor. They had all the vegetables they would need for the winter months, and Ben's share of the wheat and the corn grown by Collin on Ben's land would be taken to the mill and ground into flour and cornmeal. She gave her head a satisfied nod. She and Ben would fare quite well when nothing but ice and snow existed in the garden.

As she stood gloating over what the garden had produced, Gretchen became uncomfortably aware of her wet armpits, the back of her dress, and the large moist spot on the front of her bodice. She needed a good scrub in the small stream that ran behind the barn, she told herself. Her curls had grown long enough to be tied back with a ribbon, and she lifted the heavy mass to let the hot breeze dry her nape.

The raising of her arms constricted her movement, and she frowned in annoyance. She had let the seams out, but that had only given her a little more room. Not enough for any comfort. She had gained at least ten pounds since coming to live with Ben in the hills, due to regular good meals and less hard work.

She sighed. She hated to ask it of Ben, but she needed to make some new dresses. It was shameful the way her breasts pratically fell out of the bodices of the ones she'd sewn in the spring.

She recalled with a tickled smile the day she had met Collin's mother. The woman had looked at her full bodice with scandalized eyes, then rolled them back as though she were going to have a fit. Now, she, like Ben, pitied the poor woman who might marry the handsome young farmer someday. Gretchen had invited Collin to bring his mother into the cabin and have some refreshments, but before he could answer Agatha had replied, with her nose in the air, that they must get along, there was a lot of work to be done at home.

Collin had been obviously embarrassed at his mother's behavior, but he hadn't opened his mouth to protest. Instead, he had followed her when she went swishing out of the yard after telling Ben good-bye.

Ben had laughed and said, when the pair were out of sight, "Well, honey, I don't believe you cut the mustard with skinny old Agatha.

She'll sure try to keep her boy away from you from now on."

Gretchen had laughed with him. The woman was a harridan if ever she had seen one. But Mrs. Grady's attitude was fine with her. She had no interest in her son, other than a friendly one. Although Collin was good to look at, she found him quite boring.

A little voice inside her whispered, *With the exception of Spencer Atkins, you find all men boring.*

Truth to tell, she hadn't met many men in the area to use as a basis for comparison. And that puzzled Gretchen. The bachelors in Piney Ridge certainly ogled her enough when she and Ben went to the post, but they never approached her. Were they like the women in the neighborhood? Didn't they like her for some reason?

She had no idea that Spencer had dropped hints in the proper ears that Gretchen Ames was off bounds to the men. Only Collin Grady, whether by denseness or stubbornness, continued to stop by a couple of times a week.

"I guess that just about does it," Ben said, interrupting Gretchen's thoughts. He had lopped off the last cornstalk and tossed it across the garden to land on a pile of the others. "There's some right good fodder for old Jimbo and Beauty this winter."

Gretchen nodded agreement, then said, "Ben, I hate to ask this of you, but I need some new dresses again. I've gained so much weight over the summer, the ones I made when I first came here are too tight on me now."

"Gretchen," Ben scolded, "you don't have to ask. You know where I keep my money. Any-time you need somethin', just go to the post and buy it."

Tears moistened Gretchen's eyes. "You are so good to me, Ben," she said. "I can't seem to get used to it."

"I'm no better to you than you are to me," Ben said soberly. "Havin' you around has put new life in me. Now you go get yourself cleaned up and get on over to Jacob's and get your new dress material." He looked up at the sky, then back at Gretchen. "You got plenty of time to get there and back before dark."

With a big smile, Gretchen picked up her skirt and ran to the cabin. It took but a minute for her to gather up clean clothes, a towel, a washcloth and soap, and leave the cabin, headed for the small stream.

The haze-filled valley warned that autumn wasn't far off as the mare lunged up the hill and then started down the other side. Gretchen, perched on Beauty's back, tried to keep her mind on the dress goods she would purchase at the post. What with winter coming on, she would need to buy some heavy homespun, fustian, and twill. She would, of course, weave her own woolens. Collin had sheared his sheep and had given her two large gunnysacks crammed full of raw wool. As soon as the weather cooled she would get busy at the spinning wheel and loom. It was dreadfully hot in her loft room right now. She had been sleeping on a pallet downstairs, spread out on the floor before the open door.

Gretchen's mind wouldn't stay on the reason she was riding to the post, however. It kept drifting to a dark-haired, gray-eyed man. Would he be at the post? And if he was, would he speak to her or ignore her? Strange as it seemed, she never ran into Spencer in public. She had no idea what his attitude toward her might be. He could snub her, or he could very well insult her by words or looks. Those eyes of his could be as eloquent as his tongue.

She was well aware of what his reaction would be to her in private. Even now as she rode along she was afraid he might come along and sweet-talk her into dismounting. And she would be lost if she was foolish enough to do that. She had learned one thing about Spencer: he had only to touch her, look at her with his wicked, knowing eyes, and she was ready to melt into his arms, do anything he asked of her, even though she knew she would despise herself later.

He had proven his power over her so often, she thought with humiliation. It seemed to be a game with him to see how often and how easily he could seduce her. All he had to do was catch her alone.

Gretchen thought back to the times they had made love since Ben had ordered Spencer out of the cabin. He had come upon her fishing one time, and in a matter of minutes, it seemed, she had succumbed to his hot kisses and stroking hands. Twice she had gone into the barn for some purpose and he had slipped in behind her and without a word gathered her into his arms. Both times had been the same. Before she could cry out or protest, her body had gone up in flames. At least an hour would pass as they made feverish love.

And the last time, four nights ago, she couldn't believe his daring.

She had been asleep on her pallet in the kitchen doorway when she was awakened by hot, hungry kisses on her mouth and throat. She had jerked her head away, whispering, "Are you crazy? What if Ben should wake up?"

He had covered his mouth with her hand, shushing her. And not wanting to awaken Ben, or cause another argument between him and his son, she kept silent as the gown was pulled over her head and he began to suckle her breasts. When she gave a smothered moan of pleasure Spencer stretched out beside her, already as bare as she was. When he took her hand and moved it down to his throbbing need she forgot Ben and everything else as her fingers closed around him and stroked.

As the hours passed they explored each other's bodies with hands and lips until passion had them trembling. Spencer would then part her legs and thrust himself inside her.

Gretchen's face flamed red as she remembered how very intimate they had been that soft, hot night. While Ben snored in the background, Spencer had coaxed her into other ways she could please him. He had been just as generous to her, she remembered with a stirring in her lower body.

They had exhausted themselves, making love again and again. Dawn was breaking when Spencer finally sat up and drew on his clothes. He dropped a kiss on her nose, then as quietly as he had come, he was gone.

Tears had rolled down her cheeks as she pulled on her gown. Why did Spencer do this to her? she asked herself. Was it an act of revenge? Was it his way of getting back at her because she was the cause of the rift between him and his father? He was never rough with her in his lovemaking. Actually, he was a very gentle lover, even whispering soft love words to her when he was soaring to the crest of his passion.

She had finally fallen into a spent sleep, Spencer's scent all over her body, with a firm resolve that he would never again make love to her.

Beauty topped a rise and Gretchen came back to the present as she looked down on the post and the one-room cabins of the trappers scattered around it. Her lips curled. Trust those wild men not to get too far away from their whiskey and women.

As she rode up to the long building, dismounted, and tied Beauty to the long hitching rail, she could hear the chattering of women coming from inside the post. She braced herself for their cool politeness.

It was as Gretchen had expected when she stepped through the door that stood open. Heads turned in her direction, then cool, distant greetings were spoken. Some called her Gretchen, but more called her Miss Ames. There was one young woman among them who she hadn't met, but no one offered to introduce them. She was a pretty little delicate-looking blonde who wore sadness on her face. She neither spoke nor looked at Gretchen.

Then one of the women, Patience Hardy, a very unlikely name for such a big, forward woman, took the girl's arm and turned her around to face Gretchen. "Miss Ames," she said in her rough voice, "I don't believe you've met Ellie Allen."

"No, I haven't." Gretchen smiled at the girl and held out her hand as she added, "I'm pleased to meet you, Ellie."

The girl looked through her and ignored her hand. Gretchen felt her face burn when the other girl turned away without acknowledging her greeting, and wondered at the smothered tittering among the women. Confused, she turned to the counter to find Jacob's sympathetic eyes on her.

"What can I do for you, Gretchen?" He gave her a genial smile.

"I'd like to look at some dress goods," she answered in the silence that had descended in the room.

"You're just in time." The big man came around from behind the counter, giving the listening women a cold look. "A barge came up the river this morning, and among my supplies was some real pretty material. It's over there on the shelf. Come along and look it over." He led her to where the bolts of cloth were neatly stacked, then left her.

As she studied the prints, deciding which ones would suit her, the women prepared to leave. They looked at Gretchen's back, making up their minds whether to say good-bye to her. Jacob cleared his throat and when they looked at him, his angry black eyes ordered, *Scat!*

Most were gripped with shame as they went through the door.

Gretchen told herself that she didn't care that the women treated her so shabbily, but unshed tears glimmered in her eyes.

She had made her choices when the hairs on the back of her neck began to prickle. Someone was watching her, and very intently. She turned her head and froze, her heart beginning to pound. Spencer stood in the doorway of the connecting tavern, raw desire in his eyes as he watched her. Anger flushed her cheeks and she glared at him in icy silence. What if Jacob noticed him looking at her that way?

There was a hint of teasing laughter in Spencer's eyes as he walked over and stood beside her. "I was goin' to suggest to you the last time I saw you, in the daylight that is, that you make yourself some new dresses. You were in danger of falling out of the one you were wearing." He trailed a finger across the roundness of her breasts, which were pushing up past the dress's neckline.

"Not that I mind, you know," he said silkily.

"Stop it!" she ground out in a whisper, slapping at his offending finger. "What if Jacob saw you doing that?" She darted a look at the post owner, who had his back turned to them.

"You know you like my touch," Spencer said softly. "You like it better when my lips are on those beauties."

"I do not!" she whispered heatedly. "I hate for you to touch me."

Spencer gave a low, wicked-sounding laugh and said huskily, "We'll see how much you hate my touch when I ride home with you later."

His words sent Gretchen into a trembling mass of nerves. She clenched her fists in the folds of her skirt. She couldn't appeal to Jacob and explain that Spencer intended making love to her on her way home. The man would think she was being fanciful. It would spread all over Piney Ridge that Gretchen Ames was subject to having whimsical notions.

Gretchen knew there was but one thing to do: stick to her firm decision, make her mind stronger than her body. If she did that, Spencer would have to rape her in order to make love to her. She felt in her heart that he would never do it. He was an honorable man. If she made it clear to him that she didn't welcome his advances, his pride at least would make him leave her alone.

As Jacob measured and cut the dress lengths from the bolts of cloth Gretchen had chosen, she thought that Spencer, lounging against the counter, looked like a waiting tomcat. She geared up her fixed intention that never again would his hard body cover hers. Never again would he shame her, make her cry when he had slaked his lust and walked away from her.

Jacob had just cut the last piece when Collin Grady walked into the store. In her relief, Gretchen was overexuberant in her greeting to the young farmer. Here was her chance to get home without Spencer following her. Smiling at her neighbor, she said, "If you don't have too much shopping to do, Collin, I'll wait for you and you can ride home with me. I thought I saw a wolf on my way in."

Spencer's gray eyes took on the color of storm clouds as Collin said he would be delighted to ride along with Gretchen. "I'll just be a minute. I need to get some salt for Ma."

"Damn fool looks like a fawning puppy," Spencer swore under his breath. "She don't give a damn for you, you poor dumb bastard."

With a sardonic gleam in his eyes, Spencer watched as Jacob wrapped four dress lengths in paper for Gretchen, then measured out Collin's salt. The pair left the post then, laughing and talking, without a backward look at him.

Spencer followed them outside and leaned against the wall, wanting to spring at young Grady when he put his hands on Gretchen's waist and lifted her into the saddle. He wished the mare would turn her head and bite the idiot as he stood gazing up at Gretchen like a lovesick calf.

But as Gretchen and Collin rode away, Spencer's face grew sober. What had started out as an act of revenge, a way of getting back at Gretchen for not admitting her willing participation in their lovemaking, had now turned into a need for her that robbed him of all common sense. The compulsion to possess her, to make love to her, was a force that kept him awake nights, made him practically stalk her, to catch her alone in the cabin. When days went by when he couldn't get near her he became so irritable, his friends looked askance at him, their expressions saying that he must be losing his mind.

And what the men thought of him wasn't nearly as bad as what he thought of himself. He was a low-life dog, using his sexual experience on her untried innocence, knowing that she would be unable to resist him. In a sense he was raping her, even though she did become a wanton in his arms. It bothered him to the depths of his soul when she cried shamed tears after every lovemaking. Only his stubbornness kept him from gathering her up in his arms and kissing them away.

It had to cease, he knew that. He couldn't go on hurting her, hurting himself. He felt the same emptiness she did every time he left her; it was like he had left a part of himself behind with her. There was also the likelihood of getting her with child. He never spilled his seed outside her as he did with the others. Was he subconsciously wishing that she would get in a family way?

Good Lord, he thought, in near panic. That would mean marriage. He would never want that . . . would he?

It struck him then that he hadn't wanted any other women since Gretchen. He'd had plenty of opportunities. He could have his pick of half a dozen women every night. And there was ol' Trudie, anxious to do anything he wanted her to. So would the tavern whores . . . at a price. The trouble was, they no longer satisfied him. Only lust was involved in his coupling with them. He had no desire to stroke their bodies, to take their breasts into his mouth, to kiss their lips until a little moan told him how pleasurable it felt. He had done many things with Gretchen that he wouldn't dream of doing with another woman.

But things had a way of changing. For instance, if his seed did take hold inside Gretchen and he had to marry her, what would happen if, after a few months, he grew tired of her and started having a wandering eye? Pa would shoot him if he ever broke his marriage vows to her.

Maybe she'll marry the farmer, a voice inside him suggested. *You'd leave her alone then. You've never slept with another man's wife before.*

"Mind your own business," Spencer growled and turned back into the store, and then on into the tavern. Jacob watched him with amusement in his eyes. His friend was waging a hard battle with himself. He didn't know why the man didn't just give up and marry the little beauty.

Chapter Fourteen

When Spencer stepped out of the cabin a heavy frost lay on the ground and the air was cool and still. He breathed deeply, savoring the scent of pine and woodland earth.

It was September and the bucks were out of velvet. Winter would be here before he knew it. It was time he brought out the traps from the shed where he kept the stallion. He had to prepare them to be set out come late November.

He couldn't wait for that time to come. Running a trap line would keep him so busy, he wouldn't have time to think about Gretchen and how his body cried out for hers. And he'd be so beat when it came time to fall into bed, his sleep would be dreamless.

"Not like it's been lately," he muttered, going back inside. The rumpled blanket on his bed gave evidence of his restless sleep. Every night in his dreams he made love to Gretchen. He imagined her arms and legs wrapped around him, her hips lifting eagerly to meet his thrusting body. But just as he reached for that crest of soul-shuddering release, Gretchen would fade away and he'd find himself bucking his hips into the pillow he had dragged down between his legs.

That had been happening for three weeks now. For three weeks he hadn't been near his father's cabin, nor had he lain in wait to catch Gretchen alone somewhere. He had told himself that it was wrong, his taking advantage of her vulnerability, and promised that it would stop. He had kept his word.

And it was damn near killing him.

He had tried taking Trudie to bed again, and again he had embarrassed himself. Nothing had happened. He had remained as limp as Pa's old mule. He had tried with one of the tavern whores, and then a pretty little squaw, and had had the same results. It would seem that Gretchen had spoiled him for any other woman.

He had decided that his only hope was to stay away from the little green-eyed witch; forget all about her. Then maybe he would be able to return to his old ways.

Spencer was frying salt pork and thinly sliced potatoes for his breakfast when he was hailed from outside. "Hey, Spence, that salt pork sure smells good to an old trapper," came a voice he recognized with a broad smile. He pulled the long-handled skillet off the fire and stood up, a sparkle in his gray eyes as he hurried to the door.

"Will Smith, you old hound dog, come on in." His voice was warm and welcoming.

His friend from Squaw Hollow climbed off his mule and tied it to a tree, then stepped up on the small porch, his hand outstretched. "How are you, Spence?" the big man asked as they shook hands. "You look a little leaner than when I seen you at the rendezvous. You been losin' weight?"

He had lost weight, Spencer knew. His shirts were looser and he'd had to tighten his belt a notch. But he wasn't about to tell his friend that he couldn't eat or rest from wanting to sleep with one special woman.

"I've just honed down a little, I guess," he answered. "I've been huntin' a lot, doin' a lot of walkin'. How have you been?" Spencer asked as Will stepped inside the cabin. "How's Matty?"

"We're both fine. I left Matty over at my sister Bessy's place." He chuckled. "Poor woman, Deke was jawin' at her so fast, I was afraid he was gonna swallow his tongue. I had to get away from him before I hit him. We got in last night and I thought he was gonna talk me to death before Sister ordered him off to bed. Me and Matty's ears was ringin'."

Spencer grinned. He, like everyone else in

Piney Ridge, avoided Deke Crawford whenever possible.

When Spencer started to put another plate on the table Will said, "Not for me, Spence. I'm still about to bust from the breakfast Sister put on the table this mornin'. I'll have a cup of coffee with you, though."

Spencer filled two tin cups from a battered coffeepot, and Will asked, "Have you had any strangers around here, tryin' to talk the trappers and Indians into workin' for a big fur company?"

"We had a couple. A pair of brothers named Grundy was nosin' round the hills this summer. Claimed to be horse traders at first. When they couldn't talk any of us, including the Indians, into joinin' up with the Missouri Fur Company they left." Spencer took a swallow of coffee. "Has there been anyone around Squaw Hollow talkin' to the trappers?"

Will nodded, a worried frown on his face. "The same Grundy brothers are there now. They're giving the men and Indians all kinds of reasons they should tie in with this company out of St. Louis. I'm afraid they've almost got them convinced."

"It was the same thing here with the Indians until I pointed out a few things to their chief, made him think."

After a pause Will said, "I wonder if you would come to the Hollow and talk to our fellers. Talk some sense into them too."

"I don't know, Will. Them Grundys would like to put a knife in me as it is. If I go in there and squelch another deal for them, they're gonna come after me hot and heavy."

"Hell, Spence, you're not tryin' to tell me you're afraid of them, are you?"

Spencer gave his friend a look that said he was out of his head. "Not in a fair fight, I'm not, but those two don't know anything about fair fightin'. I'm pretty sure one of them tried to ambush me."

"Well, of course I wouldn't want you to get yourself killed." Will looked alarmed. "If they've tried to shoot you in the back, stay away from the Hollow. I'll keep talkin' to the men. Maybe some of them will listen."

"That's no good, Will." Spencer shook his head. "All the trappers have to stand together so the company doesn't get a toehold in your area. They'll back off just like they did here if they see the trappers and Indians are united."

Will looked so dispirited, Spencer gave an inward sigh. "I'll leave for Squaw Hollow tomorrow mornin', see what I can do."

"I don't know, Spence." The worried frown was back on Will's face. "I don't want to get you killed."

"I'll be careful. I'll keep a tight watch on my back trail."

"Make sure you do. I don't know if old Ben could bear the grief of losin' you."

Spencer made no response to his friend's

remark. Will didn't know the situation between him and Pa now. He leaned back in his chair and changed the subject. "What happened to Callie West—the woman I made a widow out of?"

Will grinned. "Callie is a very happy widow these days. She's livin' in the abandoned cabin that low-life husband of hers took over. She's not a bad-lookin' woman now that the bruises are gone from her face, and she's put on some weight. We all kinda look after her. Would you believe she's only thirty years old? I wouldn't be surprised if she don't get married again."

"I hope she's smart enough not to marry another Zeke West if she does."

"I'm sure she is. You can bet she'll take her time choosin' her next husband."

Will pushed himself away from the table. "I want to stop by and say howdy to Ben, then get on back to Sister Bessy's place. Old Deke has probably talked poor Matty deaf by now." He paused at the door. "Sister tells me your pa has taken a pretty young girl under his wing. A nice girl, is she?"

Spencer shrugged. "She's all right, I guess. Got her nose in the air most of the time. But she and Pa get along fine and I guess that's what counts."

Will wanted to ask if Spencer got along with the girl, but the moody look that had come over his friend's face stopped him from asking. But when he climbed on his mule a few minutes later the question was still on his mind.

For some reason Spencer hadn't wanted to talk about the girl. Will grinned to himself and said to the mule, "You know, Gray, I wouldn't be surprised if the love bug ain't bit our friend."

As Gretchen rode along, the little mare snatched mouthfuls of the tall grass still untouched by frost. Gretchen didn't mind the slow pace. She was feasting her eyes on the beauty surrounding her. In the past two weeks the forest had changed from green to scarlet and yellow. There was a steady falling of leaves in the late autumn breeze. Winter would soon be here.

But this winter she wouldn't mind the cold, she told herself. There would be plenty of food to eat, warm clothing to wear, and a warm cabin in which to pass the long winter months.

She shivered, remembering the years spent in the poorhouse, where there was never enough to eat, inadequate clothing to wear, and she had to sleep in the long room under the eaves, shivering the night away.

Gretchen pulled her thoughts from the past when, from a hilltop, she looked down on Piney Ridge nestled in the valley alongside the Ohio. *It looks so serene and peaceful,* she thought, as Beauty started down hill. The smile left her face when she recognized two mounts tied up in front of the post. One was Spencer's stallion; the other horse belonged to Trudie Harrod.

She chewed on her bottom lip as she sat the

restless mare. She hadn't seen Spencer for over three weeks and now she knew why. He'd had his fling with her, showed her that he could have her anytime he wanted to, and had then gone back to Trudie's bed.

She didn't know if she was up to facing Spencer. She didn't want to see the mocking amusement in his eyes, the knowing look on his face.

But you can't avoid him the rest of your life, she told herself. *Stiffen your spine and get yourself down there and purchase that warping you need.*

She had run out of the heavy thread needed for her loom yesterday afternoon. If she was to finish the woolen cloth from which she planned to make shirts for Ben and heavy curtains to keep out the winter chill, she had to buy more thread as soon as possible. When winter arrived it would be too cold in the loft room to sit at the loom.

Gretchen lifted the reins and the mare continued on down the hill. By the time Gretchen reached the post and stepped through its door her spine was straight and her chin was lifted proudly.

Jacob looked up from waiting on Spencer and gave her a wide smile. "Good mornin', Gretchen," he said. "I swear, you get prettier every day."

Spencer wheeled around, his face going pale and still. Gretchen looked away from him, but not before she saw the desire that kindled in his eyes. There was confusion in hers as they clashed with Trudie's. How could he desire her while the woman he lived with was in the same room?

Trudie gave her a heated glower, then walked over to stand beside Spencer, pressing her hip intimately against his. Spencer gave her an irritated look and moved away from her to continue his conversation with Jacob.

"You ridin' or walkin' this time, Spence?" the big man asked, tossing Spencer's purchases into a haversack.

"I'm thinkin' of paddlin' up the river as far as I can, then walking the rest of the way."

Gretchen pretended to be looking at dress material, but all her attention was centered on Spencer's answer to Jacob's question. Where was he going? she wondered. How long would he be gone? The supplies in his sack looked like a couple of weeks' worth. She felt a weakening in her stomach. What if he was leaving the hills for good?

"Say hello to Kile and the others when you get there," Jacob said, then turned to Trudie. "What will you be havin' this mornin'?" he asked coolly, no smile on his face for her.

"Well . . . I, ah . . . let me think what it was I wanted," Trudie stammered, making it clear that she didn't want anything, that she had only followed Spencer inside. When he picked up his sack and walked toward the door, giving Gretchen a look from the side of his eye, Trudie dropped all pretense of needing something and hurried after him.

Gretchen watched them from the window and got the feeling that Trudie didn't know where Spencer was going either. He mostly ignored the pouting woman, saying few words to her. When he had tied his supplies onto the saddle he swung onto the stallion's back and rode away, leaving Trudie glaring after him, her hands on her hips.

When Gretchen walked over to the counter to order her warp Jacob shook his head and said, "I don't know why she doesn't give up. She thinks she'll get the halter on Spence someday, but she never will. He'd never marry the leftovers of other men."

Gretchen looked at him in surprise. "Are you sure? He's living with her."

It was Jacob's turn to look surprised. "Living with Trudie Harrod? Where'd you get that notion?"

"Well, he's seen at her place all the time."

"I think that might be a lot of gossip. Spencer is livin' in that cabin he built for winter use when he's trappin'."

Over the happy thudding of her heart, Gretchen remembered it was Collin who had said Spencer was living with Trudie. Had he said it out of jealousy? It was possible.

A frown creased her forehead. Collin was becoming a little too forward these days, and she didn't like it. She had no romantic feelings for him, and she realized it was time she let the young farmer know it.

There was a sense of well-being about Gretchen as she said good-bye to Jacob and left the store. It faded a bit when she stepped outside and found Trudie waiting for her. "I noticed you and Spencer didn't speak to each other." She watched Gretchen closely.

"We nodded a greeting," Gretchen said shortly as she swung onto Beauty's back.

"Do you know where he's goin'?"

A smile of amusement twisted Gretchen's lips. "You mean you don't?"

"Of course I know." Trudie scowled.

"Are you sure?" Gretchen taunted. "It didn't look that way to me."

Temper flared in Trudie's eyes and her grip tightened on the riding quirt in her hand. Gretchen could read in her eyes that she would like to use it on someone . . . on her.

Then, with an effort, Trudie smoothed her features and said smugly, "He's gone to track down the travelin' preacher, to make arrangements for us to get married the next time he comes through."

The contentment Gretchen had known only minutes ago disappeared. Jacob was mistaken, after all. Her face carefully blank, no hint of the pain inside her showing, she gathered up the reins and said calmly, "I hope the two of you will be very happy."

Trudie stared after Gretchen as she rode

away, her body held proudly. She hadn't gotten a rise out of the little bitch and now she was very uneasy about the lie she had told. If it got back to Spencer, he'd probably never come around her again.

Her mood was as low as Gretchen's as she mounted her horse and brought the quirt down on its rump.

That night, as Gretchen and Ben sat in front of the fireplace, he with his pipe in his mouth and she knitting a sweater she was making for him, Gretchen asked, "Do you know a man called Kile?"

Ben looked at her questioningly. "Yeah, I know him. He's a trapper who lives in Squaw Hollow. Where did you hear his name?"

"At the post today. Jacob said it."

"Who'd he say it to? One of the trappers?"

"Yes. Spencer."

Ben leaned forward, his eyes brightening. "You saw Spence today? Did you talk together?"

Gretchen shook her head. "No."

"Not even to say hello?" Ben's excited expression became one of disappointment.

Gretchen was sorry she had brought up the subject. She had known that Ben missed his son, but she hadn't known how much until now. "I'm sorry, Ben," she said quietly, "but we didn't speak. Trudie Harrod was in the store too. Maybe he thought she wouldn't like it if he spoke to me."

Ben shook his head. "No, if Spencer wants to do somethin' only God could keep him from doin' it. Certainly no female like that one would stop him from speakin' to you. He's still mad at me."

Gretchen wished she could tell Ben that he had nothing to do with his son's ignoring her in the store, that it had been his way of telling her that she no longer existed for him. That he had done what he had set out to do: shame her.

But it was no fault of the father what his son did, so she said gently, "I did learn that he's not living with Trudie. He's living in the little cabin he built for the winter. Jacob told me."

"I knew he wouldn't be livin' with her even before I saw smoke comin' out of his chimney."

So, Gretchen thought, keeping her eye on the knitting needles that flashed in the firelight, Ben was keeping a distant eye on his son. An uneasiness stole over her. She hoped he hadn't been keeping too close an eye on him, especially the second time she and Spencer had made love in the barn.

She mentally shook her head. Ben would have climbed all over his son had that been the case. He would have realized, though, that this time she was a willing partner, just as she had been the first time he caught them together.

"Spence went to Squaw Hollow," Ben said suddenly, making Gretchen drop a stitch.

"How do you know that? Did Spencer drop

by and tell you?" There was hope in her voice.

Ben shook his head. "An old friend by the name of Will Smith stopped by yesterday. He lives there. It seems there was a couple of strangers, brothers, who hung around Piney Ridge for a while, tryin' to talk the trappers into joinin' up with a big fur company they worked for. When they didn't have any luck here they moved to Squaw Hollow to try the same thing. Spencer has gone there to talk to the trappers and Indians, convince them to remain free trappers."

Elation rushed through Gretchen. Trudie had lied to her. The woman had no idea where Spencer was going. Then Ben added, "Will told me that one of the brothers shot at Spencer, tried to kill him."

Gretchen stared at Ben, the knitting needles dropping unheeded into her lap. She was gripped with the terrible fear that this time the brothers would succeed in killing Spencer. How could she bear it if they did?

She and Ben sat on, both worrying about the tall, handsome trapper.

Chapter Fifteen

It was with mixed feelings that Spencer prepared for his trip. He looked forward to seeing his friends in Squaw Hollow again, but he was a little tired of trying to persuade trappers and Indians that it was the wrong move to throw in with a large fur company. Nor did he want to have another confrontation with the brothers. They were a sneaky pair, and he'd have to be on the alert all the time he was there.

But at least he would be out of Gretchen's vicinity for a while. Away from the temptation of lying in wait for her and finding a chance to seduce her into making love with him. *Maybe I should just stay in Squaw Hollow,* he thought. *Pa wouldn't care . . . nor would Gretchen.*

After a hearty breakfast of bacon and eggs and skillet bread, and with his bed made up, Spencer picked up his grub sack and rifle and left the cabin. His moccasin-shod feet left footprints in the dew-wet grass as he walked down to the river and dragged his canoe out of its hiding place in a stand of willows growing close to the bank. Pulling it across the gravelly shore, he pushed it into the water, threw the sack into it, then placed the rifle on the vessel's bottom, handy for him to grab up if necessary. He climbed into the lightweight vessel, then picked up the paddle, thrust it into the water, and pushed out into the middle of the river. The swift current caught the canoe and he began to navigate upriver.

It was quiet on the water the first hour Spencer glided along. Only the sound of the oar lifting and dipping into the water disturbed the silence. Then birds began to sweep back and forth among the trees, looking for their breakfast of bugs, while on the forest floor bushy-tailed squirrels scampered around, making their morning meal on acorns. Occasionally he heard the plop of a beaver hitting the water, preparing its quarters for the approaching winter.

Around noon the canoe swept past a group of squaws scrubbing clothes on rocks in a shallow part of the river. Spencer lifted a hand to them and they smiled and called out, "How are you, Atkins." His lips twisted wryly. If this had happened five months ago, before Gretchen came into his life, he'd have beached the canoe and led a giggling squaw back into the woods, taking his pleasure of her.

He hadn't even a stirring of interest in doing that now.

When the sun was about ready to drop behind the tree line Spencer turned the canoe toward shore. It would be foolish to try to navigate the Ohio in the darkness. Swift currents and eddies that he couldn't see, as well as floating debris like a good-sized tree trunk, could ram into the vessel, smashing it into kindling.

He dragged the canoe out of the water and turned it on its side to lean against a tree. He scrounged around beneath the trees until he had enough material to build a fire. When it flamed up, then burned down to red coals, he set a pot of coffee to brewing while he fried thick slices of salt pork in a battered skillet. As he squatted before the fire, his attention was caught by the gray shapes of wolves slipping stealthily around his camp. He picked up a short piece of wood and threw it in their direction. They gave a startled yelp and ran off among the trees.

When the meat was eaten and a couple of cups of coffee drunk, Spencer did what he'd do for the next two nights: He crawled under the canoe, placed the rifle in front of him, and fell asleep almost instantly. He was blissfully unaware that a wolf and his mate had slipped up to watch him for a moment before trailing off into the forest.

On the third morning when Spencer crawled out from beneath his shelter he knew it was time to leave the river and walk the rest of the way to his destination. The river branched off to his right, and it would flow many miles from Squaw Hollow before turning back on itself.

He pulled the canoe about three feet from the bank, then weighted it down with rocks until it sank out of sight in a couple of feet of water. It would lay there unnoticed until he was ready to retrieve it. He waded back to the shore and then picked up the rifle and his gear and struck off through the woods. In half an hour he picked up the trail he always traveled on his way to the rendezvous. Each night he camped in the same spots he always did.

It was near sundown on the third day when he looked down on the settlement of Squaw Hollow.

There was no activity on the wide paths that wound around tree stumps, reminders of those that had been cut down to erect the long building that looked similar to the post in Piney Ridge. Spencer imagined that most of the folks of Squaw Hollow would be home eating their evening meal at this hour.

When Spencer walked into the dimly lit room that could supply a customer with anything from oxen yokes to needle and thread, Pete Johnson, the store owner, was waiting on an Indian and his squaw. Spencer recognized the red man as Swift Arrow, the chief of the village a few miles down the river. He and Pete looked up at the same time and saw him standing in the doorway.

Pete's greeting was a wide smile and a genial, "What brings you to our neck of the woods, Spence?" There was only a slight softening in the chief's black eyes that showed that he, too, welcomed the white man.

Spencer advanced into the room and lay his rifle on the counter, looking from Pete to the chief. "Will Smith asked me to come here to talk the trappers and Indians out of going in with the Missouri Fur Company that seems determined to move into our territory."

"I sure hope you can, Spence," Pete said with a long face. "I might as well close my doors if they come in here." He nodded toward the Indian. "Swift Arrow, here, at least can see through them fast-talkin' Grundy brothers. He don't want no part of the company."

"I wish the trappers were that smart," Spencer said to the chief. "They don't think beyond what they want to hear."

Pete jerked a thumb in the direction of the door leading into the tavern. "Some of them are in there now, listenin' to the pretty pictures them Grundys are paintin' them. I hope you can talk some sense into their soft heads."

"I'll do my best," Spencer said, then walked across the floor to enter the low-ceilinged room. He stood just inside the door a minute, sending his gaze around the room, stopping when he spotted the Grundy brothers. They sat at a table, talking to a couple of friends of his, Kile and Ike, along with three trappers he knew casually.

The five men were listening intently to what Jeeter Grundy was saying. It was Kile who looked up and spotted him. "Hey, men," he said loudly, "look who's here!"

With the exception of the brothers, Spencer was given a boisterous welcome by everyone. Those two only gave him black looks. He was motioned forward and room was made for him at the table. Pulling up a chair for him to sit down, Kile asked, "What brings you out our way, Spence?" as he pushed a cup of whiskey across the table toward him.

"I've come to talk some sense into your hollow heads," Spencer said after taking a swallow of the raw whiskey.

"What are you talkin' about?" Ike asked.

"I'm talkin' about you fellows listening to the double-talk the Grundys are givin' you." He looked straight at Jeeter Grundy.

"Now look here, Atkins." The elder Grundy slammed his cup down on the table. "You just keep your nose out of our business. You ruined things for us in Piney Ridge, tellin' them trappers not to listen to us."

"Your business is my business," Spencer shot back, his eyes frosty. "If I can, I'll talk these men out of listening to and believing the hogwash you're telling them."

"We're not doin' that," Arnold Grundy flared sullenly. "The company treats their trappers right. It will even provide them with provisions and necessities in the summertime when they're not trappin' and have no money."

It was the first time Spencer had seen the younger brother up close. He gave him a long look before responding to the man's claim. "I'm sure the company would be happy to do that," he agreed, "and charge the men double for everything they buy when it comes time to pay up. Those who work for them will never get out of debt. Only the free trapper will ever make any money."

Kile and the others had listened closely to the exchange, and thoughtful frowns were creasing their foreheads when Spencer looked at them.

"That's the way it will be, men," he said. "Do you want to be told where you can lay your line? Told how many pelts must be delivered to the outfit each week, have your pay deducted if you come up short?"

"Hell no, we don't!" Kile scowled. "We wouldn't put up with that kind of horse dung for a minute." As the others expressed the same view, Kile looked at Jeeter, a dangerous gleam in his eyes. "You and your brother can just pack up and get the hell away from here. And you can tell the big man in St. Louis that if he sends anyone else up here, they'll get a rifle bullet in their rump."

"We won't need your furs," Jeeter, his face red with rage, declared, his hand dropping from the table to lay in his lap. Spencer's eyes followed the movement and saw that his hand rested near the handle of the knife stuck in his belt. "There are other trappers around here who will be glad to take our offer."

Kile shook his head and said with confidence, "They won't. Not after I've talked to them, told them the stunt you're tryin' to pull."

Arnold Grundy jumped to his feet, his eyes shooting hatred at Spencer. "You bastard," he shouted, "you started this. Why didn't you stay in your own part of the hills, keep watch over that purty little gal what's livin' with your pa? Ain't you afraid some man might come along and catch her alone in the barn?"

In that instant Spencer knew he was looking at the man who had tried to rape Gretchen. He jerked to his feet, the chair skidding across the floor. His eyes narrowing to glittering pin-points, he snarled, "I think the time has come for me to finish something that was started several months back."

The watching men could almost see the tremor of fear that ran down Grundy's spine. "I don't know what you're talkin' about," he blustered, a cringing indecision in his eyes.

Passion, wild and virulent, seethed inside Spencer. "You know damn well what I'm talkin' about," he growled, then he whipped his knife from its sheath. "I'm gonna slice you to pieces, you low-belly copperhead."

Arnold looked at his brother, his eyes begging for help. When Jeeter stood up, his hand on his knife, five other men stood up. His face a sickly white, Arnold knew he was on his own. This time he would not be pitting his strength against that of a fragile woman, he would be fighting a strong, determined man. With shaking fingers, he pulled his knife.

As the trappers' attention was glued on Spencer and Arnold, circling each other, feinting and jabbing, no one noticed Jeeter, who watched with furtive, calculating eyes. Nor did they note that he had palmed his knife.

When Spencer stuck out his foot and tripped Arnold, sending him sprawling on his back, Jeeter drew back his hand, the point of the knife aimed at Spencer's back.

The big blade that would have killed Spencer was never released. Kile had caught the movement from the corner of his eye. Swift as a striking snake, he jerked his own knife from the top of his knee-high moccasins and let it fly.

Jeeter stood a moment, a bewildered look on his face as the blade pierced his heart. A bloody froth trickled out of his mouth as he slowly folded to the floor. Arnold let loose a cry that sounded not unlike that of a terror-stricken animal. The brother whose hard fists he had feared, and yet looked to for protection, lay dead. When Spencer turned his head at the alarmed cry Arnold came up from a crouch, then sprinted out the door. In the tight silence that gathered in the room there came the sound of pounding hoofbeats.

Arnold Grundy was on his way back to St. Louis. It was hoped by all that they would never see him in the Kentucky hills again.

Spencer turned to Kile and held out his hand. "I owe you, Kile. You saved my life."

"You'd have done the same for me." Kile slapped him on the back. "Come on up to the bar and have a drink."

As they tossed the whiskey down their throats, a couple of trappers were dragging Grundy's body out the door. Tomorrow he would be buried out in the woods.

As their blood cooled, it became apparent to Spencer that the reaction to having killed a man was gripping Kile. There was a slight tremor in his hands and a look of regret far back in his eyes. Spencer knew the feeling; he'd had it after he had been forced to kill Zeke West. He wasn't surprised when Kile said, "I got me a pretty little squaw livin' with me. Let's head on over to my cabin and let her entertain us for a while."

"I'll take you up on a place to sleep tonight, but I'll pass on the other."

Kile leaned back and gave him an unbelieving stare. "Since when did you start turnin' down a tumble in the blankets?"

Spencer wasn't about to admit that only one woman appealed to him these days, that all other women left him cold, so he shrugged and said, "I'm beat, Kile. I just want to fall in bed and sleep for a week."

Spencer stayed on in the Hollow for a couple of days, carousing with his friends. He took a whore to bed one night, and when he couldn't do anything he muttered curses at a green-eyed witch.

Grundy's squaw lost no time settling in at the tavern. If she grieved for the loss of the brothers, it didn't show. She laughed as loud as the other whores and took her share of men into the back room.

On the morning he said good-bye to Kile and the others, Spencer's head throbbed and his stomach churned from too much corn liquor. He had over a week's growth of whiskers on his face and his eyes were bloodshot and red-rimmed. Had the young women in Piney Ridge seen him now, they would have turned their heads away from him.

He was feeling half human when he reached the river and retrieved his canoe. Three days later, when he beached it among the willows, he waded out into the river, clothes and all, and scrubbed away the stink of stale whiskey and dirty whores.

"At least I won't stink if I run into anyone before I get to the cabin," he muttered to himself as he left the river, water streaming off his hair and buckskins.

Chapter Sixteen

It was November, and there was a chill in the air. There had been needles of ice in the pail of water left out on the porch overnight. Gretchen stood in the kitchen doorway, looking down over the valley below. All the leaves were off the hardwoods, their bare limbs looking like crooked bones against the deep green of cedar and the paler hue of pine. Like bright jewels scattered about were the red and russet-colored leaves of the large oaks. Some of them would be hanging on until spring. Ben, along with some of the others, had began to lay his trap lines, a sure sign that winter wasn't far off.

Gretchen couldn't see any of her neighbors' cabins, but she could see the smoke rising among the trees in five different places. Did one spiral come from Spencer's cabin? she wondered. She hadn't seen him since his return from Squaw Hollow. Ben had heard that he had been successful there, that the older Grundy had been killed by a friend of Spencer's and the younger one had run away like a scared rabbit.

Her gaze moved to watch the Ohio flowing along. From this distance it looked like a large snake. She sighed, recalling the day Spencer had taken her there to fish in its brown, muddy waters. She hated to admit it, even to herself, but she longed for the sight of him, even the way his wicked eyes always stripped the clothes off her body.

It wasn't so bad in the daytime. She kept herself busy with household chores, working the spinning wheel and the loom. And to break the monotony sometimes she accompanied Ben as he marked the places where he would set his traps. She knew his line as well as he did.

It was the nights she dreaded, lying in bed, her body restless, yearning for the touch and comfort Spencer could bring it. Was she in love with that uncaring man? she would ask herself in the darkness, then answer that she must be; either that or she was a wanton lusting after him. She didn't like to think that she was like Trudie Harrod. One day she had overheard Ben saying to a neighbor that the woman was a lustful bitch, that she would lie down with any man who came along.

I know I'm not like that, Gretchen thought

now. Collin Grady didn't make her want to be kissed and caressed by him.

Of course, she reminded herself, she hadn't been around other men. Young, single ones, that was. But she somehow doubted they'd raise any romantic notions in her.

But Spencer—it seemed that almost any woman could heat him up. He reminded her of the tomcats at the poorhouse, kept there to keep down the mouse population. They were always on the prowl, looking for a female in heat.

Gretchen sighed again. Wasn't it just her luck that she had fallen in love with a man who had no love to give in return.

A movement to her left caught her eye and, peering against the sun, she made out the figures of two bears rooting around beneath a persimmon tree at the edge of the forest. Until the first snowfall they would gorge themselves on the delicious fruit, wild grapes and huckleberries, storing up fat for their long winter's sleep. She hoped they would leave enough of the orange-yellow fruit for her to make a pudding. It was a favorite of hers.

Gretchen was ready to walk back into the kitchen—she had some ironing to do—when she was hailed from the direction of the barn. Her lips firmed impatiently. Deke Crawford was coming up the path, a big grin on his face. He would keep her from her work at least an hour with his jawing.

But he was a good soul, she told herself,

and she forced herself to smile and greet him pleasantly.

"What brings you out so early, Deke?" she asked, wondering if it would be too rude if she didn't invite him in for coffee. She was afraid that once he sat down he'd still be here at lunchtime, and her ears would be ready to fall off.

Thankfully, Deke was in a hurry. "I can't stay, Gretchen," he said. "I gotta see all our neighbors and you're the first one. You see, the thing is, me and Bessy is havin' a cornhuskin' tomorrer night and I gotta tell everyone." He cocked an eye at Gretchen. "You ever been to a cornhuskin' party, girl?"

"No, I haven't. What's it like?"

"Well, it's a lotta fun. Everybody sits in a circle around a big pile of corn, pullin' the dried husks off the ears. Now, amongst the pile I slip in half a dozen ears of red Indian corn. Whoever gets one of them gets to kiss the girl or man of their choosin'." His grin widened. "Many a feller and gal have started courtin' because of a red ear of corn. Might be it could happen to you. I'm sure you'll get kissed by some young bachelor."

"But what if I don't want to be kissed?"

"Oh, you gotta let the feller kiss you. There'd be bad feelin's iffen you didn't. Folks would think you was stuck up if you was to refuse. 'Course, the feller would only kiss you on the cheek."

Gretchen smiled in relief. "That's good to know," she said. "I wouldn't want to kiss a stranger on the lips."

"I reckon not," Deke agreed. "Decent young women wouldn't." The next minute the grin was back on his face and he was saying that he had to get going. Gretchen felt sorry for the last neighbor he visited. That one would get his ears blasted off.

As Gretchen pressed clothes, keeping one iron heating on the fire to use when the present one cooled, she dwelled on the husking party. Would Spencer attend it? she wondered. She doubted it. It didn't seem the type of social he'd be interested in. A chaste kiss on a woman's cheek wouldn't be nearly enough for him.

Of course, Trudie would be there, swinging her hips and bouncing her big breasts, brushing up against men. She remembered how she had done that to Spencer the morning he was buying supplies for his trip. For a split second she had wanted to take her nails to the fleshy face, or tear her away from him.

Gretchen had supper waiting for Ben when he came limping home around sundown. His knees were bothering him, she knew, and she wondered how much worse they would get when the freezing months of winter arrived.

Over the meal of roast beef, mashed potatoes, and stewed turnips, Gretchen told Ben of Deke's visit. "I'd like to go," she said, "but I'm afraid that Collin will ask me to go with him. If I did, then everyone would think we're courting. I don't want that. Will you take me?"

Ben grinned in amusement. "I'll gladly take you, Gretchen, but you needn't worry about Collin askin' you to go with him. He always takes his ma to all the functions. If he tried to go somewhere without her, she'd pretend that her heart was actin' up. She does that to the boy all the time."

"Poor Collin." Gretchen shook her head. "His mother will never let him get married."

Ben crumbled tobacco into his pipe and lit it with a burning twig from the fireplace. After taking a few long puffs he said, "You know, if that little Ellie Allen girl was smart, she'd let Collin get her in a family way. That way old Agatha's heart could act up all it wanted. Collin would have to marry the girl." He looked at Gretchen through the tobacco smoke. "He was courtin' Ellie before you come along."

"I didn't know that," Gretchen exclaimed. "No wonder she always snubs me. And that's why the other women treat me so cool too."

"I reckon."

After a moment Gretchen said, "That was a terrible idea you mentioned; that Ellie should get pregnant on purpose."

"Bah," Ben scorned. "You think that's never happened before? Lots of women catch their husbands that way. In Collin's case it would be a blessin' if he was to get Ellie bigged. He'd have a wife and family dependent on him, make his ma sit back for a change."

Ben puffed on his pipe awhile longer, then said at the end of a long sigh, "That hellion of mine, he'll never get married unless some woman is smart enough to catch him that way."

A nervous little laugh escaped Gretchen. "Spencer would hate the woman who trapped him like that."

"Not necessarily. He'd have to be pretty smitten with her to get so carried away he'd forget what he should do. Of course, out of pure orneriness he'd act like a wounded bear for a while, but he'd settle down in the harness right well."

Gretchen had serious doubts about that, but she didn't voice them. She didn't tell Ben that two mornings in a row she had lost her breakfast, or that she had missed her menses twice. She didn't want to think about it, let alone discuss it. She was probably only late, or else she had eaten something that didn't agree with her. She would be getting her flow any day now.

Gretchen tugged at the bodice of the green woolen dress until it settled over her full, high breasts and hugged her narrow rib cage. With swift fingers she secured the five buttons, then smoothed the wide lace collar. It had taken her a month of evenings to crochet it and she thought it looked rather fetching. She wore a narrow petticoat under the dress so that the fine gathering at the waist fell in soft folds to the tips of her new black shoes.

She was brushing the chestnut-colored curls that now hung to her shoulders when Ben called up the ladder, "You about ready, honey? The old mule is gettin' restless."

"Coming," she called back. Giving a last look in the shiny tin mirror, she picked up the lightweight shawl lying on the end of her bed and climbed down to join Ben.

"My, oh my, just look at you." Pride gleamed in Ben's eyes. "You've got to be the prettiest little gal in all of Kentucky."

"Oh, Ben." Gretchen blushed. "I knew you needed to be outfitted with glasses." Her eyes twinkled at him. "You look pretty handsome yourself." The old man had put on his church meeting trousers and the soft woolen shirt she had made him. He had brushed his shaggy hair so it lay smooth and had given the same attention to his white beard.

"I didn't want to shame you, showin' up at the party lookin' like a shaggy buffalo," Ben said, pleased at her compliment.

Gretchen shook her head at him. "You could never shame me. I hope I never shame you," she added after a pause.

Outside, the mule stamped its hooves impatiently. It didn't like being hitched to the small buggy. This was its first experience of being harnessed to a lightweight vehicle, and it kept looking over its shoulder at the buggy. The two-seater had been put in the barn the day Ben had said good-bye to his wife and daughter and had never been brought out again. It had taken him an hour to wipe away the years' accumulation of dust and cobwebs.

Ben helped Gretchen onto the leather seat, climbed in beside her, and popped the reins over the mule's broad rump. Reluctantly, old Jimbo started out.

It was full dark when they reached the Crawford farm. A buzz of voices came from the barn, and a nervous fluttering began in Gretchen's breast as Ben helped her out of the buggy. She dreaded the cool politeness she would receive from the women. Through the big double doors that had been opened wide, she could see the men and women sitting around a huge pile of corn. There was excitement on the faces as they all looked for that special red Indian corn.

There were several lanterns placed about, hanging from pegs in the rafters. When Ben took her arm and said, "Come on, let's get in there and find us a red ear," their own lantern hung from his hand. So that was how the Crawfords had so many lanterns lighting up the barn, she thought. Each family brought their own.

Just as she and Ben entered the barn a loud whoop went up. A young man had found the red prize. He stood up and made his way to a comely young woman. She squealed excitedly as his lips smacked her rosy cheek. Was the couple courting? Gretchen wondered.

Deke spied them after everyone had settled down and called out a greeting. Bessy smiled and waved Gretchen over to sit beside her. Ben sat down a little distance from her, making sure he didn't sit too close to the garrulous Mr. Crawford.

As Gretchen sat down on the thick mat of hay that had been spread on the barn floor, the women nodded at her in their usual cool way. Ellie Allen ignored her completely.

"Grab an ear and start shuckin', Gretchen," Bessy said as she yanked the husks off an ear and tossed it to land on a pile of others.

Shucking corn was an old story to Gretchen. In her lifetime she figured she had shucked at least a ton. There were raised eyebrows and surprised looks at how deftly she stripped the covering off the yellow ears and tossed them to the growing pile of finished corn. A couple of housewives unbent so far as to give her a smile after a half hour or so. Unlike the other single girls, who giggled and flashed their eyes at the young men, Gretchen kept her eyes and her mind on what she was doing.

From the corner of her eye she had seen Collin sitting next to his mother. It was obvious that he was trying to get her attention, but she hadn't let on that she was aware of it. Young Ellie Allen was watching her like a hawk.

A surprised "Oh" formed on Gretchen's lips as she pulled down a husk and revealed a red ear of corn. It grew quiet as everyone waited to see who she would choose, sure that it would be Collin.

After a moment Gretchen rose to her feet and started walking in the direction of Collin. The smirk on his face was wiped away when she walked past him and bent over, bestowing her kiss on Deke's leathery cheek.

Everyone but Collin burst out laughing at Deke's stunned face. For once in his life the man was left speechless.

Gretchen was returning to her seat beside Bessy when Collin let out an excited yell and held up a red ear. She stood next to the open barn doors and, as the young man rose to his feet, she quickly stepped outside. She didn't know or care who he gave his kiss to as she walked slowly along the barn, looking up at the stars sparkling in a moonless sky. When she came to the corner of the structure she stopped and leaned against the wall. She sighed, wishing that it was time to go home. She didn't know how much longer she could bear the coolness directed at her. So far only Bessy had talked to her.

She gave a startled jerk when a husky male voice spoke beside her. "You just made a young girl very happy in there, and a young man very unhappy."

"Spencer," she gasped. "You almost scared the life out of me. What are you doing here? Trudie didn't come, you know."

"To answer your question, I've as much right as anyone else to be here. As to your remark about Trudie, it's nothin' to me that she's not here. I do know where she is. She's busy entertainin' my friend, Slim Peters. She's been in his cabin since he returned from runnin' his traps. She's probably forgotten all about this here party."

Gretchen tried to see Spencer's face in the pale light of the stars, to see if he was distressed that his lover was with his friend. She said, "You speak very casually about Trudie cheating on you. Don't you care?"

"What in the hell are you talkin' about, woman?" Spencer laughed in amusement and irritation. "Trudie Harrod means nothin' to me, so how could she be cheatin' on me?" He took a step closer and stroked a palm down her arm as he said huskily, "I'd have cared a whole lot if you'd have kissed young Grady back there."

Gretchen moved away from his caressing hand and snapped, "It would be no business of yours if I had."

"Maybe. But I would have made it so. I'd have wrung that young pup's neck if you kissed him."

"By what right?" Gretchen demanded, her eyes flashing angrily. "I don't belong to you, Spencer Atkins."

Spencer grabbed her arm and swung her around to face him. "Yes, you do," he ground out.

"Why, you egotistical womanizer!" Gretchen's palm struck across his cheek, snapping his face to one side. "I don't belong to you. I never have and I never will."

"Is that so," Spencer growled, jerking her up tight against his lean frame. His head lowered and his lips captured hers with fierce passion.

Gretchen struggled to get away, but her hands were trapped between their bodies and she couldn't break free. She twisted her face to escape the demanding kiss, but his slim hand came up to the back of her head, holding it still as his tongue invaded her mouth. When she felt the hard ridge of his maleness press against her stomach her body melted helplessly into his. Her tongue was stroking his when he suddenly lifted his head and released her.

"Do you still say you don't belong to me?" he asked mockingly.

While she stared at him, her body weak and trembling, he wheeled around and faded into the darkness without another word.

"I hate you, I hate you," Gretchen sobbed, her pride shattered. The devil well knew what he could do to her emotions. She prayed that he would soon tire of her and leave her in peace.

After a while Gretchen forced herself to stop crying and pulled a handkerchief from her sleeve to dab at her eyes. When she felt that all traces of her tears were gone she walked back into the barn and took her seat beside

Bessy. She noted right off that two things were different from when she had walked out of the barn. The women, married and single, smiled at her now and included her in their talk. The second thing she noticed was that Collin now sat beside Ellie Allen, and it was she Agatha Grady was shooting icy looks at. She hoped Collin wasn't trying to make her jealous. She hoped he had realized she had no romantic interest in him.

A short time later Gretchen noticed a third change in the barn: She was getting many ogling looks from the single men now. Before they had only sneaked looks at her from the corners of their eyes. Now they gazed openly, flirtatiously at her. She sighed inwardly. She wished they would all leave her alone. *Including Spencer?* her devilish inner voice teased.

Especially him! Gretchen retorted silently.

Someone picked up the last unshucked ear of corn and the party began to break up. Each man who had brought a lantern with him retrieved it from its peg, and soon only the Crawford lantern was left to dimly light the barn.

Ben, holding his at a level that lit the way, took Gretchen's arm and guided her to the place where he had tied the mule. Good nights were called out as he sent the old mule homeward.

The evening had turned quite cool, and Gretchen wrapped the shawl tightly around her shoulders. A few minutes later, as the mule clomped along, Ben said, "I noticed the womenfolk finally warmed up to you."

Gretchen made no reply. She was sound asleep, her head on Ben's shoulder. He grinned and slapped the reins on Jimbo's fat rump. "Get along there, mule," he ordered, "we got someone here who needs to get to bed."

Chapter Seventeen

It was a raw and windy day, with dismal gray skies that threatened to pour down rain. Gretchen sat up in bed and wrapped her arms around her drawn-up knees. She hoped it would hold off until Ben got home. Getting soaked wouldn't help his rheumatism any. As it was, the poor old fellow found it hard just to get out of bed in the mornings. She could hear his grunts of pain from the loft room as he limped across the floor to replenish the fire that had been stoked for the night. If he were able to run his traps when the heavy snows arrived, she'd be very surprised.

She felt sure that Spencer would help his father, but she was just as sure that the proud and stubborn Ben wouldn't accept his aid.

She gazed unseeingly at the gloom outside. Something had to be done to bring father and son back together again, though it would probably take an act of God to do it. She had never seen two men more stubborn than Ben and Spencer Atkins. It was certainly true that the apple never fell far from the tree.

Gretchen slid out of bed and shrugged into her woolen robe, then climbed down the ladder, yawning as she went into the kitchen to make breakfast. She put the long-handled skillet on a bed of red coals and quickly washed her face and hands. When she finished doing that the skillet was hot and she laid two strips of bacon in it. Then, after a slight pause, she added two more. She had a voracious appetite these days. While the cured sow-belly sizzled, sending out its delicious aroma, she sipped at a cup of coffee from the pot Ben had brewed before starting out.

When the meat was crisp Gretchen fried a couple of eggs and cut two slices of bread from a loaf she had baked the day before. Sitting down at the table, she ate her breakfast with great relish, then idled at the table, drinking another cup of coffee and wondering how she could pass the day. Ever since she could remember she had never had any time on her hands, and now, suddenly, she had more than she wanted. There was nothing for her to do outside the cabin except water and feed Jimbo and Beauty. And she was getting a little bored with knitting and sitting at the loom. She had baked enough cakes and pies and cookies to last a month.

Why don't you go make up the beds? her inner voice said impatiently.

Gretchen yawned again. It seemed she couldn't get enough sleep lately. Standing up, she went to tidy up Ben's room.

Altogether, making breakfast and eating it, making up the beds, then getting dressed, had taken a little more than an hour. Gretchen paced from family room to kitchen and back again, not knowing what to do with herself. She finally settled down in front of the fire and picked up her knitting with a sigh.

As her needles clicked together, Gretchen's mind drifted to the boys and girls still in the poorhouse. *I should be ashamed to complain,* she told herself, seeing them in her mind's eye going about in their thin clothing, working from dawn to dusk, while she sat in a warm cabin, her only task to keep it clean and cook a few meals a day.

"Count your blessings," she ordered herself.

It was a few minutes past ten when Gretchen heard heavy hooves approaching the cabin. Who could be coming here? She sat forward, the needles dropping from her nerveless fingers. Her eyes darted to the door. Had she remembered to drop the bar after her trip to the privy? She breathed a sigh of relief. The bar was in place.

Putting the needles and yarn aside, she rose and walked to the window and peeked out. Her eyes widened in surprise when she recognized the woman holding the reins to a buggy. Patience Hardy. Why was that big, rawboned woman with the rough voice coming to visit her?

She watched the woman, somewhere in her mid-forties, Gretchen thought, pull the mule up in front of the porch and tie the reins to the whipstock. She blinked when Miss Hardy stood up. The woman wore men's trousers. When she jumped from the buggy and stepped up on the porch Gretchen wiped the amazement off her face and hurried to unbar the door and swing it open.

"Good morning, Miss Hardy." She smiled. "Come in."

"Good mornin', girl." Her voice was rough, but the blue eyes were soft. "Call me Patience," she said, removing a soft, broad-brimmed hat from her thick graying hair.

"My name is Gretchen," she reminded her first female visitor.

"I remember," Patience said, hanging her hat on a peg, alongside Gretchen's heavy shawl. "A nice name. My mother was named Gretchen."

Gretchen relaxed. It didn't appear that the Hardy woman was here to say mean things to her. She pulled a chair away from the table. "Please sit down and have some coffee and a piece of cake with me. It's a spicy pumpkin cake. I made it yesterday."

"Thank you, girl, I'd like that. I don't find the time to do much bakin' myself. Never was much good at it anyway."

"Now that there's nothing to do outside anymore, I spend a lot of time baking," Gretchen said, then added, "And I've been doing a lot of knitting."

"I expect you get a mite lonesome, what with Ben gone all day runnin' his traps," Patience said as Gretchen filled two mugs from the coffeepot she took from the hearth. "Nor women comin' to visit you," Patience added when she sat down at the table.

Gretchen nodded. "None have come calling yet. I'm hoping that in time they will. Maybe now that they don't have a lot of outside work to do, they'll find the time."

"Work had nothin' to do with keepin' them from visitin' you," Patience said bluntly as she sliced her fork into the cake Gretchen had placed before her. "You see, before you came along Collin Grady was courtin' little Ellie Allen. It was understood that as soon as Collin could talk his ma into the notion of it, he and Ellie would marry.

"We're all very fond of the girl and it didn't set well with the womenfolk that a stranger would maybe take Collin away from her. Ellie has no family and she works hard for her board and keep, doin' chores for old Claude Summers and his wife, Biddy. They're good to her, but they're church-mouse poor and can only feed her and give her a bed."

Patience paused to take a sip of coffee, then continued, "Ellie is crazy wild about Collin, although I don't think he's all that much myself." She sniffed. "I wouldn't have time for a grown man who lets his ma decide who and when he'll wed."

"Ben doesn't think Mrs. Grady will ever agree to Collin's marrying anyone. He thinks she doesn't want to let him go."

Patience nodded. "He's right. Agatha can't stand the thought of it. But I'll tell you one thing, if Ellie ever gets Collin, Agatha will take second place. That girl is delicate-lookin', but she's got a will of steel. Old Aggie will think she's come up against a mountain if she tries any of her tricks on Ellie."

The big woman looked at Gretchen, speculation in her eyes. "You never did care anything for Collin, did you?"

Gretchen shook her head, then giggled. "I didn't even know he was courting me until Ben told me. He'd come over here a couple of times a week and sit with us on the porch, but I don't think he'd say more than half a dozen words to me all the time he was here.

"He brought his mother over one day." Amusement twinkled in Gretchen's eyes. "I was working in the garden and I had slipped on an Indian dress that was in the cabin so I wouldn't be dragging one of mine through the dirt. Well, Mrs. Grady took one look at me and I thought she was going to have an apoplectic fit. Her face got beet red and her lips disappeared in disapproval. She grabbed Collin's arm and announced that they had to get home, there was a lot of work to be done."

Patience howled with laughter. "Poor Collin," she was finally able to say, "he brought her here to look you over, get her approval, and there you were, dressed like a heathen."

Gretchen's laughter pealed out. "Since then, every time she sees me she cuts me cold."

"She does that to poor little Ellie all the time. I'll bet she's madder than a wet hen that them young folk are back together again."

"Are they?" Gretchen exclaimed delightedly. "I'm happy to hear that. I hope Ellie can land him this time." She looked at Patience, a crooked grin on her face. "Ben says that Ellie should let Collin get her in a family way. Then Mrs. Grady couldn't stop them from getting married."

Patience slapped her leg and laughed loudly again. "It's strange that Ben should say that," she said, wiping the tears from her eyes. "I've been tellin' Ellie to do that very thing for the past year."

"Do you think old Aggie would give Collin permission to take her to bed?" Gretchen could hardly get the words out, she was laughing so hard.

Patience joined her laughter with Gretchen's, finally getting out, "She'd be scandalized to death to think that her boy would want to do such a thing as lay with a woman."

When finally the pair got all the mirth out of their systems Gretchen said in more sober tones, "Do you suppose things have developed that far in their courtship?"

"I wouldn't be surprised," Patience said thoughtfully. "Ellie gets all flushed and squirmy when I bring up the subject. Of course, she'd never say if they had." Her wide mouth tilted in a grin. "We'll just have to sit back and keep an eye on her belly."

Gretchen thought of the probability that she was in a family way and wanted to drop her hands on her flat stomach as she asked, "Would the neighbor women think poorly of Ellie if she should come up pregnant?"

"Naw." Patience dismissed the question with a wave of her hand. "Half the women livin' here was bigged when they tied the knot. What happens is that in the winter, when courtin' couples 'bundle' so they can keep warm in cold cabins, they sometimes get carried away and the woman ends up with a little bundle in her belly. Then they can't get married until the travelin' preacher comes around in the spring."

"What exactly is this bundle thing you talk about?" Gretchen looked puzzled. She'd never heard the expression before.

"Like I said, most cabins get freezing cold six feet away from the fireplace. In order to keep warm when a feller comes to see his girl, they get into bed, with all their clothes on, and snuggle up to each other." She grinned. "Ain't no trouble at all for the man to wiggle out of his britches and the girl to heist up her skirt when it gets real warm under the covers."

Gretchen repressed a worried sigh. If she were expecting, her baby would be born in May. Would the preacher have started his travels by then? And what if Spencer refused to marry her no matter how Ben might insist? Of course, he might marry her but not live with her. Which would be all right. She didn't think she'd like to live with him. She wouldn't put it past him to bring his whores and squaws into their home, maybe even take them into their bed.

Good Lord, the things that go through your mind, Gretchen Ames. She gave herself a mental shake. That would never happen. But he could hurt her in other ways. He could stay out nights, make her fret and wonder who he was sleeping with.

Patience laid a callused palm on Gretchen's hand. "Why are you sad of a sudden, girl?" she asked. "Is somethin' botherin' you?"

"Oh no." Gretchen forced a bright smile to her lips. "I was only thinking of Collin and Ellie," she lied. "It's a shame if they have to go to such extremes to get married."

"What about you?" Patience looked closely at her. "Have you seen any young men you'd like to bundle with this winter, or are you still stuck on that handsome hellion, Spencer?"

"Stuck on Spencer?" Gretchen stared at Patience, wondering if the woman had ever seen her and Spencer making love. "Where'd you get the idea that I'm stuck on him? He and I don't get along with each other at all."

"Is that right?" Patience didn't look convinced. "Gossip has it, the two of you get along too well. That's why Ben kicked Spencer out."

"Who said Ben kicked Spencer out?" Gretchen demanded, red spots of anger on her cheeks.

"Well, it didn't come from a very reliable source, I'll give you that," Patience acknowledged. "Trudie Harrod spread the tale. Probably out of spite and jealousy."

"Even if it were true, Spencer wouldn't have told anyone, especially her," Gretchen snapped.

"That's what I said all along. But some have pointed out that Spencer was only used to livin' in his cabin durin' trappin' season . . . so's he could move a squaw in with him. In memory of his mother, he would never bring such into her home. Spencer is right honorable that way."

Gretchen was glad to hear that the womanizer had honor about some things, but she didn't say so. Some of the neighbors had their suspicions about the two of them, and she didn't want to say anything that might add to them.

"Well, Gretchen, it's been real nice visitin' with you," Patience said as she stood up from the table. "Try to come visit me before we get snowed in. There's not too much comin' and goin' between folk once the snow gets past the knees. Ben can tell you how to get to my place."

"Thank you for coming, Patience." Gretchen walked her to the door. "It was real nice talking to a female again."

"Oh, you'll get lots of female company from now on." Patience smiled as she climbed into the buggy. "Your actions at the cornhuskin' eased everybody's mind. They know now that you ain't got no interest in that spineless Collin. Had we all bothered to get to know you, we'd have known you wouldn't care for a stick like him." She lifted the reins, then looked up at the lowering sky. "It's gonna rain any minute. I hope I can get home before it starts. I got three miles to go." Gretchen watched the buggy roll out of sight, then glanced up at the sky. From the dark clouds that had gathered while she and her new friend had visited, she doubted Patience would get home before the dark mass opened up and poured down water.

The rough-spoken, gentle-mannered woman couldn't have been halfway home when it began to rain. It was a fine rain, but it fell steadily, making it cold and damp. The trees began to shed water in steady drops.

Gretchen stood at the kitchen window, watching puddles form in the yard. Poor Ben, she thought, he'll be soaked by the time he gets home. And aching in every joint. He would need a good hot supper. She turned from the window. She would put a pot of beef stew to cooking, then make an apple pie. Both were favorites of the old fellow. But first she would bring a change of clothing from his room and spread it in front of the fire to get nice and warm.

The stew was bubbling and Gretchen was rolling out pie dough when she heard the sleet pelting against the window. An anxious frown creased her forehead. It would be slippery underfoot now, and Ben would have a hard time walking. He had a hard enough time under ordinary conditions.

The rain had brought on an early dusk, and after Gretchen slid the pie into the little brick oven she lit a couple of candles, leaving one on the kitchen table and placing the other in the window, a cheery welcome for Ben. She went into the main room then and added a couple of split logs to the fire. She wanted the cabin to be toasty warm when Ben got home.

She made numerous trips to the window, peering down the trail that would bring Ben home. It was nearing twilight before she saw him trudging toward the cabin, moving slowly, stepping carefully on the ice-covered ground. She hurried to the door and flung it open just as Ben stepped up on the porch, water dripping from his clothes and beard. She unstrapped the pack of furs on his back and ushered him inside. The temperature had dropped and his teeth were chattering as she led him into the main room, where flames danced and licked at the logs in the fireplace.

"Get out of those wet clothes, Ben," she ordered. "And get into these dry ones I put out for you. While you do that, I'll get you a mug of coffee."

"Put a big slug of whiskey in it, honey," Ben called after her.

Gretchen waited in the kitchen a few minutes to give Ben time to change clothes, then carried the coffee, heavily laced with corn squeezin's, to him. When he had thanked her and taken a long swallow, she asked, "Are you feeling any better?"

"Much better, honey. I feel almost human again. I felt like a frozen totem pole before." He smiled at her. "It sure feels good havin' someone fuss over me again. I ain't had that since my Mary and Julie."

"Well, you just get used to being fussed over a lot." Gretchen returned his smile and picked up the sodden clothing and spread it on the hearth to dry. "Finish your coffee, then come on and eat your supper."

Gretchen's expression was thoughtful as she placed the stew on the table, then brought a pan of cornbread from the oven. Ben didn't know it yet, but she was going to run his line tomorrow. She knew where every trap was hidden and knew how to reset them if she had to take a catch from them. Ben was going to argue with her, though, she knew that.

As she and Ben ate supper, he exclaiming how delicious the stew was, Gretchen told him about Patience's visit and how she had enjoyed chatting with her first female visitor.

"Patience is a fine woman," Ben said. "She's an old maid, you know."

"No, I didn't know," Gretchen answered in surprise. "Now that I think about it, though, she didn't mention a husband or children. I wonder why she never married. I imagine she was quite attractive when she was a young woman. She could be much better-looking now if she didn't dress like a man and if she tamed that wild hair of hers a little."

"Yes." Ben nodded. "She was very comely when she came here with her ma and pa. She was an only child, comin' late in their lives. It was Patience's lot to take care of them. By the time she was free to marry, all the decent men her age had already taken wives. She seemed to accept that fact, and she's lived alone on the small Hardy farm all these years. She knows a lot about doctorin' and the use of herbs and such. She's delivered all the babies around here. Exceptin' the Motts' younguns. I hear tell the sisters deliver each other's babies."

All the while Ben talked about Patience, half of Gretchen's mind was on how she would slip away from Ben tomorrow morning. She had decided not to tell him of her intention to run his traps. It would save a lot of yelling and arguing. She knew that she would have to be awake earlier than he rose, and be very quiet about it. Before she went to bed she would cut a couple of thick slices of ham as usual and wrap them in oiled paper. She did this every night for Ben to take with him when he left in the morning, so he wouldn't be suspicious when she followed her usual habit.

And, she continued to plan, when Ben made his nightly trip to the privy before turning in, she would slip into his room and take a pair of his trousers and a shirt from his trunk. Her heavy jacket and scarf already hung on a peg beside the kitchen door.

Later, when Ben had gone to bed, Gretchen had everything in readiness for the next morning. Ben's borrowed clothes were upstairs in the loft room, and extra rifle shells were in her jacket pocket. Before she went to bed she pushed the half-full coffeepot closer to the live coals. It would be warm for her in the morning.

Chapter Eighteen

Gretchen awakened, leaned up on an elbow, and listened. There was no more sleet hitting against the window. She looked out the window across from the bed. The moon was pale. That meant that dawn wasn't far off.

She slid out of bed and, moving as quietly as possible, changed from her gown into Ben's pants and shirt. Picking up her boots, she slipped quietly down the ladder before pulling them on. She paused beside Ben's door, then smiled when she heard his deep snoring. She peered out the window; it must be almost four. Ben would be up in another few minutes.

Gretchen hurried into the kitchen and nodded her satisfaction when she felt the coffeepot and found it quite warm. She filled a mug, and as she sipped at it she scribbled a note to Ben. "Ben," she wrote, "I am running your line today. Stay in the cabin and keep warm. You can have supper ready tonight. Love, Gretchen."

As she signed her name, she grinned. Ben would have a howling fit when he read it. Five minutes later, she lit the candle in the lantern, pulled on the jacket, and tied the scarf over her head. Before she stepped outside she picked up the rifle and shoved the ham into a pocket, along with two apples. They would be her breakfast.

As she stepped outside and closed the door softly behind her, a blast of cold air hit her in the face. Tears sprang to her eyes as she stooped down and removed Ben's catch from yesterday from his pack. The aged trapper had been so exhausted when he came in, he had forgotten to take the furs to the barn.

With the empty pack settled on her shoulders, Gretchen stepped off the porch. Thin, transparent ice crackled under her feet as Gretchen started out on the five-mile stretch of trap line. By the time she returned home she would have walked ten miles.

But she was young and strong, and ten miles was as nothing to her. She loved the bite of cold air that was turning her cheeks rosy and her nose red. She breathed deeply as her long legs stretched out, taking her swiftly to the first trap. Kneeling down, she removed the dead marten from it, then reset the trap. As she carefully placed a piece of apple she had taken from a small bag in the pack on the trigger, she fervently hoped that any animal she found trapped would be dead. She didn't know if she could bring herself to kill it.

The sun was directly overhead and Gretchen had eaten some of the ham when she and Slim Peters ran into each other. She knew that Spencer's friend's line crossed Ben's at some point. Slim looked at her, stunned. "What are you doin' out here, Miss Ames?" He looked at the half-filled pack.

"I'm running Ben's line today." She smiled at him.

"Is the old fellow sick?" Concern jumped in Slim's eyes.

"No, he's not sick. He got caught in the rain yesterday and it made his rheumatism act up. I thought he needed a day of rest, to stay close to the fire."

"I'm surprised the proud old coot would let you run his traps."

"Oh, he didn't know I was going to. I slipped out of the cabin while he was still sleeping." Gretchen's eyes twinkled with silent laughter. Ben was probably cussing her by now.

Slim gazed at her beautiful face, thinking that his friend was a fool to let this one slip through his fingers. If ever a woman made a man think of hearth and home, it was her. "Does Spence know you're doin' this?" He frowned at her.

"He doesn't, and why should he? It's nothing to him what I do."

"Maybe so, but he's gonna have a fit when he hears about you bein' out here alone."

"He won't know if you don't tell him."

"Oh, I'm gonna tell him all right. He'd have my hide if I didn't."

"Do as you please." Gretchen shrugged. "It won't make a blind bit of difference." She borrowed a phrase Ben was fond of. She lifted her hand in farewell and struck off through the woods.

Slim shook his head as he stared after her. He knew now why his friend kept his distance from that female. He didn't know how to handle her. She had spirit, and a stubborn streak that was as wide as his.

He knew that his friend cared for the little beauty. Cared for her deeply. He was drinking too much these days, and he didn't seek out the whores and squaws anymore. In his opinion that was dead proof of a man in love. He walked on, grinning to himself. His old friend was going to have a raging fit when he learned that the delicate Gretchen had turned trapper.

Gretchen found an animal in every trap, thankfully all of them dead. They were becoming quite heavy, dragging at her back by the time dusk was setting in and she was nearing home.

Her lips parted in a wide smile when a few minutes later she saw the burning candle in the window and Ben's worried face peering over it. Bless his heart, she thought, he'd been worried all day.

She no sooner stepped up on the porch than the door was hauled open and Ben started in on her. "Have your wits wandered away, Gretchen Ames?" he half shouted. "Boy, you take the biscuit. Out there alone, runnin' a trap line. What was you thinkin' about to do such a fool thing?"

"I was thinking about you," Gretchen flared back as she undid the pack and let the furs drop to the floor. "Now tell the truth." She glared at him. "Would you have been able to get out of bed this morning and run your line?"

"It would have hurt, but I would have done it," Ben growled.

"And stove yourself up for all time," Gretchen spoke in gentler tones. "You've been so good to me, Ben. Let me help you. You know I can do it. I'm strong and healthy. It's not like you're going to catch a bear that I'd have to drag home." She smiled coaxingly at him.

Ben ignored her attempt at levity. "But what if you had come across a pack of hungry wolves?"

Gretchen held up the rifle as she stepped inside the warm kitchen. "Thanks to you, I know how to use this."

Ben nodded, remembering the summer months he had spent with her, teaching her how to aim and squeeze the trigger instead of pulling it.

"You're a right good shot," he said, "but what if you got caught in a storm, a blizzard. What would you do then?"

"I'd do the same thing you would. If I couldn't find a cave to hold up in, I'd dig a hole in a snowbank and stay in it until the storm was over."

"You make it sound real easy," Ben grumped as she shed her scarf and jacket, all the time watching him from the corner of her eye. His face was pinched with pain as he hobbled around, putting warmed-over stew on the table. She'd bet anything that he had been unable to get out of bed this morning. It had probably taken him half the morning before he could move around.

Gretchen was starved, and she dug in to the meat and vegetables like a starving animal, telling herself that tomorrow she would take more ham. It was beginning to look like she would be eating for two the next six months.

When the meal was eaten and the coffee drunk, Gretchen stood up and began to clear the table. "No, you go sit before the fire," Ben said. "I'll do up the dishes."

"Nonsense," Gretchen said, carrying the two bowls over to the dry sink and placing them in the big pan sitting there. "I'm not at all tired, and there's only a handful of them."

"If you're sure." Ben reached for his jacket. "I'll take the catch down to the barn and skin and flesh them out."

"Be careful of the ice," Gretchen called before he closed the door behind him.

She was relaxing in front of the fire, her stockinged feet propped up on the raised hearth, when Ben returned from the barn and washed his hands in the kitchen. When he came and sat down beside her, easing himself into the other rocker, she felt like crying at the sight of the lines of pain etched around his eyes and lips.

"Ben," she asked, after he had filled his pipe and lit it, "have you ever asked Patience if she had anything you could use that would ease the pain in your joints?"

"Naw, and I don't intend to. I don't need it spread all over the countryside that Ben Atkins is gettin' all stove up."

"Patience doesn't strike me as a person who would break a confidence if asked not to."

"I'm not takin' any chances," Ben said stubbornly.

Gretchen wanted to point out that anyone seeing the pain on his face when he hobbled about would know that his knee joints were inflamed and aching. But, she thought helplessly, if he wanted to tell himself that he had a well-kept secret, it was his decision. Anyway, if she explained that fact to him, he'd come back with the fact that anyone seeing her run his trap line would know that Ben Atkins was laid up. God knew she didn't want him to get that thought in his head. The proud old fellow would run his traps even if he had to crawl.

She yawned, stood up, and stretched, then said casually, "I think I'll turn in. Daylight rolls around mighty fast."

"Now look here, Gretchen." Ben leaned forward, gripping the chair arms. "I'm runnin' the traps tomorrow."

"You're doing no such thing," Gretchen answered just as firmly. "I want you to stick close to the fire the next few days, rest your knees, let the heat seep into them. You'll begin to feel much better, and then you can carry on as usual."

"But it ain't right," Ben protested, "me sittin' in a warm cabin while you're out there in the cold doin' my job."

"Ben," Gretchen said earnestly, "we both know that right now I'm more able to take care of your traps than you are. You tend to forget sometimes where I come from, the hard labor I had to do since age ten. Taking a ten-mile walk every day is nothing in comparison.

"Besides," she smiled at him, "it gives me great pleasure to do something for you. You have been so good to me, taking me in, and God knows what you might have saved me from. So please, let me do this small thing for you."

There was moisture in Ben's eyes when he nodded and said, "All right, honey, just for a few days."

* * *

Three days passed before Slim Peters saw Spencer in the tavern and told him about running into Gretchen. Admiration sparkled in his eyes when he said, "She was runnin' that line fine as you please, as good as you or your pa could do." He gave Spencer a sly look. "If you don't have any romantic notions there, I could sure get some. Besides bein' the most beautiful woman I ever laid eyes on, she's not afraid to work. She'd make a fine wife."

Spencer didn't hear Slim's last remarks. Stuck in his brain was the fact that Gretchen was running a trap line. Not only did that disturb him, but he knew that his father had to be in a bad way to allow her to do it.

"Are you sure Pa wasn't with her," he broke in on Slim, "that Gretchen was only helpin' him?"

"Nope, she was alone. Steppin' along nice as you please. That girl sure has long legs." Slim purposely brought a dreamy look to his eyes. "Can you imagine how they'd feel . . ."

The killing look Spencer shot him stopped Slim in midsentence. "We'll not discuss Gretchen in a tavern," he growled, his eyes and tone icy cold.

"I didn't mean no disrespect to her, Spence," Slim pacified. "I have only admiration for the lady."

"Yeah, I know." Spencer cooled down.

"What are you goin' to do about her doin' a man's job?" Slim asked. "She strikes me as a female who don't pay much attention to what a man has to say."

"That's no lie," Spencer grumbled, staring into his cup of whiskey. "Sometimes I could wring her neck," he said, adding silently to himself that most times he wanted to make love to her until he was exhausted. He took a swallow of the clear liquid, then pushed the cup away. "Before I start out on my line tomorrow I'm gonna drop in on Pa and have a few words with him. His rheumatism must be actin' up pretty bad that he's allowin' her to do his job."

"You never did say why you and Ben had words."

"No, I never did," Spencer answered, "and I'm not going to now."

"Hey, I didn't mean to be nosy," Slim apologized.

A few minutes later, when Spencer said goodbye and left, Slim thought to himself that he would bet a winter's catch that the little green-eyed beauty had something to do with Spencer leaving home before the trapping season.

The early dawn air was cold and Spencer's breath came out in small clouds of vapor as he stood in the woods, hidden from sight of the cabin. He had been there about fifteen minutes, waiting for Gretchen to appear, to start her rounds.

Finally, he was rewarded for his patience. The cabin door opened and Gretchen stepped out on the porch, bundled up with the pack hanging from her shoulders. His father stood in the doorway, holding the rifle that usually hung over the mantel. He handed the long firepiece to her, said something to her, and her teeth flashed in a wide, white smile. As she stepped off the porch, holding it in the crook of her arm, he wondered if she knew how to use it.

He felt his loins stir as with a wave of her hand to Ben she struck off in her smooth, graceful walk. Even though her soft woman's curves were hidden in his father's trousers and her heavy jacket, there was etched in his mind the proud tilt of her breasts, her gently rounded hips. Hips that had cradled his, reaching to meet his driving thrusts. Every night his dreams were filled with the memory of her body.

When Gretchen disappeared into the gloom of dawn he left the tree he'd been standing under and walked purposefully toward the cabin. When he pushed open the door Ben swung around, almost falling as his crippled knees didn't respond swiftly enough to the order his brain sent them.

For a moment father and son gazed at each other, both keeping from their faces how glad they were to see each other.

Ben spoke first. "You liked to have scared the daylights out of me."

"Sorry. I didn't know I had to knock."

Ben bristled at the brusqueness in his tone. "You know dad-burn well you don't have to knock. You just took me by surprise. I wasn't expectin' anyone comin' round at this hour."

"I could use a cup of that coffee." Spencer looked at the pot keeping warm on the hearth.

"Help yourself," Ben said, carefully easing himself into a chair. "I'll have one too."

Spencer filled Ben's cup and then the one Gretchen had used a few minutes before. As he sat down he had a warm, contented feeling being back in the cabin, having coffee with his father like he used to.

"I know why you're here," Ben said, lifting his cup to his lips.

"So, tell me why Gretchen is runnin' your traps. Why didn't you send me word that your hands and knees were actin' up?"

Ben turned his head from Spencer, cool and withdrawn. "Nothin' has changed, Spencer."

At first Spencer's only response was a dark scowl, then he said, "I don't like Gretchen runnin' a trap line. It can be dangerous out there for her."

"If you'd have kept your hands off her and your buckskins laced she wouldn't be out there in the cold."

"How long are you gonna jaw at me about that?" Spencer's eyes snapped angrily.

"You're gonna hear it until you do the honorable thing and marry Gretchen. She was a virgin when you took her and now you've spoiled her chances of ever marryin' a decent man."

Spencer stared at Ben, his mouth wide open. That he should marry Gretchen was the last thing he expected to hear from his father. He almost laughed at the idea. He could arouse Gretchen, that he knew, make her want him, but he had grave doubts that she even liked him.

"Look, Pa," he said, "Gretchen isn't any more interested in marriage than I am. And you know my feelin's about wedlock."

"Never mind your feelin's." Ben glared at him. "Have you asked her, given her a chance to say no?"

"Hell no. After the way she sat and blubbered, makin' it look like I raped her, I don't trust her one bit."

They stared at each other another moment, then Ben said, "After you stormed out of the barn and left, Gretchen controlled her tears long enough to tell me that she had been a willin' partner. She was cryin' because she thought I would turn against her."

"She told you it wasn't all my fault?" Spencer's eyebrows rose in surprise.

"Yeah, she did. But I don't put much stock in that. She was an innocent lamb in your hands. You knew just how to touch her, the right words to say. As far as I'm concerned, that made it the next thing to rape."

"You're wrong, Pa. It was a mutual thing that leapt between us without any warnin'."

Ben twitched his bony shoulders. "I ain't got nothin' more to say on the subject. In your heart you know the decent thing is to ask the girl to marry you."

"When wolves sleep with deer I will." Spencer slammed his empty mug on the table and stood up. He stood glaring down at his father for a moment, defiance in his eyes. When Ben only glowered back he swung on his heel and strode to the door, jerked it open, and slammed it behind him.

Damn fool, Ben thought sadly as he painfully got to his feet. Gretchen could be his salvation. With her he could settle down, raise a family, live a good, long life. The one he was living now would lead him to an early grave.

Spencer walked fast, peering ahead, looking for Gretchen's slender figure. He didn't want her running traps, and he was going to tell her so. It was too dangerous for a woman to be walking alone in the wilderness. She could be confronted with all kinds of danger; wolves, panthers, and, more important, some strange man who wouldn't hesitate to rape her. It appeared that the Missouri Fur Company had given up on trying to move into Kentucky. But they could have sent other men into the hills to try to talk their way into the fur trade. He remembered when Gretchen had been attacked in the barn, that time he'd made love to her the first time, and his heart stopped for a second. He broke into a trot and came upon her as she was removing a raccoon from the fourth trap in the line. Spencer's foot came down on a dead limb that popped like a rifle shot in the morning stillness. Gretchen came to her feet, the butt of the Kentucky rifle sweeping to her shoulder. She slowly lowered it then, the alarm in her eyes replaced with one of indignation.

"I don't like people sneaking up on me, Spencer Atkins," she shouted at him.

"I wasn't sneakin'," Spencer shot back just as sharply. "If you'd been payin' attention, as you should have, you'd have heard me comin' a couple hundred yards back."

Gretchen knew he was right. She should have been more alert to her surroundings, and ordinarily she was. But she wasn't going to admit it to him, nor was she about to tell him that her carelessness was because she'd had her mind on him.

She had dreamed of Spencer last night, and the dream had stayed with her ever since. Her cheeks, rosy from the cold air, reddened a bit more. In her sleep he had made such glorious love to her. Thank goodness minds couldn't be read. If that were possible, it would give this hellion all manner of satisfaction that she had such dreams of him.

"Shouldn't you be running your traps?" she asked when the tension began to build between them.

"Yes, I damn well should, and it's your fault that I'm runnin' an hour behind." Spencer took a step toward her.

"My fault? In what way?"

"You know damn well in what way. You have no business bein' out here tryin' to act like a man. Trappin' is not women's work."

"Is that so? Is it a law of the land that women can't trap? White women, that is. Ben told me once that it's the Indian women who snare most of the meat for the villages during the winter. I'm just as strong as they are, maybe stronger than some of them."

"That's different, and you know it."

"Only the color of our skin is different." Gretchen had placed her fists on her hips, her stance defiant.

"Well, I'm not goin' to allow you to do it." Spencer took a step toward her, his own fists clenched now.

"You're not going to allow me?" Gretchen lifted a scornful eyebrow. "How do you plan on stopping me? Lock me up in the cabin maybe?"

"Damn you, I'd like to lock you up in *my* cabin and exhaust you every night with lovemaking. Wear you out until you wouldn't have the strength to get out of bed the next mornin'."

"Oh, and how would Trudie feel about that? I don't think she would like three in a bed.

Especially if that third one was another woman."

It was on the tip of Spencer's tongue to deny Trudie was welcome in his cabin. Then he bit the words back. Let her think that Trudie lived with him; he had a feeling she didn't like the idea of that.

"I could always send her away," he said, his voice silky, the aching need inside him plain for her to see.

Gretchen's own desire for him leapt to life, and before she could gather her defenses around her he had snatched her into his arms. As his lips came down on hers, hot and demanding, she brought her hands up to push him away. But, to her shame, they only curled around his forearms and pulled him closer to her.

Even as she hated her body for its weakness, she melded herself against him, cursing the clothes that lay between them as Spencer's tongue slipped through her lips and stroked inside her mouth. She grew weak from its slow thrust and had to cling tighter to him to keep from falling to her knees. Her eyes were heavy and glazed over when Spencer raised his head and gazed down at her.

All passion left Gretchen's body when he said, "I'm runnin' Pa's traps tomorrow, Gretchen."

She pushed away from him, saying loudly in a rage-filled voice, "You will not! I want to do this for Ben, and I intend to."

They stood glaring at each other in silent combat for several seconds, then Spencer spoke, finality in his voice. "Keep his cabin neat and clean and his meals cooked. That's all you have to do for him. I'll take care of the rest."

While Gretchen's mind raced for a suitable rebuttal, Spencer turned and disappeared into the forest.

"We'll just see about that, Mr. Arrogant," she muttered, bending down and resetting the trap before moving on. She'd get up at three o'clock if necessary to get a head start on him.

Chapter Nineteen

That evening, as Gretchen and Ben ate the steaks and roast potatoes Ben had prepared for their supper, Gretchen was halfway through the meal when she said, "I saw that son of yours today."

"Oh?" Ben kept his eyes on his plate. "What did he have to say?"

Gretchen gave a short laugh and said scornfully, "He said that starting tomorrow he's going to run the line."

Ben made no response at first, then he ventured, "Maybe he should, honey. It's gonna be hard on you when the snows come." A gloominess crept into his eyes. "It don't look like I'm gonna be able to even help you, let alone gather my catch by myself. I do well to make it to the barn to feed Jimbo and Beauty."

He heaved a ragged sigh. "I'll be hangin' up my traps for good when the season is over."

"Don't say that, Ben." Gretchen reached across the table and gently squeezed the crippled fingers lying beside his plate. "You're wrong on two counts. I can take care of the traps no matter what the weather is, and once spring and summer arrive the sun will bake the swelling out of your joints. When the season arrives again we'll run the traps together."

"Maybe. I hope you're right."

They were sipping coffee in front of the fire when Ben asked, "What are you gonna do when Spencer shows up in the morning? He can be very stubborn once he sets his mind to somethin'. I wouldn't put it past him to take away your boots and jacket."

"He's not going to get the chance to do anything." Gretchen's tone said she had figured it all out. "I'm taking off at three o'clock in the morning. I'll be long gone before he shows up here."

"But, Gretchen." Worried concern looked out of Ben's eyes. "It will still be night. You mustn't do it."

"Ben, I'll be just fine. I'll have the rifle and the lantern."

"I wish you wouldn't. You're bein' as stubborn as my son."

Gretchen shook her head. "Nobody could be as stubborn as Spencer Atkins." When Ben grinned and agreed, she asked, "Would you make my lunch for me tonight? I think I'll turn in now. I want to make sure I'm up by three o'clock."

The flames from the fireplace below lightened the raftered ceiling and a candle burned in the kitchen when Gretchen woke the next morning. Ben, bless his heart, was already up and had a pot of coffee brewing.

She slid out of bed and by firelight she hurried into her heavy garb. As she climbed down the ladder, she smelled bacon frying. A soft smile curved her lips. Even at such an early hour the old fellow was seeing to it that she had a hot meal in her stomach before she set out.

"Good morning, Ben," she said as she walked into the kitchen and made straight for the basin of warm water waiting for her to wash up in.

"I wish you wasn't goin'." Ben ignored her greeting. "I feel it in my bones that it's gonna snow today, maybe storm."

"I'll be fine," Gretchen assured him as he placed bacon and eggs before her. "Besides, I'll be home an hour earlier today." She dug into her breakfast. "It will still be daylight."

"Daylight don't make much difference if you get caught in a blizzard," the old man grouched. "When you can't see a foot in front of you it's awful easy to get turned around, lose your way."

"I'll be fine, you'll see."

"I sure hope so," Ben said as he put more ham in her jacket pocket, then added two apples. He had just finished lighting the oversize candle in the lantern when Gretchen stood up, ready to leave. When she had bundled herself up and picked up the rifle and lantern he followed her out onto the porch.

"You be careful now," he said, "and don't forget to watch your back trail. Them damn wolves can slip up on a person silent as a shadow."

"I'll keep my eyes peeled for them." Gretchen gave him a cheery smile, and then stepped out into the darkness, the lantern light throwing a wavering shadow as she entered the forest.

Ben stood in the doorway a long time after the light disappeared from his sight. He was uneasy. There were patches of stars twinkling coldly in the sky and he didn't like the looks of that. Those wide black patches meant only one thing: clouds, big ones. He turned back into the cabin, a worried frown creasing his forehead.

Gretchen noted that the air had turned colder as she visited the fifth trap of the line. She pulled her thick scarf up over her lips and nose to protect them from the bite of the weather. She looked to the east as she walked on, thinking that dawn was slow arriving this morning. She'd been out at least an hour, and at this time of day the sky should be turning a pinkish gray. Maybe in her haste to outstrip Spencer she was making better time than she had realized.

The corners of her lips lifted in a smile beneath the warmness of their woolen covering.

She could just see the black scowl on Spencer's face as he hurried to catch up with her.

There was more than a scowl on Spencer's face: There was rage, as well, as he hurried along. He had thought to crisscross the forest, going from his traps to those of his father, but when he found Ben's first trap freshly rebaited he gave up the idea. That was when he became furious. The little vixen had outsmarted him. She probably had at least an hour's start on him and was laughing her head off that she had bested him.

Well, by God, he thought grimly, *I want to see her try to do it tomorrow.*

There was satisfaction in Spencer's smile a few minutes later when a threatening gray dawn finally broke the darkness. That young miss just might get snowed on today. If she froze her little rump good, she might not be so eager to run any more traps.

When finally a frosty cold dawn arrived Gretchen wasn't too enthusiastic about it. Huge black clouds floated overhead, the kind that spilled snow on the ground. She hoped it would hold off until she got home. She had half the line to run yet, then the five-mile trek back to the cabin. She hastened her pace, almost running.

An early dusk had descended when Gretchen removed an otter from the last trap. She strapped it on her back with the others and began to retrace her steps. She couldn't remember ever being so cold.

Like the dusk, twilight arrived early. Gretchen figured she was halfway home when it started snowing. She paused to light the lantern, then hurried on. Within an hour, snow hung heavy on every branch, and several inches lay on the ground. She couldn't see three feet in front of her. She walked as fast as she could, the snow crunching under her feet. She listened intently to the sounds of the night, magnified by her growing alarm. Whenever a wolf mourned or a big cat screamed, fear rippled up her spine. She expected any minute to see a pack of wolves slipping up on her, or a lean panther to spring at her from a tree.

She hurried blindly on. Once a low-hanging branch caught her across the forehead, sending her crashing back into some underbrush. She picked herself up, ordering herself to calm down, not to panic. If she kept her wits about her, she would be all right.

But when darkness came her slight courage failed her. She couldn't keep her eyes from straying fearfully on either side of her, though she knew she couldn't see any danger that might await her.

A wind came up, and Gretchen suppressed a groan. The snow would start to drift now. She was in a potentially life-threatening situation. Her alarm grew when she began to stumble over fallen logs that shouldn't be in her path.

She had gotten off her course and she was lost.

She plodded on, peering through night and snow, looking for a candle burning in a window.

She was barely dragging along, ready to drop in her tracks, when she saw the dim light through the curtain of blowing snow. She commanded her frozen feet to move, to reach that source of heat and rest.

As Gretchen pulled herself up two steps to reach the porch she realized she wasn't home. Their cabin had only one step. But that wasn't important. She had arrived somewhere. Soon she would be out of the cold and drinking a hot cup of coffee.

She lifted her hand and knocked on the door. She heard footsteps inside, then saw the curtain at the window pulled aside. She couldn't see the face, but the firelight behind the figure outlined a head and shoulders she recognized "It's Gretchen Ames, Trudie," she called. "I've been lost in the storm and I'm near frozen."

The curtain fell back in place and she waited for the door to open. Inside, she could hear Trudie speaking sharply to the black slave she had brought with her from the Carolinas.

The door remained closed, and it grew silent inside as Gretchen waited, shivering, her teeth chattering. She knocked again as she felt her legs growing weak and her vision blurring. The cabin inside remained silent, as though it was empty.

Gretchen realized then that Trudie didn't intend to let her in.

"It's all right," she mumbled, "I'm not cold anymore." She was suddenly sleepy. "I'll just take a nap," she whispered, and slid to the floor. She curled an arm under her head and closed her eyes.

She didn't see Trudie peek out the window again, nor did she hear the woman order the black woman to go get Carter, the man who couldn't speak. "Tell him to carry that piece of baggage off my porch and take her into the woods. Let her freeze to death there."

Gretchen was unaware of the hands that gently lifted her up and carried her off the porch a few minutes later. She didn't know that the black woman begged the man to get the mule from the barn and take the girl home.

"It's not right for her to die in the woods like an animal," the woman added to her plea. "I'd take her, but Mr. Atkins would ask me questions, want to know where I found her. He wouldn't ask you anything because he knows you can't speak. And Carter," she looked earnestly at the man in the swirling snow, "I'll never tell *her*."

Carter nodded and struck off toward the barn. As the old woman went back inside the cabin, she wore a solemn look. She was afraid it was too late for the beautiful young woman. She was already more dead than alive.

Chapter Twenty

Spencer had one more mile to go when the first flakes of snow began to drift to the ground. He glanced up at the sky and walked faster. Those dark clouds up there meant business. It would be no short-lived squall when they opened up fully. He prayed that Gretchen was on her way home.

By the time he had seen to the last trap and found it empty, the trigger still set and baited, the sun was only a white glow in the sky as it tried to penetrate the thick veil of snow. His long legs stretched out, cutting a cross trail through the forest. His father's line of traps lay parallel to his, about a mile away. Concerned about Gretchen, he wanted to make sure she was on her way home.

Spencer sighed in relief when he came upon her small footprints headed in the direction of the cabin. But a mile farther along he swore fearfully. Out of nowhere, there were two sets of wolf tracks behind Gretchen's. The pair was trailing her.

The fall of snow thickened, and the strength of the wind increased as Spencer's fast pace turned into a trot. Both Gretchen's and the wolves' tracks were disappearing beneath the white carpet of snow. Twilight came on and he swore at the time wasted as he stopped to light his lantern. He hurried on then, afraid of what he might stumble across at any time. But he had heard no screams of a woman being attacked by wolves, and that relieved him a little.

His keen sense of direction finally brought Spencer to the knoll where his father's cabin stood. A candle burned in the window and his heartbeat faltered. Hadn't Gretchen reached home yet? A burning light in a window was meant to guide a family member home.

He struck out running the short distance, but it seemed he had run ten miles before he reached the cabin and burst through the door. "Isn't she home yet?" he asked a worried-looking Ben after scanning the room, then looked up at the dark loft room.

"No, she's not." Ben practically wrung his hands in his aggrieved state. "She should have been home hours ago. She's lost out there in the blizzard, half frozen and likely bein' trailed by wolves."

Spencer didn't verify the fact that Gretchen was indeed being followed by wolves. "I'll find her, Pa," he said, and checked the candle in his lantern. It was tall enough to see him through the night if necessary. He prayed with all his heart it wouldn't take that long to find her.

Ben helped him unstrap the fur pack on his back and he was out the door, running now that the heavy weight of furs wasn't dragging at his shoulders. He moved in the direction of Ben's trap line, hoping he could find the place where Gretchen had wandered off the trail. Every few minutes he stopped to call her name, then waited with body tensed, listening for her to answer him.

But there was only the roar of the wind and the echo of her name bouncing from hill to hill.

The storm didn't let up and the fierce wind was piling the snow into drifts that came up to his knees in some places. Finally, he had to give up. He was almost blind from peering through the snow, he was hoarse from calling Gretchen's name, and he was ready to drop from exhaustion.

His one faint hope as he trudged along, retracing his steps, was that Gretchen had managed to get home and that she was being cared for by his father at this very moment.

A ragged sigh escaped him. If she wasn't there, he'd grab a bite to eat, change into dry clothing, and start out again, trying to find his way to the neighbors in hopes that she had found her way to one of them.

As soon as he stepped into the cabin, Spencer knew from his father's worried face that Gretchen had not returned. "I'm sorry, Pa," he said, sinking into a chair and holding his chilled hands out to the fire. "I've searched the woods within a two-mile radius and haven't found a sign of her. It's as if she grew wings and flew away."

"You don't think wolves have come upon her?" Ben hovered over Spencer, his eyes sick with anxiety.

Spencer shook his head and pointed out gently, "I would have heard them, or at least found evidence that she had been attacked."

Ben nodded, knowing to what Spencer alluded. "Maybe she's found a cave and crawled into it to wait out the storm," he said, without too much conviction in his voice.

"Maybe," Spencer agreed, "but as soon as I eat a bite and get into some dry clothes, I'm goin' out again and look for her until I find her."

"Are you sure you should, son?" Ben asked, torn between wanting Gretchen home safe and sound and hating the thought that he might lose his son to the blizzard.

"I'll be all right, Pa," Spencer said, knowing what was running through his father's mind. "Just dish me up some of whatever you've got in the pot while I change my clothes. And put some whiskey in my coffee."

Spencer had just finished wolfing down his first meal in fifteen hours and was draining the last of the whiskey-laced coffee when there came the sound of footsteps on the porch, followed by a heavy rapping on the door. He sprang out of his chair and flung open the door.

Apprehension mingled with gladness took hold of him. Trudie Harrod's handyman stood on the porch, Gretchen's limp body in his arms. He started to ask, "Where did you find her?" then remembered the man couldn't speak. He took Gretchen from him, not even noticing when the man turned and silently departed. With Ben at his heels, he carried her over to the warmth of the fireplace.

With trembling hands he ripped open her jacket and put his ear to her chest. A second or two later he raised his head and said in a hushed whisper, "She still lives, but just barely."

"We've got to get her out of them wet clothes." Ben's voice was raw with worry and concern. He sat down in the other rocker, saying, "Give her to me. While I get her undressed, go to my room and get my heaviest pair of woolen long johns and a couple of blankets. Then build up the fire."

Spencer was on his way to the bedroom while Ben was still uttering his last order. Only a moment had passed before he was back, the required items folded over his arm. In that time Ben had removed Gretchen's borrowed jacket and tugged off the soaking trousers.

He looked up at Spencer and ordered, "Turn your back while I finish undressing her."

If Spencer hadn't been half out of his mind with worry, he'd have smiled at that. He'd seen Gretchen's beautiful body bare many times.

Ben's crippled fingers finally got Gretchen out of her wet clothes and into the long-legged underclothing. When it came to buttoning them up, however, it was beyond his stiff fingers to slide the buttons into the matching holes.

Grudgingly, he said, "You'll have to do her up. It's too tedious for my fingers."

Spencer's fingers weren't all that steady either as he fastened Gretchen into the long johns. Each time his knuckles touched her icy-cold flesh he trembled with the fear that she would never be warm again.

Ben had folded the two blankets on the bear-skin before the hearth, and when Spencer had finished with the last button he said, "Lay her down here in front of the fire, then pour a mug of coffee and put plenty of sugar and whiskey in it. Meanwhile, I'll start rubbin' her hands and feet, get her blood to circulatin'."

Within seconds Spencer returned from the kitchen, a steaming mug of coffee in his hand.

"It's too hot!" Ben barked at him. "It'll scald her lips. Let it cool a bit while you roust up the fire. You can rub her feet then."

Spencer knelt down and cradled Gretchen's small cold feet in his warm palms. He held them a minute, willing his heat to penetrate the cold flesh.

"Don't just hold them." Ben flashed him an irritated look. "You gotta rub them, rub them real hard. If and when her toes turn pink, start on her legs."

Spencer welcomed his father's taking over, issuing orders, for his mind could only think, and fear, that Gretchen might die, that the small spark of life in her body could be snuffed out at any minute. She wasn't responding to their ministrations at all. She lay so still, her black lashes fanned out on her pale cheeks. He remembered how she had looked at him through that dark curtain, passion darkening her eyes as he made love to her. Her body was warm then . . . it was hot. He glanced up the length of her body and thought that she was gaining more weight. The long johns were tight on her, leaving nothing to the imagination.

His gaze moved back to Gretchen's feet. Had he felt a hint of warmth in them? He peered intently at her toes. Was there pink color to them, or was that the glow of the fire, making them look so?

"Pa," he said, afraid to hope, "do you think there's color comin' back to her toes?"

An elated smile lit Ben's face as he peered at Gretchen's feet. "You're right, son. There's definitely color in them toes. See if you can get some of that coffee down her. It should have cooled a little by now."

Spencer knelt at Gretchen's head and gently lifted it up to press the mug against her lips. When they remained closed he gently tried to nudge them open.

"Spill a little bit on them," Ben suggested. "Maybe some will enter her mouth and she'll want more."

Ben was right. When a few drops touched Gretchen's lips her tongue came out to lick at the liquid. The men grinned at each other, and Spencer offered her the coffee again. This time she drank greedily, and Ben cautioned, "Don't let her drink too fast. She might choke."

Spencer set the cup aside and began to briskly rub Gretchen's legs, slowly moving up to her thighs. In a matter of minutes her body was squirming and she was crying out as blood rushed through her veins.

Her eyes flashed open and she stared up at Ben, crying, "Oh, Ben, it hurts so."

"I know, honey." Ben smoothed the hair from her forehead. "But thank God it does. The pain means you're gonna live. We thought for a while you might not make it."

"We?" she muttered, then seemingly lapsed into unconsciousness again.

Spencer and Ben's belief that Gretchen would be her old self by morning was shattered. It was around midnight when she began to moan and toss, in the grip of a burning fever. In her delirium she took turns railing out at Spencer and speaking gently to Ben. Many times she moaned, "Let me in, Trudie. I am so cold and tired." At her pitiful plea, Ben and Spencer would look at each other and shake their heads.

"She's out of her head," Ben said. Spencer nodded his agreement. The poor little thing didn't know what she was saying.

"Let's get her to bed and start getting her fever down," Spencer said. He scooped her up in his arms, adding, "I'll put her in my room. It will be handier to take care of her."

"I'll go get some pails of snow." Ben hurried to the kitchen after he had pulled down the covers on Spencer's bed.

As Spencer gently put her down and pulled the blankets up to her chin, her green eyes opened and stared up at him. "You'll not make love to me this time," she said coldly.

Before Spencer could assure her that he had no intention of trying, she slid back into a world clouded with fever and started ranting at him again.

Ben entered the room at the end of Gretchen's words, a pail of snow in each hand, and said with disappointment in his voice, "I guess it's just as well you refused to marry her. She don't care much for you, does she? She's called you a low-down womanizer at least a dozen times."

Spencer felt a strange tightening in his chest. He was surprised at how hurt he felt, learning that Gretchen truly didn't like him. He had thought all along that the insults she hurled at him were a pretense that covered up her real feelings for him. It didn't seem possible that she could so enjoy his lovemaking while at the same time disliking him so intensely.

Why do you find that so strange? an inner voice taunted. *You don't like Trudie Harrod and yet you have slept with her countless times.*

Spencer looked at Gretchen's fever-flushed face and didn't like to think that she was like him. He didn't like to imagine that any man with the right words and experienced hands could coax her into his bed.

He suddenly found himself thinking that he would like to know her, really know her; to talk and laugh with her, to learn her likes and dislikes. She had a very sweet side. It showed in the way she behaved with his father. And she was also a caring person. Look how she ran Pa's traps so that he could stay inside and keep warm.

Ben entered the room with a fresh pail of snow, and Spencer left off his wishing as he resumed smoothing the soft, cold flakes over Gretchen's face and throat. An hour passed and she still burned with fever. And, added to the men's worries, she had developed a deep, racking cough.

Ben looked at Spencer with haunted eyes. "I think she's got pneumony, son. You'd better go get Patience. Tell her what has happened and about the cough. She'll know what to bring with her."

Spencer hurried into the kitchen, shrugged on his jacket, and picked up his rifle. He wondered when the man, Carter, had left. He had forgotten to thank him for bringing Gretchen home.

When Spencer stepped outside he found that sometime during the night it had stopped snowing. A pale moon had risen. He walked through ten-inch-deep snow on his way to the barn. The thought crossed his mind that he might have to fight his way through some snowdrifts. He wished that his stallion was here. The big, strong animal would make better time than the dainty little mare.

And time was very important, he knew.

Despite Beauty's small size, she was like her mistress, strong and determined, as she galloped through the snow. They found no drifts to battle through, and within the hour Spencer was knocking on Patience's door.

Her graying hair standing up all over her head, Patience was tying the belt around her robe when she opened the door. "Spencer," she said, surprised, "what brings you out with the wolves? Are you sick, or do you have a knife wound?"

"I'm fine, Patience. It's Gretchen who needs you. She got caught in a blizzard and Pa thinks she has pneumonia."

Patience motioned him inside and asked as she closed the door, "What are her symptoms?"

"She's burning up with fever and she has a chest-tearing cough."

"Punch up the fire and warm yourself while I go get dressed."

"If you don't mind, Patience, I'll go saddle your mule instead. Pa said to get back as soon as possible."

"You're right. It'll only take me a minute to change clothes and gather the roots and herbs I'll need."

In under ten minutes Spencer had the white mule saddled. He was walking back to the cabin when Patience stepped outside, a small haversack in her hand. Spencer helped her to mount, then swung onto the mare's back.

Patience was bundled up to her eyes and no words were spoken between them as they followed the path Spencer had made on his way for help.

Chapter Twenty-One

A highly concerned Ben waited for Spencer and Patience as they walked into the kitchen. "We got a mighty sick girl on our hands, Patience," he said by way of greeting. "She's got an awful cough and her skin near burns you to the touch."

"Calm down now, Ben," Patience said, putting her medicine bag on the table and taking off her jacket and scarf. "Poke up the fire and get a kettle of water to heatin'." She rummaged around in the bag and brought out two small, cloth-wrapped bags, then began to issue orders.

"Spencer, get me a couple of mugs," she said as she unfolded the packages. When he hurried to bring them to her she put a good-sized pinch of dried leaves into one of the mugs, explaining, "These are pennyroyal leaves for the fever, and this," she dipped her fingers into the other package, "is boneset for her chest congestion and cough." She looked at Ben and ordered, "When the water boils, fill the mugs with it. Let them cool for five minutes, then bring them to me."

She looked at Spencer again. "Go put the mare and the mule in the barn. My old plug ain't used to bein' out in the cold."

Both men rushed to do her bidding, glad to shift their anxiety onto her shoulders. They had felt so helpless.

Spencer put the animals in separate stalls and turned to leave. His eyes fell on the pile of hay where he and Gretchen had twice lain. His loins tightened at the memory of the first time. Never before had he experienced such complete satisfaction. And, unbelievably, each following time had been better yet. They knew now what pleased the other, where to touch, to kiss, to caress.

He realized then, with a shock, that making love to Gretchen wasn't enough. He also wanted her to have a good opinion of him.

This last brought a confused look to his face. He had never before cared what women thought of him after he had used them and walked away.

Understanding slowly grew in his eyes. Used. That was the word that made the difference. He had used those other women, but Gretchen—he had made love to her. "Dammit," he swore under his breath. He had a tender feeling for her and he didn't like it at all. A man didn't think straight when he became emotionally involved with a woman. He'd seen that happen with his married friends. They more or less let their wives think for them.

I think your emotions are already involved with Gretchen, Spencer's ever-ready inner voice spoke. *Look how upset you were when you couldn't find her in the blizzard. You were like a wild man.*

"You're crazy. I'd have felt the same way for anyone I was searching for."

Tell that to the moon. Maybe it will believe you.

Spencer swore again and left the barn, hoping that the nagging voice wouldn't follow him.

When he entered his old bedroom Patience had lifted Gretchen's head and was spooning one of her teas between her lips, all the time talking soothingly to her. He went to stand beside Ben, who hovered over the bed, watching the procedure intently.

When Gretchen had swallowed half the cup's contents Patience eased her head back onto the pillow and tucked the covers in around her shoulders. Then she looked up at the anxious men.

"Her fever should be going down soon," she said. "I'll let her rest a few minutes, then give her some of the boneset cough syrup to relieve her cough and break up the congestion in her lungs."

"We can never thank you enough, Patience," Ben said, a tremor in his voice. "I thought for sure we was gonna lose her."

Patience started to speak, then paused a moment. Looking away from father and son, she said bluntly, "She may lose her babe, though."

The stunned silence that greeted her remark seemed to go on forever. Finally, Ben croaked out, "What do you mean, lose her babe? Gretchen's not in a family way."

"Yes, she is, Ben," Patience said quietly, pity for the old man in her eyes. She looked at the jarred Spencer then, a question in her eyes. "I'd say she was around three months along."

Spencer's blanched face revealed his guilt, and Ben, his face twisted with rage, ground out, "You couldn't leave her alone, could you? Just to spite me, you had to use her again."

Spencer moved away from the clenched fists that were ready to strike out at him. "It wasn't like you think, Pa. I swear it. I never used her."

Ben took a menacing step toward him. "I don't want to hear another lyin' word out of your mouth. As soon as the preacher comes through here, prepare yourself to get married. My grandson is gonna carry the Atkins name."

"Look, Pa," Spencer said in a low voice, hoping Ben would lower his, "I'm willin' to marry Gretchen, but I doubt if she will have me. You heard the names she's been callin' me tonight." He looked away from the two pairs of eyes watching him. "She don't care very much for me, I'm afraid."

"That don't make a lick of difference." Ben lowered his voice when Gretchen became restless. "You're gonna be her husband. And not only that, by God, you're gonna be true to her. There will be no more whores, squaws, or Trudie Harrods in your life from now on."

All the while, Patience hadn't said a word. She spoke now. "Ben," she said quietly, "in your heart you know that Spencer is an honorable man. He wouldn't do wrong to a wife."

When Ben made no response Spencer turned around and left the sickroom. In the kitchen he poured himself a mug of coffee and sat down at the table, his mind in a turmoil. Patience's announcement had hit him like a bolt of lightning even if it shouldn't have. God knows he'd poured enough of his seed into her.

A strange excitement came over him. He was going to be a father and a husband. There would be a little one who was a part of him and a part of Gretchen. And not only that, he could make love to Gretchen every night. It didn't enter his mind that he would be giving up his old life.

Don't forget, she doesn't like you worth spit. The taunting voice was back. *If she agrees to marry you, she might refuse to sleep with you.*

Spencer refused to respond. All that his inner voice had said was true. He shook his head in amazement. There wasn't a single girl in the area who wouldn't give a year of her life to be married to Spencer Atkins, but the little green-eyed witch in his bedroom wanted nothing to do with him even though she carried his child.

Spencer lifted the mug to his lips as he glanced out the window. It was turning pink in the east. It was time to get bundled up and start out to tend the traps. He had his father's to take care of, too, now.

He rose and put the long-handled skillet on the fire and fried several slices of bacon and four eggs. His belly was crying out for food.

When several minutes later he had wiped his plate clean of every morsel of food, he rose and walked over to a large earthen jar that was kept on the workbench. He took off its lid and, reaching inside, took out a handful of pemmican and shoved it into his shirt pocket. He replaced the candle stub in the lantern with a new one and he braced himself to face his father again.

Ben looked up from his seat at the foot of the bed. He gave Spencer a cold stare, then looked away. Patience had a smile for him, though, and answered his questioning look. "Her fever is breaking and her cough is beginning to loosen." She grinned. "She's also stopped yellin' at you. She mostly berated a Mrs. Fedders and Trudie. I haven't been able to figure out who Mrs. Fedders is, or what she done to Gretchen in the past, but I imagine Trudie has said a lot of nasty things to her."

Spencer nodded in agreement. God only knew the things Trudie had said to Gretchen. She was a mean bitch. "Do you know who Mrs. Fedders is, Pa?"

"She used to be a neighbor of Gretchen's," Ben lied calmly. "She was a mean bitch, and Gretchen didn't like her."

Spencer walked toward the door. "Is there anything I can do before I leave?"

When Ben only shook his head Patience said, "We'll be fine, Spencer. Go on and take care of business."

After a lingering look at Gretchen, who now slept peacefully, Spencer left the cabin.

When he walked into the barn to get his snowshoes, pear-shaped frames with strips of rawhide woven across them, a welcoming whinny from the last stall greeted him. "Buckskin!" he exclaimed, walking up to the animal to pat his sleek head. "How did you get in here?"

He noticed the piece of paper pinned to the slatted enclosure. He pulled it free and read, "Sorry to hear about Gretchen. Have brought you your mount. Thought you might need him, Slim."

That's right thoughtful of Slim, Spencer thought, as he fed the four animals, then brought in a pail of snow for each one. It took a few minutes to fasten the webbed snowshoes onto his boots before he left the barn.

Patience saw Spencer leave out of the bedroom window. She looked at Ben and said, "Ain't you bein' a little hard on your son? He's quite willin' to marry the girl and accept his responsibilities."

"You don't understand, Patience. For years I've wanted Spencer to get married and settle down, but I wanted him to love whoever the woman was. I wanted the same thing for Gretchen. In fact, I secretly hoped that after a while the two of them would grow to love each other and have a normal marriage. Now it's a case of have to, and God knows what kind of union it will be."

"It might turn out better than you think, Ben," Patience said. "Spencer was sick with worry when he came to fetch me. And Gretchen's railing at him had as much hurt as anger in her words. There's more back of their relationship than we know. Given time, I think they'll have a fine marriage."

Patience's reassuring words brightened Ben's countenance considerably. "Sparks do fly between them, don't they? Maybe there's some kind of misunderstandin' between them that has to be cleared up." A wry grin twisted his lips. "The only thing is, they're both so stubborn. They could have six younguns before that happens."

Patience laughed so loud, Gretchen frowned in her sleep. "I kinda doubt that, Ben," she said. "I'll bet you that come spring them two will be as lovey-dovey as a pair of matin' robins."

"I sure hope you're right." Ben stood out of the way as Patience lifted Gretchen's head and slipped a couple of spoons of medicine between her lips, then stood up. "I'm gonna run home for a while, Ben. I've got to milk my cow and feed my chickens." When alarm jumped into Ben's eyes she said kindly, "You can tend to her, Ben. Just make sure she don't kick the covers off. It's real important she keeps warm."

"Yes, you go on home. I'll keep a close eye on her. I won't leave her side."

Patience was almost home when she saw Trudie galloping her horse in her direction. They both reined in when they met. "What are you doin' out so early in the mornin', Trudie?" Patience asked. "And galloping that poor animal in this deep snow!"

Frowning at Patience's chastising, Trudie answered shortly, "I'm just out checkin' how much snow we got. What are you doin' out at this hour, and with your medicine bag? Who's sick?"

Like fun you're checkin' the snow, Patience said to herself. *You're on your way to Spencer's cabin. And ain't you gonna be fightin' mad when you hear that he's gonna be marryin' Gretchen and won't be dallyin' with you no more.*

In response to Trudie's question, Patience said, "I've been over to Ben's place. Gretchen got caught in the blizzard and has come down with pneumony."

Trudie gave a start, her hands tightening on the reins. Watching her, Patience saw the anger that flickered a moment in her pale eyes and wondered just how much this woman knew about Gretchen's getting lost.

"I suppose she had a hard time finding her way home," Trudie said casually.

"She didn't find her way home," Patience said. "Spence found her and carried her home." Something told her not to reveal that it was Trudie's own hired hand who had brought Gretchen home.

"I see," Trudie said, a tic working at the corner of her mouth. Without another word she brought her riding quirt down on the mount's flank, making it rear and whistle in pain. With a jerk of the reins, Trudie pulled the animal back down and turned its head in the direction from which she had come.

"I hope that poor horse tramples you to death someday, Trudie Harrod," Patience muttered as she urged the mule to move on.

Trudie slammed open her cabin door with such force, it banged against the wall. "Mammy, you old black bitch, where are you?" she yelled, slapping the braided quirt against her leg.

"I'm right here, missy." The black woman sat up on her pallet tucked in a chimney corner, her voice filled with dread as she stared at the whip.

Trudie strode across the floor and glared down at the cringing body. "How far out in the forest did you and Carter take that Ames girl?"

Mammy scooted away from Trudie until she was stopped by the wall. "Carter carried her deep into the woods, missy," she quavered. "A long way from the cabin."

"Well, he didn't take her far enough." The whip lashed across the elderly woman's shoulders. As Mammy rubbed her back, her eyes filled with pain, Trudie shrilled, "Spencer found her and brought her home."

Mammy hurriedly lowered her lashes so that Trudie wouldn't see the relief in them. She didn't even feel the welt that had risen on her flesh, she was so relieved that she and Carter hadn't been found out. She blessed whoever it was who had told the evil woman the lie.

"Get your black ass out of bed and pour me some coffee," Trudie ordered. "I've got some thinkin' to do. The little bitch has pneumony, so I might still be able to get rid of her."

Mammy scrambled off the pallet and followed the woman she feared with every beat of her heart. When she had poured the coffee, adding just the right amount of sugar and milk to it, she stood behind her mistress's chair, waiting for any other orders that might come.

Trudie was in a deep study as she sipped and stared out the window. Mammy wondered what evil she was cooking up in her head. It was something bad, she knew. It showed in the narrowed eyes and firmly clenched lips. She shook her head, thinking of poor Miss Ames.

Mammy narrowly avoided being knocked over when Trudie shoved her chair back and stood up. "Go fetch Carter to my room," she ordered, unbuttoning her bodice as she left the kitchen.

Carter was asleep when Mammy entered his room. It had been close to dawn before he returned to bed. He came awake with a start when Mammy shook his shoulder. He stared up at her, his eyes asking if Trudie had found out that he had taken the girl home.

"She doesn't know," the old woman hastened to assure him. "Someone told her that Spencer Atkins found her and took her home. Get up now. The bitch is in heat again."

Carter threw back the covers with a sigh of relief. He wasn't afraid that his boss would take a whip to him if he displeased her, but she had other ways of punishing him, as he had discovered.

Chapter Twenty-Two

Night had settled in by the time Spencer crunched through the snow to see the candlelight in the cabin window. He smiled. It was like old times, Pa leaving a light there to guide him home.

His face wore a look of weariness. It had been a tedious day, running his own long line, then his father's shorter one. His back was beginning to ache from the catch strapped to it. As he stepped up on the porch and removed his snowshoes, he hoped that Gretchen was better and that Ben had a gallon of hot coffee waiting for him. And that the old fellow had softened toward him somewhat.

He had just slipped the furry bodies off his back when Ben opened the door, the light behind him spilling out on the porch. "You look beat and half frozen, son," he said. "Hurry on into the fire and thaw out. I'll put supper on the table right away."

"How's Gretchen?" Spencer asked, shrugging out of his jacket, then tugging off his soaked boots.

"Her fever is mostly gone, but Patience said it's likely to rise with nightfall. She was conscious for maybe a minute once."

"Did she say anything?" Spencer half hoped she might have asked for him, but he thought it was more likely she would cuss him out.

"No, she just smiled at me and then drifted off again."

"I'll go take a look at her while you get the vittles on the table."

"Go ahead. I'll just be a minute or two."

Spencer sat down in the chair that had been pulled up to the bed. He leaned forward, his elbows on his knees, gazing at the face that was no less beautiful in sleep. Of course, the beauty would be added to when the greenish-hazel eyes were open and shooting fire at him in an argument, or when the red lips curved in a smile for Pa. He had been frantic last night when Carter brought her home more dead than alive.

What if she had died? he asked himself. Could he have borne losing her? He knew suddenly that it would have torn him apart.

You love her, don't you? his inner voice asked quietly, not taunting him as it usually did.

After a moment, Spencer answered quietly, "Yes, I love her. I don't want to, for she's gonna turn the life I'm used to livin' upside down."

But maybe it will be a kind of living you'll enjoy more than your old way. And don't forget, you're going to be a father.

"Yes, there's that." Spencer smiled and realized that he was looking forward to that event. He would try his best to be a good father; a father like Pa had been to him.

Spencer smoothed back a curl that had fallen onto Gretchen's forehead. "But will you want to marry me, Gretchen Ames?" He was pretty sure she wouldn't. It would take a lot of coaxing and reasoning to convince her, of that he was sure.

"The food's on the table, Spence." Ben stood in the doorway.

Spencer rose and stretched stiff, sore muscles. "She looks a lot better, doesn't she?"

"Yes, she does," Ben agreed, "but Patience says she's gonna have a long convalescence. She says that Gretchen has to eat a lot of meat to strengthen her, and drink a lot of milk to nourish the little one she's carryin'."

"She'll get all the fresh meat she can eat," Spencer said, "but I don't know about milk. I guess I'll have to go over to Patience's place every night after I get home and borrow some from her."

"You won't have to. Patience is bringin' one of her cows over with her tomorrow mornin'.

I hope I can remember how to milk one." Ben laughed as he led the way out of the bedroom.

When Spencer had dug into a bowl of beef stew Ben said, "While you're eatin', I'll take the catch down to the barn and flesh and stretch them."

"Are you sure your fingers are up to it?" Spencer asked with a concerned frown.

"I'm sure. They've been feelin' pretty good lately, since I haven't had to go out in the cold. When you finish eatin' go and sit with Gretchen. If I'm not back by eight, give her a couple of spoons of that stuff in the short glass on her table."

Spencer nodded and watched Ben pull on his fur-lined jacket. It made the old fellow feel good to do his share of the work, he knew. Then he didn't feel so useless.

Spencer had been sitting with Gretchen some fifteen minutes when she grew restless, tossing and turning, pushing at the covers. Was her fever rising again? he wondered. He leaned forward and placed his hand against her cheek to see if it was hot.

His body grew still and he barely breathed when she smiled and turned her face to nestle it in his palm. He wasn't sure, but he thought she murmured his name. At any rate, the feel of him seemed to calm her, and he left his palm under her cheek. As he stroked her hair with his other hand, he realized there was no stirring in his loins, no desire to climb into bed with her, to make love to her. He only wanted to take care of her, to make her well again. And to marry her.

An hour later, when Ben walked into the bedroom, Gretchen's cheek was still in Spencer's palm and he was sound asleep also, his head lying on the pillow, next to hers. He gazed at the sleeping pair, his eyes soft. He had almost given up hope, but at last his son loved a woman.

He moved to the bed and gently shook Spencer awake. "It's past time for Gretchen's medicine, son."

Spencer came awake, lifted his head, and gazed at Gretchen. "She's sleepin' so peacefully, it seems a shame to wake her up."

"I know, but Patience said it was real important that she get this every four hours." He held up the glass.

Spencer reluctantly eased his hand from beneath Gretchen's cheek and she immediately began fussing. It took longer than usual for Ben to coax her into drinking the herb tea. When he laid her head back down on the pillow she took turns railing out at Mrs. Fedders and Trudie. There was so much bitterness and anger in her voice, Spencer shook his head.

"She sure doesn't like those two women, does she?" He looked at Ben.

"And with good cause, I expect," Ben said.

"Do you want me to sit with her for a while so you can get some sleep? You look tired." Spencer looked at his father's haggard face.

"No, you go on to bed. You're half asleep on your feet. Anyway, Patience will be here around midnight to watch over her until daylight."

"We can't keep imposin' on Patience much longer, Pa. We're gonna have to get some woman to move in with us for a while."

"I reckon you're right. We'll have to put our heads together and think of someone."

Spencer nodded, and after taking a last look at Gretchen, he said good night and climbed the ladder to the loft room.

Three days later, near dawn, when the hired hand had left Trudie's bed and dragged himself to his own quarters, Trudie lay awake. Her troubled thoughts were on Spencer and Gretchen. Every day she had ridden over to Spencer's cabin and every time there had been no sign he had been there.

"Damn!" she swore explosively, whacking her fist into the pillow where Carter's head had lain a short time ago. She had to know what was going on. Had Spencer fallen in love with the curly-haired bitch, or had he moved home to run his father's traps?

Trudie sat up suddenly. An idea had struck her. She would send Mammy over to tend Gretchen Ames. The old woman could soon find out just what the situation was between the pair.

Trudie slid out of bed and began to dress. If she hurried, she could catch Spencer before he started out to run his traps.

She left the cabin, slamming the door, not caring if she awakened the black woman asleep on her thin straw pallet. In the barn she saddled her horse herself, something she rarely did. Carter was always there to do it for her. This time, however, she didn't want to waste the time it would take to awaken the hired hand.

A pinkish dawn was lighting the eastern sky when Trudie rode up to the Atkins cabin just as Spencer stepped out onto the porch, ready to strike out on his daily run.

"What in the blue blazes are you doin' out at this hour, Trudie?" He frowned at her.

"I wanted to catch you before you left this mornin'." Trudie slid out of the saddle and walked up close to Spencer. "It occurred to me that Ben might need some help nursin' Gretchen."

There was sarcasm in Spencer's voice when he said, "I can't see you helpin' out with Gretchen. You hate the girl."

"I don't hate her," Trudie denied. "I don't trust her. After all, she's a stranger to these parts."

"She's only a stranger to you. Everybody else likes and trusts her."

"Well, that may be." Trudie waved a dismissive hand. "I came over here in the cold to offer you Mammy's help as long as she's needed. The old hag is good at tendin' the sick."

"That's right kind of you, Trudie." Spencer's tone softened. "Patience is about wore out, sittin' with Gretchen nights. But Pa can't be with her night and day, and I have to run my line and his."

"I'll send Mammy over this mornin'." Trudie took another step closer to him and laid her hand on his chest. "I've been missin' you," she said softly. "When will you be comin' back to your cabin?"

"It's hard to say, what with things the way they are right now." Spencer wasn't about to tell her that he hoped never to return to his cabin again, that if things went the way he wanted them to, he'd be spending the rest of his life with Gretchen in the cabin he was born in.

"Well, I hope it's soon," Trudie whined as he stepped away from her, dislodging her hand. "It's been a long time since we've been together."

Hah, Spencer thought, *from the smell of you I'd say you're havin' no trouble finding a man to sleep with. Probably as recently as a few hours ago.* He said out loud, "Pa will be grateful for your mammy's help." With that, he stepped off the porch and took off down the snow-trodden trail.

Trudie stared after him, her face working furiously. Then, from the corner of her eye she saw the kitchen curtain move. She was being spied on by that hateful old Ben. She swore to herself. Then she turned and left the porch, walking over to her horse. Swinging into the saddle, she gave it a hard kick with her heel, and the animal galloped away.

"Still sniffin' after him, are you, you whore?" Ben said as the horse took Trudie out of sight. "It ain't gonna do you a bit of good," he said with satisfaction as he let the curtain fall back in place.

Trudie had worked herself into a rage by the time she returned home and walked into the kitchen. "Make me some breakfast, you lazy black bitch," she said to the cringing Mammy, "then bundle yourself off to the Atkins's place. You're gonna take care of Spencer's new whore while she's gettin' over her illness."

When the surprised black woman put ham and eggs and hot bicuits in front of her, Trudie said, "I want you to watch everything that takes place over there, listen to everything that's said between Spencer and that little slut. Then you report back to me. I'll meet you every other day at the edge of the woods just after dark. You can pretend you're goin' to the privy." She grabbed Mammy's wrist when the old woman started to pour coffee into her cup. "If you don't tell me everything that happens there, I'll flay every inch of black skin off your scrawny body."

"Oh, I will, missy." Mammy cowered away from her. She had felt the whip too many times.

"Good. Now get your duds together and get goin'." It took the old woman exactly five minutes to throw her spare dress and petticoat and a pair of wool hose into a sack, and add a broken comb Trudie had discarded. She pulled on her thin jacket and covered her head with an equally threadbare scarf.

"I'm ready, missy," she said, looking at Trudie, who was finishing her breakfast.

"Pour me a cup of coffee, then get goin'."

When the slave had refilled the coffee cup and stood uncertainly at the table Trudie looked up at her and asked crossly, "Well, what is it? Why are you still standing here?"

"Do I wake Carter up to saddle the mule for me?"

"You do not. You can walk. It'll do you good."

"Yeah, it will do me good," Mammy muttered to herself as she stepped out into the bitter cold and started the two-and-a-half-mile trip to the Atkins's cabin. "It can do me in, is what it can do."

Ben gaped at the black woman when he answered her knock at the door. *The poor old soul looks half frozen,* he thought. He took her arm and pulled her inside. "Get over here by the fire," he said, leading her to the kitchen fireplace, where the flames leapt cheerily, sending out heat that reached across the room.

He shook his head at the condition of her jacket as he helped her out of it, and noted that she wore no gloves and her shoes were broken, probably with holes in the soles. "What brings you out on such a cold mornin'?" He eased her down into the rocker he had just vacated.

"My missy sent me here to take care of your girl, Mr. Ben. She said I was to stay until Miss Gretchen gets on her feet." She looked anxiously at Ben. "Is that all right with you, suh?"

"It's more than all right, Miss . . . what is your name?"

"My mammy named me Pansy, but I ain't heard it spoke for many a year."

"Well, you're gonna be called Pansy while you're here, which will be a while. Gretchen will need a lot of tendin' to for some time."

"I'll just take over then, Mr. Ben." Pansy started to rise.

"No hurry." Ben pressed her back down. "Gretchen is sleepin' now. You just sit there and get warmed up while I fetch you a cup of coffee."

"Oh, I'll get it." Pansy started up again. "Ain't nobody ever waited on me before."

"Then it's time someone did." Ben pushed her back into the rocker again. "Have you had breakfast?" he asked as he took the coffeepot off the hearth. "I've got ham left over from Spencer's meal. It would only take a minute to fry you some eggs."

"Well, I didn't eat yet this morning. Missy thought I ought to get right over here."

"How many eggs do you want? Will two be enough?"

"Two will be plenty, suh, but are you sure you don't want me to cook them?"

"I'm sure. I ain't much of a cook, but I can fry eggs pretty good."

Later, as Pansy ate her breakfast and Ben sat with her, drinking a cup of coffee, he said, "Pansy, I'll make you a nice pallet in Gretchen's room. I'll put down a thick mattress of straw first, then one of feathers on top of that. Do you think you'll be comfortable? We ain't got no more beds."

Pansy thought of the thin pile of hay in the Harrod kitchen pricking her through its thin covering. To sleep on feathers seemed mighty grand to her. "That'll be just fine, suh."

Gretchen was just stirring awake half an hour later when Ben led Pansy into her room. Free of her fever now, her clear eyes looked questioningly at Pansy, then shifted to Ben for an explanation.

Ben sat down on the edge of the bed. "Gretchen, honey, this is Pansy. She works for Trudie. She's come to help take care of you."

"That's very nice of you, Pansy." Gretchen offered a hand that had grown thin during her illness. "I'm sure Patience will be glad to no longer make the cold trip here every night."

While Pansy was getting over the shock of having a white person offer her her hand in friendship, Ben began explaining to her what was in the two bottles on the bedside table and what their purpose was. "But she don't need the fever medicine anymore," he said, pointing to the short glass. "Just the one for chest congestion." He held up the other glass.

Pansy nodded her understanding, then smiled at Gretchen. "Are you hungry, child?"

"I believe I am." Gretchen was suddenly starving. "Do you think I could have something other than broth?" Her eyes twinkled at Ben. "I think I must have drunk a gallon of beef broth the past two days."

"That broth put strength back in you, missy." Ben's hand tousled her curls. "And it wasn't beef broth. The first day Spencer shot a deer and you had venison broth that night. And yesterday he brought home a rabbit. It made a fine pot of broth."

A ripple of pleasure ran through Gretchen. Spencer had done that for her? She vaguely remembered him talking soothingly to her, and the touch of his hand on her face. Her brow wrinkled thoughtfully. Maybe it had been a dream.

It was no dream when, after supper that night, Ben and Spencer came to her room and very soberly told her that she and Spencer would be getting married in the spring.

Chapter Twenty-Three

Gretchen could only stare at the two men and shake her head violently, crying, "No! No!"

"Now you just stop that," Spencer ordered curtly, his ego pricked that she didn't want to marry him. "You're gonna work yourself into a fever again."

"He's right, honey." Ben sat down beside her and took her hand in his. "It's the onliest thing to do."

"No!" Gretchen denied again vehemently. "You and I can raise the child, Ben. I don't need to be tied down to a carouser, a womanizer." Tears welled up in her eyes and rolled down her cheeks. "I always planned that someday I would meet and marry a man who would love only me, not need other women, a man I could love and respect."

"To hell with your plans, Gretchen Ames," Spencer said loudly, tired of her always calling him a womanizer. He was no worse than the average single man. Pride kept him from telling her that he hadn't been with a woman since his first time with her. It was true that he had tried, but nothing had come of it.

"Look, lady," he said decisively, "whether you like it or not, you're marryin' me come spring. No child of mine is gonna wear the name bastard no matter how high you may turn your nose up at its father."

While Gretchen was mulling over Spencer's ultimatum, seeing no way out of it, Ben said in conciliatory tones, "You wouldn't have to sleep with him. Just give the little one his name."

"Thank God for small mercies," Gretchen said stiffly.

Spencer's face tightened at her sarcasm. He glared down at her a moment, then spun on his heel and stalked out of the room, almost knocking over Pansy, who stood with her ear to the door.

"Well, honey, what about it?" Ben asked after the slamming of the door made them both jump.

With a sigh of resignation, Gretchen gave in. She could remember the many fatherless children at the poorhouse, how they had suffered from being teased and called bastard. She didn't want a child of hers to suffer that stigma.

"I guess it's the right thing to do, Ben," she said finally. "As you pointed out, it doesn't have to be a real marriage. Spencer can carry on like he's always done."

"I think you're gonna be in for a surprise, Gretchen," Ben said. "I think Spencer will be true to the vows he's gonna make come spring."

Gretchen didn't respond, but inside she was thinking that when rivers ran upstream, Spencer Atkins would mend his ways.

Outside the bedroom door, Pansy, who had resumed listening, curved her lips in a wide smile. Trudie Harrod was going to have a conniption when she heard this piece of news. She looked forward to telling the brutal woman, even though she would probably feel the lash of the whip for relaying the news.

Gretchen felt as weak as water as she sat on the edge of the bed while Patience fussed with her curls, brushing out the tangles that five days in bed had brought about.

She looked down at her hands folded in the lap of her best dress, the one she had worn to the cornhusking party. In another hour or so she would be the unloved wife of Spencer Atkins.

It had been a surprise to the whole community when it was discovered that the traveling preacher, Reverend Applegate, had been caught in the blizzard and had all this time been holed up at Widow Russel's place. No one would have ever known he was there had not an inquisitive Indian peeked through heavy curtains that hadn't been drawn tight and seen the man sitting in front of the widow's fire. He had told Slim Peters the next day, and Slim had passed the surprising news on to Spencer.

Tonight, Spencer hadn't taken the time to eat his supper, in his hurry to ride the ten miles to the Russel place and bring the preacher back with him. Patience, who had stopped by to check on Gretchen, had just been leaving when Spencer arrived after running his traps, and had agreed to stay and witness the marriage. Ben, of course, would be his son's witness.

Gretchen bit her lower lip, thinking of the years stretched ahead of her, years in which Spencer would break her heart over and over. Her husband-to-be was wild-spirited and would never change his ways for a woman, much less for one he didn't care for. He would never become the sort of husband she had dreamed of having someday.

She had thought, had hoped, that in the months before spring she might be able to convince Ben that a union between her and his son could only lead to bitter unhappiness for them both, that there had to be a better way if they just thought about it hard enough. She knew in her heart that this marriage would never be in name only. This attraction they had for each other, the desire that flared up every time they were around each other would have them making love as soon as she was over her illness. This babe she carried now would have a new sister or brother regularly. All conceived in lust.

A ragged sigh escaped her as the little inner voice sympathized, *But there will be love on your part.*

"What was that big sigh all about?" Patience asked, finally satisfied with the way the chestnut curls now lay loosely on Gretchen's shoulders. "It sounded like it came all the way from your toes," she teased. "You're supposed to be makin' dreamy sounds, not like you're ready to break out in tears. You're marryin' the man every single female in these hills has tried to trap at one time or the other."

"Trapped. I'm sure that's the way Spencer feels." Gretchen looked up at her friend. "You know as well as I do that if I wasn't carrying his baby, he wouldn't be marrying me."

"That may be," Patience said as she walked across the floor and placed the brush back on the dresser, "but I'd bet my old mule that given time that old bachelor would be beggin' you to marry him. I've seen the way he looks at you."

"Well, we'll never know now, will we?" Gretchen said dully.

"Oh, honey, stop fussin' about it. You're gonna have a fine marriage, you'll see." Patience smiled down at her. "You're the prettiest bride these hills have ever seen, or likely to see again. Spencer is gonna be so proud of you tonight."

Gretchen's only rejoinder was a wan smile. Patience didn't know Spencer like she did. He might have changed his mind on his way to fetch the preacher.

Then the sound of the front door opening and the lively voices of men brought a leap to Gretchen's heart. She had detected Spencer's deep, rich voice.

"Now get that sad look off your face," Patience ordered, "the preacher is here."

Gretchen calmed her face and straightened her shoulders, her gaze going to the door, waiting to see what expression would be on his face. If he looked like he would like to be a hundred miles away, or that he was going to his own execution, she'd pretend to faint and go into a decline.

But Spencer was smiling as widely as Ben when they trooped inside, the stern-faced preacher following them. Gretchen had never met the Reverend Simon Applegate, of course, but she had heard of his hell-and-brimstone sermons. When Ben introduced the man to her she felt that he could see straight to where her baby rested beneath her heart.

There was a nervous impatience about the preacher, and Patience helped Gretchen to her feet. Spencer quickly came to stand beside her, supporting her with an arm around her waist. She was glad to lean against his strength. Patience and Ben took their places as witnesses, and Applegate opened his Bible.

Five minutes later, Spencer was slipping the wedding band he had purchased from Jacob onto her finger. She was now Mrs. Spencer Atkins. The edgy preacher didn't say the usual "You may kiss the bride now," but Spencer cupped her chin and, lifting her face, kissed her warmly on the mouth. Then, even as she was still thrilling to the touch of his lips, he eased her back to sit on the bed again. Before she knew it the men had left the bedroom and Patience was pulling the dress over her head and helping her into a nightgown. She lay back down and Patience tucked the covers around her. Pansy came and smiled down at her.

"You married a fine man, Miss Gretchen," she said. "He's going to make you very happy."

Gretchen's lips curved in a wry smile. Why did everyone keep saying that? she wondered. Could they see something in Spencer that she couldn't? All she could detect about him was desire in his eyes and biting sarcasm in almost every word spoken to her. Not in her wildest dreams could she see him making her happy.

"Miss Patience, if you don't mind, I'm steppin' outside a minute to get some fresh air while you're here," Pansy said.

"Of course, Pansy, go right ahead. I wish Gretchen could do the same. It would put some color in her cheeks."

I'm sure glad she can't, Pansy thought as she left the room. Trudie would be waiting for her, and the woman wasn't going to like it at all when she was told about the wedding that had just taken place. For sure tonight she would feel the bite of the whip her mistress wielded so freely, and in her rage she might even attack Miss Gretchen if she were there.

"Did Pansy seem nervous to you, Gretchen?" Patience asked when she sat down to visit with Gretchen a while before leaving.

"I didn't notice. I'm a little nervous myself tonight."

"Maybe I just imagined it." Patience shrugged and began telling Gretchen what little had been going on with their neighbors since winter had set in.

Reverend Applegate had left, and Ben had gone to the barn to work on Spencer's catch when Pansy entered the main room of the cabin, where only Spencer sat before the fire. He offered to walk with her when she made known her intention of getting some fresh air.

"That won't be necessary, Mr. Spencer," Pansy hurried to say. "I'm just going to walk around in the yard."

When Pansy started to walk toward the barn Trudie hissed in the darkness, "Over here." When Pansy made her way to the dim outline of the horse Trudie asked impatiently, "Well, what's been goin' on since the last time we talked?"

The black woman braced herself for the sting of the whip as she answered, "Mr. Spencer and

Miss Gretchen got married about twenty minutes ago."

There was a frightful silence for a full minute, in which Pansy held herself in readiness. Then, with a screech of rage, Trudie lashed out at her, the whip coming down across her bony shoulders. "Why didn't you stop it, you black bitch?" she screeched irrationally, and brought the whip down again.

When Pansy yelped in pain the enraged woman came to her senses. The nervous horse danced while she sat staring thoughtfully into the darkness. "Meet me here tomorrow night," she snapped at last, then, giving the mount a vicious jab with her heels, she whirled him around and he lunged into the blackness of the forest.

Pansy stared at the spot where Trudie had disappeared, pure hate in her eyes as she fingered the welts rising on her flesh. When was that woman going to pay for her wickedness? she wondered as she made her way back to the cabin. And what did she have in mind for that sick girl lying in bed?

Pansy was thankful to find the kitchen empty when she pushed open the cabin door. Mr. Ben was probably still out in the barn, and she could hear Mr. Spencer's voice in Gretchen's room. She needed to be alone, to compose herself. She hurriedly changed into her thin nightgown, flinching when the material rubbed against the lash marks on her back and shoulders. She pulled on an equally thin robe and sat down, waiting for Spencer to leave his new wife's room. With Miss Gretchen still ill, she doubted that they would share the same room, at least not tonight.

Patience was just leaving when Spencer walked into his old room. "I didn't get to congratulate you before, Spence," she said, smiling at him, "so please accept my best wishes now. Your little wife will bring you a lot of happiness through the years."

"Thank you, Patience," Spencer said soberly, his face showing nothing of what he might be thinking. "Shall I ride home with you? The wolves are probably out by now."

"No need for that, Spence. You've got to be dead tired. My rifle is tied to the mule and I know how to use it." She gave him a mischievous grin. "Anyway, it's your wedding night. I'm sure you want to spend some time with your bride."

If Spencer heard Patience's last remark he didn't let on. After a moment of strained silence Patience said to Gretchen, "I'll stop by to see you in a couple of days." When Gretchen smiled and nodded Patience said good-bye and left, closing the door quietly on the pair, who avoided each other's eyes.

He is so handsome, Gretchen had thought when Spencer stepped into the room. He had dressed up for the wedding and he looked so different in black woolen trousers, with a white shirt and a black string tie. His longish hair had been carefully brushed and his face was cleanly shaven. She blushed when she found herself wishing that he would disrobe and climb into bed with her.

Spencer had thought when he entered the room and saw her chestnut curls spread out on the pillow that no woman should be so beautiful. He remembered then that she hadn't wanted to marry him, and pride and anger held him in their grip.

He slid her a look from mocking eyes and drawled, "Well, Mrs. Atkins, how does it feel bein' a married woman?"

Gretchen wanted to cry out, *Can't you ever speak to me in a normal way? Must you always mock, use hateful tones?* Aloud, she said, "Never mind how *I* feel. How do you like being a married man?"

"Me? I feel no different than I did this mornin'. A few words spoken by a preacher don't change anything."

"Exactly." Gretchen lowered her lids so Spencer couldn't see how his words had wounded her. "My feelings haven't changed either."

She couldn't see the pain that leapt into Spencer's eyes, but she heard the coolness in his voice when he said, "That's good. I can continue my life as usual, then." He said a clipped good night and left the room.

When Pansy entered the room to go to bed on her thick pallet Gretchen's slender form was shaking with silent sobs. As she prepared to go to sleep Pansy shook her head at the foolish ways of white people. It was plain that missy and her man loved each other, but neither would admit it.

Chapter Twenty-Four

"No!" Pansy gasped, the pale moonlight showing the shock on her wrinkled face as she put her hands behind her back. "You know what that special kind of honey does to a person, missy. You fed it to your pappy until he died from it."

"Shut up, you old hag!" Trudie exclaimed, slapping Pansy hard against the mouth. "Do you want to tell them in the cabin? Now you take this and get half a teaspoonful down her every other day. After a couple of weeks give that amount to her every day for a week. Then don't give her any for a week. I want this done slowly so that no suspicions are aroused."

Pansy continued to shake her curly head. "I can't do it, missy. I can't do murder."

Trudie grabbed her arm and twisted it back

and up between her shoulder blades. "Listen to me, you black bitch, if you don't do as I say, I'll write a letter to my uncle asking him to sell your son to another plantation, and his wife to one a hundred miles away. I will also suggest that your pretty little granddaughter would make a fine bed-warmer for one of his sons."

Pansy's short-lived spirit died as Trudie heaped threats on top of her. "I'll do it," she said, and took the jar that was thrust at her.

A triumphant smile curved Trudie's lips as she swung into the saddle and with a flick of her whip sent her mount springing away.

With bowed head and slumped shoulders, Pansy returned to the cabin, the jar of honey hidden in her apron pocket.

For a while Gretchen felt a little stronger each day that passed, and she began to spend a little time out of bed. But she always made sure that she was in bed when Spencer returned from running his traps. It hurt her to look at him. His face had grown thin from the weight he had lost and his beautiful gray eyes no longer sparkled. He was miserable, she knew, tied to a marriage he didn't want.

Her spirits were low also. Her mirror showed the purple shadows under her eyes, put there from the lack of restful sleep. Each night her body cried out for his, and many times she thought of climbing the ladder to the loft room, to crawl into bed with him, to be folded into his arms.

She never had, of course, and he hadn't given the least hint that he would like to visit her bed. But she was pretty sure he wasn't going anywhere else for comfort. He returned home each evening at the same time, ate his supper, came to her room, and politely asked her how she was feeling, then left. A minute later she would hear his footsteps in the loft, then the squeak of the four-poster as he stretched out on it.

How would it all end? she asked herself wearily, staring up at the ceiling. It seemed such a long time ago that she and Ben had had the cabin to themselves, with no strain on their emotions. Even Pansy acted strangely these days. The woman avoided her eyes and mostly spoke in monosyllables, spending her time in the kitchen.

Gretchen could see through to the kitchen, where Pansy was preparing her a bowl of pudding, a dessert the old woman had started giving her a few days back. It was delicious, with just a hint of honey in it, and she looked forward to it every evening. She pushed herself up in bed when Pansy brought it to her.

After she had eaten a couple of spoonfuls of the creamy mixture she looked at Pansy, standing at the foot of her bed, and asked, "Aren't you happy staying with us anymore, Pansy? Do you want to go back to Trudie? I'm sure I can manage the cabin and cooking now." She thought for a moment that she saw fear leap into the old slave's eyes, then told herself she had imagined it. Why would the woman be afraid to go home?

Pansy's answer assured her she had been mistaken. "Oh, no, Miss Gretchen. I like it fine livin' here with you and your men. It's just that sometimes I get to thinkin' about my kinfolk back in the Carolinas, wonderin' how they're makin' out. I gets lonesome for them sometimes."

Pity and surprise came into Gretchen's eyes. It hadn't occurred to her that this black woman had a family somewhere; sons and daughters, grandchildren, maybe even a husband.

"Would you like to talk about them?" she asked Pansy, who waited patiently for her to finish eating the pudding. "How big a family did you leave behind when you came to Kentucky?"

"Two daughters and one son and ten grandchillen." Pansy sat down in the chair pulled up beside the bed. "I never got to see much of my girls and their younguns. They was sold to a plantation several miles away down the river. But Massa Harrod kept my boy. Claudie was big and strong and could work in the cotton fields. When he was sixteen missy picked out a big, strong wench for him and they jumped over the broom, then moved into a shanty of their own.

"The woman was about ten years older than my boy, but she was a good breeder. Missy was right pleased when she dropped a big, healthy baby boy ever' ten months." A dullness came into Pansy's eyes. "They was two little girl childs born, too, but missy sold them as soon as they was weaned. It was a sad time for us."

What sort of hellish woman was Trudie Harrod? Gretchen asked herself, her eyes wet. How could she take another woman's child and sell it like one would a puppy? And, my God, how could Spencer have anything to do with a heartless woman like that?

She reached over and gripped Pansy's folded hands. "Maybe someday you'll see your children again, Pansy," she said softly. "Maybe you'll go back to the Carolinas."

Pansy shook her head, a deadness in her eyes. "No, I'll never go back there again." The finality in her words led Gretchen to wonder if there was a good reason for Trudie to stay away from her home. She wondered why a woman used to the comfortable life of a plantation would exchange it for the rigorous one of frontier Kentucky. The reason must be pretty awful, she imagined.

Pansy became more her usual self after her conversation with Gretchen, even though Gretchen sometimes thought she was forcing herself to talk and laugh as she used to. Twice she had heard the old woman crying softly in the night. Gretchen told herself that Pansy was having a bad dream, and when she bent over her to awaken her, the sobbing stopped.

Two days later, Gretchen had something else to wonder about. Every time she stood up she was gripped with a weakness that almost made her dizzy. She didn't say anything about it at first, blaming the incidents on her previous illness. She probably wasn't fully recovered from her bout with pneumonia. The strange thing about it, though, was that after a couple of days she would recover and feel almost her old self.

One morning, on one of her better days, Gretchen was sitting in the main room of the cabin, working on a sweater she was knitting for Ben, when the outside door opened and Trudie strode into the room. Gretchen dropped the needles and, ignoring an amiable greeting, demanded shortly, "Have you come for Pansy? She's in the kitchen."

"I'm not here to get Mammy," Trudie replied sharply. "I'm here to give you some home truths."

Gretchen recalled all the cruel things this woman had done to Pansy. There was contempt in her voice when she said, "I doubt that I'd be interested in anything you'd have to say."

An angry flush stained Trudie's face. "You'd better be interested in what I say, you little bitch, for what I'm gonna tell you will fetch you down from your high horse."

Her arms akimbo, her hands planted on her ample hips, the angry woman glared down at Gretchen as she ground out, "You might have managed to marry Spence, but he'll never be yours. It's me he'll always belong to. Do you think for one minute that he's stopped seeing me? Well, he hasn't. He stops by my cabin every day when he's runnin' his traps. When you get over your illness he'll move back to his cabin and we'll be together again."

Pansy stared at Trudie in disbelief. The woman wasn't satisfied that the young girl was dying by inches; she had to torture her mind as well. She thanked God when she saw Ben coming from the barn. Missy wouldn't carry on with him around.

She stepped into the room and warned, "Missy, Mr. Ben is comin'." Trudie glared down at Gretchen a second longer, then wheeled and slammed out of the door. Pansy took one look at Gretchen's white face, then quietly turned and went into the kitchen.

Gretchen rose and walked to her bedroom, where she lay on the bed in agonized silence. She was too hurt and stunned even to cry. Everything was happening as she had thought it would. Why was she so surprised? Why did she feel as though her heart had been torn from her body?

She heard Ben enter the kitchen and say something to Pansy, and she closed her eyes, feigning sleep. One look at her face and he would know that something had happened. He wouldn't let up questioning her until he had the whole story out of her. Then he'd tear out of the cabin in a rage, going straight to Trudie's place, and God only knew what he'd say to her.

The sleep Gretchen pretended turned into the real thing. When she awakened it was dark outside, but inside someone had entered her room to light the candle on the bedside table. As she lay, staring out the small window, dreading seeing Spencer when he got home, the door opened and Ben walked in.

"Well," he grinned, "you're finally awake. Pansy has supper on the table. Spencer ain't home yet, but we're too hungry to wait for him any longer. I hope he's all right. He's never been late before."

Her eyes bleak, Gretchen could have told Ben where his son was. He was dallying with the woman he couldn't seem to stay away from. She slid off the bed, smoothed the wrinkles out of her skirt, and followed Ben into the kitchen.

Spencer had good reason for being late. Someone had been tampering with his traps. When he found the first one sprung he blamed a dead limb falling from a tree and hitting the trigger. But when he found a second, and then a third, he knew no accidents were involved. It was the work of a man. He started looking for tracks other than his own on the snow-trampled trail. He soon found them, and he walked a little faster, determined to catch up with the scoundrel.

At the sixth trap, also sprung, the footprints left the trail, heading toward the Ohio a short distance away. A black scowl marring his forehead, he followed them to the river and wasn't surprised at what he found there.

A canoe had been pulled up on the bank, then later it had been pushed back into the water. He had no way of knowing whether the man had paddled upstream or down. Spencer shook his head in confusion. There was a lot he didn't know. For instance, at what hour had the man done this dastardly act? It could have been at any time. He could be an hour ahead of Spencer, or he might have followed him yesterday morning, springing the traps right behind him.

Who would do such a thing? he asked himself as he tramped from one trap to another. Who of his acquaintances disliked him so much they would interfere with his livelihood? To rob a man's traps was almost a hanging offense here in the hills.

He still hadn't the slightest notion who his enemy was when he saw the candle burning in the kitchen window. He was over an hour late, and he hoped Pansy had kept his supper warm.

As Spencer stepped up on the porch and slid the furs off his back, he wondered why Pansy was still living with them. Except for an occasional weakness, Gretchen was almost back to normal. She had no need of further nursing.

As he pushed open the door and stepped inside the kitchen, he concluded that the black woman was in no hurry to go back to Trudie's harsh treatment.

His first glance at Gretchen, just finishing up her supper, told him that her mood wasn't the best. What had happened in his absence to bring that cool, aloof look to her face? he wondered as he washed his face and hands at the workbench. After he had dried off and had given his hair a couple of sweeps with a brush he sat down at the table in a chair opposite hers. Giving her a wide smile, he said, "Boy, I'm beat."

"I'll just bet you are," Gretchen snorted scornfully. Rising to her feet, she swished out of the kitchen.

Spencer looked quizzically at Pansy, but the black woman wisely kept her mouth shut, only shrugging her shoulders.

He looked down at the plate of roast beef and mashed potatoes Pansy had set before him, his face showing the strain of loving his wife and her showing no sign of loving him in return.

It was too early for Gretchen to go to bed, especially after the long nap she had taken. But she wasn't about to spend time with Spencer tonight. Nor any other night, probably.

They had gotten into the habit of spending an

hour or so with Ben in the big room each night after supper when she was up to it. She enjoyed listening to the father and son converse, sometimes voicing an opinion of her own on some subject that was being discussed. Although she felt Spencer's eyes on her almost constantly, he never had much to say to her directly.

Gretchen walked into her room, closed the door, and picked up some knitting. Immersed in the work, Gretchen didn't hear Spencer approach her door, lift his hand to knock, then let it drop. She didn't hear him walk away, nor the heavy sigh that escaped him when he eased his tired body into the rocker in front of the fire.

"You still up, son?" Ben asked on his return from the barn, where he had stretched and pegged down thirty prime pelts. "I figured you'd be sound asleep by now."

"I want to talk to you," Spencer said as he put another log on the fire.

"What about?" Ben asked as he took his pipe and pouch of tobacco from the mantel.

"Someone has been messin' with my traps." Spencer sat down. "I found six tripped today."

"The hell you say? You got any idea who would do such a thing?"

Spencer shook his head. "I've racked my brain and I can't think of a soul."

Ben puffed thoughtfully on his pipe, white clouds rising and wreathing around his head. "Have you thought about Trudie Harrod? She's bound to be pretty dad-burn angry with you right now."

"No, it's a man's tracks. Much too big to be a woman's."

"She's got that hired hand of hers. He'd do it if she told him to."

"No, the tracks led to the river, where he had a canoe waitin'."

"That don't mean nothin'. He could paddle downriver a few miles, beach the vessel, then hightail it across the woods to Trudie's farm."

"That's a possibility," Spencer said after a while. "Trudie is a spiteful bitch. If it happens again, I'll check up and down the river for a piece, see if there's any sign of a canoe landing."

When Ben knocked his pipe out on the hearth, signaling that he was getting ready to go to bed, Spencer said, "Gretchen acted a little strange tonight. Do you have any idea why?"

Ben shook his head. "I didn't notice any difference in her. She took a long nap this afternoon. Maybe she was just groggylike."

"Maybe," Spencer answered, but he didn't think an afternoon's sleep would make Gretchen cool toward him. He sat a while after Ben said good night and retired, staring moodily into the flames.

Chapter Twenty-Five

When close to a month had passed and Gretchen continued to have spells of weakness and dizziness, each attack leaving her weaker and weaker, Spencer and Ben became quite concerned. She had lost considerable weight, and her eyes seemed too large for her narrow little face.

And if that wasn't enough for Spencer to have on his mind, his traps were still being tampered with. Not only had traps been sprung, several had disappeared altogether. But what angered him the most was that a lot of his catch was being pilfered now. It had crossed his mind in the beginning that maybe a young boy had tripped his traps as a prank. But he had to conclude now that a grown man, with a grudge against him, was out to ruin him financially.

He still had no idea who it could be. He had walked for miles, first upriver then down, looking for the place where a canoe had been pulled up on the bank. He had found nothing. He returned home later and later each night. He had even slipped out of the cabin after everyone was asleep to try to slip up on the man who was his enemy.

Spencer was mistaken in thinking that no one knew when he left the cabin at night. Gretchen, a restless sleeper now, knew every time the outside door opened, then quietly closed. Tears would well up in her eyes and run down her cheeks. Her husband was on his way to visit his lover, to give to her what he wouldn't give to his wife: love and affection.

She had given up hope that Spencer would ever have those tender feelings for her. Her chances had been slim when her body had some curves to it, but now that she was nothing but skin and bones, Spencer would never feel anything but scorn for her.

She swiped at the tears that were beginning to wet her pillow. Sometimes she wanted to give up the battle against the unknown malady that was stealing her strength away. It would be easier to give in to it, to let it take her. She was so tired of the vomiting, the confusion of her mind that happened so often. Sometimes she thought she was back at the poorhouse, sleeping under the eaves, miserably cold beneath her thin blanket. There had been times when she had confused Patience with Mrs. Fedders and had fought her hands away when she was trying to bathe her. She laid her hand on the slight bulge of her stomach. Was her sickness affecting the baby? She prayed that it wasn't. She wanted this baby very badly. It was the one thing that kept her hanging on.

"She don't look at all good, Ben," Bessy Crawford said when she left Gretchen's room and walked into the kitchen.

She and Deke had only learned yesterday, from one of Big Otter's braves, about Gretchen's illness. The young Indian had stopped by their home, hoping he would be offered some cookies.

As usual, Bessy set out a plate of the sweets, and their guest had volunteered, "Spencer Atkins's woman is sick. It is said around the campfire that she will die."

"Die?" Bessy and Deke exclaimed in alarmed unison. "Die from what?"

"Big mystery." The Indian reached for another cookie. "Even the herb-and-root woman don't know. The big trapper's wife is just fading away like day into night."

"We must get over there right away, Deke." Bessy jumped to her feet. Taking a small cloth bag from a shelf, she dumped the remaining cookies into it. "Here." She pressed the bag into the Indian's hand. "Take these with you," she said as she ushered him to the door.

Twenty minutes later the Crawfords were on their way to their favorite neighbor's cabin. Soon Ben Atkins was nodding his head at Bessy's worried words.

"Yes, she's bad sick, Bessy." There was a quaver in his voice. "Patience has tried every concoction she can think of, and nothin' seems to help. The onliest thing we can do now is to keep feedin' her good, strong broth and pray a lot."

"She'll have mine and Deke's prayers too." Bessy patted Ben's arm. "We're mighty fond of the girl."

"How is Spence holdin' up under the threat of losin' his wife?" Deke asked.

"Not too good, I'm afraid. For the first time in his life my son has come up against somethin' he can't set straight. Gretchen's sickness is tearin' him apart inside."

Bessy shrugged into her jacket and motioned her husband to do the same. "We gotta get goin' home, Ben. Let us know if there's anything we can do for you folks. Anything at all." When Deke squeezed his shoulder Ben realized that in all the time the Crawfords had been there the garrulous man hadn't said a dozen words.

When he closed the door behind his visitors he looked at Pansy, sitting before the fire. As he passed her to take the other chair, he said softly, "I know that you pray for Gretchen, too, Pansy." He gave her a startled look when she covered her face with her hands and broke into loud sobs. He hadn't known the black woman had grown so fond of Gretchen.

That evening Patience arrived at the cabin shortly before Spencer did. Strapped on his back was half the catch he usually brought home. Nearly a third of his traps had either been destroyed or, most likely, thrown into the Ohio.

But the loss of traps and revenue wasn't what made his broad shoulders sag and his steps slow like those of an old man. The fear of losing Gretchen was aging him, taking its toll on his body.

When he saw Patience's mule tied up outside a mixture of fear and hope rushed through him. Had she been sent for because Gretchen had grown worse, or had she come because she had a new herb she wanted to try on Gretchen?

When Spencer pushed open the door his gaze went straight to Ben, dishing up a bowl of stew from the pot hanging on a crane. Ben read the question in his eyes.

"She's about the same, I reckon. Patience just came by to check on her."

As Spencer washed up at the workbench, Ben told him of the Crawfords' visit. When Spencer went and sat down in front of the fire, nodding to Pansy, who sat on the hearth, Ben asked, "Ain't you hungry, son? You gotta eat. We can't have you both sick."

"I'll wait until Patience comes out, hear what she has to say." He stretched his cold feet to the fire.

Patience entered the kitchen shortly after that and sat down at the table. "I'll have a cup of coffee, Ben, if you don't mind," she said gravely. When Spencer came and sat down beside her, her hand on his trembled with desperation. "I'm sorry, Spence," she said gently, "but I don't find her to be any better." She waited a minute, then said after a ragged sigh, "I'm afraid she's gonna lose the babe."

Spencer and Ben caught their breath and Pansy began to cry. Then Spencer choked out, "What about my wife? Am I to lose her too?"

Patience squeezed his shaking hand. "I won't lie to you, Spence. I truly don't know. She's fightin' hard to stay alive. All we can do to help her is to continue what we've been doin'."

Spencer stood up and left them, going to his wife's room. He sat down in the chair beside the bed and took her thin hand in his. It was cold, and he gently stroked it with his other hand, willing his warmth and strength to penetrate the almost transparent skin. He gazed at her pale face, framed by her chestnut curls, and the long lashes fanned out on her cheeks.

His love and fear for her twisted his insides. "Don't you dare leave me, Gretchen Atkins." His voice was low and tortured. "I don't know if I could face a world that didn't have you in it."

His heart gave a leap when her lips curved in a faint smile. Had she heard him? Had his words pleased her? He began to stroke her hair, saying all the things that were in his heart, things he hadn't been able to say before. As he poured his heart out, she relaxed and seemed to fall into a natural sleep.

When Ben entered the room an hour later with a bowl of stew for Spencer, he was still talking gently to Gretchen.

"That's the first restful sleep I've seen her have in a long time," Ben said, placing Spencer's supper on the small table. "I think she likes havin' you near her, talkin' to her."

"I think she does, Pa." Spencer smiled at his father, elation in his eyes. Maybe he had helped the woman who was his whole world. He picked up the fork and dug into the stew. "You talk to her, Pa, while I eat."

Ben sat down on the other side of Gretchen. Stroking her hair with his knobbed and crooked fingers, in his aged, cracked voice he told her of the deer he had seen in the meadow, digging through the snow to the summer grass below. He told her of the wolf den he had found, and of the three cubs that were inside it, and how he had brought one home and had it in the barn, so that when she got better she could tame it. He told her that Bessy and Deke had been to visit her, and Gretchen's lips curved slightly when he said that for once Deke had hardly opened his mouth.

Ben and Spencer grinned at each other when they saw that slight smile. Gretchen was listening to them; she understood what they were saying. They raised their heads and listened as, from the kitchen, they heard Slim Peters's hearty voice.

"I'll go see what that fool wants." Ben stood up. "And tell him to speak in a normal tone of voice."

Spencer stopped eating and took up where Ben had left off. He didn't want Gretchen drifting away from them again.

When Ben returned to the room half an hour later Gretchen's cheek was nestled in Spencer's palm and his head lay next to hers. Both were sleeping soundly. He hated to wake his son, but if he slept in that awkward position much longer, he'd have an awful crick in his neck. Besides, he had some news for him.

"Wake up, son." Ben gave Spencer's shoulder a little shake. "You're gonna break your back, layin' that way."

"I hate to disturb her, she's restin' so easy." Spencer eased his hand from under Gretchen's cheek and straightened up. He stretched his stiff muscles, then asked, as he massaged his neck, "What did Slim want?"

"He said to tell you that he's gonna run our traps for a few days so you can spend more time with Gretchen. Said he was also gonna keep an eye out for whoever's been messin' with your traps."

"Slim's a good friend."

"He tells me that the other trappers are keepin' an eye peeled for that polecat too."

"I sure as hell hope they have more luck than I have," Spencer said, then yawned widely. He looked down at Gretchen, who had begun to stir restlessly and mutter plaintively. "I'm gonna sleep with her tonight, Pa," he said. "Havin' someone close seems to calm her."

"I think you should," Ben said gruffly. "I think you should have been doin' that from the day you got married. I never saw two people more stubborn and prideful than you two. I'll tell Pansy to sleep in the loft room from now on."

Spencer was climbing out of his buckskins as Ben left the room, leaving the door partly open so the heat from the fireplace would help take the chill out of the bedroom. He walked around the bed and carefully got under the covers. Moving slowly so as not to awaken Gretchen, he curled his body around hers and carefully lifted her head to lie on his shoulder. When she gave a contented sigh he drew her closer, his hand possessive on the small bulge his baby made beneath her heart. Finally, he had his wife in his arms.

Somewhere on a distant, snow-covered hill a wolf raised his head and bayed at the moon as Spencer fell into a deep, exhausted sleep.

Chapter Twenty-Six

The moon had gone white and dawn had almost arrived when Spencer jerked awake at Gretchen's sharp cry. "What is it, honey?" He jerked up in bed and leaned over her.

In the candle's glow Gretchen's face was contorted with pain, her eyes dull with it. She had drawn up her knees and was massaging and holding her stomach. He threw back the covers, then groaned deep in his throat. His wife lay in a pool of blood. She was losing their baby.

"Pa! Pansy!" he yelled, dragging on his buckskins.

Ben was in the room almost immediately, still in his long johns. He took one look at Gretchen's pain-twisted face, and the blood on the sheet, and said, "I'll go fetch Patience."

"Ride my stallion and take the mare with you," Spencer called after him. "The mules are too slow."

"What is it, Mr. Spencer?" Pansy came hurrying into the room, wearing her worn robe. When Spencer answered, big tears ran down her wrinkled cheeks.

"Let me examine her while you go tear a sheet into strips," she managed to say. "I'm gonna have to pack her, stop the bleeding."

Spencer hurried away and Pansy gently lifted Gretchen's gown up around her waist. Her tears increased as she saw that Spencer's fears were well founded. The beautiful, gentle girl had lost her baby, and she was hemorrhaging badly. It would be a battle to stop the flow.

"Fetch me some towels," she said over her shoulder as Spencer came rushing in, clutching a handful of muslin strips. He tossed them on the bed, then, at a half run, he hurried to bring the towels. Pansy hadn't said how many, so he took all five that were folded neatly on a kitchen shelf.

Back in the bedroom again, he looked over Pansy's shoulder and made a sound not unlike that of an animal caught in one of his traps. The baby he and Gretchen had made together was no more.

"Lift her up so's I can get this sheet from underneath her," Pansy broke into his grief.

Spencer carefully lifted the light weight of the slight body, willing her to live. Pansy whisked off the sheet and made a thick pad out of the towels and placed it in the middle of the mattress.

"You can lay her down now," she said softly, seeing the agony in Spencer's eyes. When Spencer had done as ordered Pansy began to pack the strips against the trickle of blood seeping onto the towels. Spencer watched, sick to his soul. In her already weakened condition, his wife couldn't afford to lose much more blood. When he heard the rapid drumming of hooves he hurried through the cabin to fling open the kitchen door. Patience would save her for him.

The sky was just turning a bluish pink as Ben and Patience swung out of the saddle. Spencer stepped aside as Patience, her medicine bag clutched in her hand, rushed past him. "Put a kettle of water on to boil," she ordered as she disappeared into the room.

Ben looked at Spencer, afraid to ask the question that burned in his eyes.

"She still lives, Pa, but she lost your grandchild," Spencer said over the lump that formed in his throat.

The next hour passed in a blur for Spencer as he heated kettles of water and made teas from herbs and ginseng roots. He held Gretchen's head against his shoulder, forcing her to drink the bitter liquids while Patience worked feverishly to stop the flow of blood. Ben and Pansy huddled in the kitchen, out of the way, Ben praying and Pansy crying into her apron.

A pale dawn had peeped through the bedroom window when Patience straightened up with a wide smile. "I've got it stopped, Spence." She placed her hands on the small of her back and stretched, loosening stiff muscles. "I'm gonna go tell Ben the good news and have a cup of coffee with him before I go home." At the door she paused and added, "I'll send Pansy in to put a fresh gown on Gretchen and change the bed." She looked at the bundled-up, bloodstained sheet that held the aborted baby. "Ben can bury it next to its grandmother."

Spencer nodded, his eyes wet.

To everyone's surprise and thankfulness, Gretchen's health began to improve. Three days after losing her baby, she was sitting propped up in bed, eating solid food for the first time in weeks. Slim Peters was still running Spencer's traps, and Gretchen's husband seldom left her side. He continued to sleep with Gretchen, holding her snuggled in his arms. He was never bothered by arousal; just holding her was enough for now. Genuine smiles for each other had replaced the mockery and cynicism that had peppered their relationship before.

Even Gretchen's suspicion that Spencer had been spending time with Trudie Harrod was laid to rest when the other woman came calling under the pretense of seeing how Gretchen was coming along. She had blatantly tried to flirt with Spencer, dropped hints, alluded to things that had happened in their past. But the dislike for the woman that glittered in her husband's eyes was too real to be pretense.

Gretchen couldn't help giving Trudie a smug look as she laid a possessive hand on Spencer's arm.

Hatred had flashed in Trudie's eyes and she left soon after that, ordering Pansy to walk with her to her mount. Gretchen and Spencer looked at each other and burst out laughing. They knew that Trudie had heard them by the way the door slammed behind her.

Out of hearing distance of the house, Trudie came to an abrupt halt. She grabbed Pansy's arm and gave it a cruel twist. "Have you run out of honey, old woman, or have you stopped giving it to that little bitch? She should be dead by now."

Pansy choked back the cry of pain that rose to her lips. "I just couldn't go on givin' it to her, missy. She lost the baby she was carryin', and I couldn't bring myself to do more murder."

"Well." Trudie dropped the thin arm and started to walk away. "In that case I'll get a letter off to my uncle tomorrow."

"Oh, no, missy, don't do that." Pansy ran after her, despair in her voice. "Don't separate my boy from his family."

"All right then." Trudie swung around. "Are you gonna continue with the honey?"

Pansy drew a long breath and nodded her head, her shoulders drooping in defeat. Trudie gave her a gloating look, then strode to her mount and swung into the saddle. Pansy watched her ride away, wondering why God would allow such evil to walk the face of the earth.

The night after Trudie's visit, Spencer walked into the bedroom carrying a cloth-wrapped package. He put it on the bed beside Gretchen, and as he sat down, he said, "Do you know that Christmas has come and gone and we weren't even aware of it?"

"Are you sure?" Gretchen put aside her needlework, placing it on the table.

"I'm sure. Today is January the fourth." He nudged the package with his hand. "Open your Christmas gift."

A Christmas present. A pensive look came into her eyes as she pulled the package into her lap. She hadn't received such a thing since she was ten years old and had received a doll from her parents. Tears rushed to her eyes, blinding her so, she couldn't see to undo the string that held the wrapping together.

"I didn't mean to make you cry," Spencer said. "Maybe I should take it back."

"Don't you dare." Gretchen brushed at her eyes. "Just untie it for me."

When Spencer laughingly slipped the knot and bared the gift Gretchen gasped her delight. "Spence it's beautiful. Where did you get it?"

She held up a bright red lacy shawl.

"I had Patience knit it for me. She worked on it the nights she sat up with you." Spencer stood up and, taking the garment from her, said, "Let's put it around your shoulders and see how it looks."

He draped the light woolen covering around her shoulders, crossing the points over her breasts, then pulled her curls free to rest them against the shawl.

"You are so beautiful, Gretchen," Spencer said huskily.

"I'm glad you think so, Spence." Gretchen smiled at him, then quite naturally leaned forward to kiss him for his gift.

What was meant to be a mere brushing of the lips quickly became something else. As though they acted on their own, their lips clung together as if they had hungered for each other for a long, long time. A muffled groan escaped Spencer's throat and, unaware of his actions, he moved to sit on the edge of the bed and drew Gretchen into his arms. The kiss deepened, and Gretchen's arms crept up around his shoulders as the shawl was crushed between them.

When Spencer finally broke off the kiss and lifted his head both their faces were flushed and their eyes glittered with the need for each other.

Breathing heavily, Spencer slid back onto the chair, telling himself that Gretchen was too weak to carry their aroused passion to its natural conclusion. *Her fever could come back, for God's sake,* he told himself. He fought the wild desire, and when it slowly died away he stood up and said in a husky voice, "I think I'll go down to the barn and curry our mounts. They've been lookin' pretty shaggy lately."

"We'll be eating supper soon," Gretchen reminded him, then smiled as Pansy walked into the room. "You've brought me my pudding again," she exclaimed, looking at the small bowl Pansy carried. "I've missed it these past few days."

"How come me and Pa never get any of that?" Spencer teased as the black woman placed the dessert in Gretchen's lap, then handed her a spoon.

Pansy gave him a nervous smile and mumbled that he and his pa weren't as weak as kittens.

As Spencer walked down the snow-rutted path to the barn, he found himself whistling. He hadn't been this happy in a long time. He felt strongly that Gretchen returned his love. Certainly their desire for each other was still as strong as ever. That was more than a lot of married couples had. Many of his married friends complained that their wives seldom wanted to give them comfort.

But as he entered the barn, Spencer knew that he wanted more than passion from Gretchen. He wanted her love. He wanted her to like him, to trust him. His hopes were high, however, that the passion Gretchen had for him would turn into love.

When everyone but Gretchen had gathered at the table the roast beef that Pansy had prepared was eaten with relish. Spencer's and Ben's appetites had returned with Gretchen's steady recovery. But when Spencer carried his coffee into the bedroom to drink with Gretchen while she sipped at one of Patience's herbal teas, he found that she had eaten very little of the beef, mashed potatoes, and vegetables.

"Don't you like your supper?" He frowned down at the plate where the food had been pushed around.

"I'm not very hungry tonight," Gretchen answered. "Maybe the pudding killed my appetite."

"Maybe." Spencer nodded, then reached over to lay his palm on her forehead. Was it a little warmer than usual, he wondered, or did he imagine it because he was so afraid that the fever would return?

He straightened up and removed the plate of cold food from Gretchen's lap. "If you get hungry later, I'll bring you another plate. In the meantime, make sure you drink all your tea."

"I will." Gretchen obediently raised the cup to her lips.

Spencer finished his coffee and went to the window to draw the heavy curtains against the night air that somehow managed to creep through the tightly constructed cabin. When they were partly closed he paused and peered through the darkness. In the dim light of the kitchen candle he watched his friend Slim Peters climb off his horse. He imagined his friend was here to tell him that it was time he took over his traps.

"Slim has just arrived," he said, going to the door. "I'll see what he wants, then come right back." Gretchen smiled and nodded.

Spencer walked into the kitchen just as Ben answered Slim's knock on the door.

"Well, what brings you here, Slim?" Spencer greeted the tall trapper with a wide grin. "You tired of doin' my work for me?"

"You have lazed around for a while." Slim grinned back, leaning his rifle against the wall, then taking the chair Spencer pulled away from the table.

"Have you had supper?" Spencer asked before taking a seat himself.

"Yes, I had a bowl of venison stew at the post. But I wouldn't say no to a cup of coffee."

When Pansy had filled a mug for him and he had taken a long swallow, Slim leaned back. Looking at Spencer, he said, "I found out today why you haven't been able to catch the bastard who's out to ruin you."

Spencer leaned forward, an intense glitter in his eyes. "Tell me."

"The no-good copperhead has been paddlin' across the river. That's why we haven't been able to find any trace of his landin' on our side."

"Who in the hell would think he'd do that?" Spencer asked sharply. "The Ohio is close to half a mile wide and full of undertows in the center. What gave you that idea?"

"I had just come upon another of your traps that had been broken and this time I saw fresh footprints leadin' to the river. I hurried up and followed them, and sure enough, when I came to the river there was marks on the bank of a canoe being shoved into the water. While I stood there, lookin' up and down the river, hopin' to see the cur, I happened to look out across the water and saw a man paddlin' a canoe as fast as he could."

"I don't suppose you could tell who it was?"

Slim shook his head. "He was too far away."

"I wish I knew who in the hell he is, and what I've ever done to the man."

"Can you think of any man you've fought with, got the better of?" Ben asked, "or one that you've taken a woman away from?"

"The answer is no to the woman part. I've always been careful not to do that, but the culprit could be someone I've tangled with at the rendezvous. He could be holding a grudge against me."

"Hell, that could be any number of men." Slim grinned. "You're always comin' back from them meetin's with bruised knuckles."

On a more serious note, Slim said, "I've been talkin' to some of our friends about this. We've decided to paddle across the river and flush the bastard out. I marked in my mind just about where he intended to land. He's probably camped in one of the caves over there."

"That's damned decent of you, Slim," Spencer said with heartfelt thanks. "I'm goin' with you, of course."

"No, you're not." Slim finished his coffee and stood up. "You're gonna stay here with your wife. Three of us can easily take care of the sneakin' skunk."

"That don't hardly seem right," Spencer began, but Slim already had the door open and was stepping outside. Spencer stood, torn between going with his friends and staying behind with his wife.

When he returned to Gretchen he was thankful Slim had talked him out of crossing the river. Her fever had returned.

There was only the light of a half moon when Slim and his friends, Steph and Ivan, pushed their canoe into the Ohio, then jumped into the boat. The opposite shore was just a vague outline when Slim picked up the paddle and dipped it into the river and sent the vessel skimming across the water. The shoreline of trees shortly took shape, and a few minutes later the nose of the canoe edged up to the bank. It made no noise as it was pulled across a patch of untrampled snow.

Almost immediately, Ivan spotted a dim light through the trees and, nudging Slim, he pointed it out. Walking single file, in less than three minutes they came upon an old, dilapidated cabin. Slim motioned to Steph and Ivan to wait while he slipped up to the door and listened for sounds inside. A grim smile appeared on his face when he heard the noise of someone making supper. He waved to the men to join him, then pushed open the warped and buckled door.

"Stay right where you are," he ordered the man bending over the fire, turning a piece of meat in a banged-up skillet.

When the man gave a startled jerk, then went still, Slim moved his gaze around the room. Did the man have a companion? It was a temporary dwelling, he saw, having only the barest of furnishing. And what there was must have come from a trash pile back of some farmer's barn. Slim noted the table with a broken leg, a stick of wood replacing it, a straight-backed chair with part of the back missing, and a crudely made bunk bed with leaves and pine needles serving as a mattress. Two gray horse blankets acted as the bed covering.

Slim's eyes found a pile of traps in a corner. "Spence will be glad to see these, huh, men?" he said grimly.

"Who are you, and what do you want?" a not-quite-steady voice demanded.

"Never mind who we are. The question is, who in the hell are you?" Slim asked in a cold, dangerous voice. "Turn around and let us have a look at you."

There were sounds of surprise, then Slim swore under his breath. "Arthur Grundy," he rasped. "We should have known. We thought you went back to St. Louis."

"I did, but as you see, I'm back." Grundy looked like a cornered rat as his hand dropped to the knife at his waist. "That son of a bitch Atkins caused my brother's death, and I'm gonna make him pay for it."

"Like hell you are." Slim took a menacing step forward. "You've done all the dirt you're gonna do to Spencer."

"Oh, no, I ain't." Grundy took a step back. "I ain't even begun yet. I'm gonna ruin his trap line, then I'm goin' after his wife again. I almost got her once in old Ben's barn, but Atkins came along and beat me senseless. He won't get me the next time around. I'll get her someday when he's not around."

Slim narrowed his eyes at the raving man and was satisfied that Grundy's determination to get revenge on Spencer had driven him out of his mind. Why else was he foolish enough to think he could whip three men?

"Why don't you just pack up and go back to St. Louis, Grundy?" he said quietly, trying to calm the man. "You've done enough to Atkins. You've got your revenge."

"Like hell I have." It was plain Grundy wasn't going to be reasonable. "I ain't nearly finished. But I see I have to take care of you three first."

He jerked his knife free from its sheath and lunged at Slim. His weight brought the trapper to the floor, and they rolled around, each trying to get on top as they slashed out with their knives. Slim finally managed to grab Grundy's wrist and twist it until the knife dropped from his fingers. He jumped to his feet and, grabbing Grundy by the hair, hauled him to his knees. As Grundy glared at him, he drew back his fist and sent it flying between the hate-filled eyes. The maddened man's head jerked back, and when Slim released him he crumpled to the floor. His nose was bleeding and both eyes were beginning to swell shut.

Spencer's friend stood over him, his breath coming in pants. "If you're still here tomorrow I'll burn this shack down." His voice was like the lash of a whip. "Folk around here don't hold with a man robbin' another man's traps. They'll hang you from the highest tree they can find."

When Slim and his companions left they felt satisfied that the man still had enough sense to go back where he came from.

Chapter Twenty-Seven

Gretchen's labored breathing filled the room.

Spencer, his head in his hands, sat beside the bed while Ben and Patience stood at the foot, watching the slow rise and fall of her chest. In the minds of all three was the question: Would she live until morning?

Three weeks ago, when her mysterious illness had returned, Gretchen had grown steadily weaker, her mental confusion worsening. She was no longer aware of what was happening around her and she recognized no one.

No longer able to listen to his wife fight for each breath, Spencer jumped to his feet and ran out of the cabin. In the gray February dawn he ran and ran until he could run no more. He stopped and stood on a hill, yelling his despair to the sky. On a distant hill a lone wolf pointed his nose and yowled back in sympathy.

Spencer dropped to his knees in the snow, and in a voice raw with grief he prayed to the God he had almost forgotten. "Please let her live, God," he said over and over. He stayed there on his knees, unmindful of the cold seeping into his flesh, until the sun rose. He stood up then and made his way back to the cabin, afraid of what he might find.

When he pushed open the cabin door Patience was pouring a cup of coffee. She looked at his shivering body and said gently, "She's still with us, Spence. Sit down and get a cup of hot coffee in you. You look near froze."

"I'll go see her first," he said, his tone dead.

"Go ahead. I'll bring the coffee in to you," Patience said, then turned her head toward the door, listening. "I hear a wagon coming." She looked at Spencer in surprise. "Who could be comin' so early in the mornin'?"

She walked over to the window and looked out. "Why, it's the Crawfords with Bessy's brother and his wife and a woman I never saw before."

When Spencer opened the door for them Bessy said anxiously, "Slim Peters stopped by last night and said that Gretchen was sinking fast. Matty and Will and Callie just got in, and we hurried right over. How is she, Spence?"

"She's still hangin' on," Patience answered for Spencer. "Take off your jackets and come on in to her bedroom."

Callie stood in the doorway as the Crawfords and Smiths walked over to the bed. She was a stranger to this household, knowing only Spencer Atkins, who had killed her husband and freed her from a life of hell. When she suddenly began to smell a sweet odor she hadn't smelled in a long time, she stepped forward and looked down at the wasted body of the young girl.

"Who's been tendin' your wife?" She looked at Spencer.

"Mostly Pansy, a black woman loaned to us by a neighbor." Spencer looked at her inquiringly.

"Would you call her in here, please? I'd like to ask her some questions."

"I'm here, Mr. Spencer," Pansy said from the doorway, her eyes uneasy and red from weeping.

Callie looked at her and demanded, "What have you been feeding this girl?"

"Just regular food," Pansy said, her hands beginning to shake. "The same like the rest of us eat."

"Nothin' else? No special dishes just for her?"

"No, ma'am."

"You give her puddin' every night with honey on it," Ben reminded Pansy.

"Oh, yes, I forgot about that," Pansy muttered, and she began twisting her hands together.

"Come in the kitchen and show the honey to me."

"It's just plain honey. Mr. Ben had it in the kitchen when I first come here." Pansy made no move to leave the room.

"I'll take a look at it anyhow," Callie said in a determined voice.

Pansy seemed to shrink as she turned back toward the kitchen, everyone crowding in behind her. They all watched curiously as she took a jar off the shelf and handed it to Callie.

Callie took the cover off, smelled it, then placed it on the table and began looking through all the other jars and tins on the shelf. "Aha," she exclaimed after a minute, bringing forth a small jar hidden behind a can of bacon grease. She uncovered the container, sniffed at it, then looked at Pansy with cold, accusing eyes.

"Where are you from, woman? The Carolinas?"

"Yes, ma'am." Pansy looked down at the floor.

"Mr. Atkins," Callie said, "this is what is killin' your wife."

"What is it?" several voices demanded.

"Mad honey."

"Mad honey," Ben barked the word. "What in blue blazes is mad honey?"

"It's a poisonous honey made from the nectar bees collect from wild rhododendron and mountain laurel. It comes from southern areas, particularly the Carolinas. It causes vomiting, fever, and a weakening of the limbs.

"The effect from eating this honey once or twice is rarely fatal, but if a person is fed a daily dose of it over a long period of time, that person just wastes away."

Pansy wilted under the accusing eyes swung her way. She began to wail and wring her hands. "Why, Pansy?" Spencer clenched his hands to keep them from going around the woman's neck. "What did Gretchen ever do to you that would make you want to kill her?"

"I didn't want to, Mr. Spencer," Pansy sobbed. "God knows I didn't, but Missy Trudie said that if I didn't, she would see to it that my son's wife and chillun would be taken away from him and he'd never see them again."

She grabbed Spencer's arm and continued in a desperate voice. "I just couldn't stand the thought of that. She sold two of my daughters away once, and I knew it wouldn't bother her in the least to do the same thing to my son." Her eyes streaming tears, she gazed up at Spencer. "Trudie Harrod is evil. She even killed her pappy with the mad honey."

"I'll kill the bitch, so help me, I'll kill her." Spencer's eyes glittered with such rage Pansy shrank away from him.

"You can take care of her later, Spence." Patience laid a hand on his arm. "Right now let's see if we can do anything that will help Gretchen cling to life." She looked at Callie. "Do you know of any remedy that will rid her system of the poison?"

"Pansy," Callie asked, "when did you give her the honey last?"

"Night before last," Pansy quavered.

Callie led the way into the bedroom and looked down at Gretchen's thin, white face. "Child," she said gently, "being too weak to swallow has maybe saved your life. But you're gonna swallow for me and Patience."

She looked at Patience and said, "Her body should have lost most of the poison by now, so what we've got to do is keep gettin' your herb teas down her, and as much gingseng tea as we can. 'Sang is real healin' for one who has been sick for a long time."

"And somebody keep bringin' us pails of snow to bathe her in," Patience added. "We've got to get that fever down."

Everyone was bustling around then, Ben hurrying to get the snow and Bessy hustling her husband and relatives out of the room. "We'll be back later, Spence," she said. "We're only in the way right now."

Spencer nodded. "I'll always thank God that you brought Callie here, Bessy. We'd have lost my wife if she hadn't recognized what was wrong."

"He does work in mysterious ways, don't He?" Bessy squeezed Spencer's arm and followed the others out of the room.

In the next hour Patience brewed her different teas while Ben and Spencer rubbed the snow over Gretchen's face and body. Her skin was so hot, it melted the snow on contact, keeping them busy mopping up the water. Spencer held Gretchen up against his shoulder when it was time to get more tea down her. Sometimes he had to pinch her nostrils closed so that she would open her mouth.

It was early in the afternoon when Gretchen's skin began to cool a bit. Patience looked across the bed at Spencer, a wide smile on her face. "I think she's gonna make it, Spence."

Spencer picked up Gretchen's thin hand and held it to his lips, his eyes wet. "Thank you, God," he whispered. "And thank you, too, Patience." He placed Gretchen's hand back down and tucked it under the covers. "I don't know what I'd have done without you."

"You owe most of your thanks to Callie West," Patience said. "I've never heard of mad honey."

Spencer nodded, then stood up, purpose in his eyes. "You're goin' after Trudie now, aren't you, Spencer?" Patience read the grim look in his eyes. "You're not really gonna kill her, are you? She needs killin', I admit, but don't soil your hands doin' it. Have a meetin' with our neighbors, see what they recommend."

"I'll try to keep my hands off her, Patience, that's all I can promise. But she's got to get out of these hills. I don't want her within a hundred miles of Gretchen."

Pansy reached the Harrod farm half an hour before Spencer did. When she entered the kitchen and walked through to the main room she found Trudie and Carter lying on the rug in front of the fire, both bare of clothing. She knew by their heavy breathing and the relaxed look on their faces that they had just finished coupling. The hired hand blushed a dark red and sat up, reaching for his clothes. But Trudie shamelessly remained sprawled on her back, an arm thrown over her head.

"What are you doin' here, Mammy?" She narrowed her eyes at the slave. "Why ain't you back at the Atkinses' doin' what you're supposed to be doin'?" She sat up then, a hopeful glint in her eyes. "Or is the bitch dead?"

"It's all over, missy." Dread looked out of Pansy's eyes. "They know all about the mad honey."

"What do you mean, they know all about it!" Trudie jumped to her feet. "Did you tell them, you stupid bitch?" She grabbed Pansy's arm and gave it a cruel twist.

"No, missy, no!" Pansy grimaced in pain. "A woman who used to live in the Carolinas came visitin' and recognized what was wrong with Miss Gretchen. She looked in the kitchen and found where I had the honey hidden."

"What did Spencer say?" Trudie released Pansy and began to hurriedly dress.

"He said he was gonna kill you. I think he meant it."

Fear was plain in Trudie's small eyes. "Carter, go saddle my horse," she ordered in a shaky voice. "And, Mammy, pack me some grub and be quick about it."

"Where will you go?" Pansy followed Trudie to her room. "You can't go back to the Carolinas. The law is lookin' for you there."

Trudie wheeled on Pansy, her hatred for the woman scorching the slave's face. "Do you think I would tell you, you turncoat? You'd blab it to Spencer as soon as he got here. Now go get that food together before I take my whip to you."

While Trudie got dressed in heavy clothing and packed a small bag, Pansy hurried to throw food into a haversack and Carter stood in the barn in deep thought.

Trudie would want him to go with her, he knew, if for no other reason than to appease the lust she was never free of for long. And that trapper would catch up with them eventually. Would he remember that it was Carter who had saved his wife from freezing to death, or would he, in his fury, kill them both?

He walked past the stall that held Trudie's horse and saddled the mule in the next space. Within five minutes he and the mule were headed across country, going west. *Let the bitch die,* he thought. *She deserves it after what she tried to do.*

Barely ten minutes had passed before Trudie entered the kitchen and Pansy handed her the grub sack. She jerked open the door and ran toward the barn. Pansy watched her through the window, praying that Spencer would arrive in time to end the life of the woman who had made her life a misery ever since she could remember.

"Carter," Trudie yelled as she entered the barn. "Where's my horse? Why ain't you got him saddled?" She stopped in front of the animal's stall, not believing that it wasn't ready to be mounted.

"Carter," she yelled again, "get this horse saddled!"

It was then that she noticed that the mule was gone and realized that her farmhand was gone. She called the man every vile name she could think of as she tugged the saddle off its peg and lugged it over to the horse's stall. When she entered the enclosure the animal sensed her fury and began sidling away from her.

"You devil, stand still," Trudie ground out and brought her quirt down across his flank, laying open the skin. The horse screamed his pain and reared up on his hind legs. As he brought them down, his hoof caught Trudie on the shoulder and knocked her to the floor. Furious, Trudie lashed out at the frightened animal again, catching him on the tender underbelly. Filled with pain and terror, he tried to get away from the lashing whip that continued to flay him. He reared again and again, each time coming down on the woman who had mistreated him ever since he came into her possession.

Spencer was only yards away from the Harrod barn when he heard the screaming of human and beast. When he came to a galloping halt Pansy came running from the cabin. "What's goin' on?" he asked the wide-eyed slave.

"I think maybe missy has whipped that poor horse once too often. I think he has finally turned on her."

"I reckon she was tryin' to get away from me," Spencer said as he swung to the ground. Pansy nodded. "Where's the man Carter?" he asked, walking toward the barn.

"He left as soon as I got here and told missy that you knew everything. But you mustn't blame him for anything." Pansy hurried after Spencer. "He never knowed what missy was up to."

"I got no beef with the man. He saved Gretchen's life once."

"I know that. When Missy Gretchen came knockin' on our door that blizzardy night, near frozen, Missy Trudie wouldn't let her in. She ordered that Missy Gretchen be taken deep into the forest to freeze to death. But Carter took her home to you."

Spencer became enraged all over again, hearing for the first time what had really happened that night. "Oh, the poor animal," Pansy gasped as they stopped in front of the stall. The horse stood with drooping head and heaving sides. Blood trickled from a dozen whip cuts on his dark hide.

At his feet lay the inert, crumpled body of his mistress. Spencer didn't need to examine Trudie to know that she was dead.

"Poetic justice," Spencer muttered, then led the trembling horse outside. As he talked soothingly to him, he patted snow on his cuts until most of the bleeding had stopped. Spencer looked at Pansy, standing beside him, and said, "I'll send a couple of men over to bury her. In the meantime, rub some salve on this poor animal's wounds."

"What about me, Mr. Spencer?" Pansy looked up at him as he mounted his stallion, her eyes full of worry.

Spencer looked down at the aged slave, and all his anger at her drained away. She had been at the mercy of that witch all her life. Trudie's threats and beatings had driven the slave to do her bidding.

The hardness of his face softened a bit as he answered, "There will be a meeting to decide what should be done to you. Meanwhile, keep on livin' here." He lifted the reins and, with a nudge of his heel, sent the stallion galloping toward home and his wife.

Chapter Twenty-Eight

A week passed in which Gretchen steadily improved. Her brow remained cool and her beautiful eyes were clear. She still tired easily, however, and the neighbors who came calling were only allowed to spend a short time with her.

Bessy and Deke Crawford came often, their relatives having returned to Squaw Hollow. But Deke was only allowed to stand in the doorway of the bedroom and ask Gretchen how she was feeling. Ben would nudge him into the kitchen right away. In his opinion, five minutes of Deke's nonstop talking would make Gretchen have a relapse.

Spencer had gone back to running the few traps he had left and wasn't home the day the Gradys and Ellie Allen came calling. Gretchen was amazed at the change in Collin. He was relaxed, he smiled often, and he talked almost as much as Deke did. His eyes seldom strayed from Ellie, and he never looked at his mother unless she spoke to him. And whatever her gripe was—for the woman never had anything pleasant to say—he brushed it away as of no importance.

Gretchen studied Mrs. Grady through her lashes. The woman had always worn a sour look, but today she looked like she had eaten a green persimmon, her face was so puckered with disapproval of how her son "acted the fool" over the delicate-looking girl a strong wind could blow away.

Gretchen suspected there was steel in those slender bones. She smiled to herself. Ellie was also wily. She had managed to seduce Collin, and in so doing she had released him from his mother's stranglehold on him for all time. She had changed him into a man who no longer jumped when she gave him an order.

Later, when good-byes were said to Gretchen, the three joined Ben in the kitchen to have coffee and cookies. Ben slid a mischievous look at Agatha as he asked, "When are you two gonna tie the knot?"

Collin and his mother spoke at the same time, Agatha snapping that there was no hurry and Collin saying, as he took Ellie's hand, "The end of this month, just before spring arrives."

"It's gonna be a little crowded in your cabin, ain't it?" Ben said slyly, watching Mrs. Grady from the corner of his eye. "Your place only has two rooms, after all. You'll be underneath each other's feet night and day."

"There'll be no problem," Collin said. "I've been buildin' Ma her own cabin these past six weeks. About a mile down the road from the home place."

Agatha made a choking sound, and Ben and Ellie exchanged tickled glances. Mama Grady didn't like that at all. When Collin said, "I'll have it ready for Ma to move into in another couple of weeks," Agatha jumped to her feet, saying crossly, "Don't you think it's time we go home and do the chores?"

Ellie glanced out the window, then looked at Collin. "We've got plenty of time to visit with Ben a little longer." She gave him a flirty look as she said, "I'll help you with the milkin'."

Collin smiled at Ellie and reckoned they could stay a little longer.

If eyes could truly spark fire, Agatha's came close to doing so as she plopped back down in her chair, and she didn't open her mouth during the rest of the visit.

Gretchen was nicely tired when her company left her. She scooted down until her head rested on the pillow and then closed her eyes. The drone of voices in the kitchen soon lulled her to sleep. It was dark outside, and a candle had been lit in her room when she awakened. She smiled and reached her arms up to wind around the broad shoulders that hovered over her.

Spencer's head descended and his lips took hers in a tender kiss. He didn't dare deepen it. As it was, he had gone around all day in a half-aroused state. Gretchen was still much too weak to make love. If she only knew the hell he went through, holding her in his arms every night, not even so much as touching her breasts, let alone doing anything else.

When he lifted his head and stroked a hand down her cheek Gretchen whispered, "Ummm, you smell nice. Like pine and out-of-doors."

"You smell more than nice." Spencer smiled down at her. "Your hair smells like roses. It's silky too." He ran his fingers through her curls. "It feels like it used to before your illness."

Gretchen scooted up in bed until her back rested against the headboard. "Pansy came over early this morning and washed my hair with a bar of Trudie's soap."

Her lips turned up at the corners, and Spencer asked, "What are you smilin' about?"

"At something Pansy said while she was here. She swears that the birds won't sing within a mile of where Trudie is buried and that the snow has melted for several yards around her grave. She firmly believes that the fires of hell that are burning Trudie have reached up through the ground."

Spencer gazed speculatively at the candle flame a moment before saying, "I've heard that slaves are very superstitious, but sometimes they are right in their thinkin'."

Gretchen shivered. "I know I'm not going within five miles of that evil woman's grave."

Spencer didn't say so, but he made the same silent vow.

Gretchen picked up his hand and held it. "When are you going to decide on what to do about Pansy? I probably shouldn't, but I feel sorry for her. She's so worried about what's to become of her. She has nowhere to go if she's sent away."

"I'll go to the post right after supper and talk with the men. We'll come up with somethin' " Gretchen looked like she was going to put her arms around him again and Spencer hurriedly rose. He wasn't made of stone, he told himself. One more of those hungry kisses and he'd be crawling in bed with her even though he shouldn't.

Spencer pushed open the side door to the tavern and looked through the haze of smoke at his friends lined up at the bar. They were laughing uproariously at something one of them had said. He hadn't been one of the group for weeks, and it was hard to believe that he hadn't missed their company—that he now preferred staying home with his wife.

Maybe I'm getting old, he thought with a crooked grin, then he called out a greeting to the drinkers.

Slim made room for Spencer to join them. "How are you, Spence?" Jacob Riely boomed, slapping a bottle of whiskey and a glass in front of him. "How's Gretchen?"

"She's comin' along fine now, Jacob. She's still weak as skimmed milk, but improvin' every day."

"It's a shame she lost your babe," one of the trappers remarked.

"But there will be others." Slim slapped Spencer on the back at the bleak look that came into his eyes.

"That Trudie sure got what was comin' to her," someone else spoke up. "I saw that poor horse of hers. You wouldn't believe how she laid the whip on that animal."

"What happened to her hired man, the one who couldn't talk? I ain't seen him around lately," Jacob said.

"He lit out for parts unknown." Spencer tipped the whiskey bottle over his glass.

"He didn't go very far," Slim said. "He didn't get any farther than the Mott farm. He's livin' with them."

"That's sure surprisin'," the man on the other side of Spencer spoke up. "I didn't think Ira would let another man get near his two women."

"Didn't you hear?" Slim said. "That bastard is dead. Caught pneumony and died within four days." He gave a short laugh. "I don't reckon he got much help from his womenfolk. His sister-in-law sure wasn't cryin' when she told me that Carter arrived just in time to dig a hole and pitch ol' Ira in it."

"They might have cried tears of joy," someone said, and the men laughed.

"Anyhow, Carter has moved in with that brood," Slim continued. "Took a shine to Elvira, accordin' to her. Said they was gettin' married."

"What about the black woman?" Jacob asked. "Did she leave too?"

Spencer shook his head. "She's still at the Harrod farm. That's why I came in tonight. I want to talk to you all so you can help me come to a decision about her."

When several seconds of silence went by Jacob asked, "What's your feelin's on it, Spence?"

"Well, when I first learned what she had tried to do to Gretchen I wanted to kill her. Then, when I learned how Trudie had forced her to do it by threatenin' to have her grandchildren and daughter-in-law sold, I cooled down. All my spleen was directed at Trudie then. If her horse hadn't killed her, I'm afraid I might have. At least I would have maimed her."

"If you chased the old woman away, where would she go?" Jacob wondered. "Could she go back to her family in the Carolinas?"

Spencer shook his head. "Gretchen says she couldn't. Like Pansy, her son is a slave. It would be up to the plantation owner whether or not she could live with her son. And since she's so old, the man wouldn't want her."

"I reckon she's right sorry for what she done," Slim mused out loud.

"She couldn't be sorrier," Spencer agreed.

Jacob swiped thoughtfully at the bar. "I can't see turnin' her out in the cold to freeze to death. I'm thinkin', what if we brought Carter and his new brood over to the Harrod farm to live with Pansy? After the way the bitch treated them both I think it's only fittin' that they get her farm."

"Now that's a dandy idea!" Slim slapped his hand on the bar. "What do you think, Spence?"

"Sounds good to me," Spencer answered and, Pansy's future decided, he said good night to his friends and headed home to a night of frustration. He didn't know how much longer he could continue to just hold Gretchen in his arms.

March arrived, and the ice in the river started breaking up. Huge chunks floated down the river, making it life-threatening to venture out in a boat or on a canoe. Gretchen had steadily improved and was up most of the day, sometimes taking a nap in the afternoon. The cabin took on her feminine touch again, and every night she had a mouth-watering supper waiting for Spencer when he got home.

But it wasn't food for his belly that Spencer wanted. His desire for her was raw in his eyes every time he looked at her. It didn't help matters to see her own need for him answering back.

Then, one night he walked into the cabin and sent Gretchen a wicked look that made her heart flutter in her breast. She knew that look well. It was the same devilish one he had always worn just before he started his seduction of her.

Why tonight? she wondered, the same old excitement curling in her stomach. She had been ready two weeks ago . . . well, actually, she had been ready long before that, but her body had still been mending.

What Gretchen didn't know was that her husband had visited Patience on his way home. Nervously shifting his feet on the woman's floor, he had tried to ask her some pertinent questions relating to his and Gretchen's love life. Patience had secretly grinned her amusement at his stumbling, stammering questions and finally took pity on him.

"I think it's high time you put yourself out of your misery, as well as Gretchen's," she said.

Spencer had smiled so widely and thanked her so profusely, one would have thought that she had just told him he wasn't going to die at sunrise.

Ben tried to keep a conversation going with Spencer as the three ate supper, but he gave up when he received short answers or no answers at all to the questions he put to Spencer. His son's attention was only for his wife.

Later, when Gretchen had put the kitchen to rights and had joined the two men in the main room, Spencer, a soft promise in his eyes, pulled her onto his lap. Forgetting that Ben sat only a few feet away, Gretchen wrapped her arms around his shoulders as their lips scorched together. Ben watched them in amusement until his son's hand slid beneath Gretchen's skirt. He figured he'd better go to bed. Another minute and the pair might stretch out on the floor and make love right under his nose.

As soon as the door closed behind Ben, Spencer stood up and carried Gretchen to their room. He stood her on the bed and began to undo the buttons of her bodice. When the dress fell to her feet he slid the camisole over her shoulders and down to her waist. The aching need inside Gretchen grew as he opened his mouth over one breast, closed his lips on the nipple, and pulled hungrily. By the time the other breast had received the same attention she was so weak, she had to cling to his broad shoulders to keep from falling. Spencer laid her on the bed and hurried out of his clothes, then stripped away hers.

All conscious thought became impossible for her when his hard, demanding body covered hers and his manhood slid deeply inside her.

Soft cries of pleasure sounded many times throughout the night from the creaking bed. So much lost time had to be made up.

Epilogue

1777

It was spring. Although scattered patches of snow still lingered in the forest, the grass was turning green in the meadows. Gretchen sat on a rock in the bright sunshine, watching her husband stow away his traps in the shed. They would stay there until the next trapping season.

She looked down at her chubby son, waving his arms and kicking his feet. "You want to go to your daddy, don't you, Benny." She kissed the top of the curly chestnut head, the only thing of hers the little one had.

The baby saw his grandfather coming toward them and turned his attention to him. Ben swung him into his arms. As Benny chortled his pleasure, his grandfather carried him toward the barn, saying, "We'll go visit the old mule for a while, all right, boy?"

"Where's Pa going with Benny?" Spencer stepped out of the shed and closed the door.

"Down to the barn to visit Jimbo."

Her husband walked toward her, a noticeable bulge in his buckskins and a wicked look on his face. "You reckon they'll be gone very long?"

"I reckon." Gretchen smiled, a knowing look in her eyes. "Would you like to go look at the new quilt I put on our bed this morning?"

"Nothin' would please me better." Spencer's voice was husky.

Ben paused at the barn door, watching his son and daughter-in-law stroll toward the cabin, their arms around each other's waist. "Benny," he said, "I'd say it won't be long before you have a little brother or sister."

NORAH HESS

Best Western Frontier Romance
Award-Winner—*Romantic Times*

In the rugged solitude of the Wyoming wilderness, the lovely Jonty Rand lived life as a boy to protect her innocence from the likes of Cord McBain. So when her grandmother's dying wish made Cord Jonty's guardian, she despaired of ever revealing her true identity. Determined to change her into a rawhide-tough wrangler, Cord assigned Jonty all the hardest tasks on the ranch, making her life a torment. Then one stormy night he discovered that Jonty would never be a man, only the wildest, most willing woman he'd ever taken in his arms.

_2934-0 $4.50

LEISURE BOOKS
ATTN: Order Department
276 5th Avenue, New York, NY 10001

Please add $1.50 for shipping and handling for the first book and $.35 for each book thereafter. N.Y.S. and N.Y.C. residents, please add appropriate sales tax. No cash, stamps, or C.O.D.s. All orders shipped within 6 weeks via postal service book rate. Canadian orders require $2.00 extra postage. It must also be paid in U.S. dollars through a U.S. banking facility.

Name____
Address____
City __________________________ State______ Zip______
I have enclosed $______in payment for the checked book(s).
Payment must accompany all orders.☐ Please send a free catalog.

"Overwhelms you with characters who seem to be breathing right next to you and transports you into their world!"

—*Romantic Times*

From the moment she laid eyes on him, Rue thought Hawke Masters was the most arrogant man she'd ever seen. But once he got her home to his ranch, after a shotgun marriage, she had second thoughts. Could he be the man she had dreamed of all her life — or was she simply blinded by the ecstasy she felt in his strong arms?

_3051-9 $4.50 US/$5.50 CAN

LEISURE BOOKS
ATTN: Order Department
276 5th Avenue, New York, NY 10001

Please add $1.50 for shipping and handling for the first book and $.35 for each book thereafter. N.Y.S. and N.Y.C. residents, please add appropriate sales tax. No cash, stamps, or C.O.D.s. All orders shipped within 6 weeks via postal service book rate. Canadian orders require $2.00 extra postage. It must also be paid in U.S. dollars through a U.S. banking facility.

Name____
Address____
City ______________________________ State______ Zip______
I have enclosed $______ in payment for the checked book(s).
Payment must accompany all orders. ☐ Please send a free catalog.

CASSIE EDWARDS

Winner of the *Romantic Times* Lifetime Achievement Award for Best Indian Series!

Savage Illusion. A Blackfoot Indian raised by white settlers, Jolena Edmonds has never lived among her own people. Yet in her dreams, a hard-bodied brave comes to her, filling her with a fiery longing. When at last she meets the bold warrior Spotted Eagle, a secret enemy threatens to separate them forever.

_3480-8 $4.99 US/$5.99 CAN

Savage Sunrise. Rescued from vicious slave traders by an Indian warrior, Ashley Wyatt yearns to forsake civilized society for Yellow Thunder's tender loving. But the ruthless renegade who once took the young girl's freedom vows that Ashley and Yellow Thunder will never enjoy the glory of another savage sunrise.

_3387-9 $4.99 US/$5.99 CAN

Savage Mists. The great leader of the Omaha Indians, Iron Cloud wants only to save his people from unscrupulous government agents. He never imagines that his quest for vengeance will bring him the one woman who can fulfill all his desires—the young maiden he names White Willow.

_3304-6 $4.99 US/$5.99 CAN

LEISURE BOOKS
ATTN: Order Department
276 5th Avenue, New York, NY 10001

Please add $1.50 for shipping and handling for the first book and $.35 for each book thereafter. PA., N.Y.S. and N.Y.C. residents, please add appropriate sales tax. No cash, stamps, or C.O.D.s. All orders shipped within 6 weeks via postal service book rate. Canadian orders require $2.00 extra postage and must be paid in U.S. dollars through a U.S. banking facility.

Name___________________________________
Address_________________________________
City ________________________ State______ Zip______
I have enclosed $______in payment for the checked book(s).
Payment must accompany all orders.☐ Please send a free catalog.

Breathtaking historical romance by

Never Call It Loving. No simpering beauty ready to submit to an overbearing ogre, Marisa Fitzgerald refuses to accept that her arranged marriage will be loveless. Somehow, some way, she will tame Cameron Buchanan's brutish demeanor and turn the mighty beast into a loving man.

_3519-7 $4.99 US/$5.99 CAN

Encantadora. When Victoria refuses to choose a husband from among the ranchers of San Antonio, she never dreams her father will go out and *buy* her a man! Tall, dark, and far too handsome for Tory's peace of mind, Rhys woos his reluctant bride until she is as eager as he to share the enchantment of love.

_3178-7 $4.50 US/$5.50 CAN

LEISURE BOOKS
ATTN: Order Department
276 5th Avenue, New York, NY 10001

Please add $1.50 for shipping and handling for the first book and $.35 for each book thereafter. PA., N.Y.S. and N.Y.C. residents, please add appropriate sales tax. No cash, stamps, or C.O.D.s. All orders shipped within 6 weeks via postal service book rate. Canadian orders require $2.00 extra postage and must be paid in U.S. dollars through a U.S. banking facility.

Name________________________________
Address______________________________
City ____________________ State______ Zip______
I have enclosed $______ in payment for the checked book(s).
Payment must accompany all orders. ☐ Please send a free catalog.

By the bestselling author of *Terms of Surrender*

Running from his past, Red Eagle has no desire to become entangled with the haughty beauty who hires him to guide her across the treacherous Camino Real to Santa Fe. Although Elise Louvois's cool violet eyes betray nothing, her warm, willing body comes alive beneath his masterful touch. She will risk imprisonment and death, but not her vulnerable heart. Mystified, Red Eagle is certain of but one thing—the spirits have destined Elise to be his woman.
_3498-0 $4.99 US/$5.99 CAN

LEISURE BOOKS
ATTN: Order Department
276 5th Avenue, New York, NY 10001

Please add $1.50 for shipping and handling for the first book and $.35 for each book thereafter. PA., N.Y.S. and N.Y.C. residents, please add appropriate sales tax. No cash, stamps, or C.O.D.s. All orders shipped within 6 weeks via postal service book rate. Canadian orders require $2.00 extra postage and must be paid in U.S. dollars through a U.S. banking facility.

Name ______________________________
Address ______________________________
City ____________________ State ______ Zip ______
I have enclosed $______ in payment for the checked book(s).
Payment must accompany all orders. ☐ Please send a free catalog.

The Queen of Indian Romance

Winner of the *Romantic Times* Reviewers' Choice Award for Best Indian Series!

"Madeline Baker's Indian Romances should not be missed!"

—*Romantic Times*

The Spirit Path. Beautiful and infinitely desirable, the Spirit Woman beckons Shadow Hawk away from his tribe, drawing him to an unknown place, a distant time where passion and peril await. Against all odds, Hawk and the Spirit Woman will conquer time itself and share a destiny that will unite them body and soul.

_3402-6 $4.99 US/5.99 CAN

Midnight Fire. A half-breed who has no use for a frightened girl fleeing an unwanted wedding, Morgan thinks he wants only the money Carolyn Chandler offers him to guide her across the plains. But in the vast wilderness, Morgan makes her his woman and swears to do anything to keep Carolyn's love.

_3323-2 $4.99 US/$5.99 CAN

Comanche Flame. From the moment Dancer saves her life, Jessica is drawn to him by a fevered yearning. And when the passionate loner returns to his tribe, Jessica vows she and her once-in-a-lifetime love will be reunited in an untamed paradise of rapture and bliss.

_3242-2 $4.99 US/$5.99 CAN

LEISURE BOOKS
ATTN: Order Department
276 5th Avenue, New York, NY 10001

Please add $1.50 for shipping and handling for the first book and $.35 for each book thereafter. PA., N.Y.S. and N.Y.C. residents, please add appropriate sales tax. No cash, stamps, or C.O.D.s. All orders shipped within 6 weeks via postal service book rate. Canadian orders require $2.00 extra postage and must be paid in U.S. dollars through a U.S. banking facility.

Name____

Address____

City ____________________________ State______ Zip______

I have enclosed $______in payment for the checked book(s).

Payment must accompany all orders.☐ Please send a free catalog.